# CAUSE
# AND
# EFFECT

## Uncommon Bonds – 5

### A Novel by
# WILLIAM E. NOLAND

**CAUSE AND EFFECT**
**Uncommon Bonds – Book 5**
Copyright © 2024 William E. Noland

FIRST EDITION SOFTCOVER
ISBN: 1622537238
ISBN-13: 978-1-62253-723-5

*Editor: Lane Diamond*
*Cover Artist: Kris Norris*
*Interior Designer: Lane Diamond*

**EVOLVED PUBLISHING™**

www.EvolvedPub.com
Evolved Publishing LLC
Butler, Wisconsin, USA

*Cause and Effect* is a work of fiction. All names, characters, places, and incidents are the product of the author's imagination, or are used fictitiously. Any resemblance to actual events or persons, living or dead, is entirely coincidental.

Printed in Book Antiqua font.

# BOOKS BY WILLIAM E. NOLAND

**UNCOMMON BONDS**
Book 1: *Playing with Fire*
Book 2: *Hammer to Fall*
Book 3: *From the Beginning*
Book 4: *Day of Judgment*
Book 5: *Cause and Effect*
Book 6: *Birds of Fire [2025]*

# CHAPTER 1

**Marietta, Georgia, Sunday, October 22, 2017**

Olive jerked her head as an especially loud commercial on the television woke her.

Her neck was stiff, having slumped over when she fell asleep sometime in the middle of the third quarter. The game would be about over by now. She rubbed her eyes and waited for the particularly obnoxious advertisement to conclude, dreading the final score. The Patriots had been up 20-0 on the Falcons when she nodded off.

The game returned, and sure enough, the Pats had killed them, 23-7. She watched a grinning Tom Brady as he shook hands, yet again, with the team he'd miraculously defeated in the Superbowl earlier in the year.

*What a smug prick,* she wearily thought. *I mean, I'd have his baby and all, but jeez, I'd give just about anything to never have to watch him play football again.* "Hopefully we don't have to watch him play anymore this season, right, Mutig?"

The gray dog warily raised one eyelid from where he lay curled-up tightly in a distant corner of the living room.

"Don't y'all want to come and sit with me? Come on, boy."

She patted the couch, but Mutig didn't stir.

It had been this way since she'd returned from Massachusetts three-and-a-half weeks ago. The normally ebullient and loving animal had seemed frightened and suspicious from the minute he first saw her, and had skulked away to hide in Olive's mother's bedroom. Despite her best efforts, the dog remained sullen and withdrawn, though he no longer instantly fled whenever she entered the room, which Olive considered a miniscule measure of progress.

She had a strong suspicion about what caused Mutig's incredibly unusual behavior, but sadly, she couldn't do a damn thing about it.

"Whatever." She sighed, grabbed her phone from the coffee table, and expectantly opened her text messages in hopes Eric might have replied. He hadn't.

"What the H-E Double L?" She tossed the phone with dismay onto the couch beside her.

This was just one more strange development since her trip north. Eric was usually quick to respond to her texts, and sometimes even called her to talk, but there had been no chit-chat since he and Lotte returned from Oman. Olive had instantly sensed something was amiss when the two of them dragged into Siddique's apartment the day after they got back to Boston. She'd chalked it up to jet lag, but the more they talked about what occurred at the Majlis Al Jinn, the more she detected sadness in their voices, and a vacant distraction in their eyes.

She could sort of understand with Lotte, clearly devastated by the loss of the Afrit, who beyond anyone's reckoning appeared to have sacrificed its very existence to thwart Iblis's plan.

*Damn ol' thing. Just when I was beginning to like you, too.*

Yet that didn't explain Eric's behavior. He'd never especially cared for the dour creature.

Olive perceived something that went far beyond the Afrit's loss for both of them, as if some other sorrow, deeper and unspoken, united them in subdued anguish.

Siddique had noticed it too, and that had convinced Olive to text Eric about it after he and Lotte had uncharacteristically taken a pass on dinner and gone home. Eric had simply attributed it to tiredness and said they needed some time to recover. It sounded reasonable, but she and Siddique had their doubts, and as the weeks passed, it became clear that something in their friend's behavior was amiss.

Siddique expressed ever greater concern for them in his and Olive's increasingly regular text and email exchanges.

*Siddique.*

Originally, Olive couldn't understand why Lotte and Eric had let him live, let alone help him the way they did. It had shocked her even more when Lotte and her erstwhile kidnapper had actually become friends. Olive's impressions, however, had started to change in May, when they all went to Italy for Lotte and Eric's honeymoon—or artifact-finding excursion, depending on which narrative you chose to believe.

Siddique had been generally quiet but full of good-natured humor, and he'd been totally dedicated to the arduous process of unearthing the portal materials Lotte had found. When Lotte and Eric had desired a little "alone" time, Olive and Siddique had been forced to band together in an unusual and foreign land and had forged a somewhat uneasy truce. He was, after all, a member of the team now.

*The team that loses, even when it wins,* she thought bitterly, stroking the medallion that nestled on the flesh of her chest, underneath her well-worn blue and orange "Savannah State University" sweatshirt.

She shivered at the memory of coming-to in the back of the van, her body a firestorm of torturous, stinging lacerations. Worst of all were her eyes, a mangled muddle of gore, riddled with tiny shards of razor-sharp stones over which her lids excruciatingly scraped. Although her body had since been healed by Enki, the capricious Mesopotamian deity with whom they had unexpectedly become entwined, her mind carried the full remembrance of the agony. She often woke sweaty and tearful from nightmares of this nearly incomprehensible experience.

More than once, her cries had woken Siddique during the week she'd stayed with him, while Lotte and Eric were in Oman. Always, he abandoned the couch where he'd chosen to camp, and ran up the stairs to the loft, where she slept in his bed. He held her hand while she cried, her tears a stark reminder of the blood that had streamed from her mutilated eyes only a few short days before. He made her tea, and stroked her shoulder until she again fell unconscious, only for her to dream once more of the horror, and the possibility that the cause of this devastating memory might still lurk inside her.

She eventually deduced that Siddique watched her as they cohabited in his tiny studio apartment, concluding that Lotte and Eric had instructed him to keep an eye out for any sign of Aicha's reemergence. Siddique was many things, but deceitful wasn't among them, and his sometimes-clumsy efforts to monitor her easily gave him away. Olive didn't care, or at least, she didn't mind.

She harbored her own fears about whether some part of the nefarious Jinn might still reside inside her. Doubt about whether the medallion would keep Aicha's powers at bay also plagued her mind. She hadn't lied when she'd told her friends that she basically "felt fine," but she didn't exactly tell them the whole truth, either.

She definitely felt *something,* an almost "tingling" sensation that hadn't been there before, like the little surge of nauseated panic when the teacher hands out a test. At the time — before she returned to her mother's house in Marietta and Mutig had essentially confirmed her suspicions — she thought it might all be in her mind, like the lingering phantoms of pain after having the flesh savagely stripped from her body.

Once, while showering at Siddique's apartment, she'd defied Lotte's directive and had gingerly lifted the white medallion over her head and hung it on one of the little metal shower-curtain hooks. The tingling may have increased slightly—it had been hard to tell—but she hadn't felt the presence of Aicha's overwhelmingly powerful thoughts.

Her week together with Siddique had done much to dispel any remaining doubts she may have had as to his character. His gentle nature and attentive ministrations had ultimately won her over, not to mention his enticing smile that occasionally penetrated an otherwise shy and serious demeanor. It had come as a most unwelcome shock when Lotte finally decreed that Olive could fly back to Atlanta whenever she wanted.

Upon returning from Oman, Lotte had conducted some experiments on the medallion with the magnetometer, which had produced interesting results. Despite being innately repellent to Jinn, meaning the object must project some sort of magnetic force, the magnetometer registered no reading at all until they coupled it with another piece from Vanth's portal, at which point the reading shot to near the top of the scale. Simply resting around her neck on its leather strap, the item wouldn't pose any risk at the security gate. The screeners would think it was made of plastic, if they noticed it at all.

As it turned out, Lotte was right, but then, Lotte was almost always right.

Olive and Siddique spent that final Wednesday night together... alone. As always, he cooked an amazing meal comprised of dishes from his native Sierra Leone. Afterward, they went for a walk, talking infrequently as they coursed through darkened streets. For a time, she'd taken his hand, and felt comfort in the warmth of human contact. He'd given no resistance.

The next day, he drove her to Logan airport in the Schneider Industrial Flooring van. There, they met a bleary-eyed and still faraway Lotte and Eric, who had come to see her off.

She'd hugged Siddique, and he'd whispered in her ear, "Take care of yourself. Go slowly."

She did, bidding her friends goodbye and oh-so-slowly walking to the security line, wondering why she was doing so with every lumbering, lifeless step.

*Why? Why didn't I do something? Why didn't I act? It ain't like I didn't know how I was startin' to feel... how he was startin' to feel. I've jumped into so many dumbass relationships with boys I knew a hell of a lot less about than Siddique. Why didn't I make a move on him? At least he treats me nice.*

Was it the distance, the surety of their separation? Had her experience with Tyler, her boyfriend in high school who had broken up with her when she went away to college, colored her decision? Possibly, though Olive knew that if she and Siddique had really hit it off, she might well have moved north to be near him.

Things hadn't worked out as well as she'd hoped in her position as a Community Service Officer in the Marietta Police Department. True, the sudden need for time off last month hadn't helped, but even before that, she'd noticed that guys who were brought on as CSOs about the same time as her were getting more substantive assignments. She was beginning to doubt the department would want to sponsor her for the academy at the beginning of next year, and she felt certain that she'd need to make a fresh start somewhere else, hopefully somewhere less prone to what she saw as pretty obvious gender bias.

*Whatever. Crap, that reminds me... I have to work tomorrow. Ugh!*

In any case, she suspected geography probably wasn't the primary issue for her with Siddique. That did, however, leave other, somewhat more disturbing possibilities.

*Siddique is black, and comes from a totally different country, with different customs, languages, and culture. Plus, even though he ain't especially religious, he's Muslim by birth. Man, the good ol' boys in my family would just love that. Not!*

She wondered if either would ever be welcomed in each other's worlds, but deep down, she also worried that maybe she'd absorbed some of her family's attitudes. She'd learned about "implicit bias" at Savannah State, unknown and unintentional thoughts that nevertheless affected judgments and behavior. Olive had never dated a black guy, never even felt any attraction, and her attractions to guys were not exactly scant, much to her frequent dismay.

*I know how wrong and stupid that is, but* something *made me walk away when I normally wouldn't have. It just doesn't compute.*

Now she missed Siddique and wanted to call or text him, but it was after midnight, and she knew he worked early. She glanced at her phone, and Eric still hadn't responded to her text either.

She let out a little snort. "Some friend he turned out to be. If something's wrong, why don't he talk to me about it? Man, my life is pretty much shit right now. Even my damn dog don't like me, do you?"

Mutig cocked his head but didn't stir.

"Yeah, I figured. You're lucky I still feed you, stupid ol' thing. Well, let's check the weather for tomorrow, then I'm going to bed."

She picked up the television remote from the coffee table and flipped to the late-night local news. As she waited for the weather forecast, she saw they were running a story about Emory University, something relating to problems in their frats and dorms along Eagle Row.

She turned up the volume on an interview with a student sitting in a hospital bed. "...so incredibly weird. I woke up, and I just couldn't move. I felt totally drained, like really, no energy at all, but that wasn't why I couldn't move. I felt... like... frozen... paralyzed. Crazy thing is, my roommate had it too. Both of us were just lying there—couldn't move, couldn't yell for help. I thought we were gonna die there, but after a while, it sort of... like... wore off. It's identical to the other students who've had this. We didn't hear anything, or smell anything. It's... like... wild."

A reporter came on screen, standing outside the Emory University Hospital where the students had presumably been taken. "These are the sixteenth and seventeenth students who have experienced these strange symptoms over the past few weeks. Emory authorities are investigating potential causes and following up on all leads to see whether something in the dorm buildings could be causing students to become weakened and temporarily paralyzed. In the meantime, they're asking for patience from students and concerned parents while they conduct their investigation. For WGCL 46 News, I'm Rita Myers."

The news went to commercial as Olive sat with her jaw wide. "Y'all ain't gonna find anything in your buildings. You got a whole different kind of problem on your hands. Damn!"

She thought of what Eric told her had happened to Mrs. Binson when Aicha Kandicha had paralyzed her in her sleep while in search of the very medallion Olive now wore.

*This fits the description almost exactly.*

She snatched her phone off the couch and began to text Lotte and Eric, but then stopped.

*What are they gonna do? In the state they're in, will they even care? Lotte's so worried about school, and Siddique says Eric seems totally out of it, taking all kinds of time off from work. There's not even anything Siddique can do. He's back at work too. He can't come down here. He probably would if I asked him, but that ain't fair. He might lose his job.*

This was much the same rationale that kept her from telling her friends about Mutig's behavior. What were they going to do about it? If her dog really were reacting to Aicha's presence within her, they'd tell her to keep wearing the medallion, which she was already doing. She hoped that Mutig might eventually come around and the whole issue would just go away.

She lowered the phone.

*This probably happens all the time. It don't always make the news, but we know there's more Jinn out there... they're everywhere! We know they have to feed. Looks like one is especially hungry right now, and for some reason he's developed a taste for Emory undergrads. But he, or she, ain't harmed nobody. Not really. Looks like that boy on the TV is gonna be fine. Why bother all my friends over this? It'll just be one more thing for them to worry about, and I ain't bringin' trouble like that to their doorstep unless I have to.*

On the flipside, it worried her that maybe this was the prelude to something more ominous. *It really would be nice to at least have some sense of what the heck is goin' on over there!*

The one good thing about being relegated to doing mostly paperwork at the station was that Olive had gotten quite good with the computer systems. She resolved to do a little investigating when she went in tomorrow and began plotting how she might structure some productive data queries to see what she could learn. By the time she returned her attention to the TV, she realized she'd missed the weather report.

"Crap. I'll just look it up on my stupid phone."

<hr>

**Atlanta, Georgia, Monday, October 23, 2017**

The backup on I-75 at high rush hour never ceased to amaze Olive, especially since she was headed south, into the city, and against what should have been the worst of the traffic.

*Now I see why Momma leaves so early to get to work.*

Her mother had worked long enough in the Georgia Tech Admissions Department that they'd let her flex her hours to beat the insane traffic. It meant very early mornings, but that was better than spending an hour or more, twice a day, getting between the school and her modest little house in Marietta. Olive hardly ever made this trip, so the traffic didn't bother her too much, especially since there was a nice reward waiting for her at the end of this particular journey, after another long and frustrating day at work.

<hr>

When Olive arrived at the station, she was assigned to process and log a giant stack of reports, all while assisting in dispatch for non-emergency calls to the station, a potpourri of everything from the mundane to the absurd.

It wasn't that she especially minded these assignments—*Who knew so many dang cats got stuck in trees?*—it was more that the boys hardly ever had to do these tasks. She'd never even been trained in evidence collection or traffic accident investigations like they had, which she found incredibly discouraging, and pretty obviously unfair.

*Then again, maybe they just don't think I'm good enough. Story of my life. Maybe Daddy's right and I am a damn airhead. Maybe I should just go work for freakin' McDonald's, or something. Sheesh.*

The day, however, wasn't a complete failure. She slipped in a moment to run one of her computer queries, and to her gratification, she got a lead. The search called up all police reports since early September in the vicinity between Druid Hills and North Druid Hills, which encompassed the Emory campus. Unsurprisingly, there were quite a few, but she filtered out all the traffic accidents and stolen vehicles, then scanned through the rest. She found only one missing persons case, which made it stand out to her.

On Saturday, September 30th, Mr. Harland Cheevers of 1432 Emory Road had been reported missing by his employer, the Michael C. Carlos Museum, where he worked as a security guard. Uncharacteristically, he hadn't reported to work or called in sick for two days prior, and no one at the museum had been able to reach him. Police performed a wellness check at his house and found the door unlocked and no one home. Mr. Cheevers' car sat in the driveway, and they found his wallet and keys in a bedroom, but there were no signs of a struggle, and nothing appeared to be amiss or missing. Investigators even found his cell phone, its battery having run dead.

Unmarried, the man had lived in the house with his parents, until each had recently passed away. They'd contacted his brother, who lived in California, but he hadn't heard from Mr. Cheevers in some time. They'd done a sweep of the area around the home and come up empty. At this stage, with no leads, the investigation stalled. The Atlanta police still conducted periodic checks of the property for any signs of activity, hoping Mr. Cheevers had simply exercised his "right to go missing" and might come home, despite the suspicious nature of the disappearance.

Olive called up the address on the system, and it turned out that the man lived right nearby the student residences where the suspected "sleep paralysis" had been occurring, his house separated from Emory's campus by a strip of forest around a creek.

*Well, well. What a coincidence.*

She made up her mind to go have a look around. Given her knowledge and experience, if Harland Cheevers' disappearance was connected to the sleep paralysis happening at Emory, maybe she'd notice something the police investigators hadn't, something that might help them find him, or at least give her a better sense of what might be going on.

*It's risky, but I'm not gonna go out there unprepared.*

After work, she stopped briefly at home to grab Mutig, who reluctantly accompanied her to the car and crawled into the back seat. The dog could be a powerful ally if things somehow went sideways. Knowing she'd have to turn off her cell phone at some point, she'd rooted in a crammed drawer for the old Atlanta area road atlas — the one her mother had bought when they'd first moved to town years ago. She'd also grabbed her little Glock 19, her lockpicking tools, and some latex gloves, which she stuffed in the glove compartment of her aging black Jetta.

Based on the police report, no one currently occupied the house. Even if a Jinn were there, hovering undetected in their immaterial form, she felt it unlikely they would attack her. They hadn't attacked the police who'd investigated earlier, and as she and her friends had learned, not all of the creatures of air were like Aicha, who had her own motivations for physical violence. Most fed on the energy of humans, or other animals, while they slept, and stopped well short of causing any lasting damage or death. The Jinn operating around Emory seemed no exception. The question was, why did this one feel the need to feed so regularly, and why in such a specific area? That strangeness warranted investigation, in Olive's mind.

She took exit 249D, then turned left onto North Avenue NW. Her mood brightened as The Varsity came into view. Her promised reward beckoned. Always a sucker for Americana of all stripes, Olive had fallen in love with this iconic restaurant from the first time her mother had taken her after the jarring move from rural South Carolina to Atlanta, precipitated by the divorce. The chili dogs, signature home-cut fries, and peach pies that would sear your mouth if you weren't careful, had all become the taste of her childhood.

Best of all, though, was that you could eat in your car at what was the world's largest drive-in restaurant. It made her feel, however so briefly, as if she was living history itself, actively participating in a part of the heritage and culture of a gentler time, which had somehow been lost in the mad dash for the evidently endless string of "next big things."

There wasn't much she could do with a history degree, which is why she'd changed her major to criminal justice, but Olive's love of the past remained undiminished, even though she knew its genteel appearance often belied some deeply disturbing truths.

"What'll ya have... what'll ya have?" The ever-cheerful Car Hop took her order. His friendly smile even drew a few tail wags from Mutig.

She gave him a big tip.

The wait for her food gave her a chance to call Siddique. They'd tried to connect several times during the day after he'd texted her in the early morning, well before she'd gotten up. He'd mentioned he had some news, which piqued her interest, but a late start had prevented her from getting back to him before she jetted out to work. They were both too busy to connect during the day. She'd texted him when she got home but hadn't received a reply. He must have been busy, or driving, and she resolved to try him at dinner time.

She placed the call hopefully.

After a couple of rings, Siddique picked up. "Olive! Hi!" His words shot out in urgent whispers, as if he didn't want people nearby to hear, and she strained to understand him. "You're not going to believe this!"

She heard a voice in the background, possibly Lotte's.

"Okay, okay," Siddique responded. "Sorry. Listen, Olive, can't talk right now. I have to go. I'll call you later."

The phone abruptly went dead, and Olive pursed her lips. "Umm, okay. That was weird." *At least it sounds like they're all together, and Siddique didn't actually sound upset. He actually seemed pretty excited about something. I'll just wait.*

Her food arrived, and she gloriously pigged-out. Normally, Mutig would sit shotgun in the passenger's seat, his light-amber eyes keenly tracking the movements of each morsel as it traversed the distance from paper wrapping to eager mouth. Tonight, he seemed satisfied with a few fries that Olive halfheartedly tossed into the back seat, until he again guardedly curled up and returned to sleep.

Completely stuffed, she went inside to use the restroom before setting out. She had business this night, and dinner had merely been a pleasant distraction before the real work began. She dug out her phone, popped out the battery and SIM card so her location history couldn't be traced, and set off in the direction of the Emory campus.

Emory Road was about twenty minutes from The Varsity. After dinner, she did a quick fly-by of the house at number 1432, a yellow, 50s-style ranch that sported a fairly typical brick façade. It stood last on the outer perimeter of the road before the forest took over. A gray Buick sat in the carport, and weeks' worth of mail hung out of the crammed mailbox near the road. The houses across the street were larger, fancier, and looked a bit older.

This was a quiet and clearly a pretty well-heeled neighborhood. She couldn't just park her junky old Jetta in the driveway and saunter around the property. Even in her uniform, which she hadn't bothered to change out of, people might notice and be suspicious. She followed Emory Road as it curved south, scanning the area to her left. Trees periodically lined the sidewalk, behind which a roughly twenty-foot strip of patchy grass led to a forested area. Here, the ground sloped sharply downward toward the creek, and a sign with a little map preceded a stairway to some walking trails.

Just shy of a right bend onto Harvard Road, the grassy area ended in a stand of trees and underbrush. Despite the *No Parking* sign, Olive pulled over, jumped out of the car, and crossed the street. The vegetation was dense, but the ground here was level, and there appeared to be room to squeeze her Jetta in between the tree trunks, then park out of view behind the tangle of leaves and bushes. She made a plan to come back around 8:00 p.m., after it had gotten dark.

With a little more than an hour to kill, she drove through the Emory Campus to see the dorms where all the students had fallen ill, or more likely been drained of their energy by a Jinn.

*Whoever thought I'd believe that story!*

She hopped back in her car, continued down Emory Road, turned left onto Oxford, and then took another left onto Eagle Row. Past the parking decks and ball fields, behind which she could see the other side of the forest around the creek near Harland Cheevers' house, a cluster of fraternities and sororities lined the street. A bit farther on, larger dorm buildings appeared. Aside from confirming their relative proximity to 1432 Emory Road, her quick spin proved unrevealing, and she turned around when she reached Clifton Road, and backtracked along Eagle Row.

Unsure where to head next, she'd almost reached Oxford Road when she noticed a golden banner on a light post with the image of an ornate Greek vase. This was an advertisement for the Michael C. Carlos Museum, where Harland Cheevers worked, or had worked until about three or four weeks ago.

*Interesting.*

She pulled the car over and consulted the dog-eared road atlas. The museum turned out to be right around the corner. She hung a quick left onto Dowman, and then looped around the traffic circle onto South Kligo. The building with the museum quickly appeared on her left. It was obviously closed, being both after hours and a Monday, when few museums were open, but she pulled into a small parking area, empty as it was so late in the day.

*I'm gonna go have a look anyway. At least Mutig can sniff around and pee.*

A scan of the quadrangle and the outside of the museum didn't reveal much, but Olive was surprised how close this building also stood to the dorms on Eagle Row. She wondered if Mr. Cheevers might still be inside somewhere. The police report hadn't said anything about having searched the museum, though in all likelihood someone had looked at surveillance video to verify he'd left the premises after his final shift.

*I wonder if maybe he came back later? They probably didn't review all the video since the time they saw him leave.*

She also pondered what connection there might be between the security guard and a Jinn. It seemed unlikely that he himself was one of the creatures of air. If he were, why would he suddenly change his "feeding" habits like this? She knew from Lotte and Eric that Jinn didn't really like to switch hosts. Doing so posed risks, which, without unfettered access to the plane of air, could prove fatal.

*It just don't make sense, but I guess that's why I'm here.*

She waited for the sun to fully set, and it began to cool off. At her whistle, Mutig faithfully but unenthusiastically hopped into the back seat. She started to regret not bringing him some water and a bowl.

*Maybe I can slip him some if I can get inside the house.*

She navigated back to Emory Road, which finally stood dark and silent, idled until she saw no cars or people, then hopped the curb, steered across the sidewalk, and rambled over a short stretch of grass before entering the area of dense underbrush she'd identified earlier. She smiled at the memory of hiding the white rental van in the woods in Lumberton, North Carolina to keep it out of sight of Blake Harris.

*Hmmm. That actually didn't turn out so good, did it? Oh, well. Another ding or two on this ol' thing won't matter.*

The car scraped and pushed against some low branches but didn't encounter any major obstacles. Once satisfied she was out of view, she popped open the glove box, strapped her pistol's holster to her belt, put her lockpicking kit in her pocket, and donned a pair of latex gloves.

Quietly and carefully, she exited the car, then opened the back door for Mutig, who nonchalantly skittered out. She scampered to the sidewalk, hoping that in the dark, anyone who saw them would think she was just walking her dog. A small snap of her fingers and Mutig was at her heels.

*He may not like me anymore, but he knows to obey authority when he has to.* "Good boy, baby."

They passed by the stairway to the walking trails, now to her right, rounded the bend in the road, and quickly reached the house. Seeing no one on the street, she crouched low and sidled along the driveway, near the trees that separated the Cheevers' house from the one on its left. She and Mutig rounded the carport and entered a spit of dirt and scraggly grass that passed for a back yard, which the trees and underbrush quickly swallowed. The yard sloped downward toward the middle and opposite side of the house.

It was extremely dark back here, with no lights on in the house, and almost no illumination from the dwelling next door getting through the thick brambles that separated the two properties. Olive dug in her pocket for her key chain and activated the little flashlight she kept clipped there. She easily found a back door and looked through the glass panes. This one seemed to lead into the kitchen, nearly opposite the door to the carport. The handle seemed old, well-worn, and of perfectly standard design.

*Score!*

This would be a relatively easy lock to pick, the only real obstacle being that she couldn't hold the little keychain light while she performed the operation. She'd need to do it largely in the dark. No matter. Olive had been practicing opening locks with her eyes closed. It was more an issue of *feel* anyway.

As she began to rake the lock, she contemplated the world of shit she'd be in if she got caught, this being highly illegal. She'd lose her job, might not ever be able to serve as a police officer again, and could actually face jail time. It would be unbelievably awful, but somehow, she felt more at peace in this moment than she had since graduating from Savannah State, possibly even before that. Through her studies, she'd come to believe that what she really wanted to be was a private investigator, and this activity carried the thrill of that profession—being out there on your own, taking risks, only your accumulated knowledge, expertise, and instincts to rely on.

Mutig shuffled by behind her. "Yeah, and a magical dog sidekick." She chuckled. It sounded like the plot for a bad supernatural suspense novel. *Olivia Carter, P.I., and Mutig the Wonder Dog. They'll break a case faster than a Jinn breaks wind!*

She stopped herself from laughing out loud at her rather stupid joke, though she knew Eric would totally have her back, with his inane sense of humor.

After a bit more fiddling with her pick and wrench, the lock clicked open. She doubted there was an alarm, or that it had been armed even if there was, and thus turned the handle and pushed the door open. A terrible smell came from the kitchen—spoiled milk, no doubt. It seemed like even the police hadn't been back here since they "investigated." She left the door open to air out the stench.

"I know, it sucks," she whispered to Mutig, "but stay close to me. We'll be in and out fast, I promise." She doubted the dog could actually understand her, but somehow, he always did as she asked, though of late, cuddling on the couch or letting her pet him had been right out of the question. It was weird that he'd be so smart, but he'd been touched and transformed by a godlike entity, much as she had. "Weird" kind of came with the territory.

Once inside, a streetlamp provided some illumination through the glass of the door to the carport, so she could see a bit better. She couldn't risk turning on a light, but concluded that her little flashlight was probably safe. There wasn't much to see in the kitchen—no notes on the Frigidaire, and only a pile of old newspapers on the table. She moved through one of two doorways near the fridge to a small living room toward the back of the house. This area proved equally unexciting. Shelves along the wall surrounded a smallish TV and held some books, all pretty standard fare—novels and such. She wondered if Jinn liked to read, and whether they were into Dean Koontz and Barbara Kingsolver, two of her favorites.

A hallway at the back of the room appeared to lead to the bedrooms. Two doors stood to the left in this passageway. The first turned out to be a closet, packed with all manner of effluvium in no discernable order. If the answer she sought was in this mess, it would take her days to find it. She gave it a cursory once-over with her little flashlight before turning to the second door. This one opened to a set of stairs that led down, probably to a half-basement, with another access point at the bottom of the depression in the back yard.

"Ugh. No thanks. Let's save this one for last, huh, dog?"

A sudden blast of icy air assailed her.

Mutig let out a low growl, followed by a little yap. He then circled a few times before running farther down the hallway, where he stopped and looked right.

Olive shivered as she shook off the brief but piercing burst of cold. "What is it, boy? Do you see something?"

The dog stood perfectly still, ears and stubby little six-inch tail cocked.

Olive crept up behind him and peered around the corner. An open door stood at the end of the hall. In the room, she saw a queen size bed in the light from the streetlamp through the window.

"Probably the master bedroom. Is this where you wanna go?"

Unsurprisingly, Mutig didn't answer. He stood stock still, eyes locked on the room before them.

Olive stepped around him. "Okay, I'll go first. Y'all cover my rear. Hmmm, I'm glad I don't have a guy partner. He'd probably be making a smartass remark right about now."

She drew her trusty Glock and stepped cautiously down the hallway. An opening in the wall to the right led to a sitting room, stocked with furniture far fancier than the informal living room she'd passed through earlier. A slew of pictures sat on the end tables, and two large photos of an elderly man and woman rested on the mantle above a faux fireplace, next to what appeared to be two urns.

*Probably Mommy and Daddy. This house don't look like it belongs to a late middle-aged security guard. You inherited this here place from your dearly departed parents, didn't you, Harland? Hey, who am I to complain? I'd take it if my momma offered it to me. I ain't stupid.*

At the threshold of the door, she stopped. "Is anyone in there? Fair warning: I'm carrying a gun, and unlike most things, I actually know how to use a firearm. If you're in there, Harland, don't make a big fuss. I just wanna talk, that's all. I know more about what's goin' on than you could ever imagine. Just give me a chance. You'll see."

Mutig emitted a slight whimper behind her, but Olive's confidence ran high as she stepped into the room.

No one appeared to be inside. A dresser, a closet with its door standing open, and a bureau with a large mirror and a small TV set on its top, sat to the left. Beyond the bureau was a door, presumably to an en-suite bathroom. She shone her flashlight into the closet, empty save a few bare hangers.

She'd started toward the bathroom when suddenly the door behind her slammed shut.

Mutig instantly launched into a panic in the hallway, barking hysterically and pawing frantically to get in. Despite his efforts, the door held firm.

Olive rapidly turned. For an instant, she thought she saw something, a haze of motion moving toward the dresser, but before she could focus her eyes, it had disappeared. She lunged for the door. Mutig represented her best chance, and she cursed herself for letting him fall so far to the rear when she came into the room.

Strong arms enveloped her waist from behind and threw her forcefully onto the bed. She raised her gun, but a mighty slap sent it skittering to the floor. Her hand burned with pain from the viscous strike. She tried to get a bead on her attacker, but he moved too quickly.

She determined her assailant was male because of the brief glimpse she'd caught of the meaty arms that had ensnared her in the light from the streetlamp. They matched her impression of Harland Cheevers, whose profile in the police computer had read 6'2" and about 220 pounds. Not an especially impressive physical specimen, he seemed quite chubby and out of shape, but she recalled thinking he had a kind face with a nice smile in the photo they'd chosen to disseminate. Still, he was a big dude, who apparently knew how to leverage his weight to maximum effect. What granted his incredible speed defied her ability to explain.

She kicked out, trying to keep him at bay, but almost in the blink of an eye, he'd rounded to the far side of the bed and grabbed her tightly by the wrist. She let out a howl of pain, and she heard Mutig yelp in response as he clawed at the door. Then she looked up and was shocked to see her attacker's manhood waving just above her, beneath a protruding belly.

*Oh, shit. He's totally naked. That means....*

In desperation, she made a grab for the vulnerable member, but he was too fast. He easily parried her strike with his free hand, and despite her resistance, continued to cling to her wrist. A frustrated fury rose in her, and for a moment, she felt the peculiar and forceful urge to tear off the medallion that hung around her neck under her shirt.

There wasn't time. The man brought his fist down into her face. An explosion of impossible light erupted in her eyes, and her ears emitted a jarring and perfectly piercing high C6, as if sung by a demonic opera soprano.

As consciousness rapidly faded, Olive experienced an incongruous wave of regret that Eric would never hear her Jinn joke.

*He'd have liked it. Really. I'm sure....*

# CHAPTER 2

**Worcester, Massachusetts, Monday, October 23, 2017**

The colors, sounds, and smells of this place, which once held us in thrall, now seem dull and distant. Finding our *Sadat Alnaar* brought an end to our tortured and addled wanderings, but the termination of our madness and confusion brings only the cognizance of our diminished and piteous state.

*Once again, we are laid low.*

She tried to soothe us, tried to explain... her voice choked with sorrow, eyes wet with tears. For a time, her words were unable to penetrate our deranged frenzy and meant nothing to us. It was the sound itself that brought us focus, the signature lilt and patterns of her speech... firm, knowing, and familiar.

*Remember us in your dreams.*

Had she not, we would never have found our way back. At this moment, we wonder if perhaps that may have been for the best after all.

We sit in the welcome darkness of night atop an abandoned and decaying building, turning over in our mind what little we can recall. Nothing in the Eternal Flame goes unnoticed by us, and we remember the terrible breach. As before, so long ago, it gulped at the energy of our realm. We made ourselves small to evade detection and avoid once again being swept away, but it proved unnecessary. It was not *us* the assailant sought, but rather the heat, the burning power of the plane of fire itself.

We suspected the terrible Jinn, who had originally initiated the volatile and often uncontrollable chain of events that led us to our present state, might be responsible. We knew that the greater part of us battled in the Middle Realm to put an end to him, once and for all. We waited expectantly... and then came the explosion.

The rupture into our domain gave ingress to the force of the blast, and the ripples of the mighty conflagration pummeled us with the unthinkable and terrible truth. The horror of our violent expiration, of the sudden privation of such a significant and potent portion of us, shredded what little of us remained near the Eternal Flame into particles of traumatized and unthinking ash, and scattered them haphazardly throughout our domain.

In this state, we remained for some unknown time.

Gradually, her dreams brought us back, and the ashen cloud of our despair clustered around the images of us that clamored in her troubled and unconscious mind. First two particles, then four, then eight, and so on, until our form had reassembled, but we were not nearly whole. Our mind still swam with the incomprehensible loss, and no order could we bring to our thoughts. We called out in terror and despair, fearing that our hysterical insanity would once again blow us apart.

From the deepest void of our despondency, we howled for assistance — and she heard. She came. She opened the doorway, and then her dreaming mind led us to her, the only path back.

With time, as the sky shifted from the light of their paltry sun into blackness, she caressed our shattered consciousness and brought a semblance of order to the chaos. Stabilized, we determined to fly free in their realm once more, to soak again in the unusual charms of a world that, through happenstance, now calls to us.

If we had hoped it would be a balm for our distress, we were disappointed, but oddly we do not yet feel ready to return to the Eternal Flame. The trauma of the terminal blast still looms fresh in our mind. We prefer to remain here for now, to ponder our fate and what may come next.

When their sun again sets, we will go back... back to her and the portal she tends. We shall then see what she has to say, our *Sadat Alnaar*, upon whom we have become so disturbingly dependent.

## Burlington, Massachusetts, Tuesday, October 24, 2017

To his surprise, Eric felt happy.

He enjoyed business meetings at Olé Molé, who always agreeably scheduled the end of the session to coincide with lunchtime.

*Okay, maybe it's lunch that I really enjoy. Those fish tacos were awesome.*

The successful restaurant was planning a new location in Chelmsford, and he'd presented a proposal for the flooring that had been well received. Now, he was on his way to a warehouse facility in Acton, whose floors needed a pretty substantial new surface. Business was good, and despite a weird and wild couple of nights, he felt gratified to be back in the saddle and ready to work again. His conversation with Lotte yesterday afternoon, right before all hell had broken loose with the completely unforeseen reemergence of the Afrit, had really seemed to help.

*Note to self. Talk to Lotte more. Stop being an introverted dumbass. End note.*

He'd just matriculated onto 95 South when his phone rang. He spared a glance at the screen, conveniently tucked in its dashboard cradle, which Lotte had bought him.

"*Alter!*" she'd scolded him. "You're going to kill yourself someday, juggling your phone like that when you're driving." She was right. Of course. The adjustable little cradle was so much easier.

*Thanks, Lotte.*

He didn't recognize the number, but it indicated the call was from Marietta, Georgia, where Olive lived.

*Crap! Olive! I totally forgot to get back to her.*

He swiped to accept the call, hoping he wouldn't yet again have to suffer through some sales scam about the extended warranty on his fucking car.

"Hi, this is Eric."

The woman on the other end spoke with a thick but sweet southern drawl. "Hi, honey, this is Victoria Carter, Olive's mother. You can call me Vicky. Olive gave me your number back when she went to your wedding. I hope you don't mind me calling."

"No, not at all. How can I help you?"

"Listen, sweetie, have you heard from Olive recently?"

"Umm, yeah, I did. She texted me on Sunday night. I was at the Pats game. I was... well... I just got kind of tied up with some stuff. I'm so sorry Ms. Car... umm, I mean, Vicky. I haven't gotten back to her."

"What about more recently than that? Like, last night, or today?"

"No, I didn't... wait a minute! I just remembered. She called a friend of mine last night while I was at his place. We were... well, umm... a little busy right then. I'm not certain if he got in touch with her later."

*How can I not know this? Man, I've let a lot of stuff slip recently. I've gotta get my shit together.*

"Sweetie, can you please find out for me, or give me his number so I can call him?" Her plea sounded urgent.

"Of course. No problem. He works for the same company I do. I'll call him now and call you right back. Is something wrong?"

"Well, I got a call late this morning from the Marietta Police Department where she works. Apparently, she didn't show up today, and they have no idea where she is. I leave for work early, so she's never awake, and I let her park in the garage because it's so full of junk that only her little car will fit, so I didn't see if it was there. She came home real quick yesterday after she finished work, then shot right out again. Said she had something she needed to do. Took Mutig with her, which was awful strange. They ain't been getting along so well of late."

Bells went off in Eric's mind. "What do you mean?"

"I don't know. He just acts all funny around her, kind of mopey and standoffish. It's like he just suddenly went off her, like you do when you eat too much of a certain food, even one you like whole a lot. Do you think this has something to do with why she's missing?"

*Probably, yes.* "Umm, I'm not sure, but that's really odd. All right, let me get all this straight. You say she went out with Mutig, she may or may not have come home last night, and she was definitely a no-call, no-show at work today. I assume you've called her?"

"Honey, everybody's been calling her, including her supervisor at work, who seemed pretty pissed off. The calls just go to voice mail. He's got the department on the lookout for her, and even said he'd request a warrant to track her phone if she didn't show up eventually, but it didn't sound to me like this was his top priority."

"What about her car? Does that have a tracking chip?"

"That ol' thing? Sweetie, that's my 2006 Jetta that I passed on to her. The only chips that car has are in the paint job."

*Yikes.* "Okay. Let me call my friend and see if he got in touch with her. I'll call you right back. I promise."

She thanked him and hung up, and he immediately rang Siddique.

His friend's voice sounded in the phone's speaker, cheerful as always. "Hey, man, what's up?"

"Hey. Listen, do I remember correctly that Olive called you last night, not long after you got home? Everything was so crazy right then. I can barely keep it all straight."

The Afrit had been in a panicked frenzy after it had materialized from the un-mirror, madly flexing its wings and thrashing its barbed tail. It acted like a wild animal, cornered and ready to fight, and for some time, it wasn't apparent whether it could understand what Lotte was saying. Eric feared it might attack her where she calmly sat, just a couple of feet from the raging imp. When Siddique got home, he joined the protective vigil until the perturbed little ashen beast finally began to settle.

"Yeah," Siddique replied. "She called when the Afrit was acting all nutty. Lotte wanted me to be quiet, so I told Olive I'd call her back."

"Did you?"

"Yeah, about nine-thirty or so, after the stupid little thing finally started to calm down. She didn't pick up. I tried a couple more times, but no luck."

"Damn."

"What's wrong? Eric, is something wrong with Olive?"

"Yeah, could be. Sometime after she called you, it seems like she may have disappeared. Something's been going on with her. She may be experiencing effects from Aicha's possession. Has she mentioned anything to you?"

"No, nothing. What are we gonna do?"

"I don't know. Nobody has any idea where she may have gone, and it'll take time, and a search warrant, to trace her phone. Assuming she's still alive, there might be only one way to find her."

"What?"

"The Afrit. I have to talk with Lotte."

Never a great cell phone user, Lotte kept her device mostly in airplane mode during the day so she wouldn't be interrupted, and usually forgot to reactivate her connection until Eric reminded her in the evening. Thus, although he left her a text, he didn't really expect her to see it.

Unable to extricate himself from the meeting in Acton, he pushed ahead and tried not to look too distracted while delivering his presentation. He often had a gut sense of how a pitch went once it had been delivered, but not this time. His mind buzzed in a nervous haze. By 3:30, he was back on the road, trying to beat the worst of the rush-hour traffic.

*Rush hour. It starts about three in the afternoon and goes until seven. That's four hours, by my reckoning, but I suck at math, so what do I know? The traffic gets outrageous, so they build bigger highways, but that only encourages more people to drive. The cycle of stupidity, and I get stuck in it almost every day.*

The roadway gods smiled upon him this afternoon, partly because of the straight shot down Route 2 back into Somerville, and partly because he was going against the worst of the traffic. He pulled onto Rogers Avenue at about 4:15, parked the car in the driveway, and jogged around to the back. Lotte's bike was chained to the stairwell, meaning she was already home. He ran up the wooden stairs, but stopped dead when he reached the top.

Sitting on the edge of the roof directly above their door, claws gripping the aluminum gutter, was the biggest crow he'd ever seen.

"Holy shit." *Actually, that might be a freaking raven! Not sure I've ever seen one around here, but then I'm not so into birds, even less so after nearly being killed by that damn owl in Greece.*

He shuddered.

The creature eyed him with a sort of leisurely curiosity, tilting its head slightly to bring both of its jet-black eyes to bear.

Eric wasn't sure what to do. He didn't think it was a good idea to try and scare the thing, which looked pretty stout.

*Plus, that's probably bad luck, or something, and I don't need any more of that in my life right now. Anyway, it kind of reminds me of Lotte.*

He took a cautious step, then another. The bird tracked his movements but seemed unperturbed. He reached the door and looked up. The large corvid stared directly down at him, ebony eyes dancing with what looked almost like mirth.

*Weird.*

He didn't have time to waste, so he flashed the bird a quick smile, which he figured probably came out more like a stupid grin, then went inside.

"Lotte?"

She called from her office near the front of the house. "In here!"

He dropped his shoulder bag on the kitchen table, hustled by Langsam's terrarium, and raced to her study. "Hey, did you see the big—*woah!*" He nearly banged into her as he flew through the threshold. It seemed she'd risen to come greet him, which made him smile despite his sense of urgency.

"*Alter!* What are you doing? Where's the fire?"

He took a moment to catch his breath. "Sorry, sorry. I was just in a hurry. Did you get my text?"

A little flick of her eyebrows, and a slight scrunching of her mouth, was all the answer he needed.

"Never mind, it doesn't matter. I think we might have a problem. It's Olive. She's gone missing." He quickly relayed everything he'd learned, and posited his notion that maybe the Afrit presented their best chance of finding her.

For a moment, she didn't react. Even for her, this must have represented at least a temporary data overload. Finally, she turned, staggered to the little couch where Eric spent most of his evenings, and collapsed with a huff of exasperation.

"Seriously? I mean, *seriously*? Just when we get back to some modicum of 'normal,' this has to happen? I don't know, Eric. I really just don't know. I don't know if I can do this anymore. I'm so far behind that I might have to withdraw from some classes. I might be in jeopardy of losing some of my financial support. That's not the end of the world, as my father would pay for me to fly to the moon if I wanted, but failing to deliver on my research responsibilities would really impact my performance, and I've barely got my head above water. I've already cashed in all the chips from my work with Dr. Henriksson and the Monte Sant'Angelo find. I've got no margin of error left, and I was just getting back on track. Now this. *Scheiße!*"

Eric wasn't nearly as shocked as he felt he should have been by Lotte's reaction. He was experiencing the same conflict, and very much shared her sense of fatigue. "I... I just don't know what else to do. I don't see any other options. Wait a minute... what about Enki?"

"What about Enki? What are we supposed to do, ring him on the Enki-phone?"

He chuckled at the image. "Well, you put your arms in the water on that beach outside of Tiwi when were in Oman, and he found us pretty quickly. Couldn't you just try to do the same thing?"

"I suppose I could try, but we'd arranged to meet him there. Even though they can sense us over huge distances, we know there's a limited range to these beings' ability to communicate. I honestly doubt that if I stick my hands in the water at Revere Beach, Enki would hear me in... wherever he is."

"Yeah, but what about...." He caught himself before he could finish the sentence. He'd intended to ask, "What about Grandma?" Enki had reached out to his grandmother on the beach in South Carolina and somehow communicated with her, then used her energy to replenish the Abzu so that Eric could operate the Tablet of Destinies. Lotte didn't know this—nor that she herself had, in fact, been killed on that beach—and he intended never to tell her.

*I'll just file that question away for some other time.*

She eyed him curiously. "What about what?"

"Umm... nothing. I thought I had an idea, but it died of loneliness. You raise a good point. He probably is too far away to contact, but that just brings us back to where we started."

"Right, but there's another problem."

"What?"

She shook her head. "The Afrit. I have no idea what condition it's in after last night. It said it would meet us back at Siddique's after dark tonight, so I guess we'll be finding out, but I have no idea if the thing is up to a task like this. What happened *shattered* it."

"Well, I guess that's our starting point. Assuming it'll cooperate, we'll have to send it back home, and then truck the portal down to Atlanta."

"Exactly, and that'll take days. Plus, who the hell knows what kind of situation we'll walk into down there."

"I know, but we can't abandon Olive."

She nodded listlessly.

He tried to sound encouraging. "Aren't you at least a little bit excited and curious about this? I mean, if we can track her down and she's okay, this could be pretty amazing. Come on. What happened to 'the huntress?'"

"She's fucking *busy* right now! *Alter!* I know you're right, but this just isn't how I imagined it would be. When I said that, I was talking about hunting artifacts buried in pits, or sitting mis-labeled in museums, or serving as bloody conversation pieces in people's fishing lodges or their stupid *tiki* bars. I thought we could get to these things before more Afrits, or Jinns, or Etruscan demi-gods, or freaking Mesopotamian deities would be popping out of them! You want to know what happened to 'the huntress,' Eric? She became 'the hunted,' and so did all her friends. We're not superheroes. We should never have gotten tangled up in all of this. We're in *way* over our heads, and it's already cost us. *Dearly!*" Her head slumped to her chest.

"Wow. I mean, you're right, but still. Wow. I... jeez, Lotte... I just don't see what else to do. I don't see any way out at this point."

She lifted her head, and her shining, dark eyes froze him with an icy glare. "There's no way out. This is it, my love. This is our life, the life I led you into. You'd better call work and let them know we'll be gone for a while. I'll see if I can get in touch with Professor Sprich and let him oh-so-politely rip me a new one."

Eric started back to the kitchen to fetch his phone, but she spoke gently from behind. "You know I wouldn't want anyone else beside me, but I hope all this was worth it to you. I hope *I* was worth it."

He turned and smiled. "I'd like to say, 'every second of it,' but you can be kind of bitchy sometimes, so I gotta knock off a few seconds here and there."

She snorted a little laugh.

"I've told you before, this is what, and who, I am. It wasn't ever a choice at all, but I've never regretted anything. We'll get through this together. You'll see. It'll be okay."

"I hope you're right, Eric. I really do. I love you. You're my heart."

*And you're my brain.*

Beset by myriad and conflicting emotions, he stumbled into the kitchen and fed Langsam some food pellets while he composed himself and prepared for the dreaded call.

Once he'd screwed up his courage, he punched her number. *Margot's gonna love this. Not.*

"Hiya!" She sounded remarkably chipper for the end of a busy workday. "What's up? How did that presentation in Acton go? I was surprised you didn't call afterward."

For a moment, he didn't even remember what she was talking about. "Right. Acton. Uh, it went fine, I guess. New client, you never really know. Listen... umm... I might have to... well... Lotte needs some help again, and I might have to go out of town for a few days."

Silence.

"You there? Margot? Did I lose you?"

"I'm here. I'm checking your schedule for the next two weeks, or should I make it three?" She did not sound happy.

"God, Margot, I'm so sorry. I'm hoping it won't be anywhere near that long. Clear the rest of this week to be on the safe side. I can let you know later if I need more time."

"Honestly, your schedule is pretty light right now."

"Oh, that's good."

"Yeah, not so much, dumbass. Your schedule is light because you've been such a fuckup recently and nobody trusts you to be where you said you were gonna be or do what you fucking promised you'd do. I know you're the boss's son, but this is really starting to suck for people, me included. I'm telling you this as a friend, Eric. I know something's been wrong... I can tell... and I've tried to cut you some slack, but this just feels like a slap in the face."

He winced, and momentarily wished he could have called Professor Sprich for Lotte and gotten reamed out in a more "polite" fashion. "You're right. You're totally right. All of it. You can't imagine how sorry I am, especially that I'm letting *you* down. You're one of my best friends ever, not to mention my best work colleague, and this isn't how I want it to be."

"What is it, Eric? Why can't you talk to me? You're so together most of the time, and then it seems like you just go off the rails, and this time, it wasn't just a week or two. I'm really worried about you. I want to help, but I can't if I don't know what's going on."

"You can help. You always help. It's just that Lotte gets these, I don't know, *opportunities*... things that will really help her career in the long run. Look at what happened when she found that cave in Italy. She can't pass up stuff like this, and until she gets a real job, with a staff, and a bunch of grad students to help out, I'm it."

"Yeah, I get that. I can basically deal with that, but what's up with you drooping around the past few weeks and being so out of it?"

"I know. I'm so sorry. I don't think I even realized how bad it was until a couple of days ago. Lotte and I, we... well... we figured some things out. I was feeling better today, and I was just getting back into work. Honestly. I feel better about all that now, even after you just pummeled the shit out of me."

"Tough love, buddy. I tried everything else. Plus, you did get on my last nerve with a fucking *vacation* request right now." She let out a deep sigh. "All right, let me see what I can do. Your dad might actually have me handle a couple of your meetings, if that's okay. Speaking of your dad, he's already left for the day and I'm *not* calling him. That's on you."

"Yeah, roger that. I'll call him. And as far as you handling some of my meetings, I couldn't be happier. That's a big step for you. It shows how much my dad trusts you. You'll probably have my job soon."

She laughed. "Sooner than you think if you don't get your shit together. I don't want your job. I want *you* back. I want things back to how they used to be."

"I do too, Margot. I do too."

*I'm just not certain that's possible anymore.*

Lotte and Eric drove to Worcester largely in silence, each requiring time to recover from their respective beratings, deserved though they may have been.

After his rather jarring call with Margot, Eric had contacted Siddique to explain the plan, which was to reunite with the Afrit at his apartment this evening, return the little beast to its realm, and pack up the portal materials. Then, in the morning, Eric would rent a van for him and Lotte to transport the whole lot to Atlanta. Siddique didn't say much, but he offered to make dinner, which Eric thought was super-nice.

After braving the unavoidable rush-hour traffic, they arrived at Siddique's around 6:15. Not too bad, all things considered. Eric parked his Mazda, and they walked upstairs to the apartment on the third, and top, floor.

They knocked, and Siddique greeted them at the door. "I'm going," he said, once they'd stepped inside. "You don't need to rent no van tomorrow. I talked to Ernie. I told him my cousin down in Raleigh was in a tough spot and really needed a van for a couple of days. Ernie didn't like it, especially after I missed all that time last month when Aicha nearly bashed my head in, but I said I'd make it up to him, and he knows I will."

Lotte beat Eric to the punch. "Siddique, are you sure that's a good idea? We don't want to get you in trouble. Maybe it would be best if you stayed—"

"No!" His adamant response caused them both to jump back a bit. "I'm sorry. I don't mean to yell at you. I just, I just... I'm just going. That's all. This time I'm going, and that's final. I'm worried about Olive."

Eric was about to speak up when Lotte put her hand on his arm. "All right, it's fine. You can come. I didn't want things to be any more difficult for you at work, but the truth is, it'll be good to have you with us. Maybe you and Eric can split the driving and we can get there faster."

He smiled his enticing and all too occasional smile. "Anything you say, boss."

WILLIAM E. NOLAND

# CHAPTER 3

It had grown quite dark by the time they finished supper, aided by the storm clouds that moved in just after Lotte and Eric had arrived.

At her instructions, Siddique slid open the window and screen. Cool, autumn air drifted into the apartment, and the sound of rainfall on the metal windowsill beat a steady and soothing rhythm. They were all clearing and washing dishes when a knock came at the door.

Siddique hastened down the hall and put his eye to the peephole. "Oh, shit!" he squealed.

"Who is it?" Lotte asked.

"It's Margot!"

She and Eric both replied in unison. "Margot!"

Eric rushed to the door. "What the hell is she doing here? This is terrible."

Margot knocked again.

"Just a minute," Siddique called out, then turned to Eric and whispered. "What are we gonna do, man? All the cases and the bags with the portal stuff are here. The frame is set up in my living room, and the Afrit could fly in any second now. She could see it all!"

Eric had no idea what to do, but he knew that Margot was aware that he was here. She'd have surely seen his car in the lot. He couldn't, and wouldn't, hide from her. He lightly pushed Siddique aside, opened the door, and tried his best to act cool. "Hi."

She grinned like the Cheshire Cat. "Hi, yourself. I thought I might find you guys here. Hi, Lotte!"

Lotte sheepishly waved from where she stood near the kitchen.

"Why'd you think you'd find us here?" Eric nervously inquired.

"Because I'm not fucking stupid, Eric. You call me and say you have to go out of town all of a sudden, and then about forty-five minutes later, Ernie calls me and says he needs to find a replacement for Siddique, who has to take the van down to North Carolina to help his cousin. Coincidence? I think not! I figured you'd come here because Siddique has the van. That's what you need, isn't it? To move all *that* stuff."

She pointed at the cases that housed the papers and various parts of the Afrit's portal that lined the little hallway that connected the foyer with the doorway and the closet to the rest of Siddique's apartment. "What the hell is all this stuff, anyway? Can I see?"

Lotte dashed forward. "It's my stuff. It's... it's, like... you know... archaeology stuff. The stuff you need when you do... you know... archaeology... stuff."

Margot shook her head with disbelief, then strode toward the cases. Halfway down the little hallway, she stopped and let out a whoop. "Woah! What is *that*?" Her eyes had locked on the un-mirror that stood in glorious repose before the brick wall in Siddique's living room. "Is this 'archaeology stuff'? What are you guys, like smugglers, or something?"

Siddique looked apprehensively at Eric, who looked panic-stricken at Lotte.

Before anyone could emit a response, they heard the sound of glass shattering in the parking lot below, and a fraction of a second later, a large bird with a hooked, black-tipped, yellow beak, and tar-like, blackish-brown feathers, impossibly rocketed through the open window and into the room.

*This can't be happening.*

Having faced the Jinn-owl in Greece, Eric felt certain he knew what they were up against. His first thought, however, was for Margot. Given the givens, she appeared remarkably calm. She'd crouched down and covered her head with her arms, but he knew that wouldn't help if this powerful creature sunk its claws into her. Moreover, he recognized that things were about to happen that he didn't want her to see. He wanted to keep her from being dragged, like he, and Olive, and Siddique, and to some extent, even Lotte had been, into this world of danger and insanity.

The closet door stood open, jammed with coats and clothes on the rack, and the floor was packed with the bags that contained Enki's portal.

*It'll have to do.*

He grabbed her from behind, dragged her back into the foyer, and muscled her in, face first, against all the coats. Then, he slammed the door shut, and before she could turn to twist the knob, he grabbed the large case in which they transported the un-mirror and slid it between the door and the opposite wall.

*That'll hold her.*

He turned and ran toward the living room. Siddique swatted at the creature with a broom he'd grabbed from the kitchen as the bird nimbly sprung from one side of the apartment to the other. It looked like an eagle, but not like an American eagle. Its body was about two-and-a-half feet long, and Eric figured it had a wingspan of about six feet.

For her part, Lotte had made straight for the bowls that sat exposed on the floor in front of the large frame. She'd just protectively gathered them up and tucked them behind the TV on its stand in the corner, when the eagle made a beeline for her.

"Lotte, look out!" Eric dove over the couch while Siddique frantically whacked at the bird from behind, but it was too late. The eagle sunk its sharp claws into her shoulders, and she let out a shriek.

The monster banked to the left, back toward the open window, but to Eric's amazement, all it held in its talons was Lotte's Harvard sweatshirt, and whatever t-shirt she'd been wearing underneath. Her pants had slumped to the floor in front of the TV. She'd completely vanished, right before his eyes.

"What the...."

The eagle dropped the empty and now tattered clothes, came to rest on the windowsill, and let out a series of deep, harsh barks, almost like the croak of an exceptionally large frog. "Owk, owk! Owk, owk!"

It was about to shoot back into the room when a black figure wildly descended from outside and dug its claws into the eagle's neck. It wasn't the Afrit. To Eric's amazement, it was a large black bird, almost undoubtedly the raven he'd seen earlier at their house.

*This is just getting weirder by the second.*

The raven madly and repeatedly pecked at its opponent's head, and blood oozed onto the creamy, golden buff feathers of the eagle's majestic crown. For a moment, it looked as if the smaller bird would bore a hole straight through the larger creature's skull and pick out its brain, but the injured and infuriated blackish-brown avian suddenly vanished.

The raven flew inside and perched on the half-wall that ran the perimeter of the second-floor loft. There, it furtively scanned the room below. For a moment, all was quiet.

Eric grabbed a lamp from the end table and quickly discarded the shade. He and Siddique stood back-to-back in the middle of the living room, breath heaving, and sweating from their exertion and extreme apprehension.

"I guess that eagle is a Jinn?" Siddique rhetorically asked.

"All signs point to yes, unless you know of a species of eagle that can disappear like that."

"That black bird, too?"

"Yeah, I think so. I can't think of any other explanation for why it did that."

"Well, this broom isn't gonna cut it. We need iron. That's how you killed Aicha, and that owl. Right?"

*Why the hell didn't I think of that?* "My friend, you've never been more right. Let's get to the kitchen. Steel knives may be the best we've got."

Before they could move, a loud rapping and a muffled voice came from the closet in the foyer. "What the fuck, guys! Let me out of here! What the hell is going on?"

The noise seemed to trigger the end of the detente. From out of nowhere, the eagle reappeared and grabbed the raven in its powerful claws. Feathers flew as the black bird desperately cawed and struggled, before it, too, vanished into thin air.

Eric and Siddique both ducked down and raced past the couch toward the kitchen, but the eagle swooped down and dove straight for Siddique. Eric threw his lamp, but the unwieldy projectile wildly missed the mark. The glass bulb exploded on the kitchen counter. The huge bird was almost on top of his friend, and he felt anger boil inside him. He wanted to punch this damned thing right in its hooked beak, and for some unknown reason, that's exactly what he did.

He should have used his little elbow trick, the one he'd learned in the abandoned gravel plant in New Hampshire right after he'd nearly broken his fingers on a biker's face... but he didn't. He punched the menacing eagle with his fist, right in its hardened bill, made harder by the fact that this bird was exponentially tougher due to its superhuman possession. He expected to break every bone in his hand, and maybe his wrist. He'd never scroll on a cellphone again, or write another letter to a girl in really tiny print.

To his wonder, it wasn't like that. Not at all.

His fist struck the beast's beak, and the great eagle's momentum inconceivably shifted. Its entire body lurched 90 degrees from its target and directly into the brick wall, where it impacted with a shuddering *thud*, mercifully still a few feet away from the un-mirror. The ancient glass would have shattered with certainty had the creature made contact at such force.

Siddique stared at Eric, who shrugged his shoulders and said, "Dude, I have no idea. Something just came over me. I was scared for you. I got really mad, and that angry feeling just spiraled out of control, all in the space of a nanosecond. I thought I was gonna break my hand, but I couldn't stop myself."

"Well, thanks. I think you might have saved my life. Again."

"Don't mention it. Look, that thing isn't dead. It's probably just stunned. Let's get knives from the kitchen and finish it off."

They heard a sound behind them, and turned. The now miniature Afrit, barely three feet tall, crouched in the window, wings twitching. It currently appeared uniformly black as the night sky, but that was clearly by choice, to blend into the darkness. When it had emerged from the portal the day before, its monotone ashen form bore the marks it had gained after ingesting Ninurta. Its eyes had glowed like molten magma, horns had pulsed from blue to orange to a hot yellow, and a spiderweb of incandescent veins had illuminated the creature's wings.

*'Where is she? Where is our* Sadat Alnaar? *We sense her not.'*

Eric stepped forth. "Your guess is as good as ours. She just... *disappeared*."

The little beast scanned the room. *'What happened here? There has been a struggle.'*

"You're not kidding. It was that bird over there." He turned to point, but the eagle had vanished. "Oh, shit. It was right there a second ago. It just disappeared again. It's not a normal bird. It's possessed by a Jinn."

At that moment, Lotte reappeared, in the precise spot in front of the TV where she'd stood when she'd been attacked. She was completely unclothed.

Siddique rapidly turned away. "I'll just be in the kitchen. I have to clean up all that broken glass. That's what I'll be doing. I didn't see anything."

Eric rushed to her. "What the hell happened? Where did you go?"

She seemed completely confused. "I... I don't know. I don't think I went anywhere. I could have, but I somehow knew I was safe. Eric, I think I was like a Jinn, when they go into their immaterial form. It's all kind of vague and hazy, but I could sort of sense you and Siddique around me, as well as the eagle that attacked me. Then, for a while, there was something else in the room, too, but it left out the window."

"That must have been the raven."

"The *what*? You're saying there was an eagle *and* a raven?"

"Yeah. I even think I saw that raven before, at our place, but I'd forgotten about it. I'll tell you about that later. How did you manage to come back, or be material again, or whatever?"

"Well, I sensed when the Afrit came in through the window, and right after that, the eagle left as well." She turned to the little ashen creature who had hopped into the room. "Didn't you see it? It passed right by you, right out the window."

*'We are not Jinn. We cannot detect these creatures when they vanish, but apparently, they possess the ability to do so. For a time, it seems, you were as they are. Why, we do not know.'*

"I don't either, but when I sensed the threat was gone, I just... I don't know... I just... *rematerialized*. I can't explain it any better than that."

Another loud knock sounded from the foyer. "Guys! What the fuck?"

Eric grimaced. "Shit. I had to lock Margot in the closet. What are we gonna do?"

Lotte jumped into action. "Go close the window. I've just got to find my underwear. Mighty Afrit, could I impose on you to fly up to the second floor and hide yourself for a short time? I promise, it won't be long."

The beast momentarily seemed to glower at her as it swayed from side to side. Then, it rapidly took to the air and disappeared over the half-wall that encircled the loft.

She turned back to Eric. "Whew. All right, go let her out. I'll be right there."

As he went back down the hall, he chuckled as he noticed Siddique doing everything possible to *not* look into the living room. "Margot, it's okay. I'm gonna get this case out of the way, then we'll let you out."

He waited for Lotte to locate her undies, then don what remained of her tattered Harvard sweatshirt. She skittered down the hall to join him, and he pulled the case out of the foyer and opened the door.

Margot had somehow managed to turn herself around. She sat on the bags containing Enki's gateway, her back pressed awkwardly against the coats on their hangers. She didn't look especially happy. "Eric, did you lock me in a fucking closet?"

He started to squirm. "Uh, there was a bird. Big bird. You saw it. I didn't want you to get hurt."

"So, you locked me in the closet? I could have helped you get it out! Have you lost your mind?"

Lotte came to the rescue. "Eric is such a gentleman. He tried to push me into the bathroom to 'protect' me, but I wasn't having any of it. Don't take it personally."

Margot's eyes widened as she gawked at Lotte. "Why aren't you wearing pants?"

"Oh, that. Well... I took them off. Yeah, to fight the bird. I took off my sweatshirt first. Look what it did to that! Then I took off my pants."

"And your socks?"

"Umm, they kind of went with the pants. Listen, whatever. It worked, right? The big bird is gone."

"Does this happen often, birds flying into Siddique's apartment?"

"Siddique," Lotte called out, "do birds fly into your apartment on a regular basis?"

Siddique rounded the corner to join them, a dustpan and small brush in his hands. "No, this is pretty much a first, and hopefully a last."

Margot shook her head. "Un-fucking-believable. I'm really starting to think you people are crazy, not to mention artifact smugglers!"

"We're not smugglers, Margot," Lotte calmly explained.

"Then what is that thing in the living room, that big frame-thing with glass in it?"

"That's... umm... that's Siddique's."

Siddique started. "It is? I mean, yeah, it is. It's mine."

"What is it?" Margot asked.

"It's... well... It's kind of... umm—"

Lotte interrupted. "It's part of his religion. He's a Zoroastrian."

"Zoro what?" Margot squealed. "Is that like Rastafarian? I thought that was Jamaican."

"No, not Rastafarian. *Zoroastrian*. It's an ancient religion from Persia. The frame and glass are part of his worship, like a shrine. He doesn't like to talk about it much."

Siddique vigorously nodded. "Yeah, it's a kind of private thing."

Margot scraped her hand through her hair. "Okay, I give up. Are you guys gonna tell me what's up or not? This is getting ridiculous."

Lotte placed her hands on Margot's shoulders. "It's just like I told you. It's archaeology stuff. I have this specialized equipment from Germany that I know how to use, and people call me from time to time to have me help them look for things. It's proprietary technology, and I'm responsible for keeping trade secrets, as well as keeping it out of the hands of people who might put it to use in dirty industries, like mining and fossil fuels. So, I have to keep a close eye on it, and do all of the work myself. I need Eric, and sometimes Siddique, to help me out—just grunt work, since they don't know anything."

"That might be the only truthful thing you've said to me all night."

Lotte snickered. "You've got that right. Look, *Liebchen*, I can't tell you how much what you've done for Eric in the past has meant to me, last month in particular. I try to keep these things to a minimum, but this is one I just can't pass up. Hopefully, this will be it for a while, and things will get back to normal. My studies are falling behind. I can't keep doing this, but just help us out this one time. *Bitte*?"

Margo deeply sighed. "All right. I'm not sure why you couldn't have told me that before—*Eric!*—but I'll let it go this time. You're pretty slick, Lotte, and you're damned cute too. Not sure I've ever seen you without pants. If we weren't both spoken for, I'd make a play for you. For the record, you pretty much had me at 'Liebchen.' Call me when you know how long this is gonna take. You can count on me to cover all your Zorofarian asses, or whatever."

They shuffled Margot politely but firmly out of the apartment, over her protestations that she'd help clean up the mess or help load the cases of "archaeology stuff" into the van, since they'd told her they needed to leave that night. When she was finally gone, the three stared at each other with a mixture of relief and utter confusion.

Siddique broke the silence. "So, can anybody explain what just happened, or what this weird 'Zoro-whatever-thing' religion is that I'm supposed to belong to?"

"No to the first, yes to the second," Lotte distractedly replied, "but we'll do that later. Right now, I've got to talk to the Afrit. Before we do anything else, we have to determine if Olive is even still alive. Actually, before *I* do anything else, I'm going to put on my pants."

Siddique and Eric followed as she padded down the hall and into the living room, where she slipped into her pants and fumbled for her wedding and engagement rings, which had bounced under a chair and the coffee table after she'd disappeared.

*Good thing Margot didn't notice those weren't on her hand. That would have been* really *hard to explain!*

They were about to head up the stairs to the loft when a bright, bluish-red light beamed in from outside. Everyone scrambled to the window and saw a police car in the parking lot. About half-a-dozen people had gathered around a small, red vehicle, parked a few spaces down from Eric's Mazda and the Schneider van. It appeared that one of the side windows had been shattered. Glass littered the asphalt around the little car.

"That must have been the sound we heard right before the eagle flew in," Eric said. "I wonder if there's any connection?"

"It's entirely possible," Lotte replied. "It could also be a normal break-in, or just vandalism. What's the crime rate like around here, Siddique?"

"Yeah, stuff happens. Just kids acting crazy, mostly, or drug-related stuff. But, sure, cars get broken into, especially nice ones like that. Never seen it happen in our parking lot, but it's not so surprising."

"Well, either way, nothing we can do about it. Come on." She scampered up the stairs that led to the loft. Eric and Siddique moved in her wake but stopped near the top of the stairway as she inched into the room.

The Afrit huddled in the corner on the opposite side of the bed. It didn't register her presence as she approached, or when she sat cross-legged on the floor a few feet away.

"How are you?" she tenderly asked.

The creature raised its horned head, and its bony wings twitched. *'We are. No more, no less. Our cohesion grows. We have once again assumed control of our faculties and powers, diminished though they may be.'*

"I'm very glad to hear that. I can't imagine what a being like you might be going through, but I've experienced loss. Terrible loss. I know the sense of being 'blown apart' and having to put yourself back together, and I know the feeling of not wanting to bother, of just wanting to disappear to nothing."

The Afrit remained silent, but cast its empty gaze upward, as if looking toward the heavens.

"I coped by retreating into a shell, trying to keep others away and give time a chance to heal the pain. It worked, I guess, for a while, but it was through friendship and a shared sense of purpose that I truly found my way back."

Eric beamed and twirled the wedding band on his finger.

"We have need of you, great Afrit. Your friends, those who care deeply for you, have need of your powers. Diminished they might be, but you can do things no mortal can. Do you feel up to trying to help us?"

Eric heard the beast's barbed tail whip on the hardwood floor. *'Feel? We know not what this means. The bargain is either worth our while or not. Make your offer. If we deem it within our abilities, we shall comply.'*

Lotte stiffened. "Let me explain. There's one you know. You've gone into battle with her against Ninurta. Her name is Olive."

She paused, and Eric sensed she was probably projecting their friend's image into the Afrit's mind.

"She's gone missing. No one can find her. We don't even know if she's alive."

The Afrit jumped to its feet, and Eric almost knocked Siddique down the stairs when he reared backward from surprise.

Even Lotte had started at the sudden movement and had scooted back a couple of feet.

The creature extended its wings and swayed for a few moments before it again settled to the floor. *'She lives. She is far away. That is all we can say.'*

"That's excellent news," Lotte gushed. "This makes us very happy. Can you help us find her? Will you?"

The beast began to cackle, its grating and unintelligible words like the sound of a dying man's last breath. As always, its meaning rang clear in their minds. 'Sadat Alnaar, *you know better than this. What is the bargain? What shall be our spoils for aiding you once again? We hope the prize is a worthy one. Our dealings with you have proven rather, shall we say... risky.*'

Lotte shot a nervous grimace toward Eric, who simply shrugged. *This is your department, sweetheart.*

She paused in thought for a long moment, then returned her attention to the Afrit. "It isn't like it used to be, back when they sent you out to settle their blood feuds, or to eliminate their enemies. The world has changed. Well, maybe not all of it. I'm sure there are those out there who'd use you to kill, or to threaten, or to collect *dirt* on others to bring them down. They'd say they were doing it for 'good,' but in truth, it's just power most of these people want. Even if good comes of it in the short run, eventually, that kind of power corrupts, and history has shown that violence is rarely a long-term solution to anything. You can win the war, and easily lose the peace afterward."

She shifted to her knees and crawled closer to the little ashen monster where it hunched against the wall.

"I've never asked you to do anything like that. At worst, we needed your help to eliminate those who had first threatened *our* lives, and the lives of our families. At best, we asked for your aid to protect others, people that we don't even know, from the harm of dangerous supernatural entities. It's harder to make a bargain under those circumstances. Generally speaking, we knew what we were going into. There were enemies to fight, and the likelihood that there would be people for you to consume was reasonably high. This time, I really have no clue. I have no idea what's going on. All I know is that I want to find out what happened to our friend—your friend, whether you know it or not. I'm asking you to take the chance. There's always risk, but you know the rewards have sometimes been great for you. You also know that in this, I'm yours. You bargain with *me*, and *I'm* ultimately responsible for fulfilling my end of the deal. Make of that what you will."

The beast didn't move—no flutter from its wings, no quiver from its tail. Its stony gaze locked on Lotte, whose face had come within a foot of the monster's jagged fangs. Glacially, the Afrit raised its arm and extended its clawed hand.

A relieved smile spread on Lotte's face. "Eric, get the rings, if you'd be so kind."

He dashed down the stairs, trying to remember which case contained the box that held the gold ring and the bent filigreed bracelet. He'd just reached the hall when he heard a loud knock on the door. It didn't sound like Margot. He anxiously tip-toed to the door and looked out the peephole. A police officer stood in the hallway, hands on his hips.

*What else is gonna happen tonight, a plague of toads?*

"Guys, it's the police!" He opened the door, and once again tried to play it cool. *I need freaking acting classes.* "Hi, officer. What can I do for you?"

"Sorry to bother you, Mister...."

"Schneider-Schwarz. Just call me Eric."

"Okay, Eric. You live here?"

"No, I'm just visiting my friend. He was busy cleaning up a little mess."

Siddique joined him at the door. "It's my place, sir. Is there a problem?"

"Well, maybe you can tell me. We're here investigating a vandalism, or attempted theft, of a vehicle downstairs."

"Yeah, we heard the glass break earlier," Eric offered.

"That right? Did you call the police?"

"Umm, no. We didn't."

"Why not?"

"That was right when the bird got in. That's what caused all the mess we were cleaning up. It just flew right in the open window. Weirdest thing ever. Well, maybe not *ever*, but it was pretty weird. We thought it was weird, anyway. I'll shut up now." *Idiot!*

"I see. That must explain why people said they heard a lot of noise coming from up here. Lots of bangin' around."

"Yeah, we were chasing the bird with a broom, and whatever else we could think of. We broke a lamp, knocked over a couple of chairs. It was kind of stupid. The bird finally flew out on its own."

"Mind if I have a quick look around?"

Eric's heart began to race. "Umm, no, I guess not. Is that really necessary? We didn't have anything to do with that car." *Not that you can prove, anyway.*

"I'd just like to take a quick look. Just trying to be thorough."

*Yeah, thoroughly dead if the Afrit sinks its tail into you, but by all means, come on in.* He stepped aside and let the officer through.

The man gave a cursory glance into the closet, then strode down the hall. He performed a quick sweep of the living room, and unsurprisingly, his eyes came to rest on the Amazing Technicolor Dream-frame. "Wow, that's impressive. What the hell is it?"

"It's for my religion," Siddique tentatively put forth. "I'm a Zoro... Zoro—"

"Zoroastrian," Eric interrupted. "He's new to our little family, hasn't got all the nomenclature down quite yet. I'm helping him. May the blessings of Zoroaster smile upon you." He waved his hand in ceremonial fashion and flashed his pearly whites.

The cop furrowed his brow. "Thanks, I guess. Man, do you all have these giant things to pray in front of? Bet that's hell when you have to move."

"You have no idea. It's a tough religion. There aren't many of us out there, as you might imagine."

"Good thing you didn't break it when the bird got in." He bent to inspect something near the couch, but Eric couldn't see what it was. Seemingly satisfied, the officer moved on. As he approached the kitchen, he noticed the broken glass on the counter and floor that Siddique had swept into little piles.

"Lamp," Eric helpfully offered.

The man didn't respond. "What's up there?" he asked, pointing toward the loft.

"That's where my bed is," Siddique replied. "Nothing broken up there."

The officer glanced at the stairway, and for a moment it looked like he might go up, but then he turned and headed back to the foyer. "All right, I've seen enough. Sorry to trouble you." He was about to open the door when he stopped. "What kind of bird did you say flew in here?"

"Umm, we didn't say," Eric cautiously answered. He felt uncertain mentioning the eagle, a bird highly unlikely to fly through an open window. "I'm not sure. It was big, and black. Maybe a crow, or a raven."

The officer held up a black feather. "Sure was. Mighty big one too. You're lucky more stuff didn't get broken. I'd tell you to call animal control next time, but they probably wouldn't come until the next day, or maybe even the day after that." He guffawed. "You might be better off just leaving and checking into a hotel. Of course, there probably won't be a next time, will there?"

"If there is," Siddique said, "I think I'll just move."

# CHAPTER 4

**Location and Date: Unknown**

*Great, here it comes again.*

The pattern repeated, always the same. Olive would hear some sort of door slide open, and bare footsteps pad to where she lay on what felt like an unfinished cement floor, cold and damp against the fabric of her uniform. He'd lift her. Impossibly strong, he would hold her at arm's length, like one might a reeking carcass, as he carried her. He'd deposit her in a spot that reverberated slightly with the sound of a tile floor and walls.

"Relieve yourself," he would say. "I wish not the foul stench of your waste to attract attention."

*Dude, like it could be any worse than the freaking rotten milk smell?*

It hadn't taken her long, however, to realize she no longer smelled the spoiled milk in the kitchen of the house that she and Mutig had so ill-advisedly broken into.

*Where am I, anyway? There's some kind of machine that keeps going off right next to me, like the furnace in my momma's house. Maybe I'm in the basement. That smell probably don't get down here.*

She couldn't ask. Like her ankles and wrists, her eyes and mouth were bound with duct tape, sticky and hot despite the faint chill in the air. It made it awkward and unpleasant to pull down her pants to follow his wishes, and doubly so due to uncertainty of whether he watched her. It also felt like he'd unbuttoned her shirt. A queasy feeling came over her when she thought of his fat, stubbly fingers groping her breasts while she lay unconscious.

She couldn't say how much time had passed since he'd knocked her unconscious. She desperately longed for water, and for ice to soothe her eye that throbbed incessantly beneath her blindfold. More than anything, she worried about Mutig, and whether he'd been able to escape, or had fallen into her captor's clutches.

The slide of the door began the cycle anew, but this time, she felt a tug at the side of her face, and then the excruciating shock of the duct tape being ripped from her mouth.

"Who are you?" he demanded. "*What* are you?"

"W... wa... water... water, please. Please."

A moment's hesitation, then she heard his steps trail away. Soon, he returned and forced a plastic cup into her hands. She shakily brought the vessel to her mouth and greedily gulped it down.

"Now. Talk."

"I'm... I'm Olivia Carter. You can call me Olive, or 'stupid' if you prefer. At this point, either is fine with me. I'm a Community Service Officer with the Marietta Police Department. I came here to investigate what's been goin' on over at Emory. I thought there'd be some clues here. Guess I got a little more than I'd bargained for, huh? Why'd you attack me like that, and where's my dog?"

"The dog."

"Right. Mutig, my dog. Where's he at?"

"I know not. The dog is the answer to your first question. In my weakened state, he noticed me, detected my presence. I tried to flee, but then I sensed... *you*. I feared for my existence, a power sent to entrap me once again before I could regain my strength. I struck, before you could strike at me."

"But I told you I wasn't gonna hurt you! I just wanted to talk!"

"Probable lies."

"Oh, thank you very much, mister jump-to-conclusions. You made pretty short work of me. Why'd you think I'd pose any kind of threat to you?"

He was momentarily silent. "I ask again, *what are you?*"

"I told you, I'm a Community Service Officer! What more do you want me to say?"

"Tell me about the object that hangs around your neck."

A very uneasy feeling began in the pit of Olive's stomach, and it wasn't hunger. "That's, uh... that's a little hard to explain."

"Try."

"Well, it's just something I gotta wear. Something to keep something else inside me... well... quiet, like."

"Finally, a truth from your prattling lips. That was not so hard, was it? Now, tell me why it is that you came here."

"I told you! I came here to investigate the sleep paralysis cases that've been happenin' over at Emory. Unlike most humans, I know what causes that. You're a Jinn, aren't you? You've been feedin' on those students. I was just trying to figure out who was behind it, and why. The body you're in, or at least the one I *think* you're in, came up as a missing person. Like I said, I work for the police, so I can look stuff like that up and make connections that other people might not be able to. That's what brought me here. What I don't understand is why you haven't just been feedin' on me? What am I, too *old* for you?"

"You speak like the Idigna and Buranun when they swell with water and overflow their banks. I drown in your ever eddying currents. To respond to one of your myriad ramblings, I did not feed upon you because of the amulet you wear, and when I tried to remove it, I did not feed upon you because of what you *are*."

Olive felt the sting of tears under the duct tape that bound her eyes. "What *am* I?"

"In truth, I know not. Something lurks within you. If I am correct in my identification of the object you possess, then I suspect you wield great power, or truck with those who do. You represent danger to me, and until I gain the strength to reunite with my brother, I must keep you under my watchful eye."

"Why don't you just kill me? Really, I don't mind. I'll probably starve to death before anyone finds me here anyway, unless you plan on feedin' me. I don't think I'm good for much anyway. I'd probably fuck-up at McDonald's too. It's hopeless. Seriously, finish me off. Just please make it quick and painless, unlike what most of my life has been to this point."

"I yet may. A part of me, however, senses that you might be telling the truth, in as much about your ignorance as anything. And contrary to what I have come to gather is now widespread belief, I am not evil. Vengeful, yes, at times, but not evil. So, tell me, strange little chattering being of uncertain provenance, what can I get you to eat?"

<hr />

## Worcester, Massachusetts, Tuesday, October 24, 2017

"The blessings of Zoroaster? Seriously?" Lotte still couldn't get over Eric's remark to the police officer. "The older you get, the more it seems like your 'inner six-year-old' leaks out into public. They say women marry their fathers. I certainly fell into *that* trap!"

Eric snickered. "Hey, you knew what you were getting into. Come on, I know you think it's funny. I see that smile." He poked her, and she let out a little squeal of laughter.

Crowded around the window, they watched the police cruiser and the tow-truck begin to pull out of the parking lot below. A red Mini Cooper, with a white roof and white stripes on the hood, trailed behind, sans driver's side window.

She retreated and sighed in disgust "*Alter!* Finally! What the bloody hell took so long? Are we ready to go?"

He joined her in the living room. "Yeah, I mean, unless you want to try again with the Afrit. I don't mind unpacking what we need."

The little beast had declined to return to its Eternal Flame. Lotte had argued with it briefly, saying it couldn't fly to Georgia, especially in the daylight when it might be seen, though the monster did seem to be adept at avoiding detection. It had flown all the way to Oman and gone unnoticed, but that trip had been mostly over water. They'd reached a begrudging compromise that it would find them before sunrise and ride with them in the van during the day.

"No," she replied. "In a sense, it might be better to have the Afrit with us after what happened. If we're attacked again, its protection might make all the difference."

"You really don't have any idea what that was all about?"

"Well, I have ideas, especially since you told me you saw that raven at our house, but who knows if I'm right. You remember what Aicha said to you when you first talked with her on the phone?"

"Umm, vaguely."

She tsked and rolled her eyes. "A mind like a steel trap, except that the trap's *broken*. Whatever. She said something like, '*We've* been looking for Vanth's portal for a long time, and *we* were all so excited when someone discovered it.' Aicha had associates, likely Jinn associates, if they'd all been looking for the box for a long time, and they knew about me. It was probably some of her people that attacked the Tower of Heaven and Earth at Metéora."

"Could have been Iblis's minions, too."

"Possibly, but Aicha also said that he liked to work alone. I take that to mean he didn't work with other Jinn, because he obviously had humans with him in Oman. I also except... *her*... because she was his prisoner."

He noticed she still had trouble saying Dimme's name. "All right, but if Aicha sent her own people, why didn't she lower the barrier around the tower? She created the sigil, right?"

"Right, but try to keep up. Utnapishtim told us she needed to be quite close to the sigil to lower the protective field. She was in Worcester at the time, first in Siddique's body, then in Olive's. She needed people there fast. That owl we fought was probably the closest of her associates to Metéora, along with the men that attacked the tower. They almost got us. In any case, it's doubtless her other partners are curious about what happened, and if you think about it from their perspective, the trail goes cold with us. She likely called Iblis when we were driving to New Hampshire, not them. They may not even know what *happened* to Aicha, or that Iblis wound up with the key and the scroll."

"So, they're looking for information."

"That's my guess. That Jinn-eagle was trying to take me out the window, in all likelihood to be interrogated by someone who can communicate with me. It would have worked if I hadn't suddenly vanished."

"Seriously. Any ideas about *that*, or the raven?"

"Not really, but you can only conclude one thing: we have some allies. Some Jinn are after us, but others seem to be protecting us. I have no idea what caused my little disappearing act, or you suddenly gaining superhuman strength, but I suspect some kind of Jinn magic is behind it. It probably saved our lives. Come on, we've wasted enough time waiting. Let's get out of here before something decides to try again."

They'd already packed everything up: the Afrit's portal and all of Lotte's Grandparents' papers, Enki's gateway, along with Vanth's portal, which Siddique had crammed into his closet upstairs. All the cases and bags sat in the hallway and foyer, ready to be loaded into the van once the police and onlookers had cleared out. The Jinn-eagle had surely seen the frame. Siddique's apartment was no longer safe — if it ever really was. They'd have to find a better solution, but for now, the irreplaceable artifacts would ride with them.

They laboriously loaded the van with all the gear, the cases with the Afrit's portal being the hardest to transport. Siddique had packed up some of his clothes, but since Lotte and Eric hadn't anticipated leaving so soon, they needed to stop by Rogers Avenue to gather some things for the trip, and also leave a note for Mrs. Binson to please feed Langsam for a few days, or possibly more. Siddique drove the van, and Eric followed behind in his Mazda, not willing to abandon his car if the broken window was the result of routine vandalism.

He worried the whole way back, picturing the Afrit plunging through the window of Blake Harris's SUV. The man never had a chance, and neither would he, or Siddique, if that eagle decided to pull the same move. *The difference is, the Afrit is guarding us. That raven may be as well. Of course, it's probably Lotte who they're watching over, but that's fine with me.*

As it turned out, his worries were for naught. They reached their house without event, and quietly slipped inside to gather the few things they might need, including some pillows and blankets to soften the ride for those in the back of the van. Eric snuck downstairs and taped a note to Mrs. Binson's door about Langsam, thanking her profusely. By about 11:30 p.m., they were on the road to Atlanta.

For once, traffic wasn't an issue. Siddique took the first driving shift, and Eric squeezed in beside Lotte where she'd nestled into the cramped space between the side door and the various cases. Exhausted, he fell asleep almost immediately.

Eric woke when he felt the van come to a halt. The first hints of dawn poked through the windshield. "Where are we?"

"Just outside Baltimore," Siddique replied. "We're making great time. I'm gonna go inside and pee. Our little friend did a fly-by a few miles back. I took the next exit I could that had gas. We're around back of the station, so nobody should see. Open the side door so it can get in."

Lotte and Eric groggily stumbled out of the van. Soon the ashen monster descended and landed gently near the aged pump that advertised "free air." Eric suppressed a giggle at the filigreed bracelet they'd jammed onto one of the little beast's horns, its talons having been too small to accommodate the ersatz ring.

*'Your vehicle moves with the lumbering speed of a chariot with a broken wheel, pulled by a lame steed. We must circle endlessly to keep you in our sight. Can we not simply fly free and rendezvous when you arrive?'*

"We've been over this," Lotte explained. "We're likely in danger. We need your protection, and I don't want anyone to accidentally see you. Plus, being together will give us a chance to talk, if you like."

The monster swayed briefly before it marched to the van and hopped inside.

"Sheesh," Eric observed. "Chuckles has sure been in a bad mood since the big 'reappearance.' What do you think is up?"

"I don't know. The Afrit says it doesn't have feelings, but I'm not sure that's true, or maybe it simply doesn't recognize or acknowledge feelings for what they are. All creatures deal with trauma in their own way. If you ask me, I think *that's* what's going on, but I'll try to get more information if I can."

They stocked up on some very unhealthy prepackaged foods and hit the road, hoping to cut the drive time. Eric took the wheel and Siddique slumped in the passenger's seat to try and catch some sleep. Being so early, they slipped through Washington, DC with remarkable ease, but lost some time around Richmond during their morning rush. Seeing signs to Durham a bit before noon, Eric found he couldn't resist pulling in for a longer stop. Once he got oriented, he easily found the German restaurant on Durham-Chapel Hill Boulevard.

Lotte was stunned. "Cool! How in the world did you know about this place?"

*Kuuuul.* "I have an incredibly keen, but very narrow sense of smell. I can detect German food from about a hundred miles out. It comes in handy on occasion."

She rolled her eyes.

"But seriously, I ate here with Olive the day you got kidnapped. I figure it brought us good luck then, so why not give it another shot?"

After a wonderful and refreshing lunch, Siddique again took the wheel. Not wishing to disturb Lotte and the Afrit, Eric rode shotgun. The little monster perched on one of the cases, swaying in sympathy as the van rocked. Lotte hadn't gotten much out of the beastie. Talking didn't seem to be on its agenda, so now she had her laptop out, working on something for school.

Past Charlotte, they hit a long, straight stretch of I-85 that took them through a corner of South Carolina. A bit shy of Anderson around 3:30, Siddique woke Eric with a little whistle.

"Whew. Man, that was close."

"What?" Eric asked.

"Big truck back there. It pulled out to pass some guy, but he jumped into the left lane. The truck had to jerk away really quick. Almost hit somebody to his right."

Eric looked in the mirror outside his door. In the distance, he saw a little red car with a white roof in the breakdown lane, trying to reenter the highway. "Holy shit! Siddique, is there an exit coming up soon?"

"Umm, I think there's a rest stop just a couple of miles away. Why?"

"I think we're being followed. Stay in the right lane and let's take the next exit."

Lotte joined them in the space between the seats. "What is it?"

"It could be a coincidence, but I think I saw another red Mini Cooper behind us. It got forced off the road by that truck."

"It can't possibly be the same car. They couldn't have gotten it back from the police, fixed the window, and caught up with us by now."

"You're right, but it just seems suspicious. There's a rest area coming up. We'll pull in, get some gas, and be on our way if it turns out to be nothing. I'd just like to see what that car does."

"All right. That's actually good thinking. Nicely done."

*Woo-hoo!*

The exit ramp for the rest stop came up quickly. Eric scanned behind in his side mirror, but he couldn't see the red Mini. "Okay, when you pull over, go really slow on the ramp. I want to make sure they see us."

Siddique hit the turn signal and guided the van up the ramp as it curved away from the highway. He slowed to well below the speed limit. Eric rolled down his window and adjusted the mirror so he could see behind. After a moment, the red Mini came into view. It drove in the right lane, behind a ten-foot U-Haul moving truck.

The Mini started to slow down as it approached the ramp. For a moment, it looked like it was about to take the exit, but then it signaled for a left turn and swerved into the middle lane. Eric whipped his head around and leaned over Siddique to track the car as it zoomed by. It had almost been eclipsed by the U-Haul that it had suddenly decided to pass, but he still caught a glimpse of it.

"Is it the same car?" Lotte nervously asked.

"No, definitely not. It's red with a white top, but no stripes on the hood. It looked like a woman was driving. She had really thick, wavy black hair, and she was wearing sunglasses. I couldn't see much else. Weird she decided to pass at that moment after poking along behind that U-Haul for two or three miles."

"Well, it's probably nothing, but you never know. Good eyes, my love. Better safe than sorry."

---

The final hop into Atlanta was about two-and-a-half hours. Once again, Eric drove, and the van's passengers descended into road-weary silence. As they neared the city on a predictably traffic-packed I-85, the Afrit suddenly spoke.

*'Should you continue on your current course, you will pass her by. I sense her in the direction of the Southern Winds.'*

Eric took exit 89 off the highway and banged a quick left onto North Druid Hills Road. "Better?"

The creature was silent but popped from its perch and stood by Lotte on the floor of the cargo space. They drove about half a mile before it spoke again. *'Go this way.'*

"It wants you to go right," Lotte informed him.

He engaged his signal and turned onto Briarcliff Road. They wound along for over two miles, passing by some tall TV towers on the right, while he waited for his next instructions.

They finally came, rather cryptically, from the mouth of the Afrit. *'You must soon reorient yourself in the direction of the rising sun.'*

"That's east, right? Lotte, which way is east?"

"Left, I think," she replied. "Go left when you can."

He looked out the window and saw a solitary, and even taller, TV tower to the left. A road soon appeared that led to a complex of buildings near the soaring structure, presumably a television broadcast station.

"That's Fox Lane," Siddique reported, eyes on his cell phone.

"Well, I guess we know what station it is," Eric said. "It seems unlikely that Olive would be here, but in the Afrit we trust." He took the left but came to a quick stop when he saw that the road toward the buildings had a guarded checkpoint. Likewise, a large metal gate blocked a small road to their right. He quickly turned the van around and jumped back onto Briarwood in the direction they were heading before.

"I guess I'll just take the next left. What street will that be, Siddique?"

"Looks like Emory Road."

"We must be near Emory University," Lotte observed. "They have an archaeological museum that's probably the best in the Southeast. I'd love to see it, but we probably won't have time."

Eric made the turn onto Emory Road, and the Afrit pushed into the space between the van's seats. *'She lies directly ahead.'*

They traversed several monstrous speed bumps and were about to follow the road as it curved to the right, when the little creature yelled, *'Stop!'*

They came to a halt in front of a house with somewhat aged, yellow aluminum siding, and a brick façade. A generic gray sedan sat in the carport, and a raft of uncollected mail had been stuffed into the mailbox, which bore the number 1432.

*'She is there.'*

"Is anyone with her?" Siddique eagerly asked.

The ashen beast steadily turned its head in his direction and almost imperceptibly lowered its horns. *'We cannot see through walls. If there is another who you suspect lurks inside, project their image into our mind. Otherwise, stay your tongue.'*

Eric winced slightly at his friend's discomfort and tried to change the subject. "What the heck would she be doing here? Are we anywhere near Marietta?"

Siddique scrolled on his phone. "It's like, twenty miles. Not so far, but not really that near where she lives."

"Well, there's way too much light to do any snooping around right now, and I think people might get suspicious if they see our van parked out here, or even worse, see Chuckles flying around. I'm exhausted, and I think we could all use a shower. Is there a hotel nearby?"

Again, Siddique consulted his phone. "Yeah, there's one like five minutes down the road. The University Inn at Emory. Doesn't look too expensive."

"All right, let's go there, get a couple of rooms, and regroup after dark. I just don't see what other choice we have. I hope she can hold out that long."

### Location and Date: Unknown

Apparently, a bacon cheeseburger from Five Guys wasn't on the menu. Olive settled for some slightly stale Triscuits, and some manner of cornflakes that she had to pour into her mouth directly from the box. Obviously, these were things her captor, or the man her captor now controlled, had handy in his cupboards.

*Not exactly fine dining, but at least I ain't Starvin' Marvin no more.*

When she'd finished eating and drinking, he suddenly and unexpectedly replaced the duct tape gag. She futilely thrashed in protest as he carried her, once again at arm's length, into the bathroom to relieve herself. When she was finished, he deposited her back onto the damp and cold cement floor.

She willed herself to keep from crying tears of frustration, which just tended to clog up her nose with snot and make it hard to breathe. Countless hours passed, and she drifted in and out of troubled and restless sleep. She'd almost begun to think he'd abandoned her, when she finally heard the door slide open. After another trip to the bathroom, he propped her against a wall in her now familiar cement floored prison and ripped the duct tape from her mouth.

"Ouch! Damn, can't you give me a little warnin' before you do that? Where the H-E Double L were you? I thought you'd left me here."

"Drink," he said, as he pushed the plastic cup filled with water into her hands.

She fervently drained the contents while, to her great surprise, he answered her question. "I was forced to replenish the energy I lost while battling you and your beast. I gorged, then rested to digest what I consumed, but I am still appallingly enervated. In retrospect, it was a mistake to so utterly expend my powers when they tricked and attacked me, but how was I to know? The pestilence I wrought devastated their minions, and for a time kept *them* at bay as well, giving me hope. In the end, however, I fell. We both fell."

"I don't understand what you're talkin' about. Who was after you, and who fell with you?"

"My brother, but it matters not. That is long in the past. Now, it is decided. You shall lend me aid."

She nearly snarfed her water. "What? You want *my* help, after the way you done treated me? That's rich! And maybe you haven't noticed, but I ain't exactly some super-powerful 'Genie with the light brown hair' who can bob my head and make things happen. Wait a minute, she was blonde. Whatever. What I'm sayin' is, how can *I* help *you*? My damned dog's stronger that I am!"

"That is a lie."

"Listen here, mister whoever-the-hell-you-are, we're gonna get one thing straight right now. *I don't lie!* I may not always answer the question the way you want me to, or say the right thing, but that don't mean I'm lying to you!"

"It is not me to whom you lie, but rather yourself. This is why it is decided that you will lend me aid."

"Decided by who? You? Man, you are a piece of work. What if I don't wanna help you?"

"It would be an easy matter for me to bring an end to your existence. You will help me, or you will expire. What you desire is irrelevant."

Her spine tingled. "I told you already that you could kill me! But then you fed me. I guess you really do want my help, even if I am totally useless. Okay then, I'll help you. You could've just asked me nicely, though. *Sheesh.* What do you want my help with, anyway?"

"I will require your assistance when I reunite with my brother."

"The one in California?"

"I know not the name of the place where he is located. I sense his spirit far away."

"Well, California is a long way away. I've never been to California. Sounds exciting. When do we leave?"

"Soon. If his present state is like mine was until a few days ago, he is weaker even than me, but that could change rapidly, which would be especially inauspicious for me, and for him... and for *you*."

The tingling feeling returned. "Why?"

"Because then we must take by force what we can now take without violence. It is a race, and he knows this, but there may be little he can do. He may not enjoy the fortune that smiled upon me."

"I'm totally confused."

"As I say, it matters not. You will do as I ask of you when instructed. It is decided. For now, I need to return you to silence."

"Seriously? You're gonna put that damn gag on my mouth again? Why? You seem to believe I'm not lyin' to you, and I told you I'd help you."

He paused a moment before answering. "You did not volunteer your aid. You first resisted my decision, but that is of little consequence. I do believe you tell me the truth, but I know not who may come into this dwelling while I gather my strength for the journey. I do not wish them to find you, and I am uncertain whether you would call out to them for help. If such an event occurs, stay still and quiet until they leave. That will do much to quell my suspicions, and perhaps the restraint on your ever-active mouth can be discarded."

With that, he restored the duct-tape gag. This time, she didn't resist.

*If I'm gonna get out of this, I've gotta play it cool... look for an opportunity. He can't keep me bound and gagged all the way to California. Someone will surely see me. Unless he sticks me in the trunk. Oh, shit. What the hell have I gotten myself into?*

### Atlanta, Georgia, Wednesday, October 25, 2017

After checking in at the University Inn and showering, the somewhat rejuvenated trio walked to Dave's Cosmic Subs on North Decatur and got some sandwiches and drinks to go. 1432 Emory Road was only another ten minutes by foot up the road, and they resolved to walk after it had gotten dark, rather than take the van. The vehicle might draw suspicion, and if they needed to run, a perusal of Google Maps revealed there was a forested area to the east, around a creek, which would provide decent cover. They agreed to meet near the Emory University baseball and softball diamonds on the opposite side of the trees if they became separated.

By the time they'd finished their informal dinner, it had grown dark. The sky was clear, but it was surprisingly cool as Lotte and Eric skipped down the stairs and out to the van, which he'd parked in a spot near the rear, close to some trees and vines that had overtaken an old, wooden fence.

He opened the side door and Lotte pulled herself into the vehicle to address the Afrit, who had returned to its perch on the flight case. "Can you still sense Olive? Has she moved? Is she still alive?'

*'All is as it was.'*

"Good. We're going to let you out so you can scout around. We'll come later, after we've rested a bit, and after the people in the surrounding houses have gone to sleep. We'll walk up near the house and produce a small flame from this lighter. Come to us then and tell us if you've seen any activity inside. Agreed?"

The creature gave a curt nod and quickly darted for the open door. Eric had to duck as its wings flapped sharply above his head.

*Jeez. Careful there, Chuckles.*

Lotte clicked on the cargo space light and snatched Siddique's flashlight from the toolkit behind the driver's seat. Eric hopped in and located the sharp knives they kept in the cases. The one that had belonged to Dr. Esfahani had once kissed his throat on a crisp fall night like this one, almost exactly twelve years ago. He'd once thought it gone forever, but now it would be pressed into service again, just one of many dangerous but advantageous items they transported.

*Wait a minute.* "Hey, Lotte, should we leave all these cases and bags in the van? The Afrit isn't here to guard them anymore, and when we go up to that house, neither will we."

"*Alter!* You're probably right. If a Jinn is dead set on stealing them, there's not much we can do, but at least moving them into the rooms will make it a bit harder. I'll bring along a piece of Vanth's and Enki's portals, so at least they won't be functional if someone takes them. The bowls are too fragile to be transported like that, but I'm not as worried about the Afrit's portal. It's too hard for someone to just walk off with that frame. It's a gigantic risk, but we'll just have to hope we get lucky, or that one of our Jinn friends, assuming we still have any, will help us out. Let's go get Siddique to help us move all this stuff."

The pair closed up the van and traipsed back up the stairs, their dreams of a nice nap before rising at midnight to investigate the house frustratingly postponed.

Suddenly, Eric stopped. "Hey! When we get up, you know what it will be?"

She looked puzzled. "What?"

"Your birthday!"

"Ooh, you're right. I'd totally forgotten. Twenty-eight years old. That's almost dead. Do you still love me, now that I'm old and decrepit?"

"Eh, I guess. You know what the real draw for me is, though."

"No, I can't imagine, but I'm sure it'll be highly entertaining. Do go on."

He grinned and accepted the challenge. "It's my great weakness. I just totally *dig* chicks who are into archaeology."

She covered her eyes with her hand. "Little shit! You've probably been waiting to spring that one on me for years. You're never serious, are you?"

He wrapped his arms around her and hugged her tight. "You want me to be serious, huh? Okay." He took a deep breath. "You know that tree at the back of my parent's yard?"

She nodded, her head snuggled against his shoulder.

"It was looking a little rough a couple of years ago, so my folks called a tree specialist to get an expert opinion about whether to save it or cut it down. I went out to watch. He climbed up there with a bunch of ropes and pulleys, and he had this short but super sharp saw that would slice through a pretty decent sized limb. I was impressed. Anyway, he shimmed up to the top, cut out a bunch of deadwood, and then rappelled down like a professional mountain climber. The guy was a total pro. Wanna know what he said?"

She held him tighter and nuzzled her forehead into his neck.

"He said, 'That's not one tree, it's two trees that grew up in unison. They're big enough now that they're pulling apart, and that's causing stress, but if you just link them with a little cable, they'll sway together in the wind, and all the stress will be gone.' He said it would be a cheap, easy fix, and that the tree would be healthy and happy for decades to come. My folks gave the go-ahead, and sure enough, now it's the most beautiful tree in the neighborhood. That's what I think we are—two weird and different trees that've been linked to sway in the wind in some kind of bizarre unison. I'm glad the circumstances that brought us together happened. I've grown taller, and straighter, than I ever would have alone, or with anyone else. You don't look old and decrepit to me. You look healthy and happy, and I think you always will."

They stood for some time in each other's arms outside the University Inn at Emory, the warmth from their bodies staving off the chill of the fall night.

"It's incredible," Lotte finally said, sounding a bit teary.

"What is?"

"How you can go from infantile to sagacious in the blink of an eye."

"Hey, it's just another one of my many talents, underappreciated as they all may be."

She pulled away, but grabbed his hand and dragged him up the stairs to their room. "Okay, Mr. Underappreciated. Take me to bed and show me one of your other talents. I'll consider that my birthday present, since I know you've been busy and haven't had time to think about what to get me."

Eric kept his mouth shut, knowing he was getting a fantastic deal, especially since he'd been as clueless as she that tomorrow was her birthday, until it had accidentally dawned on him.

# WILLIAM E. NOLAND

# CHAPTER 5

*Nah, this doesn't look suspicious... not at all.*

The trio traipsed up Emory Road in the darkness, hugging their bodies for warmth. Their hoodies and windbreakers that had been fine during the day were totally insufficient for near 40-degree cold.

*I thought this was supposed to be the South. I think it's warmer in Boston right now.*

The temperature was the least of Eric's worries. If a cruiser happened to drive by, he knew they'd be screwed.

*Yeah, this is great. Three young people, one carrying a large flashlight, and two others with knives in their pockets they can barely conceal. We're the very definition of* suspicious. *No cop would pass up investigating us, and we really have no good excuse for being in this neighborhood at this time of night. 'Really, officer, we're from out of town and just thought we'd do a little sightseeing.' Man, it doesn't get much lamer than that.*

Fortunately, it was only a twenty-minute walk from their motel, and they'd already covered most of it. They hadn't even brought their phones, having no need for directions, and fearing that if trouble found them, it would be best to leave as little trace as possible. They stayed on the side of the street near the trees, opposite the row of big, fancy houses that made the one in which Olive was located seem a bit lowly.

They neared the bend in the road. Number 1432 was about a football field away, when suddenly, Siddique stopped dead. "Did you hear that?"

Lotte and Eric came to a standstill.

"Hear what?" she asked.

"Something in the trees, right there... like a rustling... something moving."

"We're too exposed out here for me to shine the flashlight. Let's get a little closer to the house, duck behind a bush, and I'll call the Afrit."

They skulked cautiously forward along the sidewalk, listening for any noise.

"There!" Siddique whispered, and again they all came to an abrupt halt.

This time, it was unmistakable. Something was in the bushes, moving with them, stalking them.

"What are we gonna do?" Eric asked.

"Come on," Lotte directed. She gingerly stepped onto the grass and inched toward the trees. Eric and Siddique followed and flanked her. She'd bridged half the distance to the tree line when she stopped. "Is anyone there?" she quietly called out.

Something zoomed out of the bushes as if shot from a cannon. In the darkness, Eric couldn't see what it was, but before he could react, it slammed directly into Lotte, and she tumbled backward onto the grass. Some beast pinned her to the ground and tore at her. Eric grabbed for it, but it skipped away. The creature rapidly repositioned itself above her head, then appeared to viciously bite down into her face.

"Eww, gross!" she squeaked.

She pushed at the shape that assailed her and it darted straight for Eric. He felt the thrust of powerful, meaty paws on his chest as the animal reared up on its hind legs and repeatedly forced its rough and slavering tongue over his face.

Realization dawned on him. "Mutig!" The frantically overjoyed dog bounced back into Lotte, once again knocking her to the grass just as she was about to get up.

She began to giggle. "All right, all right. I know you're happy to see us, but you have to calm down. And no barking. Do you hear me? None. I don't want to hear a peep. *Jetzt, ruhig!*"

The gray dog instantly sat down beside her and put its head on her thigh. She scratched him behind the ears, and he vigorously wagged his stubby tail. "There, that's better. You poor thing, you must have been out here for days! What have you been eating? It's all right. Everything's okay now. We're just going to find your mother, then we'll get you some food. Is that okay? Do you want to find your mommy?"

Mutig let out an almost inaudible little whine, and his tail slowed.

"That's what Olive's mom said," Eric interjected. "It's like he's gone off her."

"More likely, he's just scared. Olive probably doesn't smell or feel right to him, off in some way that he can't understand. Remember, he's been touched by Enki and the power of the Abzu... enhanced. Maybe he senses Aicha's magic, or the medallion, and it makes him wary. He stayed here, though. He knows his master is in trouble, and he didn't abandon her. He wants her back, wants her to be safe, despite everything else."

Eric nodded. "Speaking of which, we better get a move on. I hope we're far enough from those houses that they didn't hear anything. Gotta say, though, I'm glad to have Mutig with us if the going gets rough."

The dog fell in step, close at Lotte's thigh, as they hurried toward the house. They slipped into the side of the yard where it met the trees and crouched behind a bush, out of view from the street. Lotte dug the lighter out of her pocket and clicked until it sparked into flame, then held it forth and gently waved it in the darkness.

They all jumped when the Afrit spoke from behind. *'Nothing has changed. The one you seek remains inside, stationary. She is near the center of the structure, but beneath its upper story. There is an access point to this area on this side of the building. Come, we will show you.'*

"Have you seen anyone else in the house or detected any movement?" Lotte inquired.

*'No. All is still. If anyone else is inside, they did not announce their presence.'*

The little ashen beast led the way as they cautiously prowled deeper into the back yard. The ground precipitously sloped downward at the back right corner of the house. In the dim light from a streetlamp, Eric could see narrow, basement-like windows near the top of an exposed concrete wall in the divot at the bottom of the incline. They slipped around the corner onto a small, stone patio that barely accommodated a couple of wrought metal chairs and a small table. To his left, he could barely make out a plain but sturdy door in the inky blackness.

"There's another window there," Lotte whispered. "Move that chair over and I'll try to get a look inside. No one will see the flashlight back here. We're behind the house, and the slope up into the rest of the yard will block off the view from the house next door."

"What if someone inside sees the light, or hears us?" Eric whispered.

"The Afrit has been here for nearly four hours and seen no movement. Eventually, we're going to have to try to break in, so if anyone else is in there, they'll hear us at that point for sure. I'd rather know what we're getting into, if possible."

*She has a point.* He quietly lifted one of the chairs. It was old, heavy, and by its feel under his palms, rusty. He positioned it under the narrow window, and Lotte stepped up.

She braced her arm on the slender windowsill, held the flashlight against her ear, and clicked it on. *"Verdammt!"*

"What?"

"There's a bloody curtain. I can't see a damned thing." She clicked the flashlight off and hopped down. "That sucks. I don't think it's worth trying those other windows. Too much risk of being seen along the side of the house. I also think this window is way too large to try and break. It'll make too much noise, and I think we risk getting badly cut trying to crawl in through that cramped space. I also don't believe we're going to get in through that solid door." She crouched down to face the Afrit. "Is there another way in back here?"

*'Up this slope, near the other side of the house, there is a door into the upper level of the structure.'*

They scampered up the little hill to have a look. The door they found had nine panels of transparent glass that dominated its upper half.

Lotte clicked on the flashlight and scanned inside. "It's the kitchen. Looks pretty normal." She shut off the light "There's a door on the opposite side that probably goes into the carport. It's got glass like this one. I don't want anyone to see the light."

Eric pulled the sleeve of his hoodie over his hand to prevent fingerprints and tried the knob. "It's locked. I hate to say it, but I think this may be our best bet."

Lotte glanced at Siddique, who shrugged. She nodded and passed the flashlight to Eric.

He removed his hoodie and handed it to her. "Hold this over the lower right pane of glass. It'll soften the blow and make less noise."

She did as instructed, and he drove the butt of the flashlight into the door. It took him a few tries, but finally the glass gave way and he heard the shards as they tinkled on the tiles of the floor inside. "Well, they'll know we're here now, assuming anyone else is home."

"I think that's a pretty safe assumption," Lotte said as she handed him back his hoodie. "Or unsafe, as the case me be. *Alter!* What's that awful smell?"

"*Yeesh.* I think it's rotten milk. There was all that mail in the mailbox. Maybe nobody's here after all, except Olive, of course. That doesn't make a lot of sense, though, does it?"

He again pulled the sleeve of his hoodie over his hand, reached inside to unlock the door, then pushed it open. He gestured to the Afrit, whom he could barely make out in this especially dark spot behind the house. "After you."

The beast strode by him, hooves surprisingly gentle and quiet on the ceramic floor.

Eric could see better for a spit of light from the streetlamp that leaked through the glass in the door to the carport. He spared a quick glance over his shoulder and saw that Lotte followed behind him, her hand on Mutig's collar, while Siddique guarded the rear, knife already drawn.

There were doorway-sized openings near each other in the far corner of the room. One led toward the front of the house, one to a room at the rear.

"Which way?" he whispered over the little monster's twitching wings.

It didn't answer, but marched to the leftmost opening, toward the back.

Eric and the others followed, past the refrigerator from which the offending smell emanated, and through the opening. Pitch darkness again descended.

"I can't see a damn thing in here" Lotte groused. She clicked on the flashlight and waved it around the room.

Eric took in what looked like an informal living room, or "TV room," as he and his folks might call it. *Do they call it a* TV room *in the South?*

Nothing appeared amiss, or especially interesting in this area. When Lotte relocated the Afrit in the flashlight's beam, the creature's attention had locked on a small hallway across the room, past a large couch.

It strode into the hall, stopped, and looked at the floor. *'She is below... beneath us. We must go down.'*

The trio, plus Mutig, whose collar Lotte still clutched, crowded into the hallway. The flashlight revealed two doors to their left, and they could barely see a third, across another hallway that ran perpendicular to the one in which they stood.

"That's probably a bedroom over there," Eric speculated aloud. "Let's see if either of these doors lead down." He tried the first. It turned out to be an incredibly overstuffed closet that reminded him of those in his parents' house. He shut it, and everyone shuffled a bit deeper into the hallway. "Okay, here goes."

He pulled open the door. Instantly, he felt a strange, frigid breeze around him.

The Afrit at his hip seemed to feel it too. It shot its wings wide and sharply whipped its barbed tail above the horns on its head.

Mutig began to growl threateningly, and urgently tugged at Lotte's restraint.

As quickly as it had come, the odd sensation passed, but Eric's heart pounded in his chest, and he sensed that all his companions likewise remained on edge.

The flashlight Lotte held revealed the top of a stairway leading down. Eric couldn't see the bottom because the light came from the side. Undeterred, the Afrit skittered past him and down the stairs, and Eric followed, feeling the little beast's sense of urgency. He detected a bend to the right in the stairs, just as Lotte's flashlight illuminated the remainder of the passageway.

A gigantic red- and blue-faced man, mouth wide and uvula dangling between crooked teeth, silently screamed directly in front of him. The man's tormented eyes intently focused down and to the left, as if he witnessed something so terrible, it was literally driving him to instantaneous madness.

Eric's heart leapt again, until he realized the discomfiting image was merely a poster. "Jeez! What the hell are these people who live here, a bunch of doomsday cultists?"

Lotte spoke softly in his ear. "No, it's a record cover, some band from the early 70s, or some-such. King Diamond, maybe. No, that's not it. It's King something, though."

"Yeah, King Fuckin'-Scared-The-Hell-Out-Of-Me." The Afrit had already disappeared around the corner and into the room below, so Eric began to sidle past the disturbing poster.

At that moment, Siddique screamed above and behind him as the door violently slammed shut. Mutig ripped free of Lotte's grasp, dashed up the stairs, and began to furiously paw and scratch. Eric realized that Siddique must still be upstairs. He pushed past Lotte, who pointed the flashlight at the door, and twisted the handle. It turned with ease. It wasn't locked, but neither he nor Mutig could budge it, despite how hard they pushed. He heard a struggle from the direction of the TV room.

Suddenly, the top of the door smashed open with the piercing sound of splintering wood. The Afrit had flown over Eric's and Mutig's heads and bashed straight through. Even though it had been hollow on the inside, the feat was still impressive. The remainder of the door suddenly flew open, all resistance gone, and Eric and Mutig spilled into the hallway.

The dog scampered into the TV room while Eric righted himself. He'd just gotten up when he again felt the rush of freezing wind around him. This time it carried the chill of death, and it made him tremble like the near-arctic blast of a New England Nor'easter. He heard Lotte moan behind him, probably experiencing the same thing. Like before, the ghastly feeling quickly passed, like a fast-moving cloud that briefly obscured the sun.

He reached behind and extended his arm. Lotte grabbed his hand, and he helped her up into the hallway. Then they both rushed into the TV room where she frantically shone the light, trying to locate Siddique. Their friend lay at the opposite end of the space, just under the television. He massaged his jaw and sported a nasty looking cut on his lip. They both ran to his side.

"What happened?" Lotte asked with alarm.

"Somebody attacked me. From the size, I think it was a guy. He must have come from that other hallway. I never saw him, it was too dark, and I was looking down the stairs. Man, he was strong. He pushed me from the hall and I landed here. Banged my head pretty good on this cabinet. I couldn't see shit. I tried to get up, and he smacked me in the jaw. I was seeing stars. I thought I was a goner, but then, he just left."

"Where did he go?" Eric prompted.

"I have no idea. I didn't hear him run away, but I was so out of it, who knows. If you didn't see him, I'm guessing he went into the kitchen."

"I doubt it," Lotte said. "I think he vanished when the Afrit broke through the door. I mean, vanished, vanished. Like a Jinn. I think that's what we both felt a minute ago. I think he dematerialized and that he's back downstairs, or who knows where by now. He could be anywhere." She scanned the room with the flashlight and located the Afrit perched on the back of the couch. "Is Olive still downstairs?"

*'She has not moved.'*

"Can you sense the one who attacked us now?"

*'We did not see him, did not register his face. We are blind to his presence, but if he truly is a Jinn, then perchance we would not be able to perceive his location. Never have we been able to do so with a Jinn, and take our word, we tried many times to pinpoint Iblis.'*

"*Verdammt!* That puts us at a disadvantage, but there's nothing for it. We have to try to reach Olive. That broken window won't go undetected for long, and when the police come inside, they'll find that smashed door. Plus, this Jinn knows we've found him. This may be our only chance. We just have to stick close together."

Siddique brushed himself off and located his knife, then nodded that he felt good enough to go.

The party assembled in their previous order. Led by the Afrit, they trooped into the hall, and then crept down the stairs. Eric shivered as he passed by the creepy poster and rounded the corner. He hovered on the bottom step while Lotte surveyed the room with the flashlight. It wasn't anything like what he'd expected.

The far wall was lined with shelves that must have contained thousands of compact discs. To the left, near the door that led out to the patio, a large wooden stand housed a 65-inch flat screen TV, and an impressive variety of audio components. Tower speakers stood to either side of the console, and a desk with a computer and fancy gaming chair sat under the window that Lotte had tried to peek through earlier.

Across the room to the right, a couch and a coffee table were perfectly positioned to watch the TV and hear the formidable looking speakers. Above the couch were more posters. He saw odd looking spaceships with sails, upside down triangular land masses landing into some alien seascape, and one that had a strange, spiked, semi-circular shape beneath golden words on a black background:

MEKANÏK DESTRUKTÏW KOMMANDÖH

# MAGMA

"Umm, another band?"

Lotte snickered. "Yeah. I've heard of them. They're French."

"That doesn't look like French to me."

"No, it's not. Magma made up their own language. I can't remember what it's called. It's all very hermetic. The people who like this stuff lap it up like it's the key to understanding the universe. I think we've stumbled into the den of a 'Prog Rock' fan. Not surprisingly, it's in the basement. I wonder if his parents live upstairs."

Eric shook his head in disbelief, as much that Lotte knew anything about Magma, or "Prog Rock," as anything.

He tried to refocus. Beyond the couch, a door opened into a darkened room. Hard to his right, another hallway led to a door at the end, barely visible in the roving beam of the flashlight. The "Prog Rock den" appeared to be empty, but if they were dealing with a Jinn, he knew the entity could be standing right next to him, and he wouldn't know it.

He felt Mutig strain to enter the room, but Lotte held firm and chided the dog to be still. He knew Siddique was behind her, close at her back and guarding against any strike from behind, as best he could. The Afrit stood in the room, near the coffee table, twitching with agitation as it looked down the hallway to the right.

'Down there. She whom we seek is close, behind one of those doorways.'

Eric could only see the one door at the end of the hallway, but shrouded in darkness, the right wall was still invisible to him. He took Lotte's arm, and together they gingerly stepped into the room.

Suddenly, something, or someone slammed into his back. It felt as if he'd been pummeled with a sack of rocks, and the blow knocked his breath out. He collapsed to the floor and fought to suck in air. The light from the flashlight winked out, and he realized Lotte had probably been knocked down as well. It was almost pitch black. The curtains on the windows blocked most of what little illumination might filter in from outside.

He heard a struggle around him. Mutig fiercely growled and seemed to be tearing at something, while a voice he didn't know bellowed screams of pain and bitter anger.

Unexpectedly, the room flooded with light. Eric looked up to see a rather portly, and very naked man, struggling with Mutig and the Afrit. The dog had clamped his teeth into his ankle, and despite a mighty punch, which Eric assumed was not the first the animal had endured, Mutig held on tenaciously as blood spattered on the light blue wall-to-wall carpeting. For its part, the Afrit had sunk the tiny but still deadly barb of its tail into the man's back. Having picked his poison, their naked assailant struggled with Mutig, and seemed to ignore the painful injury from the Afrit.

Siddique launched into the fray from the stairwell, where he must have found a light switch. Savagely, he drove the blade of his knife into the man's shoulder. Again, their attacker howled in agony, and swatted at Siddique with the back of his hand. Siddique tumbled into the desk and knocked over the leftmost speaker, which toppled into the console behind the TV.

Eric was about to try and get up, to attempt a similar maneuver as Siddique's, but the man swiftly brought his hands together, then cast his arms out, palms wide. A wave of nausea assailed Eric, and his body instantly felt wracked by fever. He curled into a fetal ball, and tried to ride it out, but he couldn't avoid expelling the contents of his stomach onto the rug. He heard Lotte retching beside him where she still lay, and even Mutig let go of his forceful grip on the naked man's ankle and retreated to the corner of the room to gag and barf.

By the time Eric could look up again, the large man had reached behind him and pulled out the Afrit's barb. He held the little beast by its tail and tried to batter it with his clenched fist. The Afrit, however, was too quick. With almost lightning speed, it flapped its wings and darted out of the way, then clonked its chubby aggressor under the jaw with a sharp kick from one of its little cloven hooves.

The man stumbled backward into the wall to the left of the desk, knocking several framed LP record covers to the floor, along with a rather psychedelic poster of a hippie surrounded by rainbow hues, wearing a long coat while standing on one leg playing the flute. Above him was the name:

# Jethro Tull

*Poor Jethro*, Eric thought, as he located his knife and again attempted to rise.

The man had lost his grip on the Afrit's scorpion-like tail. The little monster twirled to the couch, bounced off the back cushions, and landed on the armrest near the far door, where it quickly sprang to its hooves and let out a threatening screech.

The man regained his bearings, bowed his head slightly to his little ashen opponent, and then vanished from sight... except, he didn't. Eric could track him by the wake of disturbed air that swirled and rippled as he streaked away. Like an intermittent video signal, his body flashed in and out of focus as he sailed toward the Afrit. It appeared the child of the Eternal Flame could see him as well. It easily took wing and flew over to the desk, where Siddique miserably hunched on the floor in front of his own pool of vomit.

After that, Eric lost track of their assailant. The translucent man either went through the door beyond the couch, or he'd managed to fully dematerialize. Eric didn't know, and he didn't care. *This might be our best, and maybe only chance to rescue Olive. It looks like we hurt him. He's having trouble with his powers.*

He got shakily to his feet and shouted over his shoulder to the Afrit. "Watch that door over there, or for any sign of him. I'm gonna see if I can find Olive. Lotte, Siddique... you guys okay? Stay close to the Afrit. That dude could come back any second."

He saw Lotte begin to crawl through the displaced LP covers toward the desk before he bolted for the hallway. To his surprise, Mutig galloped alongside him, seemingly recovered from his bout of illness. The light revealed that there were, indeed, two doors in this space, the one at the end of the hallway he'd seen before, and a large sliding door to the right, which Eric assumed was a closet. He bypassed that and went straight for the door at the end and threw it open.

"Fuck! Closet!"

He turned and saw Mutig whining and scratching at the base of the sliding door, and he quickly backtracked to join the dog, then grabbed the handle and pulled. The door slid somewhat hesitantly into a recess in the wall, and he saw a washer and dryer before him. This part of the house seemed unfinished, with visible wooden studs on the walls, and a cement floor.

He reached inside and clicked on a light. To the left of the washer, he saw a tall water heater, and beyond that, a large furnace. Pipes and aluminum vents trailed into the ceiling, apparently a unit, or perhaps two units, which supplied both heating and cooling.

Mutig scrambled past him and went instantly behind the machinery. *Of course!*

He followed after the dog, squeezed by the large contraptions, and there she was. Olive lay on the cement floor in a narrow space between the various furnace components and the back wall. Her ankles, wrists, eyes, and mouth were all bound with silver-gray duct tape. In the corner, not far from her head, sat a couple of cereal boxes, a plastic cup like you'd use in the bathroom for toothbrushes, and the remains of what he presumed was once her cell phone. It had been pulverized, ground nearly into dust, a few cracked shards of the plastic case the only clue as to the object's identity.

Mutig had settled tentatively at her feet, just barely nosing her shoes. Eric pushed past him and bent over his friend. She lay very still, but she was obviously alive. The buttons of her uniform's blouse had been unfastened, and he spied the bulge of the white medallion nestled under her t-shirt.

"Olive, it's Eric. Listen, I'm gonna take off this gag. It may hurt, but we don't have a lot of time."

She stiffened as if in surprise, then gave a little nod.

He ripped the duct tape from her mouth.

She coughed a bit, then spoke. "Gawd damn! I hope that's the last bleepin' time I have to go through that! How the hell did y'all find me?"

"Long story, I'll tell you later. I have a knife. I'm gonna cut your hands loose, then I'll get your ankles." He quickly but carefully sliced through the duct tape that bound her wrists, which she stretched and massaged while he freed her legs.

By the time he'd finished, she'd propped herself up and was fiddling with the tape around her eyes. "Help me unwrap this," she pleaded. "Oh, man, it's all gummed up in my stupid hair. Don't you dare be rippin' that off my head! Just try to get it loose so I can see."

He quickly peeled away the portion of tape that covered her eyes and pulled it back over her head like a hair scrunchie. He gasped when he saw her left eye, which was horribly swollen and bruised. "Olive, did he hit you?"

"Sure did." She touched the wound. "Ouch! That's gotta look pretty awful, huh?"

"Yeah, pretty awful. Listen, we don't have much time. Can you stand up?"

"If you help me. I may not be too stable, but I'll be gawddamned if I'm stayin' here!"

He pulled her to her feet, then had to hug under her arms to keep her from collapsing. After a moment, she seemed steady enough to stumble along with his aid. They'd just begun to retreat from the space behind the furnace when Mutig emitted a low rumble. The dog faced back toward the washer and dryer, and as Eric rounded past the furnace, he discerned the reason for the animal's agitation.

The still naked man stood by the doorway. He'd grabbed a broom from near the dryer and held it forth in both hands as if it were a halberd. Eric would have laughed at the ridiculous image before him if he didn't grasp how much trouble they were in.

"Not so quickly," the man said, palpable menace in his tone. "She is mine. I have need of her. You cannot take her."

"Try to stop me, asshole." Eric lunged at the man with his knife, his courage bolstered by Mutig's presence. "Guys! A little help here!"

Far quicker than he was, the dog shot out first and leapt for the man's throat. Their opponent reacted with the speed and technique of a Major League Baseball batting champion. He swung his broom, contacted Mutig in mid-air, and sent the dog sprawling into the washing machine, where he landed with a resounding *thunk*.

The man then deftly stepped aside to avoid Eric's knife thrust, causing Eric to stumble forward, his target having suddenly shifted position. He felt the broom push against his back, forcefully sweeping him out of the room and into the hallway. Here, he collided first with the Afrit, who flew into his head, and then into Siddique, who unwittingly knocked him to the floor.

The sliding door slammed shut.

The Afrit pounded against the portal, clearly held in place by Jinn magic, but unlike the one at the top of the stairs, this door was made of solid wood.

Siddique desperately tried to pull it open, but his efforts were futile.

As Eric frantically tried to think of something that might help them get leverage, a shot rang out from inside the room, and he again felt engulfed by a frozen wind that pierced his body like a million microscopic icicles.

Siddique collapsed to the floor, but his hands, locked on the latch of the door, inadvertently slid it open. Olive staggered into view in front of the washer and drier, where she collapsed, gun in hand, while Mutig limped out of the room, past all of them, and down the hall.

*Lotte!*

She was the only one back in the den area, and Eric felt certain that was where the Jinn had gone. He bolted down the hall behind the obviously injured dog and saw the computer desk under the window before him, but Lotte wasn't there.

He launched into the room, but meaty hands grabbed him from the right. The naked man stood on an end table next to the couch. He lifted

Eric high into the air and flung him across the room, where he crashed into one of the CD racks near the outer door. His back and right shoulder screamed in pain as countless CDs cascaded from the shelves and battered him from above.

For a moment, he couldn't see anything, eyes clenched in agony and arms feebly protecting his head from the plastic onslaught. When Mutig snarled angrily and then let out a yelp of distress, Eric opened his eyes. The dog lay in a heap on the floor in front of the door beyond the couch, breathing heavily. The Afrit now fluttered about the room but kept a discrete distance from the enraged and powerful man.

The man flailed ever more wildly, blood spattering from the gunshot wound to his arm, and flowing from the slice in his shoulder from Siddique's knife, and running from the puncture wound in his back from the Afrit's barbed tail.

*What are we gonna do? What am I gonna do? Should I go for Olive's gun? Too far. Siddique will grab it. What can I... wait a minute! This guy is Jinn. They don't like iron.*

He hauled himself to his feet, ignoring the shooting pain from his shoulder, grabbed the handle of the outer door, and twisted the locking mechanism to the open position. He threw the door wide and stumbled onto the little patio. The chairs were too heavy to lift and wield, especially in his current condition.

*That little table, though....*

He picked it up by the top and looked through the see-through lattice at the legs below. Once, they'd probably had little plastic end caps, but those were long gone. Now, they were naked, jagged metal that had scraped and sharpened themselves across the stone of the patio for a decade or more.

*Perfect!*

He brought the top of the table to his chest, legs pointed straight outward, and charged into the room. He leapt over the pile of CDs, which it would probably take somebody hours to carefully re-file in their previous order, and brought his ersatz weapon to bear.

The Afrit seemed to sense his plan. It flew toward the stairs, and the man, who'd jumped from the end table to the coffee table, tracked his tiny but dangerous foe. His back was now largely exposed to Eric, who didn't hesitate. He drove the legs of the little wrought iron table into the man's lower back and buttocks.

Their naked opponent screamed in shock and torment, and to Eric's utter amazement, once again vanished.

*Wait a minute, that wasn't supposed to happen! That should have been enough iron to stop a Jinn cold, like that spike did to Aicha. He should be disintegrating into dust right now, or at least be frozen in place. What the fuck?*

He circled the room, trying to find any sign of their assailant.

The Afrit landed on the coffee table beside him. '*He is gone, out that door and into the night. We should not be able to, but we can track him, intermittently. He sputters, in and out of our ability to sense him. He flees in the direction of the tall tower we briefly saw earlier today through the glass front of your vehicle. We should make haste and retreat from this place, lest he return and assail us once more.*'

Lotte appeared from around the corner in the stairwell and ran up to Eric. "Are you all right? I heard what the Afrit just said, so I came out from where I was hiding. I'm sorry, I didn't have a weapon. I didn't know what else to do."

"It's fine. You're safe, and that's all that matters. Go check on Mutig and see if he's okay. I'll go back and grab Olive and Siddique. You heard Chuckles, we've gotta get out of here. Do you think anybody heard that gunshot?"

"Hard to say. It came from deep in the house, underground, and all the doors and windows were shut when it happened. Still, we better get a move on just in case."

He dropped the table and tottered down the hall, back and shoulder a cacophony of discomfort. He reached the sliding door and found Siddique and Olive sitting on the floor, locked in an embrace.

*Umm, okay.*

Siddique looked up. "Sorry, man. She wouldn't give me her gun, and she wouldn't let me go. I didn't know what to do."

"It doesn't matter. I think we drove him away, but we have to get out of here right now."

"I didn't think you could fight him if I couldn't kill him with my gun," Olive said with misery. "Dumbass put it right back in my holster. Probably figured I'd never get at it, and if you hadn't found me, he'd have probably been right. I was gonna give up if he promised not to hurt you and let all y'all go. He ain't right. He's weak. Fightin' uses up his energy real quick. He might have taken the deal."

Eric nodded vigorously. "Okay, makes sense, but now we have to get out of here. Can you walk?"

"Yeah, I think so, as long as we don't go too fast." Eric and Siddique helped her to her feet, and they all stumbled back toward Prog den. "Ewww, what is that *smell*? Did y'all have a barf party in there?"

"Yeah. He has some kind of power that made us all sick for a minute. It must have cost him. He didn't try it again."

She halted the instant she entered the room, eyes locked on the miniature Afrit. "What the.... I... I thought you was *dead*! And what the H-E Double L happened? Did somebody run you through the drier one too many times?"

Eric suppressed a little laugh. "Like I said, it's kind of a long story. We'll explain all that to you — "

"Mutig!" Olive raced to where Lotte crouched by the dog, who sat on his haunches as she stroked his chin. "Is he all right?"

"I don't know," Lotte replied. "He's pretty shaky, and his side is really tender. I'm not sure if anything is broken, but he's badly bruised. He doesn't seem to want to walk. Eric, can you try and pick him up? I'm sure he'll let you politely know if that's not what he'd prefer."

"I'd be happy to, but I really took it in the shoulder and back. I don't think I can carry him."

"We don't have that far to go," Olive interjected. "My car is right outside. I hid it in the trees."

"Perfect! That'll be way better than having to walk back and potentially attract attention. Okay, Mutig, let's see if I can lift you."

Siddique gently pushed past him. "I'll do it. My head and lip hurt, but my arms and back are fine." He briefly brushed Mutig's neck and ears, then bent down and delicately embraced the dog. Mutig gave no protest, so he lifted him up. "Okay, let's go."

Lotte located the flashlight where it had skittered under the couch, whose ruff extended to the carpet and had blocked it from view. It was still on and working. They all performed a rushed wipe down of any surfaces they might have touched, and then quickly exited through the back door, the Afrit flittering above and keeping a watchful eye.

Lotte breathed a sigh of relief. "Bloody hell, that's better! Fresh air at last. It was absolutely putrid in there."

Everyone muttered in agreement as they scampered through the yard, then hugged close to the trees along the drop-off to the creek to avoid detection.

It took Olive a few moments to locate her Jetta, but once she'd found it, she tossed the keys to Eric. "I'm too wobbly to drive. You do it, and I'll help you back out. Keep the lights off until we're on the street so, hopefully, nobody sees us doin' this."

With hers and Lotte's direction, he reversed the car out onto Emory Road. Everyone climbed in, save the Afrit, which would make its own way back, and they drove carefully toward the University Inn. Fearing security cameras along North Decatur, Eric diverted onto some side streets, and eventually wound his way to Emory Drive, where he parked the car on the roadside a few blocks from the motel.

He and Lotte slipped back to the parking lot and grabbed the blankets out of the white Schneider van, which they'd use to sneak Mutig into one of the hotel rooms.

As they locked up, the Afrit swooped overhead and disappeared into the tangled mass of bushes and vines near the old wooden fence that separated the University Inn from some houses beyond.

Lotte approached and whispered into the underbrush. "Can you still sense him?"

The Afrit's voice came from a tree near the tumbledown fence. *'He is near where he was before. He has not returned to the house. We shall watch from here and knock upon your window if he ventures toward us.'*

"Thank you. Thank you for everything. You... you didn't get your spoils. Can we discuss that tomorrow? We're all pretty exhausted."

*'Our bargain is not complete, but we sense our troubles with this entity are just beginning. We shall see what happens. Sleep now and regain your strength. Doubtless, you will need it in the days to come.'*

# CHAPTER 6

A faint scratching on the window screen woke them.

Lotte bolted from the bed. "*Scheiße!* What time is it?"

Eric tried to focus his bleary eyes on the digital clock on the nightstand. "Umm, four-twenty-four a.m. Well, that was the best two-and-a-half hours of sleep I've ever had. I'm totally ready to face this day. *Not.*"

She rushed to the door and eased it open. The Afrit stood just outside on the exterior walkway. It spoke quietly to her, then she shut the door and traipsed over to her bag on the floor. "Come on, we have to get up. The Afrit says that man is on the move."

He dragged out of bed and clicked on a light. "Great. Just what I wanted to hear." He fumbled for his pants where he'd left them on a chair, but then decided to start with a fresh pair that didn't smell like puke.

She was ready to go by the time he'd found his bag. "When you get dressed," she said, "go get Olive and Siddique, then meet us down by the van. I'll see what's going on."

"Okay, but just one thing."

"What?'

"Happy birthday."

She breathed a little laugh, then quietly slipped out the door.

Sleeping arrangements had briefly been a matter of consideration once they'd returned to the motel and lurched up the stairs to their rooms on the top floor. Utterly spent, and worried about attracting unwanted attention, they'd decided to wait until morning for a full debrief, but they only had two rooms, and at nearly 2:00 a.m., it was hardly worth trying to procure another. Lotte had suggested Olive might be more comfortable sharing a room with her. Eric didn't care. He felt so exhausted, he could've slept with the Afrit at that point. However, both Olive and Siddique had politely declined, saying they'd gotten used to sharing close quarters in his apartment last month.

Once dressed, Eric tiptoed to their room and quietly knocked.

Siddique finally cracked the door. "Whew, it's you. I was afraid it was the hotel manager coming to give us trouble for having a dog in the room."

"I doubt they saw us bring him in. We hid him under a freaking sheet. This hotel actually allows dogs in certain rooms. I have no idea if this is one of them, and we didn't pay the extra fee, but I'm hoping they'll be a little lenient if we get caught. How is he, anyway?"

"Quiet. He's sleeping in the chair. He drank some water from the tub, but we don't have any food. We need to get some tomorrow, or I guess later today, given what time it is, but I was hoping to get a little more sleep."

"Me too, but we might have trouble. The Afrit woke us up and said that guy's on the move. Grab Olive and meet us down by the van. By the way, is she okay?"

Olive pulled the door wider and yawned. "I'm fine."

She wore only a t-shirt and her underwear, and looked so much like Lotte that Eric experienced an almost autonomic attraction. She'd somehow managed to remove the sticky residue of the duct tape from her hair, perhaps with scissors, as it looked a little ragged in spots.

She smiled at Siddique. "I'm more than fine."

He flashed a sheepish grin. "We'll be right down."

Eric gave a little whistle when the door closed. *Okay, then.*

He hustled down the stairs and sprinted through the parking lot to the van. When he arrived, Lotte called to him from behind the decaying fence at the perimeter of the little overgrown area behind the motel. He twisted through some branches, then crouched down beside her.

"The Afrit says it's lost him," she said.

He could see the frost of her breath in the early morning chill. "That's not good."

"Well, I'm not sure. For a time, it seemed like he was headed back to the house, but then he kind of went past it, farther to the east. I think that's where Emory University is, right?"

"Your guess is as good as mine. I'd need to look it up on my phone, but I left it in the room. Did he disappear there?"

"Yeah. The Afrit said he just suddenly—"

*'We can again sense him,'* the little beast interrupted from a low branch of a tree above them. *'He has not moved far, and no closer to us.'*

She sighed with relief. "Well, that's good. Keep monitoring him. Maybe we should get the weapons out of the van."

"Good idea, but I left the keys in the room too. Want me to go get 'em?"

"No, don't bother right now. We'll see what this guy does next. Here come Olive and Siddique. I want to ask her more about what happened."

"Speaking of Olive and Siddique, I think something might be going on. Like, going on *between* them, if you know what I mean."

"Really? Interesting. Siddique always thought Olive was a bit standoffish toward him. I wonder if that week together changed things."

"Could be. By the looks of it, the last couple of hours may have changed things, too. If so, I'd be happy for both of them. I honestly worry about Siddique sometimes. Dude lives like a freaking monk."

"Mmmm. He's a very serious young man. I think he still takes what happened, with the kidnapping and all, very personally. His sincerity when we talked... well... you can't imagine how much that helped. He's lived up to all the promises he made, some to me, but mostly those he made to himself. I think he wanted to find his own way before he brought anyone else into his life. It's quite remarkable, really."

Their friends looped around the van. Lotte gave a signal, and they crawled through the underbrush and joined them.

"What's happening?" Siddique whispered.

Lotte filled them in, then said, "Olive, what's over in—"

'He has once again vanished.'

"*Verdammt!* Let's give it a minute and see what happens. Anyway, Olive, do you know what's over in that area just to the east of the house?"

"Sure do. That's Emory University, Eagle Row, more specifically, where the frats and dorms are. That's where he's feedin'."

"How do you know that? In fact, how did you even get involved in any of this? Tell us what's going on."

Olive pursed her lips. "Well, I don't know *everything* that's goin' on, but I sure know I messed up. I saw on the news the other night that students at Emory were experiencing sleep paralysis, just like y'all told me your landlady had after Aicha found her sleeping. I did some investigating at the station on Monday and saw that this guy named Harland Cheevers had gone missing. His house was just a stone's throw from Eagle Row and those dorms. Guy even worked at the Carlos Museum as a security guard, which is also right nearby."

Lotte grasped Olive's arm. "What? This man works at the Michael Carlos Museum? You realize that's an extremely prestigious archaeological museum, right?"

"Well, sort of. I know it's kinda famous, but I never went. It didn't seem to have the kind of archaeology stuff that would interest me. Them old Greek and Roman things are more up your alley."

"All right. It's just that after our experience with Sharur breaking out of the Louvre, I look at all these artifacts with a very different eye. It's an awfully big coincidence all this is happening in proximity to a museum like this, but anyway, keep telling us what happened."

"Yeah, so like I said, I thought it was super suspicious this guy goes missing at almost the exact same time as those students started having sleep paralysis. I thought maybe if I investigated, I could help the police find him, or figure out what was goin' on in the Emory dorms. So, I picked up Mutig after work, waited until dark, and snuck into his house."

Eric cut in. "Olive, just out of curiosity, if you really suspected a Jinn might be involved, why didn't you call us?"

She scoffed. "Why didn't you call *me*?"

"Huh?"

"Eric, I texted you on Sunday night. You said you might go to the game. I watched it on TV... well... most of it, until it got boring, and I fell asleep. I thought it would be fun to hear your voice at the game or get a picture... or *something*. You never even texted me back. Did you not get my message?"

Despite the chill in the air, he suddenly felt quite warm. "No, I got it. I was kind of... I don't know... distracted. I'm sorry, I really am."

"Well, apology accepted, but if you wanna know why I didn't call y'all, that's why. You've both been all sad and distant since you got back from Oman. Siddique told me you were calling out sick a lot from work, which isn't like you at all. He was worried too. I tried to stay in touch, but all I got back from you were one-word replies—if I even got a reply at all. I figured you two had your own row to hoe. Lotte was behind in school, and you were behind at work, so what was I gonna do... call you down here to go snoopin' around for some hungry Jinn and make your lives even more miserable? I'm sorry, but—"

'*He has reappeared.*' The Afrit's interruption created a stony silence. Even the little creature was quiet for a time, until it finally spoke again. '*We sense him not far from his previous location. He is no nearer to us.*'

Lotte stroked Olive's shoulder. "It's all right. I think we both understand now. You're absolutely right in your perceptions. We were so caught up in our own troubles, we didn't even realize how it was impacting you... or you, Siddique. Neither Eric nor I are very good communicators, me especially, and this was a particularly difficult issue to talk about. It still is, so I ask that you please bear with us on that. Just know, Olive, that the second your mother called Eric and told him you were missing, he knew we had to drop everything to find you, and I did too. You and Siddique are two of the most important people in our lives. Don't take our shortcomings personally. This was totally on us."

In the darkness, Olive leaned over and wrapped her arms around Lotte's neck. "Not totally. What I did was pretty dang foolish. Y'all saved my worthless life. I love you. You too, Mr. Eric Schneider, who owes me at least a picture from that football game, even though your rotten ol' Patriots beat my Falcons—again! I'm sorry y'all have troubles like that, but if there's anything I can do, please let me know."

"Me too," Siddique softly added.

Lotte's voice trembled slightly. "Thank you, both of you. There is something you can do, Olive. Finish telling me what happened. You seem to know more about this man who took you captive."

Olive gave her another quick hug, then pulled away. "Yeah, I do. For a while, all he did was take me to the bathroom, but later, he took off my gag and started talkin' to me."

"What did he say?"

"Well, he said lots of things. He told me he has a brother. I think he lives out in California. I saw that in the police report. He said once, a long time ago, he and his brother were defeated in some kind of battle. I got the impression he used up most of his powers trying to win that battle, that's why he's all weak now, and why he's feeding all the time on all those undergrads. He's trying to store up power, then he's gonna reunite with his brother. He wanted me to come along, said I could help him, even though I don't really see how. He said he had to do it real quick, though, before his brother changes into a different *state* and gets stronger. He said if that happens, it might lead to violence, which would be bad for everybody. That's basically it. What do you think?"

Lotte brought her hand to her chin. "I don't know what to think. That's a lot to digest, and without more context, it's hard to understand. How long ago—"

*'He has vanished once again.'*

"I'm tellin' ya," Olive said. "He's feedin'. There's gonna be lots of paralyzed kids at Emory tomorrow mornin', but they should be okay. He don't kill 'em. That fight we just had probably took as much out of him as it did us, and he's trying to replenish his power for the trip."

"The trip to California," Eric posited.

"That's what I assume."

"Possibly," Lotte interjected, "but that's what I was going to ask you about. You said that battle where the brothers fought together happened a 'long time' ago. Do you have any sense *how* long?"

"Not really."

"Right. It could be centuries... millennia! Why would Harland Cheevers feel compelled at this particular moment to reunite with his brother in California? I think Harland is a new host for a Jinn... a Jinn who's only recently become somehow... I don't know... *reactivated*. I don't think his brother in California has anything to do with this."

"Too bad. I was lookin' forward to seein' California."

"Well, he may yet go to California. We have no idea where he might go. It seems the Afrit can track him, as long as he stays in physical form, or his powers malfunction due to weakness, but that brings up another issue."

"What?"

"Is this really a Jinn we're dealing with? I mean, it *could* be. Maybe his weakness renders him trackable by the Afrit when he's in physical form, but that's not normally how it works. Something just doesn't seem *right* about all this."

"Yeah," Eric added. "I drove an iron table into his ass, and he was still able to vanish. That didn't happen with Aicha when I stabbed her with that rail spike, or when Vanth ripped her to shreds with the remnants of Charun's portal."

Olive moaned. "Y'all, I am actually sittin' right here, and that was *my* body that got all torn up!"

"Sorry, sorry. I didn't mean it that way. I was just... oh, never mind. I'll shut up now."

"It's all right. It just brings up bad memories. So, anyway, now that we know all this, what are we gonna do?"

"I'm not certain," Lotte said. "I don't know *what's* going on, or what to do about it. We've gotten you back. That was our primary goal. I'm not sure this guy is any of our business, or that we have the power to interfere with what he wants to do even if it is. You're right, he's not killing the students that he's feeding on. Jinn do this, we know that. They've lived amongst us since before the dawn of civilization. Now he wants to reunite with his brother. So what? Does it really have anything to do with us? Do he or his brother pose any threat? I have no idea, and even if they do, what are we going to do about it? We need more information, and there's only one place I can think of to get it."

"The museum!" Olive sang.

"Right you are. See, you get to visit after all, and so do I. On my birthday, no less."

"Dang! It's your birthday today? Happy birthday! I'm glad we get to spend it together, even if we're all sitting on the dirt in the cold behind a stupid parking lot."

*'He has materialized once again. He has moved. He is closer to the structure where we battled him and hastening in that direction.'*

Lotte scratched her cheek. "Weird. I wonder what he wants there. Maybe he's absorbed enough energy and wants to pick up the fight again, but that seems dubious. He's been feeding for some time and his powers were still spotty enough that we could fend him off. Maybe he somehow knows his house is free. If he can sense us like the Afrit can track him, that might be possible, but it's another thing that I don't believe Jinn can do. Either way, he has to know it's not safe anymore — or won't be for long. It didn't seem like anyone heard that gunshot or called the police, but someone's bound to notice the broken window eventually."

"Yeah," Olive affirmed. "The Atlanta police are still monitoring the property, at least the outside. Crap, speaking of which, it's Thursday, right? What time is it?"

Siddique consulted his phone, the only one to have brought one along. "It's almost five-thirty."

"Damn. I gotta call the station and talk to my momma before she goes to work, if she isn't staying home all worried sick about me. What the hell am I gonna tell 'em? Man, am I screwed, or what?"

"What if you told her you were in an accident?" Eric suggested. "That would explain your black eye."

"What, like a car accident? Then my car would have to be bashed up. I'm not sure that's gonna work."

"No," Lotte said. "A bike accident. You were in a bike accident."

"Well, I've got a bike... haven't ridden it in years. It's home, sittin' in the garage with all the other junk that's there. I can barely open my car door. Pisses me off. Anyway, that won't work either."

"Yes, it will. You got a new bike. It's a mountain bike. You've always wanted one, or you've wanted one recently. You just bought it used from some person on Craigslist. You decided to take it for a quick test ride. There have to be some trails for that around here somewhere. Siddique, can you look for nearby mountain bike trails on your phone, please?"

He began to type and scroll.

"Anyway, it was your first day. You got lost, took it too fast. You fell down a cliff into a ravine. You couldn't get out, and your phone disappeared, likely broken."

"Fer real!" Olive huffed. "Did you see what that guy did to my dang phone? Crushed it near into beach sand! Why the H-E Double L would he do that?"

Lotte pondered for a moment, then spoke. "As we know from Aicha, Jinn are quite conversant with mobile phones. They easily use them as tracking devices because they're *already* bloody tracking devices. He was holding you captive and didn't want you found. Eliminating your phone was quite logical."

Olive nodded. "Yeah, makes sense. I'd already removed the SIM card, but he probably didn't know that. What he did would have crushed the daylights out of the NFC chip. Nobody would have been able to track that phone. I wonder if he knew exactly what he was doing?"

"It's possible. As we've also learned, Jinn can access their host's memories. You say this 'Harland Cheevers' worked as a security guard at the museum. Perhaps he knows something about things like this, or one of this Jinn's previous hosts did. It's hard to say. In any case, let me finish: you fell into a ravine and you couldn't get out, and you couldn't call for help. You were stuck there for two days. Finally, some people out for an early morning ride noticed Mutig in your car. You left your window down far enough that they were able to unlock the door. They let him out, he found you, and the nice people helped pull you out. I've seen signs for Emory Hospital. It seems to be right across the street. Go and call your mom from over there, that'll lend credence to your story. You might also want to have them do something for your eye while you're there. Siddique, can you go with her? Maybe they can look at your lip, too. Speaking of, did you find anything?"

"Ira B. Melton Park," Siddique chimed in. "It's like a five-minute drive from here. They have mountain bike trails."

Lotte smiled. "See? That could work. Of course, the story's got more holes than a wheel of Swiss cheese. I mean, who knows if there's a ravine in that park, for example, or why no one could hear you yell for help, but how deeply do you think your mother, or the station, will look into that? They'll just be glad to have you back."

Olive looked dumbfounded. "How the H-E Double L do you come up with stuff like this off the top of your head?"

"That's what I've always wanted to know," Eric quietly griped.

"All right," Lotte said. "Eric, go up and grab our phones. We'll stay here and call Siddique if anything suspicious happens. You'll still be close enough to us that if our Mr. Cheevers risks coming our way, we can let you know. Call us when you have an update. Also, give us your room key so we can look in on Mutig. There's a CVS right by where we got sandwiches last evening. I think they'll have dog food. If not, we'll find some." She clasped Olive's shoulders. "Speaking of Mutig, later, you're going to have to tell us what's going on... *everything*. I know this is difficult and confusing for you, but we're your friends, and we're all in this together, *ja*?"

"I know," she meekly replied. "I'm sorry. I shoulda' told y'all sooner, but I just—"

"Never mind. It doesn't matter. We're just happy you're with us. Now, go make your calls, and we'll see you later this morning."

Siddique passed Lotte the key, then he, Eric, and Olive wriggled out of the bushes and strode back through the parking lot. At the stairs just beyond the van, Eric bid them farewell. He dashed up to get his and Lotte's phones and their vehicle's key, along with an extra sweatshirt for Lotte, who had started to shiver in the cold, then bolted back to their little hiding place.

As he settled next to her, she gave him an update. "The Afrit says he's entered the house. Pass me my phone." He did, and she rapidly thumbed a query. "*Alter!* I can see what Olive was talking about. I just searched 'Emory news,' and all this stuff about the sleep paralysis in the dorms came right up. It's been going on for about three or four weeks, just one to three students every few days, but then the pattern changed. He took four on Monday night, and six on Tuesday. Now, he's just taken another... how many times did he vanish near the dorms before he headed to the house... three? That would be up to six more students, assuming two per room. He's definitely trying to replenish what he lost, or he's stocking up. I'm not sure what his—"

'Yet again, he moves, more rapidly than before.'

"Is he coming toward us?"

'No. He travels in the direction of the setting sun... wait... he has stopped. He has changed course. Now he approaches the tall tower... he has passed it. He travels swiftly, navigating in reverse the course we originally charted to reach this area.'

"He's in the car! He went back to the house to get his car, maybe even some clothes, one could only hope. He's headed north, probably back to the highway. Unbelievable. It looks like he might be done with us. Now, the question is, are we done with him?"

## Marietta, Georgia, Thursday, October 26, 2017

Olive stared blankly out of the passenger side window of her Jetta as it motored along 75 North. At nearly 11:00 a.m., traffic wasn't so terrible. She knew she'd be home soon and looked forward to a shower and a change of clothes, save the fuzzy hoodie that Lotte had loaned her when they'd gotten back from the hospital. She nestled in its comfort, trying to forget the ordeals of the past several days. Four hours in the Emory emergency room had been the last straw, though at least most of that time had been spent waiting, and she'd nodded off to sleep on Siddique's shoulder.

There hadn't been much the doctors could do for her. Nothing was broken, and the time for ice to have been much benefit to her eye had long since passed. The hospital staff clearly didn't believe her story about a mountain bike accident. They pressed her to be honest about whether someone had hit her, perhaps the young man with the bruised and cut lip who'd accompanied her to hospital but had refused treatment himself. Her rather testy rebuke put an end to that line of questioning.

One of the nurses had taken pity on Olive and let her use the phone after Siddique claimed he didn't have one. She really wanted the call to come from the hospital as Lotte suggested. Her mother had been frantic, and demanded she come home immediately, but Olive explained she was in the emergency room receiving treatment for minor injuries, and promised she'd see her later that afternoon. Though not satisfactory in any way, the ploy nominally succeeded. Her mom couldn't afford to miss any more time from work, so she couldn't afford the time to drive out to Emory Hospital.

Thankfully, her supervisor hadn't been in when she'd called the station. She left a message that she'd be out for a few days while she recovered from her "little accident."

She groaned and pressed her cheek against the cool glass of the window. *Assuming they even want me back at this point. What a mess.*

"You okay?" Siddique asked from where he sat behind the wheel of her car. "You seem quiet."

She flashed him a feeble smile. "I'm just tired. I feel like such an idiot. I really didn't expect any of this to happen, though I probably should have. Now... I don't know. I don't know what's going on, about *anything*."

"Lotte's really smart. Don't worry, she'll figure things out."

"Yeah, that may work for some stuff, but not for the disaster I've made out of my life, and not... well... never mind. No need to get into all that right now."

"What? Tell me."

She sighed and covered her forehead with her hand, but jerked it away when her left eye screamed in protest. "Darn it. This hurts as bad as it looks. I need to grab my oversize sunglasses from home. They're all scratched up, but they'll be better than walkin' around lookin' like I was in an Ultimate Fighting match."

"You don't look so bad, not to me. Anyway, say what you were gonna say."

She scowled. "I wasn't planning to say anything, but I guess it probably needs saying. Lotte ain't gonna help me figure out what's going on between you and me, now, is she?"

He smiled and waggled his eyebrows. "Try her. You might be surprised."

"Very funny. You know your exit's coming up, right? Take a left onto Windy Hill Road when you get to the end of the ramp. I know you and she are pretty good friends, but I don't see her havin' much to say about us. I mean, assuming there even is an *us*."

He hit the blinker and steered along the exit ramp. "Is this a question you're asking me?"

"Kinda, yeah."

After a short wait at the light, he hung a left and drove quietly for a time. "Hmmm. I'm not sure I can answer. It's not only my decision. You know I care for you. I was really worried when you went missing, and I felt wonderful when we found you."

She snickered. "Yeah, I could tell. You were pretty much all over me last night. Guess I was all over you, too. I was surprised you stopped, not that I minded falling asleep in your arms, or waking up there, it's just that most boys would've, well...."

"Man, don't think I wasn't tempted. It's just that... like... with us, there's more to it, right? If things don't work out, we can't just say *a de go* and never see each other again. We know stuff, and we have to work together, or we may all be in big trouble. You also live a long way away, and maybe I'm not the kind of person you want to have *that* kind of relationship with."

"Meaning what?"

"Well, I mean, I don't have that great a job. Not that I don't like it, I do, but I didn't go to college, and I don't have a lot of options where I can work. I don't make a lot of money. I can barely afford the place Lotte and Eric found for me. It's nice, but sometimes, I don't think they really *get* it. I come from a very poor country, but it's almost harder to live here. Everything is so close, all that you could ever want, but it all costs so much money, and if you don't have a lot of skills, or if you don't really fit in, all that stuff is out of reach, even the basic things you need to live a happy life. Sometimes I want to go back to Sierra Leone. Maybe that's crazy, but that's how I feel in my heart, like maybe I'm not good enough to be here. You and me, we were brought together by these nutty circumstances. We have things in common, and we like each other, but if you could choose, would you really pick somebody like me?"

Olive was flabbergasted, and for a while didn't know what to say. "My gawd. You and me really are peas in a pod, aren't we? 'Not good enough.' Sounds like something I'd say, but those would be about the last words I'd have ever expected out of *your* mouth. I don't think I've ever met *anyone* who thought they weren't good enough for *me*. Mostly the exact opposite. It's funny."

"What?"

"They call humans 'social beings,' but it seems like all we do is float around in our own little worlds. Our heads are full of all kinds of fool stuff, a bunch of worries that usually turn out to be totally off base — prejudices and assumptions based on crap we've been fed by other people — but we act on all that nonsense anyway. Then we actually *talk* to somebody — or experience something directly — get an entirely different perspective, and wish we hadn't done what we did. By then, though, it's too late. A card laid is a card played, as they say, and you deal with the consequences." Under her breath, she whispered to herself. "Like walkin' into the security line at the airport, when you should have stayed with somebody who cares about you."

"Sorry, I didn't catch that last —"

"Oh, crap! That was our turn. Sorry, I'm spacin' out. Dang it, too late to take Atoka. Go up to the next street and take a right. We'll just turn around. That's Olive Springs Road! Ain't that funny?"

Siddique chuckled as he bore right, then turned into the first driveway. He put his right arm on the back of her seat and looked over his shoulder as he threw the car in reverse. He'd just started to back up when he slammed the brake. "What the...."

"What? What is it?"

"Oh, man, this is *not* good. I think we're being followed! Did you see that red car that just went by?"

"No, I wasn't lookin' that way."

"It looks just like one we saw back in Worcester, and on the highway coming down here."

"That's not *that* unusual. Lots of cars look alike. What makes you think they're following us?"

"It's a long story, and I haven't had time to fill you in. The emergency room wasn't safe, plus you were really tired. We have to hide out, try and lose them. Where can we go?"

She rapid-fired through their options, none especially enticing. "Umm, there's a shopping center right across the street. Turn around, go straight, and pull into the lot. I guess we can drive behind the building, see if we can lose 'em."

He swiftly backed out onto Olive Springs Road while she looked behind her. She didn't see a red car. In the back seat, Mutig stirred as the little black Jetta jerked, and the bag of dog food Lotte and Eric had bought slid onto the floor. The light was green, and Siddique sped through the intersection, hung a quick left into the parking lot of the strip mall, banged a quick right past the Pizza Hut and the dumpster, then banked left again behind the building. This section of the back of the building was quite small, cut off by a ramp that connected the rest of the shopping center's rear with a small, parallel street to their right.

"What should I do?" he urgently inquired.

"Try to pull up behind that big electrical junction box over there. That might do it."

He pulled the car around a yellow, cement stanchion and maneuvered the front bumper up to the large, green electrical box that sat near a set of metal stairs painted a bright red. He wiped his brow. "I don't know. This isn't the best cover, and if she takes a left on the street to our side, she'll see us for sure."

"How do you know it's a she? Did you see the driver?"

"No, not just now. Eric did on the highway. I'm just guessing it's the same car."

"Well, all right. I guess there's no harm in sittin' here for a while. Maybe we should get out and watch the road."

After a moment's thought, he gave a deep sigh. "Okay, but we'll leave the doors open and the engine running, in case we have to get out of here fast."

They slipped out of the car and peered around the corner of the junction box onto Olive Springs Road. It couldn't have been five minutes before a red Mini Cooper with a white top passed slowly by, coming from the direction of Windy Hill Road. A woman with black hair, wearing large, round sunglasses sat behind the wheel. They both jerked their heads out of view and pressed their backs against the big, green, metal box. Fortunately, the car went straight, as it didn't appear on the little street to their side.

"Is that the car?" she asked.

"Man, it sure looks like it to me! If she comes back, she'll see us for sure, even with the trees there. We have to go, now!"

They bolted for the Jetta, slammed the doors shut, and Siddique steered out from their hiding place. Instead of going right, he exited left onto Barrett Circle, the little street that ran parallel behind the shopping center, then sped to Bouldercrest Drive, where he veered left, and eventually back to the right onto Windy Hill Road. Timberly Drive, where Olive lived, was just a half mile away. Cars quickly filled in behind their black Jetta, and they felt well obscured in the traffic.

Olive nervously monitored out the back window after Siddique made the right onto Timberly. Her house was barely 60 seconds away, tucked amongst the trees that straddled Nickajack Creek. When her mailbox came into view, she saw no cars on the road behind her.

"It's this right," she directed. "Just follow the driveway around the house. The garage is in the back."

He looped around the building and came to a rest in front of the white garage door in the lower level of the house, under a narrow, wooden back porch.

"Let me get the garage door, and you can pull in."

He gently squeezed her arm and smiled. "I'll do it. Just hang tight. I think we made it." He got out of the car, jogged to the large door, pulled it open, and then hustled back.

He had just rounded the open car door and was about to hop in, when Olive heard the rustle of mighty wings above her. Siddique yowled in pain and surprise as something swept him from his feet and lifted him into the air. She screamed as he quickly and horrifyingly disappeared into the trees that nearly engulfed the back and side of the house.

# CHAPTER 7

Olive threw open the passenger door to her Jetta and spilled into the driveway. Whatever had whisked Siddique away had come over her side of the car from slightly behind, making use of the open space provided by the driveway. She scanned over the roof of her vehicle, where a commotion rustled branches and leaves in the thick cluster of trees near the left side of the house.

"Olive!" Siddique croaked. "Help me! I can't hold out here much longer!"

"Hold on!" she shouted. She couldn't see him for the dense foliage which had only just started to exhibit the colors of fall. One large branch of the tree waved tantalizingly near the roof on the side of the house, above the kitchen window.

*I'd have to get the dang ladder to get up there. That'll take too long. Shit! What the hell am I gonna do?* She seethed with frustration, and for a moment thought about grabbing her gun from the glove box. *Oh, good thinkin', dumbass. I'll just shoot into the tree where I can't see a fuckin' thing, kill my friend, and make a whole lotta noise in the process. That'll sure solve the damn problem once and for all. Stupid* airhead!

The word felt like a direct strike to her heart from a bolt of white-hot lightning. It seared her with the purity of all-encompassing torment. A lifetime of her father's belittlement surged from the depths of her soul, and for a moment, she felt as if she might be torn in twain. She snarled with an utterly unrecognizable rage, and savagely spit through teeth clenched so tightly, she could have gnawed through iron.

Far beyond rational thought, she madly thrust her hand under the hoodie that Lotte had loaned her, and frantically fumbled at the collar of her Marietta Police Department blouse. Her trembling fingers grasped the leather strap that suspended the white medallion with the symbols of An and Ki embossed on its surface. The object lay pressed between her breasts and had begun to burn with a chill so cold, it seared her flesh, as if she touched the very essence of fire itself. She writhed and tugged until she'd pulled the amulet over her head. Once free, she held the offensive item aloft by its strap and let out a defiant howl, then threw it brutally to the ground and burst into action.

She ran about ten feet behind her car, then hurled herself forward toward the vehicle. Through eyes red with murder, she saw Mutig gaze at her through the back window as she leapt onto the trunk, then to the top of the car, before she launched herself upward and grabbed the railing of the porch just above the garage. With inhuman strength and agility, she hauled herself up, balanced precariously on the top of the slightly unsteady fencing, and then vaulted onto the roof of the house.

Without hesitation, she shimmied to where the branch swayed near the eaves. She needed to grab the limb closer to the trunk, lest it break and send her to the ground. There wasn't time to climb up. She backed up several paces, then sprinted full speed toward the edge of the roof and sprang high into the air.

To Olive, it seemed as if the entire universe moved in slow motion. She studied every detail of the branch before her, calculating where best to set her grip, and how to then propel herself farther into the thick leaves that obscured the struggle in which she hoped to intercede.

Her senses guided her faithfully. She grasped the limb, then robustly pulled her body forward into the mass of finer branches and foliage. They raked at her shoulders and sides and tore ragged holes into the soft fabric of Lotte's hoodie. Her hand and forearm guarded her face through the obstacle, and she quickly zeroed in on her target.

A huge blackish-brown bird with a hooked beak held Siddique ensnared in its claws as it strained to lift him upward. Blood streamed from her friend's shoulders where the avian's sharp talons had pierced his flesh. He clung tenaciously to a limb just below the one she'd employed to gain entrance to this lofty space, though it was clear his endurance was diminishing rapidly.

She didn't think. She acted with the instincts of a predator, intent on nothing less than the death and dismemberment of her prey. The bird hardly had time to register her presence before she dove downward, clenched her hands around the beast's throat, and delivered a bloodthirsty twist. This would slake her wrath. This would put to right the wrongs of the past. This would prove her worth, once and for all, and for evermore.

Her balance gave way as the creature in her clutches abruptly vanished, leaving her with fistfuls of downy feathers. With blinding speed, she grabbed the branch above her, then swept down with her free hand to catch Siddique by the arm before he plummeted to the ground. Their eyes met, and for the briefest of moments, she felt the terrifying urge to repeatedly and ferociously flail his dangling body into the trunk of the tree until nothing remained but a bloody and unidentifiable pulp.

He smiled, and a sudden wave of nausea assailed her. Reality flooded back like waking from the most terrible of nightmares, but she knew it was no dream she'd experienced. In her heart, she realized she'd likely seen reality, a truth she'd buried behind a lifetime of equivocation and denial to mask how deeply the wounds of her life had penetrated.

She started to tremble and cry. "Why? Why would you do that?"

Siddique strained to speak. "Olive, what's wrong? Do what? What did I do?"

"Why would you do something like that... make me feel so bad about myself? I was just a little girl. I was *your* little girl."

"Olive, I don't know what's happening, but I can't hang on like this much longer. My arm is killing me. I don't know how you do what you're doing right now, but can you just help me get back to the branch? Olive? Do you hear me?"

As her anger faded to sorrow, her strength began to fail, and Siddique's full weight began to assert itself. She spent the last of her fading power positioning him on a decent-sized limb, then shakily lowered herself and stood beside him. Steadied by the trunk of the tree, she wiped her nose and cheeks with her free hand, oblivious to the pain in her left eye.

He touched her thigh. "Are you all right?"

"I... I honestly don't know. I have no idea what just happened. Actually, I do, but that don't make me feel any better. I'm sorry. I was kinda out of it. Don't pay any attention to what I was sayin'. I think I was just blabbering nonsense. You're bleedin' pretty bad. I think we better try to get out of this tree. Do you want me to get down and fetch the ladder?"

He wrapped his arm around her leg. "Let me rest for a minute, then we can try. I'm afraid if you go, that eagle might come back."

"If it does, we're screwed, 'cause I ain't strong enough to fight it no more. Maybe I gave it enough of a scare that it'll just stay away."

Wordlessly, they each struggled to catch their breath and calm their racing hearts. Finally, Siddique said he felt ready to attempt the decent. Olive led the way and helped him as he fought through the pain and unsteadiness in his injured arms and shoulders. Blood seeped through the tattered punctures in his shirt, and he complained about lightheadedness just as they arduously reached the ground.

She supported him as best she could as they staggered back to the car. Mutig met them in the driveway, apparently having slipped out through one of the open doors. He tottered suspiciously above the discarded amulet.

Siddique fell to his knees and picked the up artifact. "I think you should put this back on."

She remembered the searing pain and numbness she'd felt when she'd ripped the object from her chest. "It hurt me. I needed to get it off. If I didn't, I couldn't have saved you, but it hurt to have it gone, too, just in a different way. It's like trading one injury for another, and they both hurt real bad."

"Listen, I'll put it back, and if you feel pain, I'll take it off again. I promise. Do you trust me to do this?"

She nodded and kneeled, and he cautiously slipped the medallion over her head. She felt the cool stone touch her breastbone, and the last vestiges of her ire subsided. Strangely, a sly sense of accomplishment overtook her. She wasn't sure exactly what she'd accomplished, and in some sense wondered if, indeed, it was *her* feeling of accomplishment at all.

Eric followed Lotte as she scooted through the automatic doors and into the waiting area of the Wellstar Cobb Hospital emergency care unit. They instantly spotted Olive where she sat in an empty corner of the room, eyes obscured behind a pair of oversize sunglasses. Her hands had disappeared into the sleeves of her Savanah State University sweatshirt, and she'd wrapped her arms around her shoulders, trying to stay warm in the near meat-locker temperature of the waiting room.

*Why the hell do they have to keep it so cold in these places?* Eric wondered.

A faint smile crossed Olive's lips when she saw them approach, and she fell into Lotte's embrace when they reached her. "Please don't tell me the Afrit's out there waitin' in the van in the middle of the hospital parking lot."

Lotte gave a little laugh. "No. Our little friend is hiding out in the trees behind the motel. We need a guard for the portal materials in our rooms. How is Siddique?"

"Got me. At least they took him in right away 'cause he was bleeding, but they ain't exactly keeping me posted with regular updates."

"We'll go ask someone in a minute. First, I want you to tell me what happened. I know you were attacked, but you said something to Eric about being followed as well."

"Yeah, we missed my street, and while Siddique was turnin' around, he saw this red car that looked like one you might have seen before. There was a woman driving it wearing sunglasses."

"That's almost undoubtedly the same car I saw," Eric affirmed. "Red Mini with a white top, right?"

"That's the one. I think we lost her, but maybe not, because when we got home, that's when the eagle attacked us."

Lotte pulled out her phone and held it out. "Did the eagle look like this one?"

"Basically, yeah, I guess. I only saw it for a second, but that's what I remember."

"That's an Eastern Imperial Eagle, native to southeastern Europe through West and Central Asia. Basically, unheard of over here, unless it's someone's pet. Did Siddique tell you that a bird like this, probably this *very* bird, flew through his window before we left for Atlanta?"

"He told me all about that once I got him inside the house while I was tryin' to fix him up. I figured he needed stitches for some of those cuts, though, so I brought him here. I didn't know what else to do."

Lotte squeezed Olive's shoulders. "You did exactly the right thing. We should have been far more careful. I had no idea that bird followed us here, and we really weren't sure if that red car was related to the one we saw in Worcester. Now, I think we know, but we were incredibly fortunate neither of you were more badly injured, nor taken away by that Jinn-eagle. How did you stop it?"

She put her feet on the seat of the chair and sunk her chin into her knees. "I don't think you're gonna like my answer to that particular question."

Eric sat next to her and put his hand on her back. "Olive, you're our friend. Whatever you tell us won't change anything."

"I guess not, but that's just because the change has already happened. It's already done, and there ain't no goin' back. When that eagle took Siddique, I was goin' crazy! I didn't know what to do. I was frustrated and mad, and then I got even madder at myself for not thinkin' straight. That's when I did it."

"Did what?" he gently prompted.

"I ripped off that dang old necklace, and I just let the anger wash over me. It made me strong, y'all. I literally jumped up to the roof of my house, then I threw myself into the tree where Siddique and the eagle had gotten all tangled up. I felt like Spider-Man, or something. I got that eagle in my hands, and I was about to twist the nasty ol' thing's head off. That's when it vanished, and that made me *furious*! Got me two nice fistfuls of feathers, though."

"Wow. That's... amazing. I experienced something similar when that eagle got into Siddique's apartment. I got really mad, and I punched the damned thing right in the beak, but my strength had somehow been... *enhanced*. What you did may well have saved Siddique's life. You should be proud."

She scoffed and jerked away. "Right. I'm so proud. I caught him as he was about to fall, then I near bashed him to death myself! There's something not right with me. She's still in there, *Aicha*. Ol' Harland Cheevers, or who-the-hell-ever he is, sure told the truth. I have me some power, but I have no idea what I did to start using it, and I couldn't control it when I wanted it to stop. I'm not right. I don't think I'm really even *human* anymore."

Eric glanced at Lotte, who frowned and gave a flick of her eyebrows before she again took hold of Olive's shoulders and brought her back to face them. "I know this is incredibly difficult. I can't imagine what you're going through or how you must feel. This is why we try so hard to keep others at arm's length, even you and Siddique. None of us belong in this hidden world, a world of monsters, and gods, and almost magical powers. You can't get into this world without it changing you, and some changes are far deeper than others. But Olive, Eric told you the truth. For *us*, this changes nothing, and I think you have another power inside of you that you've overlooked."

"Whuut?" she morosely asked.

"The power to choose. The amulet gives you a choice. As long as you keep it on, it's *you* that's in charge... not Aicha. It all comes down to you, and in the end, I don't think there's anything more human than that."

Lotte took a seat to Olive's left, so that she and Eric flanked her. They all huddled close, sharing the warmth of their bodies to fend off the piercing, industrial chill. Eventually, she fell asleep between them, and Eric caught Lotte's eye. She smiled sadly, and slowly shook her head.

All the hope that her words had inspired in his heart flickered, and then faded like the flame of a cheap candle, set delicately in a bowl lined with *Alkuartiz Alnaar*.

*So much for Lotte's birthday.*

Eric couldn't really complain that much. He'd only spent about two-and-a-half hours in the emergency room today, compared to Olive's and Siddique's nearly nine. Their comrade's injuries had not proven too severe. Olive's instincts had been right about needing a few stitches and staples, but he'd gotten off easy compared to what could have happened.

It was nearly 3:30 p.m. when they finally limped out of the hospital, Siddique wearing some fresh clothes that they'd fetched earlier from his room at the University Inn.

"Y'all, I *have* to go home," Olive said with dread. "We left Mutig at the house, and my momma will know I've been there. She's gonna be madder than the snake that married the hose pipe, but she'll kill me for sure if I'd don't show up at all. It'll be like the atomic bomb. Half of Marietta will go up with us."

Lotte was pensive. "It's a huge problem. I don't think we should be separated. As we've learned, it just makes us more vulnerable. I also don't want whoever's after us to see your mother. They could easily decide to take her hostage, force us to come to them, though I'm actually not certain why they haven't tried that yet. If they were following us in Massachusetts, they could have gone for my father, or Eric's parents, or really anyone close to us."

"Maybe they're afraid," Eric posited. "You said you thought we had allies... people, or Jinn, or whatever they are, who are protecting us. Maybe the ones trying to grab us don't want to expose themselves that way."

"That's plausible. From what we know of Jinn, they usually like to work behind the scenes, stay out of harm's way as much as possible. So far, it seems like they've tried to quickly make off with one of us to somewhere they hope we can't follow. Taking a hostage would attract a lot of attention, and we can't control what the entities who appear to be protecting us might do in retaliation. We're not even in contact with them. That may be the very thing that's keeping our families and friends safe."

"So, what does this mean about me goin' home?" Olive asked.

"I don't know. It still feels incredibly risky. It would be so much easier if we could all go with you, but that's obviously impossible."

"No, it's not. That's the best idea *ever*! My momma wouldn't pitch nearly so much of a fit with y'all around."

"*Alter!* How would we explain our presence here?"

Eric cut in. "We'd tell her we were worried and that we decided to drive down here. We were gonna call her mom to get an update when we got here, but then Olive called us early this morning, so we just went ahead and met her at the hospital."

"That's perfect!" Olive squealed. "Then we'll say we're all goin' out for Lotte's birthday tonight, and I'm staying at the motel with you guys, because friends don't let friends drive drunk. Then we're goin' to the museum tomorrow. Sorry we couldn't go today, Lotte, what with Siddique, and all. Happy birthday, anyway."

Both Olive and Eric smiled broadly.

Lotte's eyes repeatedly darted between the two of them. Finally, she shook her head. "All right, you win. I guess it's no crazier than any of the *Tüddelkram* we've already told her. Siddique, ride with Olive, and make sure you stay close. I hope this doesn't come back to haunt us. I really don't like making decisions with so little information, but sometimes, I guess you just don't have much of a choice."

Whatever concerns Eric harbored about Vicky Carter's reaction to their unexpected presence, or to Olive herself, were quickly allayed by the shower of joyful tears and hugs the woman extended to her daughter and her friends. Even Mutig made a groggy appearance, weakly wagging his stubby tail a discrete distance from his mysteriously altered mistress.

"Good thing he's recovering," Lotte whispered in Eric's ear. "We might be needing his help at some point, maybe sooner than later."

With Lotte's assistance, Olive was able to parry her mother's thorniest questions, and the relief of having her child home soon mollified any lingering apprehensions. They all had a nice visit, and Vicky enjoyed meeting in person the friends Olive had spoken so highly of, and who had been so unusually kind to her daughter.

*If you knew what we knew, you wouldn't think it was so unusual. You'd also probably never let her out of the house again.*

After a tense discussion behind the closed door to her mother's bedroom, Olive emerged a bit past 6:00 p.m. and announced it was time to go. "She don't like it much" she confided as they walked out to the van, "but she can't keep me here. I'm almost twenty-four years old. I told her y'all would run me back tomorrow after the museum. She's worried about work. I guess I should be too, but I'm not even sure I *want* to go back there."

They returned to the motel, then wandered into Emory Village for dinner, finding a wonderful little Italian restaurant nearly right across the street from the sub shop and the CVS they'd stopped in before. The four friends reveled in each other's company, and celebrated Lotte's somewhat stymied birthday with great food, and at Olive's urging, a few drinks as well. With a little cajoling, she even convinced Lotte to teach them "Ein Prosit," so they could give her a proper German toast at the end of the meal.

Sufficiently humiliated by some odd looks from the other restaurant patrons, and a bit tipsy, they laughingly exited and trekked back to the University Inn. Once out of sight behind the van, the four friends slipped into the underbrush near the old decaying fence. Lotte pulled out her lighter and clicked until it sparked into flame.

The Afrit spoke from the low tree branch, just above them. *'He has traveled farther from us, in the direction from whence we came.'*

"That would be north," Olive grumbled. "So much for California."

*'He moves at a staggered pace, stopping with regularity, and for substantial periods. At these times, we briefly lose track of his presence, but always, he returns. It is the pattern we observed when he fed, and we suspect he continues to do so.'*

Lotte spoke into the darkness. "What are you up to, whoever you are? We'll check the news when we get up to our rooms, see if more cases of sleep paralysis start popping up, or even worse... *deaths*. I still think the Carlos Museum is our best bet to gather information. I'd have browsed their collection online today if there'd been time. Now I'm too tired, and frankly, too drunk. Thanks a lot, *Olive*."

"Y'all hush," she snickered. "You know you had fun."

"I did. I was just kidding. I think we all needed that after everything that's happened. In any case, I know the museum opens tomorrow at ten. That's soon enough. Our Jinn friend, or whatever he is, doesn't seem to be in a tremendous rush, and we still don't even know if this is any of our concern, or what we'll do about it even if it is. So, we'll group up tomorrow and see what we can find out. Great Afrit, are you satisfied staying here until we come back?"

*'We find very little about this situation* satisfying*, but here we will stay. Dally not,* Sadat Alnaar. *Our patience is not infinite, and we yearn for the conclusion of our bargain, in one manner, or another.'*

The sharp rustling of branches signaled the rapid departure of the nearly invisible monster as it took flight higher into the trees. A cold breeze stirred the leaves above them, which to Eric seemed to underscore the grim creature's ominous and foreboding words.

# CHAPTER 8

Atlanta, Georgia, Friday, October 27, 2017

Eric drained the last of his coffee and briefly contemplated getting a refill before the complimentary breakfast area of the University Inn closed. He'd already downed four cups, hoping to dispel the fog from last night's indulgence. As always, once his inhibitions had been lowered, he found it hard to turn down "just one more." Egged on a bit by Olive, "one more" had proven "one too many," and now he was paying the price.

From across the table, Lotte looked up from her phone. "You ready to go?"

"I was actually thinking about a little more coffee, and maybe some orange juice. I need to take some ibuprofen."

"You all right?"

"Yeah, fine. It's been a while since I drank that much."

She tucked her phone in her bag. "Same here. I got a little carried away too, but it was nice to just let it all *go* for a while. Everything's been so stressful. I'm sorry, though. I should have paid better attention."

"Hey, it's not your fault. You're usually my safety valve. It's easier to stop when I see you stop, but when you don't, I tend to forget that you still only drink a fraction of what I do. In any case, this isn't your responsibility. This is a lesson I need to learn for myself, but I still screw it up."

"Occasionally, but I can't remember the last time this happened. Don't beat yourself up. You can't control everything all the time. Take it from me, I've tried." She winked.

He faintly smiled. "Thanks. I appreciate that, although I have to confess, I'm not exactly devastated that you failed in your attempt at world domination. You'd drive people nuts."

"Ha, ha. Guess you'll just have to suffer on the world's behalf."

"It's a grisly job, but somebody's gotta do it. Hey, speaking of control, what do you make of what the Afrit said last night? What are we gonna do if we don't find *spoils* for the freakin' little thing?"

She shrugged. "I haven't the faintest idea. It's strange, but this feels like a step backward in my relationship with this creature. It's almost like it was the first time we performed the summoning, all very perfunctory and 'by the rules.' I thought we'd gotten beyond a lot of that. In fact, if we hadn't, I'm not sure the Afrit would have sacrificed itself in the Rope of An and Ki. But that was another Afrit altogether. This one lacks some of those experiences, and might still be reeling from the impact of having lost so much. I just can't believe it would truly take *me* if no other solution can be found."

"Yeah, I don't believe that either, probably because it'll happen over my dead body."

"Let's hope it doesn't come to that. There's still time, and we don't even know the full extent of what's going on, which reminds me... I'm really eager to get over there. Get your coffee while I go up and see how Olive's doing. I think she's worse off than you. Siddique brought her some things from the breakfast bar, so hopefully she'll be all right."

She grabbed her bag and scurried off while Eric went for a refill and a glass of juice. By the time he'd finished and strolled outside, his three companions were walking toward the entrance. Olive wore her oversized sunglasses to hide the ugly bruise around her eye, and seemed a bit pale and sluggish.

"Cool!" Lotte effused. "Are we all ready for the museum?"

Siddique happily nodded until the less than eager looks on Olive's and Eric's faces tempered his enthusiasm. Unperturbed, Lotte led the way, and they trekked out of the parking lot and down North Decatur.

The Michael C. Carlos Museum was only a ten-minute walk from the motel. They found the entrance in the center of the long building that dominated one side of a grassy quadrangle on the Emory University campus. A few passersby traversed this fairly quiet spot on their way to classes or other academic business, but theirs was the only party that waited in the shadow of the towering Italianate marble entranceway for the museum's doors to open. At just past 10:00 a.m., a cordial security guard ushered them inside, and they strode past the gift shop toward the ticket counter.

"Look, y'all." Olive pointed at a colored flier on the wall opposite the shop, between a doorway and a rack that held various postcards, and they crowded around. The smiling face of Harland Cheevers greeted them, under the words, "Have You Seen This Man?"

"As a matter of fact, we have," Eric muttered. "He looked a little different without any clothes on. Unfortunately, we're not gonna be alerting the museum or calling the police like they want us to."

"Come on," Lotte said. "If anyone can help Harland at this point, it'll be us. Let's see what we can find out."

They followed her to the admissions counter, purchased their tickets, checked their bags, and grabbed maps to get oriented. The museum was divided broadly into two wings, one that presented the arts of the ancient Americas, and the other which housed just about everything else. Lotte led the way through a large room packed with Greek and Roman statuary and down a corridor toward the Egyptian and Near Eastern exhibits.

"I want to start with the Mesopotamian artifacts. That's the most likely place to find what we're looking for. Not that we know what we're looking for, but I'm hoping we'll recognize it when we see it."

They took a right in front of a huge, Egyptian stone sarcophagus that brooded at the end of the long hallway and emerged into another large room. This chamber contained an assortment of ancient wooden coffins decorated with innumerable hieroglyphics that covered their surfaces. Many stood upright along the walls like the one in the hallway, but four in the middle of the room lay horizontal and contained mummies.

Eric's attention was drawn sharply by a female security guard who stood at the far end of the room, next to a passageway that led the Galleries of Ancient Near Eastern Art. She had a distinctly "goth" appearance, with a long, black leather coat, black platform boots, and sculpted, flowing, jet-black hair that framed her pale but attractive face. Dark mascara around her eyes completed the picture. Only the badge she wore on a lanyard around her neck gave any indication she worked for the museum.

"Holy shit," he said, agog.

Having not realized he'd actually spoken aloud, Olive's reply startled him. "I know, it's amazing, isn't it?"

"Seriously. If you'd known Lotte in high school, that's essentially what she looked like."

"Huh? What in the world are you talking about? That mummy don't look nuthin' like Lotte, unless that's how she sleeps, which is really TMI."

He turned to face Olive and realized she was looking in the opposite direction, where a wooden barrier separated a portion of the room from the main chamber. On the far wall of this smaller space, a glass case contained a mummy lying on its side, legs interlocked, neck cradled in a wooden headrest, and arms jutting straight downward with palms clasped together, as if locked in eternal prayer.

"I ain't never seen a mummy like that," she said. "Let's go check it out."

He followed her into the segregated space while Lotte and Siddique briskly headed past the security guard, intent on investigating the rooms beyond.

Once inside the little alcove, Olive inspected the label on the case. "Hmmm. Says here this is an older mummy. 'It is not until after the Old Kingdom that mummies were uniformly buried in a prone position.' I never knew that."

"Neither did I. I guess that's why we go to museums. I've never been such a big fan, but Lotte loves them. We might be here all day."

"Great. I may just have to curl up with this old guy and take a nap. Truth is, I'm still a little hungover from last night. Had fun, though, that's for sure. I like hangin' out with y'all."

"We like hanging out with you, too. Siddique seems especially happy. I think he was worried about you. He wasn't gonna let us go without taking him along... not this time."

"Really?"

"Yep. If I'm reading things right, I'd say you were pretty pleased to see him too. That's none of my business, though, if you don't want to talk about it."

She gave a wan smile. "I don't mind. There ain't really much to talk about, though. We like each other, but there's... I don't know... all these *obstacles*, all this practical stuff that gets in the way. Or maybe it ain't so practical. Maybe it's just *stuff*, like stuff that gets in your head and won't get out. I've got stuff, he's got stuff, and it all just piles up, like all the crap in your garage, until finally you can barely get your dang car door open. Plus, there's this whole crazy thing with *Aicha*! What a mess *that* is. Whatever, it's fine. We're taking it slow, seeing if we can work things through. It's just that what you probably *think* is going on really isn't, at least not yet."

Eric slowly nodded. "I hear you. It might be hard to believe, but I've been there. Not exactly the same issues, but I know all about 'stuff.' It takes a while to sort through, and even then, more stuff will come up... guaranteed. For me, it all came down to being true to myself, but that's harder than it might sound when you're not certain who you really are. I know both you and Siddique. You're good people. You'll figure it out. If there's anything Lotte and I can do, just let us know."

"Thanks. I got me some thinkin' to do, but I may take you up on that. *Yeesh*, this mummy is startin' to creep me right out. It looks so *human*. I keep thinking it might wake up."

"Would that really surprise you given the crazy shit we've seen?"

"It probably wouldn't, which is pretty weird, if you think about it. Anyway, let's go see if those two have found—"

Eric heard Lotte emit a doleful howl from just beyond the entryway to the next room. He and Olive sprinted toward the passageway, through which the security guard raced ahead of them. Once past the opening, they hung a right, then spilled into a smaller room with many tall, narrow glass cases on the walls. Lotte and Siddique stood in front of one of these displays, next to an emergency exit door, and just beyond a wooden bench that dominated the center of the room. She'd wrapped her arms tightly around his waist, and he gently stroked her back, trying to comfort her.

Eric maneuvered past the confused security guard and skidded to a halt next to them. "What happened?"

"I don't know," Siddique answered, stress in his voice. "We were just looking at the cases, and she was telling me about all the stuff. Then, she cried out and threw her arms around me. Lotte, look, Eric's here."

Mechanically, she released Siddique and instantly clung to Eric like a magnet.

He hugged her closely. "Lotte, are you okay? What is it?"

She didn't look up, but the signature scalpel of her tongue slashed words into his shoulder. "What is it? It's what it *always* is... cause and effect! It's all just cause and effect, isn't it? Except we don't know what we're doing, do we? We do what we think is right, but who knows if it really is. You knock one down, and another one just *pops* up. How were we to know? Is this one better or worse than the last one? We had no way of telling, but I'm pretty bloody certain we'll find out now!"

"I... I can't understand what you're trying to tell me. What brought all this on?"

She pulled away slightly, deliberately lifted her arm, and pointed. He glanced over his shoulder and saw that her finger aimed directly at the case behind him. He turned to face the display of artifacts while Olive and Siddique gently led her to the bench. A cursory scan of the objects quickly told him all he needed to know, and an icy chill ran down his spine.

A sturdy, rectangular amulet, perhaps six inches long and four inches wide, caught and dominated his attention. It bore the image of a monster that stood in relief against a flat background. The beast was bipedal, humanoid, and judging from the protruding serpentine penis, clearly male. He appeared emaciated, and etchings on each side of his elongated torso seemed to suggest he possessed scales. Ruffs of hair like high, furry boots ringed the top of each of his bird-like feet, while two pairs of impressive wings spread wide on the creature's back.

Like the Afrit, a scorpion's barbed tail menaced from behind his legs. The being's right hand was raised in the air, while his left hand pointed downward. His face was a sinister mixture of canine and human features, with a doglike muzzle, sharp fangs, bulging eyes, and a ridged and wrinkled brow.

*I recognize this thing, but I don't know how. Where have I seen this before?*

Most alarming to Eric, however, was something he could instantly identify. The amulet was constructed of six, small wrought iron plates, bound together by golden seams and encased in a frame of gold. It was unmistakably identical in composition to Dimme's unnerving collar, which he'd seen in the great chamber in the Rope of An and Ki. It was labeled as item number six in the case, right next to a ceramic head of what appeared to be the same entity. He scanned the list of descriptions and read the text.

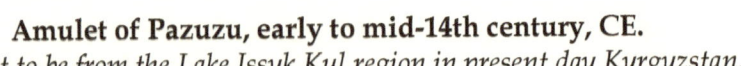

### Amulet of Pazuzu, early to mid-14th century, CE.
*Thought to be from the Lake Issyk Kul region in present day Kyrgyzstan.*

An unusual and puzzling piece, purchased in the 1920s by Professor William A. Shelton while on vacation in Southern France. The amulet clearly depicts Pazuzu, personification of the West Wind, and master of the lilu wind demons. However, this artifact post-dates all other known worship of this deity by nearly 1,500 years. Mineralogical analysis has traced the gold to the mines near Kumtor in Kyrgyzstan. The metallurgy and construction place it in line with traditions from the Issyk Kul region. The piece appears to have been separated from a similar charm depicting Pazuzu's brother, Humbaba, or Huwawa, once connected to the back of this artifact by strands of gold that have been severed. What is thought to be the accompanying medallion now resides in The University of Pennsylvania Museum of Archaeology and Anthropology. Scholars are uncertain whether these items are replicas of now lost originals, or if worship of these ancient Mesopotamian gods continued well into the common era in remote and isolated areas.

"Pazuzu. Now I know where I've seen this thing before. It's from the freaking *Exorcist*!" He walked back to where Lotte sat on the bench in mute dismay. "Did you read the description of that item?"

"No. I saw that thing and...." She ceased speaking and cautiously turned her head to meet the gaze of the still worried security guard. "I'm terribly sorry. I didn't mean to make a scene. Something in that case over there just reminded me of... well... something *else*. Something that brought back some bad memories. I'm all right now, really. I hate to have troubled you."

"It's okay," the young woman said. "I'm just glad you weren't hurt. That would've been a mess of paperwork, and a ton of questions. We've all had our share of *those* recently, not that it did a lot of good." Her tone conveyed a touch of anger.

"Questions about the guy in the flier near the gift shop," Eric proffered. "He worked here, right? Did you know him?"

She sighed forlornly. "I knew Harland. I worked with him quite a bit. He was a security guard, same as me, except he'd been here a lot longer, so he helped me out when I was new. He's a sweet guy, but really... kind of... socially *awkward*. He's smart, but super shy, and really uncomfortable around people. He told me folks had always made fun of him and called him 'weird,' and picked on him. I know the feeling, being treated differently because of your looks or how you want to dress, but at least I have a lot of friends. Harland was mostly on his own, especially after his folks died. I guess he spends a lot of time online and playing games, and every so often he goes to music festivals in other states. We got along pretty easily because I like music too, and we could talk about that, even though I don't know any of the bands he's into."

"Join the club," Eric quipped.

"Excuse me? Do you know Harland?"

"Uh, no," he fumbled. "I was talking about my wife. I don't know any of the weirdo bands she likes either." Lotte shot him an annoyed glance. "Anyway, I'm sorry, I didn't mean to pry. You just seemed upset."

"*Frustrated* is what I really am. After all we went through, I don't believe the police are going to find him. I think he just decided to leave it all behind. I think he's dead, lying in a ditch somewhere, or at the bottom of some river, and it really tears me up."

"That's awful. I'm really sorry... we all are."

"It's me that's sorry. I didn't mean to lay all that on you. It's just been a really emotional thing for a lot of us, and it drives me crazy that the police don't have any leads. Strange as he can be, everybody here loves

Harland. He never caused any trouble, and he was always really polite and professional, even if he doesn't say much. I also tend to think about him when I'm stationed here because this was his favorite spot to work. He loved the mummies, and all the ancient displays." She turned to Lotte. "In any case, are you feeling better? Can I get you anything, some water, maybe?"

Lotte smiled weakly. "No, but thank you. I'll think I'll go read that description now. My husband seems to think it'll make me feel better, and he's usually right about things like that. Again, I'm really sorry."

"It's fine. It'll probably be the most interesting thing that'll happen to me all day. I'll just be in the next room if y'all need anything."

As she departed, Olive turned and whispered into Eric's ear. "That's what Lotte used to look like?"

"Pretty much. Lotte looked a bit, *tougher*... I guess... but that's the basic idea."

She beamed. "I like that! I bet she was kinda scary."

*You have no idea.*

Lotte sluggishly got up and dragged over to the case.

Eric followed, but indicated Olive and Siddique should give her some space, so they discreetly moseyed into the adjoining room.

It took Lotte a few moments to bring herself to look at the items, but once she'd worked up the courage, she quickly digested the descriptive text. "Pazuzu. So *that's* who you are. It makes sense."

"How so?" Eric asked.

"Remember what Enki said, that Pazuzu was Dimme's sworn enemy? He took it upon himself to act as a guardian against her. He was probably able to do this because he has Jinn-like powers as well. He might be similar to her, part god, and part Jinn. That would explain a lot."

"Yeah, about his powers, but I don't understand why he's inside Harland Cheevers now. How did that happen, and why did it happen now and not in the last ninety years this thing has been sitting in this museum?"

"It's like I was saying, cause and effect. *We* released him! We just didn't realize we'd done it. As you clearly noticed, the amulet's construction is identical to Dimme's collar. That means this was Iblis's magic. He'd somehow trapped Pazuzu's spirit inside this artifact, likely to placate Dimme as a setup before he imprisoned her as well. When Enki destroyed Iblis's staff, the charms on *both* items were nullified. Dimme got free, and so did Pazuzu, but Pazuzu didn't have a *body*. He was stuck inside this item until someone nearby fell asleep, and like a Jinn, he could infiltrate their mind and take them over."

"Shit. Poor Harland."

"No kidding. He clearly liked being stationed in these rooms. Maybe on a slow day, he sat down on the bench, right where I was, just to rest for a minute. If he drifted off, even for only a second, that's all it would have taken. Now, Pazuzu's got him, and we have no idea what that might mean."

"I'd guess it means he's headed to that museum in Pennsylvania to reunite with his brother, Rum Baba, or whatever."

She giggled slightly, which he took as a good sign. "Humbaba. I don't know much about him, though it's probably more than I know about Pazuzu. He's a pretty significant character in *The Epic of Gilgamesh*. Not that I give a lot of thought to meeting Mesopotamian gods, but I'd never have given the slightest consideration to meeting *him*."

"That's right, I remember now from that book on Mesopotamian myth. Gilgamesh killed him."

Her eyes grew wide. "Good for you! The little hamsters in your head are clearly working overtime. What I'm not certain about is whether Pazuzu might have had another brother. I'll have to do some research, but for now, your guess about what he's up to is as good as anything."

"So, where does that leave us?"

"I'm not sure. I know Pazuzu has a bad reputation, primarily because of that stupid movie, but we know all the entities we've encountered can have violent and vengeful traits as well as benevolent characteristics. His representation certainly looks pretty nasty, but so does the Afrit. One thing does give me some comfort."

"What?"

"He seems to hate *Dimme*, and so do I. I want her dead for what she did, for what she's done to other women... what she's probably doing now, and what she'll surely do in the future. I know I'm supposed to be scientific and rational about this, but I've read up on her. Even the other gods thought she was an abomination. Her Jinn heritage must have allowed her to avoid the worst of their wrath, and Pazuzu might not have been powerful enough to kill her by himself. But this has to end, and I'm going to see to it that it does, if it's the last thing I do. I can't believe I'm saying this, but I think we might need Pazuzu's help. We need to talk with him. If he can exterminate Dimme, with or without our assistance, then—as we've discovered in the past—the enemy of our enemy may very well be our friend, even if he's a dangerous son of a bitch."

Eric had the strange sensation of being, for once in his life, completely free of mental conflict. "I'm totally with you. Anything that spells the end for that shrew from hell is worth it to me, even if we have to fight Pazuzu when it's over. I just disagree with you on one point."

"What?"

"*The Exorcist* is *not* a stupid movie. Have you actually seen it?"

She rolled her eyes. "Really, like a six-year-old. Come on, let's go find Olive and Siddique and get going. I think we found what we came here for."

*Add one more museum to the list of places I'll probably never see.*

"Hey," he said, "are we gonna take them along? This might be dangerous. What am I saying? This already *is* dangerous, but confronting Pazuzu again after what happened? That might be asking for serious trouble."

She shook her head. "This time, there's nothing for it. We need Olive with us. She's the one card we have to play with Pazuzu. He said he needed her. We'll give him what he wants. We also can't strand Siddique down here alone, and you know he'll never let us take Olive away without him anyway. They've always wanted to get in on the action. This time, they'll get their wish, which only proves the old adage: be careful what you wish for."

They crossed into the room to their left, which also housed ancient Near Eastern artifacts, and found their companions examining the back wall. Coincidentally, the large display in this area depicted various elements from *The Epic of Gilgamesh*.

"That's him," Lotte exclaimed as she made a beeline for the first item displayed in the case, a roughly four-inch diameter, round ceramic plaque depicting a wrinkled and distorted human-like face, mouth wide and teeth clenched.

"That's who?" Olive asked.

"Humbaba, Pazuzu's brother. Pazuzu is the entity that's taken over Harland Cheevers's body. We'll explain how we know that later. I never realized he and Humbaba were related until I read the description of the amulet in the other room. This is most likely the brother Pazuzu is after, except it doesn't make sense. Humbaba is supposed to be dead. The little plaque in this case is meant to represent his severed head that Gilgamesh and Enkidu put into a leather bag. I believe they presented it to Enlil, who was none too pleased, but I need to reread the story to be sure. In any case, the Pazuzu medallion in the other room was fastened at one time to a matching piece that portrayed Humbaba. It's in the Penn Museum in Philadelphia, and I'm pretty certain that's where Pazuzu is headed."

"So much for California," Olive griped, "but I guess Philadelphia will be fun."

"I rather doubt it, given why we'll be there, but I'm glad to hear you're up for coming along. Still, I need to be absolutely certain you know what you're getting into. I know it sounds crazy, but I want to find Pazuzu and talk with him, and I think he'll be far more likely to listen if you're with us. He wanted you for something, something related to his brother, and I'm guessing he still does. It's bound to be incredibly dangerous, but we need you, and it might be even more perilous and unpredictable if we don't act. Are you in?"

Olive's eyes widened "Am I in? Are you kiddin'? Of course, I am. I just want to take Mutig with us. I know he don't like me right now, and he's a little banged up, but I feel safer with him along. I need to leave my momma a note anyway. She's gonna be fit to be tied, but I'll deal with that later."

"All right, that's wonderful. We'll go and pack up the van, then swing by your house. Once we're on the road, I'll explain everything, but I think we need to get going now."

"Let me just use the restroom before we leave," Eric interjected. "All that coffee from breakfast is hitting me. I'll meet you in the gift shop."

He hustled back toward the large chamber with the mummies. The gothy security guard still stood vigil, though the room was vacant of visitors.

"Y'all leaving already?" she asked.

"Yeah, story of my life. We go to all kinds of interesting places, but priorities always seem to change, and I rarely wind up seeing anything. Thanks for being so nice."

She smiled. "I hope you can come back and visit us again soon."

"Me too!" *Assuming I'm alive, there's nothing I'd enjoy more.*

He encountered a group of visitors in the room with Greek and Roman statuary, and a few purchasing tickets in the central foyer. The restroom was downstairs, through the door near the entryway, next to Harland Cheevers's missing persons flier. Staff were just opening up the gift shop as he passed by.

The lower level, which seemed to be an administrative area, appeared utterly vacant, and he had the bathroom all to himself. He quickly peed, washed his hands, and rounded the corner for the exit. He nearly jumped out of his skin when he almost ran into a man wearing a ski mask, standing with his back to the door and blocking the way.

"What the—"

"Relax, Eric," the man calmly said with a lilting Middle Eastern accent. "I'm not going to hurt you. I just want to talk. I'm sorry I wasn't able to make your acquaintance at Metéora."

Eric's mind and heart raced, but he knew he was trapped, and doubted yelling for help would do anything but put his life in further jeopardy. He decided to try and play it cool. "You were there, huh? Sorry I missed you too, but we hung out with your pet owl for a while. That was a swingin' time."

The man gave a sinister laugh through the ski mask. "Such wit. You realize the being you killed had lived in this realm for over six-thousand years?"

"I didn't do the math, but if we hadn't done what we did, we wouldn't have lasted another six seconds. Am I supposed to feel bad about saving my own life?"

"No, my friend, you acted according to your nature, just as I would have. Understand, however, that the beings whom I serve, and whom you appear to have dealings with as well, possess their own nature, their own motives, and will also do what they feel they must in order to get what *they* want."

"And what exactly might that be? What the hell do they want from us anyway?"

"They want the truth, Eric. You don't mind if I call you that, do you? They need accurate information."

"Then why don't they just ask us for it?"

"They won't believe you until they've proven for themselves that you're telling the truth. Their methods are perhaps a bit *extreme*, but their results are impeccably reliable."

"That's ridiculous. Why would we lie to them?"

"Tell me, Eric, what happened to Aicha Kandicha? Where is she now?"

"Umm, she's dead. She got eaten by something tougher, and smarter, than she was."

The man shook his head. "You see... you lie. Uri felt her touch him ever so briefly when the girl attacked him in the trees. He knows Aicha's aura well. Do not take us for fools."

"I... well... I'm not lying. It's just complicated."

"Of course, it is. Our goal is to make things simple for you. Give us what we want, and we'll leave you in peace."

"Sounds more like you'll leave me in *pieces*. No thanks. You actually expect me to walk out of here with you to go get *tortured*?"

"That would never work. You are under close scrutiny, and I wouldn't get far with you before meeting my end. The only reason I could get near you is that I'm not a Jinn, and those who watch you don't know me. I could have killed you, but instead, I'm extending an offer. Call off your protectors and send us one of you to be... *questioned*. Once we have what we want, we'll be off. You have our word."

"Why would I do that?" Eric scoffed. "If we're being protected, why would I just give myself to you?"

"Because things are about to change. All our attempts to capture one of you have ended in failure, often to my employer's great surprise. You have resources they never anticipated, but the balance is about to shift, and the game of cat and mouse will end. When it does, we shall have the upper hand, and we'll exercise our advantage through increased violence that will threaten all of your lives. Some of you will almost surely die, and in the end, we'll get what we want. I'm giving you the opportunity to avoid such an outcome."

The cool frankness with which the man spoke caused Eric's bravado to fade. "All right, let's assume I believe you. There's still a major problem. I have no idea who's protecting us. We have no contact with them. Things have happened that we can't explain. I assume this was their doing, but I can't say for sure. We can't control what they might do if one of us goes with you."

"Hmmm, a pity. They are wise. They conceal their identities from you in case we successfully abducted one of your little group. Like you, and us, they have things to lose, things that can be taken from them, if we know who they are. This poses a problem, but it is your concern, not ours. You have proven quite capable. There may be a solution to your conundrum, should you put your minds to it. I leave that to you. Know with certainty that your window of time to act in accordance with my offer is open only for so long. All too soon, and I mean that in all sincerity, we will possess the capability to *take* what we want, and we won't hesitate to do so should the opportunity present itself."

"I understand. I'll pass the message along, and we'll consider it. I wouldn't hold your breath, though."

He nodded. "Very well, then. Return to the sink and count slowly to twenty, then you may leave. It was a pleasure to speak with you. Understand that only fate puts us on opposite sides of this matter. I bear you no malice, and hope you heed my words. It would be a shame to see the end of so many promising, young lives."

# CHAPTER 9

Lotte and Eric sat in the shade of a scraggly tree. The woebegone plant jutted out from a layer of reddish mulch on an island in the parking lot of the strip mall. She munched on a powdered doughnut while he took another bite of his bagel with cream cheese. It wasn't much of a lunch, but neither were especially hungry.

After leaving the museum, they'd returned to the University Inn and hurriedly transported the boxes and bags with the portal materials from their rooms into the van. Lotte coaxed the reluctant Afrit out of the trees and grudgingly into the vehicle, and they set off for Marietta.

Olive's house had been the first stop. She hadn't taken long to leave her mother a note, grab the few things she might need, and corral a seemingly improved Mutig into the van's now crammed cargo space. They'd have hit the road then, but Olive absolutely required a new phone. The T-Mobile store was only ten minutes away down Windy Hill Road, past the shopping center where she and Siddique had evaded their pursuer the day before. Conveniently, a doughnut shop just a few doors down was still open, and Lotte and Eric had a chance to grab a quick bite to eat while Olive and Siddique were inside picking out the new phone.

"You sure about this?" Eric asked, wiping cream cheese from his lips.

"Sure about what, not having one of us give ourselves up to be tortured? Yes, I'm pretty sure about that, *danke schön*."

"What if they catch us, though? What if they catch *all* of us? Then we're *all* going to get tortured, unless they don't even bother. Maybe they'll just kill some of us and torture whoever's left. That's what I'm trying to avoid."

She gave an exasperated sigh and rubbed her temples. "I understand. I'm trying to avoid that too. I just think we have a better chance trying to enlist Pazuzu's help. They can't possibly have anticipated *that*, and I don't believe they brought enough firepower to deal with an angry god. If we can get to him before they get to us, nobody has to put themselves at risk."

"What if he doesn't help us?"

"Why wouldn't he? He already wanted Olive's help. Now, we're bringing her back to him. We'll explain what happened and offer our assistance as well. These beings are used to being served by humans, and we know that Pazuzu granted his protection from... well... you know, to those who honored his name."

"Right, or he brought famine and disease when they let him down. It just seems kind of chancy."

"Well, then we can't let him down, can we? I know it's risky, but it's our best chance. The alternative is out of the question—unless I'm the one who goes."

"Yeah, hard no. We've been over that already. I'm the logical choice. Unlike you, I have the willpower of a defective toothpick. I'll crack the minute they look at me sideways."

"*Tüddelkram!* You're a stubborn little turtle, always hiding away your troubles inside your shell. But this isn't the point. I don't want *any* of us to go. I don't believe what that man said. I don't think they'll let you go, and I don't believe they'll leave us alone. If anything, I think they'll come after us even harder to try and get the portal materials once they figure out what's happened. They don't understand that they're not nearly as close to breaching the doorway back to the An as they think they are. As long as we have a chance to keep away from them, I want to take it, and I think Pazuzu gives us that chance."

Eric shrugged. "Okay, I surrender. We'll do it your way. Not that I'm crying... getting tortured by a Jinn wasn't exactly on my bucket list. Look at freaking Utnapishtim. *Yeesh!* In a sense, I guess it's no different from our original plan. I hope Pazuzu finds us useful enough to give us all this help, and eventually try to track down Dimme."

Olive's voice startled him. "Why are y'all so dead set on that, anyway?"

Eric turned to Lotte and held her gaze until she covered her eyes with her hands, like she had in the MFA cafeteria what seemed like 10,000 years ago.

Sensing her distress, Olive sat next to her. "Sugar, what is it? What's so awful about this that you'd be so upset in that museum? Does it have anything to do with why you and Eric have been so... I don't know... down in the dumps and all? Please tell us. We're your friends. We're on your *team*. You know we'd do anything to help y'all. We just have to understand what this is all about."

Lotte haltingly lowered her hands, revealing tear-stained eyes and cheeks. As usual, her runny mascara completed the portrait of misery. "I'll tell you. It's time you know. We bought doughnuts if you'd like some. Bagels, too, with cream cheese. I'm sorry, that's all this little plaza had, unless you wanted Vietnamese. That seemed like too much trouble for the road. I'm sorry. I really am...."

Eric put his hand on her shoulder. "Lotte, it's okay. I can tell them—"

"No," she cut in. "I'll do it. I need to do it." She wiped her nose and took a deep breath. "Her Akkadian name is Lamashtu, but in the original Sumerian, she's known as *Dimme*. Like Enki and Enlil, she's a daughter of Anu, so she's considered a goddess in her own right, but her mother was... well... it's not really known. I believe she was a mortal woman possessed by a Jinn, and Dimme is frequently classified as being a Jinn. Enki said the union fell far short of the sum of its miraculous parts, and ancient mythology surely bears this out. Dimme acted in malevolence of her own accord, rather than at the gods' instructions. She was known for slaying infants, gnawing on their bones, sucking their blood, and causing harm to mothers."

She began to shake, and dark tears once again coursed down her cheeks. "Her victims included unborn babies... and expectant mothers. Of all the tales we've learned that told a hidden truth, I'm sorry to say, Eric and I can vouch for the genuineness of this story. Before she fled the Rope of An and Ki in Oman, Dimme took our unborn child, and for this, I'll never forgive her. Never."

Cars whizzed by on Powder Springs Road, creating a rhythmic backdrop to Lotte's gulping attempts to cease crying. Olive threw her arms around her and cried as well, while Siddique sat quietly next to Eric. They stayed that way until Lotte finally reached out, picked up what remained of her doughnut, and stuffed it into her mouth.

"Pazuzu is Dimme's sworn enemy," she said, mouth full of crumbs and powdered sugar. "The ancients invoked him to protect them from his malicious rival. It looks like what's old is new again. Our actions unwittingly let this god loose in the world once more. Cause and effect. Now, we have to make the best of that unforeseen opportunity, try to enlist Pazuzu's assistance, and hope something far worse doesn't result from our efforts. In all honesty, I'm not sure I care, as long as Anu's defective daughter pays for what she's done. Come on. Grab the doughnuts and let's get going."

---

Eric's companions nodded off, one by one.

Lotte collapsed first, emotionally exhausted after her harrowing confession about what Dimme had done to them. Tears not fully spent, she lingered in Olive's embrace before she crumpled into the makeshift bedding on the floor of the van. Mutig eagerly commandeered the space beside her. The dog pressed close to her body and rolled on his back in a stupor of bliss. Olive soon joined them, sandwiching Lotte with their warmth.

Siddique fell last, head propped on a sweatshirt that served as a makeshift pillow against the glass of his window. He'd offered to drive, but Eric needed time to process what had happened, and he knew his friend wasn't completely comfortable operating the van in the incessant onslaught of traffic in the Metro Atlanta area.

*Actually, we got lucky. Traffic isn't so bad at two-thirty in the afternoon.*

He planned to drive for an hour or two, then let Siddique take over when they stopped for gas on I-85. For now, he enjoyed the hypnotic pattern of the van's forward progress. Like riding his bike, this always calmed him, cleared enough of his mind that he could think without really thinking, feel and then quickly let the feeling pass, like the road signs that whizzed by—there, but rapidly relinquished to the past, processed, and then discarded.

Unexpectedly, Eric felt his seat pull back, like someone using it to hoist themselves up in the row behind you on an airplane. Simultaneously, the curling, scorpion-like tail of the Afrit snaked firmly around his shoulders and neck, its nasty little barb barely tickling his left earlobe.

"Umm, did I do something wrong?"

The creature hissed quietly in his ear. '*Calm yourself and keep your voice down. We must stabilize ourselves upon this precarious perch. You will not be harmed... unless you displease us. We would speak with you, and do not wish to wake those who slumber.*'

"Sure, whatever you want." He rolled his window down a bit more, increasing the white noise from the rushing air. "How can I be of service, oh great one?" *Hey, if it's good enough for Lotte....*

He felt a slight flutter from the little beastie's wings. '*What distresses our* Sadat Alnaar? *Why does she weep?*'

"Riiight. Well, she had to tell the others about something bad that happened to us. They needed to know because it has a bearing on this *entity* we're tracking down right now. By the way, are we still on course?"

'*In essence, yes. Flight would be swifter, but we know your roads interminably weave and wind. You are on the fastest route.*'

Eric snickered. "You sound like Google Maps. Anyway, we had to explain the situation to them. Truth is, we should have talked to them long before this."

'*Why did you hesitate?*'

"Because... well... it's just not so easy talking about some things. This had to do with another one of these damn godlike beings. You actually met her in the Rope of An and Ki, but I guess that was a different 'part' of you, or whatever, so you don't remember. We thought we had her trapped, but she got away, and she wound up... oh, jeez... how can I say it? She basically *ate* our unborn child. Umm, having a child is how we mortals make more, er, little mortals who grow up—"

*'Cease! We are not ignorant of your kind's method of reproduction, incomprehensible as it may be.'*

"Gotcha, sorry. I had no idea you knew about all of that. I'm not sure how that makes me feel." He shivered slightly at the thought. "Whatever. In any case, stuff like this brings up a lot of emotions that are hard for us to experience. It's also tough on the people you talk with. They don't know what to do, or what to say. Sympathy only goes so far. It doesn't really *change* anything. Actually, that's not completely true. It can be extremely helpful to have someone to talk with about your problems. There's a guy whose books I've read who popularized the idea of a 'talking cure,' basically the notion that just expressing your troubles aloud can be a path to feeling better."

*'Feelings. The scourge of your ilk. So much energy squandered on things of such scant import.'*

"Hey, guilty as charged. That's just how we roll, like it or not, but I'd be willing to bet that's part of what makes us such tasty morsels for all you 'creatures from the eighteenth dimension,' or what-the-heck-ever. All I know is, our 'ilk' can experience pretty intense sorrow, and we have to find ways to deal with that. Lotte sobbed when she told Siddique and Olive about what happened with you... well, the part of you that went with us to Oman, anyway. Hard as it was, I think she felt better after that, and I think she'll feel better for having talked with them about losing our child, just like I felt better after I spilled my guts to her—even if she did fall asleep on me."

*'You also wept?'*

"Like a baby, and for the baby neither of us will ever get the chance to know. It almost destroyed me. For a while, I think it did."

The Afrit clung silently to the back of Eric's chair for a few moments, then the beastie whispered in his ear. *'We understand.'* The barb of the creature's tail slipped delicately across Eric's neck as the diminutive monster retreated rapidly to the back of the van.

Once again, Eric found himself alone with his thoughts as they hurtled into the immutable past.

Siddique took the wheel after a brief stop along I-85, and Eric replaced Olive in the back of the van with Lotte, who became engrossed in her laptop. He glanced up several times at the Afrit, who brooded above him atop its favorite flight case, but the creature stared stonily forward. Eventually, Eric fell asleep.

The weary, and now hungry, passengers arrived in Blacksburg, South Carolina around 6:30 p.m., where they found an unassuming little café that served breakfast all day, along with burgers, sandwiches, and "such." Eric was disappointed they didn't have cheese grits but enjoyed his plate of fish and hushpuppies.

"I saw you had your laptop out before I fell asleep," he said to Lotte as she nicked one of his hushpuppies. "What were you working on?"

She scowled. "I was trying to reread *The Epic of Gilgamesh, aber ich vergaß, dass es viele Versionen gibt!*"

"Woah, slow down there, *Fräulein.* You *forgot* there's lots of *what?*"

"Sorry, I'm just frustrated, and tired. Good job you caught as much of that as you did. I said I forgot there were so many bloody versions, and various translations, too. I had to download a bunch of them. I used my phone as a hot spot, but we kept losing the signal. So annoying!"

"Did you get anywhere?"

"I suppose. I think I've got all the materials I need. Now, I just have to piece them together, try to figure out the most consistent narrative, and separate the original, core text from later accretions. It's not so easy. Scholars have been at this for centuries. I just come at it with a slightly different eye, knowing what we know."

He laughed. "Yeah, sometimes the craziest parts of these stories turn out to be true." A man in the next booth warily looked over his shoulder, and Eric quickly went back to his food.

After supper, the four friends cleaned up as best they could in the restroom, then took a short walk to stretch their legs.

*If what the Afrit told us is right, we'll get close to Harland Cheevers, or I guess I should call him Pazuzu, some time tonight, depending on whether he stops to feed. I'm not sure if that's a good thing or not.*

It was after 8:00 p.m. when they got back to the van to resume their journey. Darkness had descended on the little town of Blacksburg, so the Afrit speedily zipped into the air. Siddique drove for nearly two hours up I-85. After a quick pit stop, Eric took the wheel, feeling refreshed after another nap and having digested his food. He wanted Siddique to get some rest and give his stitches time to heal. Olive redressed his wounds with materials they'd received at the hospital, then joined Eric in the passenger's seat. Lotte remained in the back, absorbed in her studies.

*Or maybe she's playing Might and Magic III?*

Just past Durham, around 11:15, the Afrit swooped down and clung to Olive's side mirror. She rolled down her window and listened to its instructions.

*'He has ceased his progress, as is his pattern. If he remains stationary, you will come upon him soon. We shall fly ahead and determine which route you must take in your incommodious vehicle.'*

Olive fumed once the creature had again taken to the air. "Did that damn ol' thing just say we was driving around in a toilet?"

"I have no idea," Eric replied. "It has a better vocabulary than I do, which I guess isn't saying much, but still.... Can you tell Lotte to get ready and have her wake up Siddique? I think we're about to meet your old friend Harland again."

"Can't wait," she said morosely, but then changed her tone. "Oh, Eric, that ain't true. After what Lotte told us, I'm happy to do this. That Dimme woman sounds downright *evil*! I know these things have their own thoughts, and their own way of doing stuff, but even the other gods seem to realize that she's totally bonkers! I'll do anything I can to help stop her, and to get her back for what she did to both of you. You know I will."

"I do, and you can't begin to imagine how much what you just said means to me, and to Lotte. The problem is, this time, I think I'm gonna have to take you up on your offer, and as we're beginning to realize, we totally suck at predicting the outcomes of our actions. If anything happens to you, I don't know what I'll do."

She smiled and grasped his arm. "Yes, you do. You'll carry on, just like I would. It's too important not to. That's why I'm on this team in the first place, and why you told me everything right from the beginning. Because the details are important, and we have no idea who's gonna survive to carry forward what we know. It's just like your damn Patriots: 'next man up.' I really hate em', but you gotta respect a team like that. That's the team I'm on, and so are you."

He marveled at her assessment as she edged into the back.

*Sheesh. She's cut out for this better than I am. At least, she is now. She's not the Olive I got to know two years ago, that's for sure. It's like going to war. You adapt pretty quickly, or you don't survive. How I've gotten this far is a total mystery.*

Olive turned and gave Lotte a quick update, and she and Siddique soon crowded behind the van's seats. They drove in tense silence until nearly midnight, when the Afrit finally reappeared.

*'Leave this road at the next available opportunity. When you can travel no farther, navigate toward the side by which you steer this conveyance. We shall provide additional guidance when necessary.'*

"I think the last sign I saw was for Middleburg and some other town," Eric said. "Exit 220. It's coming up in a couple of miles. Assuming we have a signal, can somebody call up directions on their cell phone?"

Olive squirmed in the passenger's seat. "Umm, I don't think that's such a hot idea. Cell phone data can be traced pretty easily. If we're tracking this here Pazuzu guy to where he's feedin' and there's trouble, the police are bound to investigate eventually. We don't want our cell phone signals anywhere near something like that. Y'all were smart not to bring your phones to Harland's house before, but I think we need to do what I did... take out the SIM cards so we're not sending out any signals at all."

"She's right," Lotte declared as she handed Olive her phone. "Here, do mine for me. I'm a complete *Evolutionsbremse* when it comes to these stupid things."

Eric blinked a few times as he wracked his brain, but then gave up. "Wow, that's a new one. Care to fill us in on what that means?"

She slyly chuckled. "Well, if you'd actually *studied* back in high school, you'd know that Bremse means 'brake.' So, it literally means 'evolutionary brake,' or in my case someone who's such an idiot with cell phones that my existence on Earth is actually holding up the advancement of humankind... kind of like you with your sense of humor."

They all laughed heartily as one by one they handed Olive their phones for her to perform the necessary operation. When complete, she stacked the devices and their disassembled components into the glove box.

After a brief time, another sign appeared announcing that Exit 220 was coming up in one mile. When the ramp came into sight, Eric hit the blinker and began his turn. Just as he started to veer off, a flashing red light went off in a vehicle about 100 yards behind the van. It sped toward them, high beams reflecting irritatingly in the side mirrors.

"Crap!" Eric groused. "Looks like the police are stopping us."

Lotte poked her head between the two seats. "Were you speeding?"

"Well, that depends on what you mean by 'speeding.' I was definitely going over the speed limit, but not by much in this clunky van.

Cars were passing us pretty often. I wouldn't think we'd especially be a target for a speeding ticket, unless this is one of those speed traps you hear about in the South."

Olive frowned. "That's usually in small towns, not on the interstate, and it mostly ain't true anymore anyway. Better pull over and see what they want. Maybe we got a taillight out."

Figuring that might be possible, Eric steered to the side of the exit ramp and rolled down his window. The vehicle with the flashing light pulled in behind them. It appeared to be an SUV, and the twirling red illumination came from the dashboard, not the roof. From behind the intense glare of the high beams, a door opened.

"This ain't right!" Olive yelped, her eyes transfixed on the passenger side mirror. "They're gettin' out on my side, too, and I think that guy's holdin' a rifle! Eric, move! *Now!*"

After a moment's panic, he threw the van into drive and floored it. They quickly left the SUV behind, but by the time they reached the end of the exit ramp, Eric could see it had pulled into the road. Remembering the Afrit's instructions, he ignored the stop sign and banged a left onto Route 1. They quickly passed a school on the left, and were approaching a Dollar General store, when the little ashen creature plunged out of the darkness and grabbed the side mirror.

*'Follow us!'* it bellowed, before it darted in front of the van.

Eric could track the beast in the headlights, and it quickly swerved to the left. He slammed the brakes, navigated the treacherous turn, then gunned the engine. They whizzed past a couple of churches on the right, screamed under the bridge that carried I-85 away to the northwest, then emerged in a dark and quiet stretch of rural roadway.

"They're gainin' on us!" Olive reported. "That SUV is way faster than we are. They'll catch up with us in no time."

Eric spared a glance in his mirror and saw she was right. The vehicle had made the sharp turn he'd maneuvered and rapidly closed on them. "Olive, are you sure this isn't the police?"

"Positive! Never been surer of anything, unless this is some kind of crazy case of mistaken identity—like they think we're runnin' drugs or something. What are the chances of that, though? You told us that man in the bathroom said they'd act if they saw the opportunity, and here we are, coming off the highway out in the middle of nowhere. He also said they'd be comin' for us soon. I think we're in way deeper shit than just the police! Pardon my French."

"What can we do?"

"We have to buy time," Lotte interjected. "We have to get to Pazuzu, see if he'll help us. At least he might spare Olive if he needs her so badly. That's better than nothing."

"What about the Afrit?" Eric asked. "Can't it help us if we have to fight?"

"It's so diminished," she fretted. "These men might be soldiers, like the ones at the Majlis al Jinn. Remember what damage they did with their weapons? That Afrit was enormous. This one couldn't withstand a battering like that. They might disrupt the force that binds the creature together, like we did when we fought the imp in my old kitchen, and that would *really* be the end—and likely for nothing."

"Slow down," Olive said.

Eric was incredulous. "What, slow down the *van*? Why the hell would I do that?"

"Because I'm fixin' to take a shot at 'em, and it'll be easier if we're going slower." She pulled her pistol from its holster and rolled down her window.

"Are you sure that's smart?"

"Y'all have a better idea? Lotte says we need to buy time. If I can scare 'em enough, put a shot through their windshield, they might pull over. I might even get lucky and hit the driver."

"What if they shoot back?"

"Seems like we're gonna be in that pickle one way or another. They might not think we're armed. This at least gives me the element of surprise."

Lotte touched Eric's shoulder. "She's right. We have to try it. This may be our only chance."

Eric reluctantly let his foot off the gas. The van slowed, and the Afrit quickly disappeared from sight.

Olive knelt, facing the back of her seat, then leaned out the window. "I gotta use my left hand to shoot, but that don't matter."

The SUV rocketed toward them, and Olive delivered a salvo of bullets from her Glock 19. Amazingly, their pursuer swerved wildly, then skidded off the road and into a cornfield to the right.

"Got 'em!" Olive shrieked with delight. "Y'all messin' with the wrong people if you think we're gonna go down without a fight!"

Siddique helped her squeeze back into her seat, and Eric floored it. After a few moments, he saw the Afrit glide back into view. They followed the creature along the darkened road, which began to curve to the right. A flashing sign appeared in the distance. As they grew nearer, it revealed itself to be an arrow, pointing left. They blew through a makeshift stop sign and the road quickly narrowed to one lane.

*Wait a minute, we're on a bridge.*

The right lane was under construction, blocked off by orange barrels and yellow tape. The van passed a two-wheeled trailer with a service body bed and bundles of rebar stacked to its side, then whipped by another trailer-mounted sign with a flashing arrow for those approaching the bridge from the opposite direction.

Eric hit the brakes, and the van came to a halt.

"What are you doing?" Lotte cried out with alarm. "Why are we stopping?"

"Because I'm getting out," he replied. "I'm gonna block the road with those flashing signs so they can't get by. You all take the van and go find Pazuzu. Hopefully, this will buy you the time you need."

"Eric, it's too dangerous! You'll get—"

"It's too dangerous *not* to!" he barked. "Those guys aren't gonna give up. They'll be here sooner than we think. If they catch us, they catch *all* of us, plus all the portal materials! This will give you more time, hopefully enough."

He unfastened his seat belt and began to open his door when Siddique spoke from behind. "I'm going with you."

Lotte, Olive and Eric all screamed "No!" in unison.

"Yes," he calmly replied. "Eric, you can't move those signs by yourself, they're too heavy. You need me."

Eric sighed with exasperation. "All right, fine. You're probably right. Let's do it, though. We're running out of time."

"Then I'm staying too!" Olive insisted. "I can cover you with my gun if they show up."

"No, you can't. You need to drive the van because *Fräulein Evolutionsbremse* can't drive! Plus, you're our only bargaining chip with Pazuzu. You have to go with Lotte."

The Afrit landed with a light *clip-clop* on the roof of the van, and its horned head quickly appeared, upside down, in Olive's open window. *'What is the meaning of this delay?'*

"No delay," Eric said as he opened his door. "We're splitting up. Olive's gonna drive. Just lead the van the rest of the way to the guy we're tracking, then stay with her and Lotte while they talk with him. If there's trouble, they'll need you."

He began to jump out, but Olive stopped him. "Here. At least take my gun. Let me grab you another magazine, too." She pulled a little rectangular metal case from her jacket pocket. "It's got fifteen shots, and there's probably eight or nine left in the gun."

Not wishing to waste any more time, he took the pistol and hopped to the ground.

Siddique quickly followed, and Olive climbed into the driver's seat. "We'll be back," she said with an unconvincing smile, "and we'll bring help. Promise."

Lotte appeared behind her, a worried look on her face. "Don't let this be the last time I see you—either of you! Just block the road, and then hide. We'll be as fast as we can. *Ich liebe dich, und ich hab' dich lieb.*" She tapped Olive's shoulder, and the van sped away.

"What did she say?" Siddique asked.

"She said she loves me, and that she likes you a lot. Come on. Let's go try to not get killed."

# CHAPTER 10

Eric and Siddique raced back across the bridge to the first flashing arrow the van had passed. They planned to topple this one, then return to the one on the opposite shore if time allowed. Despite having been built as a trailer with two inflatable tires, the metal sign was heavy and unwieldy.

*Siddique was right. I couldn't have done it without him.*

They arduously dragged the mechanism into the open roadway and upended it. Glass from the flashing lights shattered as the face of the arrow smashed onto the pavement. Siddique drew his knife from under his sweatshirt and slashed the tires. This would make the demolished sign even harder to move, and the broken glass might puncture the wheels of the SUV should it attempt to cross the bridge.

Once finished, they dashed back to the other side and began to work on the other flashing arrow. Like the first, it fell with a mighty crash, and glass littered the ageing asphalt. Siddique was about to cut one of the tires when a shot rang out, and a bullet ricocheted on the metal fender around the wheel.

Siddique shrieked in surprise and dropped his knife. Eric grabbed him by the collar and began to retreat, but suddenly realized they'd both be in the line of fire until they cleared the bridge.

*That's too much of a risk.*

He changed direction and headed for the nearby trailer, parked amongst the construction materials near the bridge railing. The thick bundles of long rebar rods on the ground would prevent bullets from coming in from under the chassis, and Eric could monitor the fallen sign with his pistol from this position if their pursuers tried to move it.

"This isn't such a bad spot," he said. "We might be able to hold out here for a while. They must have been driving with their lights off. I didn't see them pull up."

Siddique shook his head. "Me neither. I wonder if anybody heard that shot. Maybe they'll send help."

"Maybe. This seems like a pretty remote area, though. Plus, I'm not sure I want the cops to show up. That'll *really* complicate things."

All was still for a time, until he heard a familiar voice from the opposite shore. "Eric, is that you? You don't mind if I call you Eric, do you? I thought I spied you with my thermal imaging goggles. Such handy devices, don't you agree?"

"Oh, shit," Eric groaned. "It's that fuckin' dude from the bathroom at the museum. Looks like Olive was right, Lotte too. These guys are soldiers, and it seems like they brought all their happy little toys with them."

"We have to get outta here," Siddique said. "We did what we came to do."

"You're right. The problem is, where do we go? We can't use the road. We'll be sitting ducks."

"What about over the side, into the water?"

"That's not a bad idea, but they might be watching the water, and if whoever is watching can see in the dark too, it's that whole sitting duck thing again. Let's keep that as our last-ditch option. Honestly, I think we're just gonna have to hold out as long as we can, and then surrender. This is why I didn't want you to come. I have no idea what they'll do with two of us."

"I hear you, man, but I'm not sorry I came. You had the idea, but it took both of us to do it. I'm also glad to be here with you."

"I'm glad you're with me, too. We've sure come a long way since we met in that house two years ago, huh?"

"Feels like another lifetime. I'm a different person now. A better person."

The man on the opposite side of the bridge shouted again. "What do you say, Eric? You know we've got you cornered. I'm former Deuxième Bureau, and these are all trained mercenaries with me. You got lucky on the road back there, but that won't happen again, I assure you. Why don't you come out now, and I'll take you both in. I can't control what will happen after that, but this is the best deal you'll get. Come on, Eric, let's get this over with before the authorities show up and we have to kill all of *them* as well."

"Save your breath, bathroom guy! The longer you spend here, the better off our friends are. If you have such awesome military intelligence, why don't you come get *us*?"

Siddique looked at him quizzically. "Did you really have to say that last part?"

"Very well," the man countered. "We'll do it your way. I'll have one of you in my grasp all too soon. The other, well...."

After a few more moments, a hollow *thumpf* sounded, and a reddish glow permeated the air around the little bridge as a flare arced into the night sky.

"What's he doing?" Siddique enquired.

"You got me. I was expecting a full-on assault. It's not like they need light."

The flare dimmed as it slowly dropped, when suddenly, something rammed into Eric's shoulder. The blow dislodged the gun from his hand, and it skittered into the road behind the trailer.

"What the hell was that?"

"Oh, man," Siddique wailed. "It's that damn eagle! I just barely saw it. It came out of nowhere!"

"We have to grab the gun!"

"Get under the trailer. I'll get it!"

Eric was about to shout "no," but his friend acted too quickly. He dove for the Glock, landed right next to it, and batted it back toward Eric, who grabbed it and retreated under the back of the service bed. Another shot echoed from the far shore, but the bundles of rebar blocked their assailant's angle, and a shower of dislodged concrete rained from the bridge's guard rail onto the chiseled pavement.

Siddique rolled to the base of the railing just as the eagle swooped in. The great bird banked to avoid a collision with the thick cement fencing. Eric fired the Glock, but the avian deftly swerved. The shot went wide, and the creature vanished into the darkness.

Siddique began to wriggle on his belly back toward the trailer while Eric cautiously peered over the bundle of rebar, fearing what might be happening on the bridge. To his horror, he saw a man crouched by the first toppled arrow sign. He took aim with his pistol and pulled the trigger. The man let out a stifled cry and collapsed backward.

*Holy shit, I got him.*

He felt Siddique press against his back. "Damn, that was close. What happened?"

"They tried to use the eagle as a distraction. Somebody was crossing the bridge, so I shot him."

"Really?"

"Yeah. I think I got him pretty good. I might have killed him. I'm sorry to say, he isn't the first person I've killed... like *really* killed, not just been responsible for their death."

"Wow, man. That's not easy, especially for you. That isn't the world you grew up in. Right now, though, you just gotta let it go. We aren't done yet. I need some kind of weapon if that stupid bird comes back. I can't get to my knife. Stay down as much as you can. I'll just be a second."

Eric considered telling him to stop, but he knew Siddique was right. He hunkered under the trailer as best he could and spared brief glances over the rebar at the roadway beyond. He couldn't see the man he'd shot. The light from the flare had gone out, and the bulk of the overturned sign obscured details in the darkness.

Siddique fumbled with a hatch on the outer side of the service bed, near the cement railing. It finally creaked open, and he started rooting around. "Toolbox. I'll see what's inside."

"Watch out for that bird," Eric cautioned. He could see Siddique's feet and lower legs as he rifled through the contents of the toolbox.

"I don't think it can get me so easy here," his comrade replied. "It's a tight squeeze with this door open. I got a couple of things, just one more... what the—"

Eric heard three throaty trills from a bird as Siddique's feet surged backward toward the railing and the box of tools clattered to the ground.

*That wasn't the eagle. It made that weird ass* owk, owk *sound. That was a different bird.*

He rapidly swung to the other side of the trailer and gaped around the corner. One of the mercenaries had come up over the cement fence and had grabbed Siddique from behind.

*Jeez, maybe this wasn't such a hot spot to make a stand after all.*

The two men struggled, each trying to gain some advantage. Eric pointed his gun but couldn't shoot for fear of hitting his friend.

The soldier had his arms around Siddique's neck, but then lifted one away and raised his fist. Siddique used the extra bit of freedom to twist his back and slam his opponent into the open service bed hatch to his left. The man grunted in pain. Siddique then took hold of his arm, lifted him off his feet, twirled around, and fell over backward on top of the stunned mercenary, driving him into coarse underbed of the stripped roadway. They landed in a heap among the scattered tools.

Siddique rolled off the man and grabbed a long screwdriver. "I've got him! This guy's soaking wet. He came through the water. He had a gun, but something knocked it out of his hand right before he grabbed me. I think it was another bird, maybe that raven from my apartment. I heard it caw. It probably saved my life."

Eric shook his head, confused, as his companion straddled his dazed opponent. Just then, the open door of the service body compartment slammed shut. The eagle blasted through and sunk its talons deeply into each of Siddique's shoulders. He screamed as the ferocious avian lifted him into the air.

In desperation, Eric reached out and tried to catch his friend's leg, but the second he did, more gunshots sounded from the far shore, and someone jumped on him from the bed of the trailer above. He vainly watched as his comrade looped over the cement railing and vanished into the darkness over the water. He struggled to break free, but a powerful blow to his head from a hard, blunt object quickly put an end to his resistance.

Olive frantically tracked the Afrit as it fluttered before them. To her surprise, they'd only traveled about a mile before the ashen beast banked right, down a nondescript dirt road. The van jolted on the rough, rocky ground and the flight cases bumped loudly against the walls of the cargo space. They quickly passed a few houses, then drove through an undeveloped area before the road abruptly ended. Their winged guide slipped down an even narrower dirt track to the right, lined closely with trees.

She followed as best she could in the clumsy van, and finally emerged near a darkened house, nestled in a small clearing. A light on a pole near the dusty driveway revealed Harland Cheevers's gray Buick sedan, alongside a pickup truck and beat up old hatchback. Olive pulled up behind the cars and shut off the ignition.

The Afrit landed as she and Lotte hopped out. *'He is here, the one you seek, the one we battled before. He is situated on the upper story of this structure. Doubtless, he is aware of our presence. Your noisy vehicle made certain of that.'*

"It doesn't matter," Lotte replied, tightening the leash affixed to Mutig's collar. "We want him to see us. We're here to talk with him, not take him by surprise. If you can sense him, he must be in his material form. Let's hope he stays that way and doesn't launch a preemptive strike."

They strode down a stone walkway and climbed the three steps to a creaky, wooden porch. Olive tested the front door. Finding it unlocked, she pushed it open, and the unusual little band went inside. By the exterior light, they could see they were in an entry foyer. The stairs stood immediately ahead to their right.

Lotte called into the darkness of the second story. "Great Pazuzu, hear my plea! We fought with you before, but not by our choice. We were looking for our friend, the one you held captive, and the one whose help you wanted when you reunite with your brother. I know of your brother. If I'm right, his name is Humbaba. The stories we inherited from our ancestors say the hero Gilgamesh killed him in Enlil's Cedar Forest. I don't know if that's true, but our myths say things about you as well. They call you the enemy of Lamashtu, or Dimme, as she was known before that. If this is true, then we may have much in common. We, too, are enemies of Dimme, and if you do oppose her, we propose an alliance whereby we help each other. As part of that help, we're here to offer our friend's assistance with your brother. She's here now, and she comes to you willingly. We all do. Will you speak with us?"

*Damn*, Olive thought. *That girl really does have a silver tongue. She could sell a pair of underwear to a nudist!*

The house sat silent for several nerve-wracking moments, but then a light went on in the stairwell, and a man slowly walked down the stairs. Olive recognized Harland Cheevers, or at least, his *body*. She took great pleasure in the fact that he wore clothes: jeans and a rumpled and untucked button-down over a black t-shirt.

He stopped near the bottom of the stairs and surveyed the beings before him. "Given your words, I accept your invitation to parley. Woe be unto you if duplicity is your aim, but you speak the truth that it was *I* who drew first blood. As such, I shall grace you with the benefit of the doubt. I confess, I am impressed that you deduced who I am. I would have anticipated it to have been far harder to make such a determination, based upon what I know from the memories of this *oaf* whose body I now inhabit."

Lotte stepped forward. "You were very lucky, or we were. There aren't many who know what we know or could have made the connections that led us to discovering your identity. That amulet in the museum... I know who made it. I think he trapped you there, and I think I know why. What I don't understand is how your brother fits into all of this. At one time, there was another amulet depicting Humbaba, connected to the back of yours. It's been separated and is now in a museum in a city we call Philadelphia. That's where you're headed, isn't it?"

The mysterious god nodded. "I know not the specifics of his location, but there is veracity in your speculation. I do seek my brother. He needs me. In truth, I now need *him* in a way I could never have envisioned. We have become... alike. Both of us were imprisoned long ago, victims of deception as we pursued Dimme."

"So, Gilgamesh didn't kill Humbaba after all. He was there with you."

"You misunderstand. Your myth speaks true. The warrior Gilgamesh and his traitorous friend, Enkidu, did, indeed, slay my brother, but there is more to the story. I was present during the fearsome battle, hiding amongst the great cedars of Enlil's forest. I witnessed firsthand Gilgamesh's merciless act of barbarity, goaded on by Enkidu's cowardice and jealousy. What the two 'great warriors' failed to comprehend was that, as the children of our father, the Jinn Hanpu, both Huwawa—or as you know him, Humbaba—and I possess some of the powers of those beings. My brother's energy vacated his decapitated body, and he and I became one. Individually, each of us had formidable capabilities, but debilitating shortcomings. Together, however, we became mighty, much more than the sum of our parts, and we swore vengeance on the one responsible for my brother's demise."

"So, you went after Gilgamesh and Enkidu," Lotte surmised.

"Of course not," Pazuzu chortled. "The gods already had their eyes on those two, and soon enough, their friendship would end in epic calamity. No, child of wisdom beyond her years, Humbaba and I set our sights on the one who had stoked Gilgamesh's hubris at the outset, the one who exhorted him to rule Uruk through terror and selfishly indulge his appetites with any woman he wished, and finally, the one who persuaded him to reject the romantic advances of Inanna, daughter of Anu himself! Your stories mask the truth that even the gods were loath to accept. This was *Dimme's* doing, a ploy to enhance her power by creating chaos among the people and the gods alike, and to rule in the shadow of the great warrior-king. For a time, it worked, but I knew the truth, for I was likewise tormented by the same stunted and inconsistent abilities from which she suffered. For a time, we had commiserated in our states of misfortune, both outcasts to our birthright, so I knew her ways, and the telltale signs of her involvement."

The sound of gunfire echoed in the distance.

Lotte exchanged a worried glance with Olive, then turned back to the uncanny being on the stairs. "This is astonishing! You can't imagine how overwhelming it is to hear the unknown details of the oldest known story in human history. I understand now what you're trying to do, and what it means to reunite with your brother. But listen, those are my friends out there... my *husband*! We're all being chased, for a complex variety of reasons that I'm happy to share with you, but not right now. We need your help. These people know nothing about you, or the power you possess. Help us deal with them, and we'll help you with your task. Believe me, the sworn enemy of Dimme is a friend of ours. Do this one thing, and we'll be at your service."

Pazuzu's face darkened. "You do not understand. Yes, I have powers, but I am *severely* diminished."

The Afrit's wings briskly twitched.

"I live, in spirit, but this is not my body. This is not the way in which I once ruled over my domain. I lost most of my power trying to save myself from the trap laid by Iblis and Dimme. Now, in this form, I feed, but so much is lost, so little absorbed, and the process is interminable. Scarcely have I garnered enough strength to reassimilate my brother, perchance not enough, and if that fails, I fear that I am doomed. This is why the girl is of such value to me."

Olive shivered as he pointed directly at her.

"She is a reservoir of energy," he quickly went on. "I, on the other hand, have nothing to spare. I cannot afford to go into battle, either with you, or against you. I am too weak, and there is too much at stake. If you lend me aid, you shall have your ally against Dimme, my eternal foe. This I swear. But I am in no condition to help your friends, and that reality is as devastating to me as I know it must be for you."

Olive heard a strange noise and looked out the door. "Weird. The sky looks kinda red. What the hell are they doing, shootin' off fireworks out there?" She turned back to the distraught god. "Okay, Mr. Pazuzu, we hear you. We *will* help you with your brother, promise. Right now, though, our friends are in deep trouble, and we need to go help 'em. Problem is, there ain't much we can really do. They're most likely well-armed soldiers. I don't even have my Glock no more. I gave it to Eric. I hope he's gettin' some use out of it."

As if in response to the statement, more shots resounded into the night air.

"You're right," Lotte said with grim determination, "but we have to do something. We beg your leave, great one. Please hope that we can return."

The desperate party turned toward the door, but Pazuzu stopped them. "Wait!" He focused intently on the Afrit. "What manner of creature are *you*? I have heard tales of one such as yourself, but never did we meet. Odd. I pictured you as being... *larger*."

The little beast's tail whipped furiously, but the god ignored its outrage.

"A creature of fire, or so the stories say. Is this accurate?"

Molten orange veins began to bulge on the monster's hitherto ashen body. Its eyes began to burn like small suns, while its horns and wings exploded into a vibrant panoply of blues, reds, and blazing yellows.

"Impressive," Pazuzu murmured. "Once, I cast a visage such as this. Can this being renowned for surreptitious abduction and probable murder not dispatch your assailants?"

"Under normal circumstances, perhaps," Lotte replied. "But the men we face are well armed, and we believe they work for Jinn, and are prepared for supernatural threats in ways the ancient victims of the Afrit were not. Also, as you observed, the creature isn't quite as *robust* as usual, but that's because it recently sacrificed most of itself battling Iblis, just as you once did. It would be far too much to ask our friend to risk its existence in battle alone, but we'll meet this challenge together. We're allies, even though the arrangement is a bit uncommon."

The Afrit swayed from side to side as the enigmatic god surveyed the creature from horns to hooves. Once complete, he shook his head. "I hoped to sway you from risking your lives, and I know from experience that opposing your wishes with force will bring little good. You have proposed an alliance, of sorts, with me, not unlike your arrangement with this creature. Perhaps I have been too hasty. Our interests are now intertwined, and I do not wish to lose the girl's assistance."

"My name is Olive," she grumped. "I told you that before, in case you forgot."

"Olive. Yes, I remember. All right, Olive, let us proceed together and assess the situation with your friends. I will follow in the amazing horseless chariot in which the man whose body I inhabit travels. Many wonders in this new world, but the old patterns of strife and violence I find entirely recognizable."

Eric heard a series of confusing and distant noises that gradually came into focus. They were voices. One of them sounded like the man from the bathroom in the museum.

"...can put him in the back and bind his arms and legs. I can't lift him right now after being shot. Good thing we put on our vests, though we should have done it before. I didn't expect them to be armed. In any case, we have to get out of here. I'll watch for that raven. Did you hit it while I was in the trailer?"

"Nah," another voice answered, this one bereft of the Middle Eastern accent. "Fuckin' thing is too quick. I missed, then it just vanished, like they all do. It looks like I kept it from coming back, though... for now. Where's Uri, anyway? Isn't he supposed to be watching out for us?"

"Disposing of his prey, no doubt. He'll probably bash in the poor devil's skull on a rock and drink what remains of his essence before he dies. He's expended much energy traveling. It's no matter to us, but I wish he'd hurry back. You're right, that raven is no match for Uri, and I'd feel safer with him here. Hmmm.... It looks like our friend is coming to."

Eric felt an arm on his shoulder and some light slaps against his face.

"Wakey, wakey," the second man prodded.

"Stop," the first chided. "He might have a concussion. I hit him quite hard. He needs to be in decent shape for Ornias and Uri. What happened to Conor?"

"He's getting his gear back by the river. He'll be here in a second. Man, is he pissed. That fuckin' black kid did a number on him! Guess that's the last thing *he'll* ever do. Uri will see to that!"

Eric sputtered as he tried to suppress a wail of grief.

The Middle Eastern man crouched near him. "Ah, there you are, you poor soul. I tried to warn you, but I admit, in your shoes, I'd have done precisely the same thing."

Eric woozily opened his eyes. "What, hold the fort for, like, ten minutes, then get knocked out and dragged off to be tortured?"

He chuckled and rubbed his forehead. "I might have held out a bit longer. I merely admire your willingness to fight for your friends, and for yourself."

"I guess. It didn't seem to make much difference, and I almost got killed, although I may wind up regretting that I didn't. I guess I almost killed you too."

"This is a lucrative but dangerous line of work."

"Maybe you need find a different way to make a living."

"Perhaps. I became careless. I didn't anticipate you being such a good shot."

"It was pure luck, but I've found that sometimes it's better to be lucky than good."

"True, my friend, but your luck has now run out. We'll be off with you shortly. Here comes our comrade now, a bit wetter and slightly battered for his trouble."

Eric heard a man who he presumed to be Conor approach from some underbrush near the shore. He spoke with an Irish accent "Very fuckin' funny. I had him dead to rights. You know it was that black bird what got in me way. Uri was supposed to protect me. Instead, he used me as bloody bait! What are you two doing lounging around here, anyway?"

"Waiting for you. My chest is bruised from that gun shot. I can barely breathe. We got him this far, but I couldn't go on. I don't want to risk injuring him further. He must be carried with care, plus someone has to watch for that damned bird. Help Kane get him in the car, and we'll get out of here."

Conor gave a snort of disdain. "Right. Okay, come on, Kane, you ludder. Grab his feet and I'll take his arms."

Before he knew it, Eric felt himself lifted into the air. The rapidly forming lump on his head screamed in protest, and waves of dizziness washed over him as he bounced in the grasp of the two soldiers. They'd already transported him back across the bridge, and the SUV quickly came into view by the side of the road, engine running and headlights now aglow. In the light, he saw two spiderwebs of circular cracks in the windshield where Olive's bullets had penetrated, one positioned near the steering wheel.

The two men carried him to the back of the large vehicle, where the tailgate stood open. For a brief moment, he considered trying to break free as they laid him on the carpeted floor of the SUV's trunk space, but he lacked the strength or stability to put up any meaningful resistance.

Eric felt Kane bind his ankles with a thick, plastic tie, while Conor bent over him and positioned Eric's arms behind his back. "That's right, josser, just relax while we get you squared away, then we'll be —"

The man let out a stifled gag, and a sudden gush of liquid sprayed across Eric's face and into his mouth. He tasted the salty, metallic flavor of blood, like sucking on a briny penny, as Conor collapsed on top of him.

"What the fuck?" Kane screamed as he lifted the man's motionless torso.

In the SUV's dome light, Eric saw a bolt sticking straight out of Conor's neck, blood still pouring from the fatal wound.

With a look of angry determination, Kane let the dead man's body slump to the ground, swung his thermal goggles into place, and brought the rifle around his shoulder to bear. "Rashid! We got trouble!" He turned to Eric. "I'll be back for you later. If you know what's good for you, you'll stay put!" He slammed the SUV's tailgate shut.

For a few moments, Eric hawked bloody spittle onto the carpeted flooring, trying to clear his mouth of the taste of death. Outside, his two captors shouted terse instructions at one another, searching for their assailant, and seeking defensible positions.

"There!" Rashid called from the passenger's side of the vehicle, near the road.

Two shots resounded, but then Kane cried out in pain and backed into to side of the truck by the window of the trunk where Eric lay. "Fuck! Cover me. I got a bolt in my arm. I need to pull it out."

"All right, but hurry," Rashid hissed. "They know we can sense them with these goggles, so they won't come too close, but we're completely exposed in this spot. Do what you need to do, then I'll try to get in the car."

Through gritted teeth, Kane stifled a howl of pain as he wrenched the bolt from his arm. "Damn! Okay, got it. It's bleeding pretty bad, man."

"There's nothing we can do about it right now. Just stay low and keep on the lookout."

Eric lifted himself on shaking arms and peeked cautiously out the window. All seemed still, but then Rashid appeared as he popped up from the ground and scurried around the SUV's hood. He didn't get far before he yelped in pain and fell against the front bumper. Kane let off a volley of shots into a stand of scraggly trees near the shore on the opposite side of the road, then staggered in the direction of his fallen compatriot.

*They're both hurt, they're both distracted, and they're both at the opposite end of this disgusting land yacht of an SUV. Maybe I can get out of here.*

Eric strenuously repositioned himself, then cautiously reached for the latch to the tailgate. He was about to throw it open when he felt the barrel of a gun pressed against the back of his head.

"Not so fast there, hot shot." The woman's voice was smooth and soft, even though the pistol in her hand quavered slightly. "You're not going anywhere, except where I tell you. Now, slide in here with me, nice and slow." She released the catch, and the back of the rear passenger's side seat dropped down.

Eric warily maneuvered himself through the opening, gun to his head the entire time. Once settled, he spared a glance at his newly discovered captor, a black woman wearing army fatigues, a helmet, and more infrared imaging goggles. A white tourniquet stained with blood swaddled her right shoulder, and the gun wagged falteringly in her right hand.

"Yeah, you got me pretty good," she said, sensing his eyes on her wound. She quickly squatted down to the floor. "I nearly wrecked the car, but that ain't gonna stop me now. Here, take this and cut your legs free."

She handed him a knife, still in its leather sheath. He noticed her left hand sported what looked like brass knuckles from which a nearly four-inch iron spike jutted cruelly outward from the middle.

"Are you gonna let me go?" he hopefully asked.

She snorted a quick laugh. "Are you kidding me? You're my ticket out of here. You need your feet free so you can drive. Now... cut, and don't try anything. I'm weak from blood loss, but I ain't *that* weak."

Eric freed the knife, which felt distressingly like Dr. Esfahani's in his hand, and began to saw at the plastic tie. The sharp weapon quickly freed his legs, so he returned it to its sheath and handed it back to the woman.

She nodded, thick goggles bobbing with each motion. "Good. Now, climb into the front. No funny business."

Having few options, he obeyed, though the motion made his head spin, and he began to feel nauseous. He positioned himself behind the wheel and was about to put the SUV into drive, when he heard Rashid begin to yell.

"Naomi! Can you hear me? Are you awake? You have to open the door. Naomi! We're trapped out here! Naomi!"

Eric hesitated. "What do I do?"

"Drive," she calmly said, poking the gun through the seats and into his right ribs. "Rashid trusted his partners and they let him down. I'm not taking the fall for that fucking guy. Drive."

"Where do I go?"

"The bridge is still blocked, right? That much I caught when I started to come around. Circle around and go back the way we came."

He threw the SUV into reverse and backed up, ignoring the vigorous remonstrations of the men lying near the front of the vehicle. When the rear window contacted the underbrush past the grassy part of the roadside, he shifted into drive.

Kane suddenly stood and aimed his weapon.

Eric ducked just as his window exploded in a shower of crystalline shards. Panic stricken, he reached toward the passenger door, but the barrel of Naomi's pistol in his forehead stopped him cold.

"Just hit the gas," she snapped. "We have to get out of here!"

He arduously pulled himself up and poked his head over the dashboard, just enough to see. As he started accelerating, he saw Kane near the road, almost directly in SUV's path of escape. The man pointed his rifle at the windshield, but then suddenly collapsed to his knees. The point of a small spike emerged from his cheek, right under his infrared goggles. Blood streamed down his face like crimson tears as he clutched feebly at the offending object, then fell forward and smacked headfirst into the pavement.

Naomi screamed behind him. "Drive!"

Eric gunned it.

To his left, Rashid came into view, lying by the side of the road, makeshift tourniquet around his right thigh. He aimed his rifle and fired as the SUV turned hard into the road. A stream of bullets riddled the back of the vehicle, and the window of the tailgate shattered as the projectiles tore into the roof, but they were soon clear of the gunfire.

The frantic activity and adrenaline rush of the escape caused Eric's head to throb, and a deep tiredness besieged him. His muzzy eyes wove between the cracks in the windshield as the trees by the roadside whipped by. He didn't even realize he'd almost lost consciousness when his captor screamed behind him. He shot to attention and glanced over his shoulder.

Naomi fiercely struggled with someone in the back seat. Her gun discharged, but the bullet struck the roof.

Unable to see anything, Eric reached up and fumbled for the dome light switch. When he found it, he threw it on, then looked around once more.

A completely unclothed woman with beautiful, olive-brown skin held Naomi's right wrist pressed against the back seat, gun pointed directly upward. Eric couldn't see the rest of the brawl, but the sound of desperate gasps indicated that the SUV's new passenger had the mercenary by her neck and was strangling her. He turned to refocus on the road when he caught a glimpse of Naomi's left hand. She had just freed it from behind his seat, and now brought the forbidding iron spike to bear on her nude assailant's exposed flesh.

Without thought, Eric grabbed Naomi's arm just as the thick barb drove into the woman's abdomen. The strike didn't penetrate deeply but it produced an instantaneous effect. The naked woman froze, stiff as a board, and collapsed on top of her opponent. Naomi quickly pointed her pistol at the woman's head.

Eric wasn't quite certain what happened next. A cacophony of chaos erupted around him as the sound of shattering glass and shearing metal roared through the SUV's cabin. His already bruised head experienced another colossal jolt as something exploded into his chest, pinning him to the back of his seat.

Unable to move, he gave in for a time and let dizziness overtake him. The spinning sensation was so intense, he momentarily thought he rode the Ferris wheel at the annual fair on the Southby common. Terror overtook him, and like he had when he was a child, Eric reached out for his father's steadying hand, knowing that with his dad's support, he'd never fall, despite his almost complete certainty to the contrary.

To his amazement, someone met his grasp. He squeezed, and they gave a slight squeeze in reply. He felt hands clearing away some kind of fabric that draped across his chest and legs, then unbuckling his seat belt. The hands moved to his shoulders, and with almost impossible strength, lifted him firmly but gently out the door and onto the grass.

There he lay, asleep, or passed out, when the sound of a car awoke him. Once more, he felt the powerful but tender grasp lift him off the ground. Fighting his woozy reeling, Eric opened his eyes and saw a red Mini Cooper with a white roof parked by the roadside. The door stood open. The passenger's seat had been turned down to expose the back, his apparent destination, but in the front, he could barely make out a small crossbow where it sat among a pile of discarded clothes.

Once inside, he happily curled up along the back seat, and caught a quick glimpse of the unclothed woman hop in the driver's seat before the little car sped off.

WILLIAM E. NOLAND

# CHAPTER 11

Olive briefly caught a glimpse of the Afrit, once again ashen black, as it darted through the van's headlights before settling on Lotte's open window. The beast had flown ahead to reconnoiter while the two clumsy vehicles traversed the dirt tracks and then the paved street back to the vicinity of the bridge, which had not quite come into view.

'They are separated,' the creature announced as Olive steered to the roadside. 'One is on the shoreline to this side of the waterway, though the trees in the direction of the rising sun. He is immobile and appears injured.'

Lotte gasped. "Is it Eric, or Siddique?"

'The latter, the one with darker skin. Yours is on the opposite shore, entangled in some sort of skirmish.'

As if to underscore the monster's gravely words, gunfire sounded from beyond the bridge.

"What do we do?" Olive frantically asked. "If they blocked the bridge, we can't get over there, unless we go through the water, but we ain't armed. We'd be useless in the middle of a firefight."

Lotte anxiously rubbed her temples, then turned to the Afrit. "Is Eric hurt? Is he awake?"

'He has been imprisoned by those who pursued you. They have carried him to their vehicle, but someone, or something, assails them. We could fly there and attempt to render assistance, but it would not be without risk. Meanwhile, your other compatriot languishes in a wretched state. We leave the choice to you.'

Olive jumped when Pazuzu appeared by her window, having left his car parked behind the van. "Do they yet live?"

"They do," she gushed, "but they're not together, and both of them are in a heap of trouble. Siddique is easier to get to, and it sounds like he might be hurt, but I don't wanna... well...." She turned to Lotte, then lowered her eyes.

"If your friend is injured," the god interjected, "I could perhaps be of aid, though it would tax my energy."

"Seriously? Does that mean you could've fixed my eye back in that basement? If so, thanks for nuthin', mister 'I've got better things to do.' *Sheesh.*"

"You had yet to earn my trust, and I shall not reiterate my struggles to gain strength. I offer this now as a gesture of good faith. Decline if you will."

"No, no," Lotte stammered. "We appreciate your generosity, great one. We gladly accept. Olive, get out and have the Afrit lead you and Pazuzu to Siddique."

"But what about Eric?"

"Much as I hate to admit it, you're right. There's no sense in us walking into a gunfight, and I'm not willing to risk the Afrit against well-armed mercenaries. Hopefully, whoever is fighting with them frees him. If not, I can't believe they'd go to all this trouble to capture Eric and then just kill him. We can track him down later. Siddique may be in worse trouble." More gunshots rang out on the opposite shore. "Right, go on then! I'm too upset to be any good right now. I'll stay here with Mutig in case anyone comes. We can hide in the trees. Go on, go!"

Olive gave Lotte a quick hug then jumped out of the van. The Afrit swooped over the vehicle and into the trees, and she and Pazuzu hastened behind. The pines were not densely packed, and the carpet of fallen needles prevented the growth of excessive underbrush, yet the route, and the darkness, challenged them. They fumbled along as the god tracked the ashen monster that buzzed above them.

"I could locate your friend myself," he grumbled beside her, exhibiting no signs of exertion despite the swift pace and the unfavorable footing, "but I did not see him clearly enough. Never did our eyes meet, and never could I gather a full enough picture of his nature to discern his signature from all others of your kind."

"Well, that's fascinating," Olive heaved. "I'll be sure to fill Lotte in about all that later. Right now, though, I'm just tryin' to stay on my feet and not run smack into a tree, thank you very much."

"Why do you not access your powers? Just the tiniest amount would make this activity as child's play for you."

It gave her pause that the thought had never crossed her mind. *Why did I feel so compelled to strip off that amulet when Siddique was in trouble before, and now, I don't feel anything?*

She filed away that line of questioning when a rapid burst of rifle shots, and the sound of shattering glass, echoed in the chilly night air.

As tranquility returned, the pair resumed their trek, and sloshing water lapping gently against the shore came into focus.

Olive's pulse raced. "We must be gettin' close!"

She quickened her pace, and soon emerged on a muddy stretch where the trees gave way to the expanse of the reservoir. Pazuzu casually joined her as she frantically surveyed the moonlit water, but darkness, and many rocky outcroppings in the shallows, restricted her visibility.

The mysterious god beside her pointed. "There... on that rock lurks your winged companion."

Olive squinted and could just barely make out the Afrit's silhouette, crouched on a boulder that jutted out of the water, perhaps 20 feet from the shore. Without consideration, she drove into the gentle waves and splashed toward the creature. The water had reached her mid-thigh when her hand found the rock, against which she steadied herself as she tottered around to the far side. She hadn't quite completed the circuit when her knee made contact with something solid.

Siddique lay with his back to her on a flattened, ramp-like rim of the boulder, his legs still submerged in the water. Stifling tears, Olive reached for his shoulder to pull him onto his back, but jumped when her fingers grasped several large, fibrous feathers. She prodded in the dark and finally discerned the shape of a bird's wing, which she traced back to the creature's body, nestled by Siddique's side as if cradled in a loving embrace.

'Fear not,' the Afrit pronounced. 'The creature is paralyzed. Once, long ago, we battled one such as this... an owl whose presence threatened the lives of those trying to help us gain our freedom, though we knew it not at the time. We surprised the beast in midair and ran it through with our horns. The owl first froze, then began to disintegrate to dust before we dashed its remains on the stones of the street below. This bird has not begun to dissolve. Perhaps its wound is less severe, but something noxious to the being's nature has penetrated its flesh, as did my horns with the owl, and it will be helpless as long as this remains the case.'

Pazuzu waded around the boulder and joined Olive where she hovered above Siddique's motionless form. Her friend's labored breaths were shallow and irregular, and he gurgled with each heave of his chest.

"I have no idea what's wrong or where he's hurt," she morosely muttered. "Can you help him?"

The strange god touched his hand to Siddique's back, then slowly slid it to his shoulders, then to his neck and the back of his head. "There are many wounds... broken ribs, deep piercings from the bird's talons in his shoulders, and, by appearances, a gash in his neck from the creature's beak. He will die without assistance. As fortune would have it, his injuries have rendered him unconscious. His mind is open to me, and through that, I can reach into his body. It will deplete what energy I have acquired, but there is yet time to replenish what is lost. I will help him, secure in the knowledge that your loyalty is mine when the time arises."

Olive shivered, knowing she would likely have to once again experience the terrifying power she'd unleashed when she'd removed the amulet, but she didn't hesitate. "I gave you my word, Mr. Pazuzu, and I give it again. Help my friend, and anything I have to offer is yours. I'd swear to Jesus Christ on a stack of Bibles—if any of 'em were handy here in this freezing cold water—although I'm not exactly sure how that would go over up there in Heaven."

"A follower of The Nazarene, I see," Pazuzu commented as he gently laid his hands on Siddique's head. "His star rose as mine descended, though never did we find ourselves in opposition... merely a case of the new replacing the old in the minds of your sort. His cult has prospered, though I sense he and his fishers of men would be aghast at the many atrocities committed in their name. In this, your savior and I endure something in common, though in vastly different degrees. Be still now, child, while I help your friend, in amused defiance of all that your Christian brothers and sisters believe about me."

Olive didn't bother trying to contradict him. *Truth is, nobody I know ever heard a damn thing about any ol'* Pazuzu, *or your brother, or your father, or any of your other weirdo family—unless some bookworm at school read it in a dusty old history text, or somebody saw it in a movie, like Eric did. I guess it must be tough being a forgotten god, though, and this really is another perfect example of how people come to conclusions without knowing diddly squat about what they're talking about. So, whatever, as long as this works.*

By the time she'd returned her attention to Siddique, his breathing had calmed. A police car's siren wailed somewhere in the distance.

She whispered to the Afrit, who still crouched on the rock above them. "Is that coming from the north, where Lotte is, or the south, across the bridge?"

*'The echoes across this water make it difficult to determine precisely. We can fly above and find the source of the noise, but we sense that your other friend, the servant of the* Sadat Alnaar, *moves back in the direction from which we originally came.'*

"Dang, they must have him prisoner. Maybe the police will catch 'em, although that might not be the best thing either. You can follow him from really far away, like you did with me, right?"

*'As long as he lives, we can ascertain his whereabouts.'*

The piercing sound of the siren drew closer, almost surely on the opposite shore to the south, but the trees in this small inlet obscured any view of the bridge. The noise abruptly ceased, and a bright light illuminated the sky past the treetops. Olive heard distant shouts, and then several more volleys of gunshots before all once again went still. Ominously, the bright light suddenly winked out, and whatever optimism she'd harbored for the presence of the police vanished along with it.

Siddique stirred, and his legs contacted hers in the water.

Pazuzu slowly lowered his arms and leaned heavily against the boulder.

"Is he okay?" Olive anxiously enquired.

"Ask him yourself," the god replied, fatigue in his voice.

She put her face near Siddique's. "Sweetie, can you hear me? Can you talk? If that didn't work, I don't know what we're gonna do! I've tried everything I know how. I won't be able to take it if you don't live. I don't know what I'll do. I'm not sure—"

"Olive," Siddique sputtered.

"Oh, honey, thank God! What is it?"

His phlegm- and blood-clearing coughs soon turned into a jaunty chuckle "Shut up. You're making my head spin."

"So it is with this one," Pazuzu drily observed, "ever prattling and making the possibility of a rejoinder virtually unattainable."

Olive stuck her tongue out at the beleaguered entity, then secretly hoped he didn't see her impetuous slight in the darkness. She returned her attention to Siddique. "What happened? How did you get this way, and how did you subdue that bird?"

Siddique gave a slight jerk as he looked down, almost as if seeing the beast for the first time. "Oh, man, I got it! I can't believe it. I thought it had me for sure. Back on the bridge, I lost my knife, so I grabbed a long screwdriver that fell out of a toolbox. When the eagle snatched me up, I still had it in my hand. The damn bird sunk its talons into my shoulders, like before. I could barely move my arms, so I tucked the screwdriver in my belt. Good thing, too. The eagle dragged me across the water, and it got shallow, and it started banging me into rocks like this one. I'd have dropped the screwdriver for sure. It knocked my breath out, and it felt like my chest was totally smashed in!"

"It was," Pazuzu interjected. "You had several broken ribs, and a pierced lung, among other injuries. You are fortunate we found you quickly."

"Thank you," Siddique solemnly said. "I guess Lotte and Olive talked you into helping us."

"They promised their assistance with my slight... dilemma. I agreed to aid them when feasible. We made a bargain of equals, an arrangement to which *you* are now bound. Finish telling me, my newest associate, about your prowess in battle."

Siddique hesitated, so Olive put a calming hand on his shoulder. "It's okay. He's telling the truth. We're in this together. It seems like Lotte wants what he wants as much as *he* does. That can't be a bad thing, right?"

He nodded, then continued. "So, where was I? Right, the eagle smacked me around real good. I'm sure it thought I was dead, or at least unconscious. Maybe I was, but when it dropped me into the water, I woke up. It came down on me and bit right into my neck. I knew this was it. I went for the screwdriver, and it was still there! I must have stabbed the stupid thing. It couldn't have seen the strike coming from under the water. Then I must have grabbed the eagle and stumbled to this rock. I don't know, I don't remember, but look at it... still right here with the screwdriver stuck in its pretty neck. Not deep enough to kill it, apparently, but just one more little push...."

'*Stop!*' the Afrit commanded from its perch.

Surprised, Olive confronted the little beast. "Why? Why not kill the thing? It tried to murder Siddique, and if it's the same eagle, it tried to take Lotte back in Siddique's apartment. It's allied with the people threatening all of us. Why not kill it? It is a Jinn!"

'*Precisely. Were it simply an eagle, we would care little how you dispose of the creature, but this is not* simply *an eagle. This is a being of substantial potency that is almost impossible to encounter in such a state of debilitation. We claim it as spoils. Bring it to the gateway to our Eternal Flame. We shall consume this entity and recoup much of what we have lost, and we will mark your bargain with us completed.*'

Eric had barely settled into the surprisingly spacious back seat when the little car screeched to a halt and rapidly reversed direction. A moment later, they banked hard right, and he could tell that his unknown driver, and savior, had shut off the vehicle's lights. In the distance, he heard the wail of a police car's siren that steadily grew louder as it approached.

They drove a short way, then cautiously rolled left onto a side road, or perhaps a long driveway, lined on both sides with trees. There, his still unclothed chauffeur idled the car, and began to rifle through her belongings that sat in a heap on the front seat, or on the floor where they'd fallen when the vehicle's momentum shifted.

Eric unenthusiastically sat up, head still reeling, and body screaming from more aches and pains than he could count. "Are they coming this way?"

The uncanny woman turned to face him. "Pray they don't... if you pray, that is." She had a strong Middle Eastern accent, with just a touch of something else that danced smartly from her lips.

*French, maybe?*

"But I think not," she continued. "Surely the noise alerted someone who called the authorities. They rush to the bridge. When they pass, we'll be on our way. There they go now."

The pitch of the police car's siren warped from high to low as it raced by. She threw the Mini in reverse, backed into the side street onto which she'd diverted, and hit the accelerator. They zipped back to the main road, banged a hard left, and quickly streaked under the I-85 bridge.

Eric fastened his seat belt, as much to steady his unstable and shaking body from the movement of the car as from fear of an accident. "Where are we going, back to the highway?"

She laughed. "Well, that's a start. From there, you'll have to tell me. You've taken us on quite a journey, Mr. Schneider-Schwarz. It's made things most difficult, indeed. Do you care to tell me what you and your friends are up to with all this traveling about?"

He clung to a handle above the door as they made the right onto the road that led to the interchange. "I'm not sure where to start. We've traveled to various places for different reasons over the past... what... three days, going on four? I don't know. We were following somebody when we got off the highway. Apparently, somebody was following us, too."

"Oh, we know. We've been trying to keep you out of their hands since Tuesday night. We're running out of schemes to help preserve your safety. In fact, this may be our final gambit." Just past the Mobil station, she steered onto the onramp for I-85 north.

"So, Lotte was right. Somebody *has* been protecting us. Are you partners with that raven that we've seen a few times?"

"Mmmm... Karšift. My oldest and dearest companion. He flies above us now, watching for signs of trouble. Yes, you could say that we undertake this effort together."

"Well, that's awfully nice of you, but can I ask *why?*"

She sweetly giggled. "Because we were asked, and we couldn't refuse. Karšift understood the summons. Had he not, it would have gone unheeded. It came from the shoreline in the calls of innumerable gulls who swept the city, almost darkening the sky. I heard, like countless others, but I couldn't comprehend. Never had that tongue graced my senses, almost the sound you hear when you press a conch shell to your ear. It vanished from our world nearly eighteen-hundred years before I was born."

"Let me guess... Enki?"

"Close. Enki was there as well, and his advocacy for the wellbeing of you and your loved ones is why my companion and I are here now. The directive, however, came from Enlil, and Karšift make it quite clear that a request for assistance from such a powerful entity is *not* one from which a servant turns their back."

It gave Eric some cheer that Enki had thought of his and Lotte's safety, but he still felt confused. "Why didn't they come themselves? Why send you?"

"The Lords of the Abzu told us that they once again had business in this world, and one doesn't question a god, especially when they're standing knee deep in their own element. Not that Karšift would have challenged either of their authority. He's been loyal from time immemorial. He accepted his task, and I refused to let him fly into danger alone. Enki and Enlil promised they would come when they could, or else send additional aid. I pray to Allah they speak the truth."

"Aren't you a Jinn?"

"I'm half Jinn, but I've inherited far more of my father's ethereal power than most children of mixed parentage. Why do you ask?"

"I'm just surprised you're religious. I figured all you 'beings from the tenth dimension,' or whatever, thought our gods were just... well... I don't know... *made up*, I guess... that you'd have some different perspective on it because of what you know."

She scoffed. "What I *know*? What exactly do I know? Far less than you presume, I assure you. I know our powers seem extraordinary to you, perhaps godlike, but if you perceive us to be superior to humans, why would you find it difficult to believe that something in the universe could be greater than us? In any case, appearances can often be deceiving. The reality of my kind is vastly more complex and dangerous than you imagine. If you want proof, just look at my side. It bleeds from that woman's weapon, fashioned to strike at me in the way that I'm most vulnerable. It nearly worked. Your actions, and quick thinking, saved me."

"Yeah, you've definitely confused me with somebody who, like, knows how to do shit... and stuff. I do vaguely remember trying to keep

Naomi from stabbing you, but if I recall correctly, I failed miserably. In the process, I'm guessing I wasn't watching the road and slammed the SUV headfirst into a pine tree. Not that I shed a tear over that... stupid gas-guzzling piece of crap."

"Well, your actions saved my life, and probably yours as well. If that woman's spike had penetrated deeply, I wouldn't have survived. The accident jarred it loose, and I was able to get free and snap her despicable neck."

Eric felt a moment's sadness knowing Naomi had been killed. Something about her told him that had they met under different circumstances, they might have gotten along. Strangely, he felt the same about Rashid, orchestrator of the band of mercenaries that almost captured him and sent him to be tortured at the hands of irrepressible Jinn.

*I'm really not cut out for this stuff. I'm like my mom, always looking for the best in people. Pathetic!*

"Whatever the fact is," she went on, "you have my thanks. Our lives are now in each other's hands."

As they crested a hill, she suddenly pumped the brakes and came to a near standstill behind a semitruck. Vehicles lined the highway as the right lane merged into the left. Flashing police lights indicated there might be some sort of accident not far ahead.

"Oh, *'enta betharrag ma'āyā*, what is this? The traffic is completely backed up."

"It doesn't look too bad," Eric said. "We're lucky there aren't many cars on the road this time of night. Once we get through this mess, we should be okay. Hey, speaking of 'okay,' do you have any idea what might have happened to my friend? He was on the bridge with me, but that eagle grabbed him and carried him away."

"I'm sorry," she somberly replied. "I don't know. Perhaps Karšift might. He monitored the eagle, until we both had to flee, as well as your strange, winged companion who only appears to come out at night. The infamous Afrit, I presume. I never saw the creature, but my father did."

The revelation jolted him to alertness and kept him from drifting off. "What? Your father met the Afrit? When?"

"In the days when he held sway with the Caliphs, from the time of Muhammed until the incursions into Iberia and France in the early eighth century. He oversaw the creature's protection from threats of an *otherworldly* nature. As a Jinn himself, indeed one quite powerful, he knew how to keep their curiosity at bay, and how to punish those who transgressed. In the end, he suffered a fate similar to that of the beast he helped shelter, though in his case, the effects were final and irreversible. Many times, I asked him if I could just ever so briefly lay my eyes on the terrible monster of such renown, but he always scolded me, saying it was not my business, and that it presented an existential danger. Little did I know at the time how truly he spoke."

Eric tried to get his sluggishly moving head around what she'd told him while the various vehicles on the road jockeyed into position. They finally fell into a single file that moved at a slow but steady pace, as each driver inevitably gawked at the accident scene. It seemed to have happened near the entrance to the offramp for exit 223. One vehicle, a Jeep by its appearance, had slammed into a grassy embankment by the side of the road. An ambulance stood nearby, rear doors open, but he couldn't see inside. Another car seemed to have lost control and lay on its side on the highway's shoulder at the bottom of a small hill just past the exit sign, surrounded by a panoply of broken glass and other debris. When they passed this wreck, Eric saw another red Mini Cooper with white stripes on the hood, and a white top that had been crushed into the cabin as if swatted by a gigantic roll of newspaper.

Dumbfounded, he asked, "What the hell was *that*?"

"That, Mr. Schneider-Schwarz, was our final ruse, one that kept the balance ever so slightly in our favor and prevented you from being captured. I pray to Allah my pupil, Nadia, found her way to safety. She and I have been using nearly identical cars to fool the people pursuing you and your lovely bride, and your ever-growing menagerie of friends."

"So, that was you in the parking lot outside Siddique's apartment in Worcester?"

"Quite so. I followed both of you there from Somerville in the first Mini I'd rented. Right before the eagle attacked you, another Jinn assailed me. He smashed right through the window."

Eric nodded knowingly. "Yeah, trips like this are hell on rental vehicles. Looks like you got a new one. I knew you couldn't have fixed the window that fast. Was that you I saw later when we were headed for Atlanta?"

"Yes, that was me, though you can't imagine what I went through to get there. As you know, they towed away the poor little car, with all my belongings in the trunk, except the clothes I'd left on the driver's seat. I'll bet that raised a few eyebrows. I had to sneak into the impound lot and get it all back, especially my crossbow."

She tapped the little weapon on the passenger's seat beside her. "Once I had my things, I called Nadia. She'd been watching your house and saw you return to Somerville, and she and Karšift, who'd followed you back from Worcester, tailed your van out of Boston. We stayed in touch by phone, so I knew where you were. I arranged an Uber to take me south so I wouldn't get too far behind. Don't ask how much *that* cost! The next morning, I had to rent another red Mini that looked like Nadia's, not the easiest task. Why couldn't she have driven a gray Toyota Camry? I picked up some time when you stopped for lunch in Chapel Hill, then followed you the rest of the way to Atlanta so Nadia could get some rest. She's not like me. She needs to sleep."

*So do I,* Eric mused, but curiosity got the best of him. "Why did you abandon your car in the first place? Why didn't you fight the Jinn that attacked you?"

She sighed. "I'd anticipated a strike such as that at one point or another, but I confess, he took me unaware. I didn't know what I was up against—I didn't even find out this Jinn inhabited a male body until we started observing them in Atlanta, just as they'd been watching us in Somerville—so I fled in immaterial form. He hounded me for quite some time. He knew he couldn't touch me, but I think he simply wanted to keep me occupied so his accomplice could grab one of you and get away without my interference. They didn't anticipate the supernatural powers with which I'd endowed you."

"Supernatural powers? What do you mean? Wait a minute... that's how Lotte disappeared, and how I was able to punch that eagle so hard. How did you do that?"

She flashed a smile over her shoulder. "Your myths about Genies having the ability to grant wishes aren't completely without merit. We do so by using our energy to enchant items. In this case, your beautiful golden wedding bands suited me perfectly. We'd been watching you for some time, all without incident, until Tuesday when our adversaries surprised us. Each night while you slept, I dematerialized, snuck in, and fashioned the charms to serve you in whichever way you needed aid the most at a critical moment... your wish granted."

"Well, we appreciate that—even though it's kind of creepy thinking about you sitting over us without any clothes on while you cast your spells—but we both still wear our rings, and I haven't been able to do anything like that since then. If I could, I would have saved Siddique from that fucking eagle!" He instantly regretted getting so worked up. His head pounded and stars appeared before his eyes as he woozily braced himself on the back of the woman's seat.

"Easy, Mr. Schneider-Schwarz. You've had quite a rough evening. To set your mind at ease, the enchantments on your rings could only function once, and I haven't had time, or the energy, to replenish them. All this driving about and having to watch you around the clock has its drawbacks. It's not like your silly fairytales where we can grant 'three wishes,' or *unlimited* wishes... such foolishness. My resources are finite. I needed assistance, and a variety of alternative tactics, to oversee your protection, but now we've essentially gone through our bag of tricks."

"You mean after the accident we saw back there."

"Precisely. Nadia was closest when the SUV pulled you and your friends over. I was a few miles back, out of sight. She called me and I told her to speed ahead and intercept the Jeep in which the other Jinn, the one who'd attacked me in Worcester, drove. One good turn deserves another. This time I wanted her to keep *him* from interfering. He took the bait and followed her along the highway, thinking he was chasing me. I don't know how she did it, but somehow, she forced him off the road, obviously at the expense of her own car."

"Do you think she survived?"

"By the grace of Allah, yes, but my confidence is high. Like you, she possessed a charm that allowed her to dematerialize, or invoke some other superhuman ability. This item of her own creation, with my assistance, of course."

"Are you saying humans can enchant magical items? This is like a fantasy role-playing game."

"Some humans... only those with Jinn blood, and typically women who seem to inherit greater capacity than most male children. Through the centuries, I've instructed brightly shining daughters of certain families with long lineages. Nadia's branch emigrated from Lebanon years ago, but I've stayed in contact. Fortunate that I did. Her assistance has been indispensable, but that's the last I'll call on her. She's done more than enough, and without her magic, she's completely exposed. It's just us now, Mr. Schneider-Schwarz, and I'm afraid brute strength will be our only recourse from here forward."

"You can call me Eric."

"That's lovely. Thank you, Eric. And you may call me 'Most Regal Heiress to the Throne of Jupiter.'"

He scratched his increasingly weary head. "Seriously?"

She heartily laughed. "No, I'm just joking, but that would be awfully fun, don't you think?"

*Sure, whatever you say.* "Actually, you told me you begged your father to let you see the Afrit almost thirteen hundred years ago. You can check my math if you want. I suck at math. Now you say you've been teaching women to enchant magic items for hundreds of years. Who are you, anyway, and what makes you think we stand even half a chance against these Jinn, and the mercenaries they'll undoubtedly keep hiring, to hunt us down?"

The mystifying woman took her eyes from the road and looked proudly back at him. "I am Tamanna Ibnat Shamhuresh, daughter of Shamhuresh, the Fifth King of the Jinn, and we stand a chance because my father taught me the ways of warfare, and how to survive against odds of the most unfavorable sort."

# CHAPTER 12

Some exceptionally glorious smell caused Eric to gradually open his eyes. He squinted in the morning light and wondered how he had once again come to lie across the back seat in the comfy little car. The sounds of the highway had vanished, and the vehicle sat stationary with the engine off. His head throbbed and spun, and his mouth felt like someone had wiped it repeatedly with a bag of cotton balls. He urgently licked his lips and tried to regain some memory of what had happened the night before.

Once Tamanna had introduced herself, they'd talked a bit longer, but Eric couldn't remember anything else. He recalled beginning to drift away when she started delving into the details of multiple Mini Coopers driving around everywhere. By the time she got to "Tamanna's Academy of Magic for Promising Young Women," he'd pretty much lost it and must have finally fallen into blissful unconsciousness.

Having generated enough saliva to separate his tongue from the roof of his mouth, he intrepidly attempted to speak. "Where are we?"

She turned to him and smiled. She looked like a movie star in her oversized, round sunglasses, black hair billowing in disheveled elegance. She'd gotten dressed, which came as a mild disappointment, her clothing stylish but economical and well suited for activity. "Ah, welcome back to the land of the living. How do you feel?"

"Like somebody chopped me into little pieces, then sewed me back together without the instruction manual. I'm like the Ikea version of myself. The setup was a disaster, and the final product is about to fall apart."

She laughed. "At least you still have your sense of humor."

*You say that now, but just wait....*

She consulted her phone. "Let me see. It appears we're in Elkton, Maryland, in the parking lot of a restaurant called *Waffle House*."

"Are you serious? Can you read minds? This is, like, my favorite place."

"No," she chuckled. "I can't read your thoughts unless I take full charge of your body, which I have no interest in doing, but my 'supernatural powers' told me you'd be hungry when you woke up, and this place seems to specialize in breakfast items. It seems I chose well."

She produced a large cup of orange juice, which he downed without taking a breath, then she handed him a Styrofoam container, still warm on the bottom. He opened it as if it held the Crown Jewels, and given his hunger, the waffles, bacon, and hashbrowns seemed of far greater value.

*No cheese grits. Oh, well.*

He applied the requisite syrup to the waffles and was about to dig in when he suddenly stopped. "Hey, you have a phone. Can I call my wife?"

Tamanna flashed her eyebrows. "I don't see why not. Nadia called me a couple of hours ago, and I'm not expecting to hear from her again anytime soon."

"Is she okay?"

"Thankfully, she's fine. She's in the hospital for 'observation.' She turned herself in to the police early this morning and told them she hit her head during the accident after she'd fallen asleep at the wheel. She needed an excuse for having wandered off."

"Without any clothes on."

"Quite right. That always poses problems for my kind when we can't get back to our discarded garments. A small price to pay, I suppose. Nadia's smart. She'll get them to believe any story she tells them. In any case, the police are probably talking with her now, so go ahead and call your wife, but then you'll have to explain to me what's happening and where we're going. I've been operating on the assumption that we're headed back to your home near Boston."

Unable to resist, he sporked a helping of hashbrowns and popped them into his mouth. "Much as I'd like to go home, I think we have to stop somewhere else first. If I can make that call, I'll doublecheck if that's still the plan, or if something has changed. Then I'll tell you everything I know."

She handed him the phone.

With syrup-sticky fingers, he dialed Lotte's number and put the device to his ear.

She answered on the third ring, her voice guarded. "Hello?"

"*Guten Morgen, Fräulein Evolutionsbremse.* I see you got your phone working again, or did Olive do that for you?"

"*Alter!* Eric!" she excitedly squealed. "I can't believe it! Are you okay? We thought you'd been taken captive!"

"Yeah, they *did* capture me, but it turns out you were right. We have people looking out for us—well, more than people, really, but that's beside the point. One of them rescued me. I'm here with her now."

He heard her apprising Olive of the situation, who gave an enthusiastic whoop before Lotte returned to him. "Where are you? Are you safe?"

"I'm in the parking lot of a Waffle House in some town in Maryland. I guess we're safe. Who really knows anymore, huh? I wanted to see if you and Olive were all right. I... I don't know what happened to Siddique. That eagle got him. I tried, but I couldn't help him. Lotte, I'm so sorry... so, so sorry."

"Well, you can tell him how sorry you are yourself, but later. He's sleeping with Mutig in the back of the van."

Eric almost dropped his precious strip of bacon. "What?"

"It's a long story. I'll fill you in later, but the eagle didn't kill him. Siddique stabbed it with a screwdriver that just happened to have one of those magnetic tips. In fact, I think the whole shaft was magnetic as well, probably made of chromium-vanadium steel."

"You just know that right off the top of your head?"

"No. I was curious why the screwdriver had that kind of effect on a Jinn creature, so I looked it up when we turned our phones back on, after we left Middleburg about an hour ago."

"Why did you hang around there all night?"

"Oh, that's an even longer story, but in short, both our otherworldly companions wanted some 'late-night snacks.' We went back to the house where we confronted Pazuzu, and he finished feeding off of the residents, a husband and wife and their three young children. They were all fast asleep, even when we left around seven a.m., and he swore to us that they'd be fine. I guess I believe him, but it still gives me the creeps."

"Me too!" Olive hooted in the background.

"So where is he now?" Eric asked. "I assume you got him to help us?"

"In a manner of speaking," Lotte replied. "He's following behind the van in Harland Cheevers's Buick, but he's incredibly weak and has little energy to spare. He definitely wants our help with his brother, especially from Olive, and he did save Siddique's life, though it's pretty clear his powers of healing aren't even remotely comparable to what Enki can do."

"What do you mean?"

"I mean... well... you'll just have to see for yourself. Siddique was badly injured. He's lucky to be alive, but he'll bear the marks of that battle, and he's still utterly exhausted."

Eric shook his head. "Wow, that sucks. I guess we knew going in what this might be like. It's just hard to face the reality of it. It's weird. Even knowing what *could* happen, you never really believe it actually *will* happen... until it happens. It's like death. You just can't believe it's something you'll ever experience, even though it's inevitable. Speaking of which, who'd you have to kill to satisfy Chuckles?"

Lotte sighed. "You're going to love this... *not*. Siddique's screwdriver didn't kill the Jinn-eagle. The Afrit demanded it as *spoils*."

"You've gotta be kidding me. What the hell effect will *that* have on the damn thing, and where is it now?"

"It returned to the Eternal Flame. We set up the portal in the living room of the house while Pazuzu was feeding upstairs. The Afrit devoured the eagle and then went back to its realm. It always needs time to digest, and in this case, it might need more than usual. I don't think it would be a good idea to summon it for at least a few days, unless it's really an emergency."

"So, where does that leave us? If Pazuzu is that weak —"

"Pazuzu?" Tamanna interrupted. "He's been gone from this world for centuries! What in blazes are you talking about?"

"Yeah, I'll explain all that. Just give me a second, please." He returned to Lotte on the phone. "Sorry, my new friend got a little freaked out when she heard Pazuzu's name. Can't say I blame her. I was about to ask that if Pazuzu is so weak, what'll you do if you get attacked again? The Afrit won't be there to help you."

"Well, I didn't think there would *be* much chance of being attacked since they already had you prisoner. Pazuzu says he'll be far stronger once he reunites with Humbaba. We planned to help them get back together as quickly as possible, then I intended to ask him to help rescue you, maybe with the Afrit's assistance, if Pazuzu was still too feeble. In a sense, I think that remains our best course of action. A strong Pazuzu would be a fabulously powerful ally and protector. The museum is open until five o'clock today. We can be there between two and three. That's gives us plenty of time for a Mesopotamian family reunion, *ja*?"

Eric laughed. "*Jawohl, Kommandant!* We get to have a reunion, too, huh?"

"We do! Eric, I was so worried. I thought I'd lost you. I didn't know what to do."

"Yes, you did. You totally had a plan, like you always do. I suck at that. Every time I have to plan something, I ask myself what *you* would do. I've been doing that since I met you, and if I hadn't, I'd probably still be transfixed in front of an Xbox like a zombie. I'm glad you were planning to come rescue me. It would have made getting kidnapped totally worth it."

They both laughed and signed off with tender words and the promise to speak again once the van had arrived in proximity to the Penn Museum. Being just an hour away from their destination, Eric and Tamanna decided to go inside the Waffle House where he could use the restroom, get more orange juice and some coffee, and finish his breakfast at a real table. As he got out of the car, he noticed the raven, perched in vigil on a telephone wire above them. It cocked its head and stared at him as he stumbled toward the restaurant.

They sat in a secluded spot, and he began relating his tale as he finished his food. He didn't start on Tuesday night, when he'd first unknowingly encountered Tamanna outside Siddique's window, or even that afternoon, when he'd seen Karšift on the roof over the back door of their apartment. Instead, he went all the way back, back to high school, back to when he first saw Lotte in full goth regalia reading a book on that low stone wall. He didn't have to, but they appeared to have time, and he wanted Tamanna to understand the complete picture of what he and Lotte had been through together, what forces and decisions had brought them to this moment, and the entire succession of cause and effect upon cause and effect upon cause and effect that had forged his uncommon group of lovers, friends, and otherworldly associates into the beings they were today.

She listened in silence, only occasionally batting her elegant lashes, or raising her thick eyebrows above her sparkling amber eyes. He knew it would take much to surprise or impress an individual with such substantial longevity, but her subtle responses betrayed the moments when certain incidents found their mark. It was after 10:00 a.m. when he finished his account, and despite frequent coffee refills, he once again struggled to stay awake.

After a final stop in the Waffle House restroom, and a brief diversion to a nearby pharmacy to pick up several bottles of water and some ibuprofen, Eric climbed back in the Mini, curled up on the back seat, and instantly fell asleep.

---

Something in the reverberation of the road finally woke Eric from deep slumber. He groggily rose and glanced out the window. Clouds had rolled in since morning, but rain didn't appear imminent. The little car traversed a bridge, and the Philadelphia skyline came into view on the right. Huge cranes lined the shore they were approaching on the left.

He rubbed his eyes and cleared his throat. "How long have I been out?"

"Several hours," Tamanna replied. "It's nearly two in the afternoon."

"Jeez, what took us so long to get here? Four hours for what should have been a one-hour trip? You must have hit the worst traffic jam ever!"

She laughed. "There was some traffic, but it wasn't *that* bad. I-95 was a bit backed up, so my phone diverted us over the river into New Jersey. Now we're crossing back into Pennsylvania. We'll arrive at the museum in about fifteen minutes, but we only left Elkton about forty-five minutes ago. I decided to take a little... *detour*."

"That sounds ominous."

"Nothing so awful. I'd noticed several hotels near the Waffle House. I decided to see if I could find any late sleepers, replenish a bit of my energy. That battle last night took a lot out of me."

"Any luck?"

"Oh, yes. Hotels almost always provide opportunity. I regained enough strength to finish healing my side, perhaps a bit more. I feel far better."

As they left the bridge, Eric noticed all the electronic billboards flashed a message about an Amber Alert for a missing child. "What's that all about?"

"I have no idea. There were similar signs in New Jersey. There's a number you can call for more information. I hate to be crass, but it doesn't have anything to do with us, and the likelihood of us seeing something useful is inestimably small, plus I needed my phone for directions, so I didn't bother. Do help yourself if you like, just be quick."

He shook his head. "Nah, you're probably right. Who knows how old that notice is. I was just curious."

The looming light towers of Citizen's Bank Park, home of the Philadelphia Phillies, caught his attention on the left as they passed. "Wow, nice looking park. I've never been to any baseball stadium except Fenway in Boston. Is baseball popular where you're from?"

"I'm from many places, Eric. I can't say any have especially embraced your game of baseball, but I've seen my share of boring cricket matches. Football, or what you call 'soccer,' is popular in Lebanon, but I don't like it. I grew up on very different sports, like archery, and camel racing. I still practice with a bow and arrow, but the crossbow is so much more practical when I have to travel."

Eric shivered, remembering a similar weapon Aicha had used to threaten him and Lotte. *I wonder if they both shop at the same crossbow store.*

I-76 wound to the north, then crossed the Schuylkill River before they took exit 346A and banged a left onto South Street, headed directly for the museum. The parking garage came into view on the left, right across the street from the University of Pennsylvania football stadium, but the road leading toward the entrance was blocked off by yellow tape and a police detail, while multiple emergency vehicles clogged the entryway.

"What's going on?" Tamanna asked.

"I have no idea. Maybe there was an accident. Whatever it is, we aren't parking there. Give me your phone and I'll find something else." She handed it to him, and he performed a quick search while they crawled along in the traffic. "It's no problem. Just take a right up here past the museum, then there's one between Chestnut and Ludlow Streets just five minutes away."

This garage presented no difficulty, and soon the Mini sat in a spot overlooking Ludlow Street.

"While I've got the phone, maybe I should call Lotte. We can find out where they are, and I'll tell her not to park in the museum's garage." Tamanna assented, and he punched in the number. This time, he put the phone on speaker so she could hear as well.

Lotte picked up quickly. "Eric, we're almost there. We had to stop to get some food, and we hit some traffic on the highway, so we're still about thirty minutes away."

"That's fine," he replied. "The museum will still be open. Don't park in their garage, though. Something's going on there and the police have it closed."

"Mmmm... actually, Olive and I were discussing this. We have no idea what might happen when Pazuzu tries to reintegrate with Humbaba. If there's trouble, we might want to have some discrete distance from both of them. There are bloody cameras everywhere nowadays. We thought it might actually be better if we parked in separate garages and arrived at the museum at different times so it's not obvious that we're all together."

"That's good thinking, Lotte," Tamanna interjected. "It's a pleasure to make your acquaintance, by the way."

"Oh, truly, the pleasure is all mine. I don't even begin to know how to thank you for saving my husband. We'll do everything we can to repay your kindness."

"All of you have won the favor of two incredibly potent beings. If they say your protection is vital, I'm happy to help in any way I'm able. You mention cameras. I have a way of dealing with that in the museum, and it might be to all our benefit if I remain hidden. If something goes awry, I'll be at an advantage. Plus, we save on the price of one admission, right?" They all giggled. "When you get to the museum, Eric will fill you in. You won't be on camera while you're there, for about an hour. Just park in separate garages and don't arrive together. That will definitely make it harder to associate you with Pazuzu if something goes wrong."

"That's wonderful," Lotte gushed. "Before we get too much closer to Philadelphia, we're going to get off the highway and try to find an out-of-the-way spot to fill him in on what to do. We'll also get some cash, so we don't have to use our credit cards in the museum. We should still get there around three, so we'll meet you in the lobby then."

"We shouldn't bring our phones either, y'all," Olive piped in. "If you're afraid of being traced, that's one of the surest ways."

"Agreed," Tamanna said. "That won't be an issue for me as I'll temporarily be without hands to hold anything, but for all of you, this is another wise precaution."

The plan having been hatched, Eric signed off. "So, how will you disable those security cameras?"

"As you know from your experience with Aicha that you told me about, all these electronic devices are quite easy for our kind to manipulate. I'm going to find the central computer system that controls the cameras and set them all in a loop that shows and records the past hour, or so. More than that might start to look fishy with variations in sunlight, volume of patrons, things like that. If we need more than an hour, I'll go and reset it, but my sense is that will be enough."

"Okay, what do you want me to do?"

"I'm going to head to the museum shortly. You take my car keys and leave in time to get there at three o'clock. It's probably a ten-minute walk. Once you're all together, just stay in a group and follow Pazuzu's lead. I'll be with you, but you won't be able to see or hear me, and I won't be able to communicate with you. If you need my assistance, separate yourself from the group and find an out of the way spot. I can materialize enough that we can talk. Hopefully, all these machinations will be for nothing and everything will go smoothly."

He snorted. "If so, that'll be a first for us, but I guess there's a first for everything, huh?"

When Eric walked into the museum just before 3:00 p.m., he was surprised to find Lotte, Olive, and a bedraggled-looking Siddique meandering around behind a huge Sphinx just beyond the ticket counters.

*They got here faster than I expected.*

Lotte spotted him and ran to meet him at the bottom of a small staircase leading up to the monumental statue, where she threw her arms around him. "*Alter!* Eric, you look awful... *ugh*... and you smell even worse. How can Tamanna stand to be in the car with you? Don't Jinn breathe?"

She instantly covered her mouth, fearing she'd spoken too loudly. Fortunately, the museum seemed extremely quiet, possibly due to the lateness in the day. Only a bored-looking young woman sat behind the one of the ticket counters, and she gave no indication of having heard what Lotte said.

"Sorry about that," she muttered. "I was just so excited to see you. Don't pay any attention to what I said. I know what you went through."

He smiled. "It's fine. I feel almost as bad as I look... and smell. That guy from the bathroom in the Carlos Museum hit me on the back of my head, and there's a massive lump there now. I don't know if I have a concussion, but I've been super tired and I've been sleeping a lot. I'd be asleep now if it weren't for this."

She nodded. "I know. Hopefully it'll all be over soon. I think I know where we need to go. The Middle Eastern rooms are just off the lobby. I have all our tickets. We're just waiting for... well... our *friend* to show up." She eyed the woman behind the ticket counter, who seemed completely engaged with her phone.

Siddique and Olive joined them, arm in arm. He walked stiffly, and Eric saw a deep scar from a huge gash in his neck. It seemed healed over, but the skin remained rough and fibrous, and Siddique clearly had trouble moving his head.

Still, he smiled as he reached with open arms and hugged Eric. "Oh, man, am I glad to see you! I thought they'd taken you prisoner. I didn't think we'd see you again."

As he returned his friend's embrace, Eric felt rough pits on the backs of Siddique's shoulders, more byproducts of his battle with the Jinn-eagle, and evidence of Pazuzu's less than thorough healing. "I was in the same boat. I heard those guys who captured me talking. They thought you were dead, and they said that the eagle was gonna drain whatever energy you had left. I'm so sorry I couldn't help you."

"Yeah, Lotte told me. You really shouldn't apologize for things that aren't your fault, but I tell you this, and you do it anyway. You're crazy — all of you — but even though I almost died, I don't think I've ever felt so alive in my life. I'm glad to be crazy with you... all of you."

He grinned at Olive, who clung to his arm and pulled him close before she turned to Eric. "Not to be selfish or nuthin', but do you still have my gun?"

Eric reflexively patted his hands to his sides, searching more for the extra magazine that should have been in his pocket than the gun itself. He couldn't find it. "Fuck!"

That word, delivered with sincerity and echoing in the empty lobby, finally drew the attention of the woman behind the desk. She lowered her phone and glowered at the group of friends gathered on the little stairway.

Lotte came to the rescue. "We're so sorry! We're so excited to see the museum, we just kind of, umm, lost track of where we were. We'll just wait over there for our friend. He won't be long. Really... sorry."

The woman flashed a strained smiled then went back to her phone while the group sidled over to the entrance into the Middle Eastern rooms.

"My bad," Eric said, once they'd established a sufficient distance. "I didn't even think about your gun until just now. The magazine might have fallen out of my pocket, or they might have taken it, but I had the gun in my hand when I got hit. I have no idea what happened to it."

Olive sighed deeply. "Well, there's not much we can do about it now, but that gun is registered in my name, and if the police find it on that bridge, I may as well give my heart to Jesus, 'cause my butts gonna be theirs."

They silently pondered the truth behind her colorful phrasing when the body of Harland Cheevers, under control of the god Pazuzu, strolled through the entryway and joined their little party. His eyes nervously scanned the Middle Eastern rooms ahead from floor to ceiling.

Lotte handed the jumpy god his ticket. "Here. We think what you're after is in one of these rooms. Are you ready?"

He seemed confused as he took the little slip of paper, head quickly darting up and down and from left to right. "Up," he finally said.

Lotte balked slightly. "You think Humbaba is upstairs?"

"Up," he repeated.

"Well, I suppose that's possible. I think your brother's medallion is normally housed on this level, but it may be part of a special exhibit or something. If so, they'll probably have a placard there telling us where it's currently on display. Since we're here, let's have a quick look. I'm sure we'll find it."

He nodded and fell in line next to Eric as Lotte eagerly led the way.

Few other patrons were in this section of the museum, and silence pervaded. The first room contained displays related to early Mesopotamian settlements, living in cities, and household items, including items of religious worship. Eric smiled knowingly at the variety of cylinder seals and tablets that depicted or referenced Enki, Enlil, and many of the other gods with whom he'd become familiar.

*Or met in person, as unbelievable as* that *might be.*

The group wound their way around a wall into an area featuring pottery and metalworks, including a mold for making bronze tools. Wasting no time, Lotte led them toward the next room, showcasing treasures from the Royal Tombs of Ur, prominently advertised in gold lettering at the entryway. She hung a quick right into an area with glass cases along the wall, and the partial reconstruction of a great stele that separated this section from the rest of the space. She quickly scanned the cases, then made a beeline for a spot in the middle of the far wall, beneath lettering that read, "I am Shulgi, King of Ur! My Words Must Never Be Forgotten!"

*Sorry, Mr. Ostentatious, that ship kind of sailed.*

When Lotte reached her destination, she froze stiff and mutely pointed at the item at the bottom of a row artifacts related to *The Epic of Gilgamesh.* The rest of the group quickly huddled around.

The amulet looked exactly as Pazuzu's had, several small wrought iron plates, bound together by golden seams and encased in a frame of gold. The archetypal image of Humbaba's writhing and tangled face, identical to an artifact molded in clay that sat directly above, gaped at them with empty, tear-shaped eyes. No photograph sat on this shelf. This was the amulet itself, there for all the world to see.

Wide-eyed, Lotte turned to Pazuzu. "Tell me your brother is here."

He met her gaze, shook his head, then raised his eyes to the ceiling, and with his right index finger deliberately pointed upward.

"*Scheiße!* Can you find him?"

"Of course. Now that we are close, discerning his exact location is a simple matter. From a distance, small variations in position are harder to detect, and the greater the distance, the less likely I am to notice. My brother is above us, and from what I can tell, not on the second level of this structure."

"How many levels are there in this building?" Olive asked.

"I think just two," Lotte replied. "If he's not on the second level, he must be on the *roof*. The stairs are back this way. Come on!"

She began to bolt back toward the lobby, but Eric grabbed her arm. "Hold it! We have no idea what's going on here, or how to get onto the roof. Give me a second."

He slipped past the stele toward the back of the room, passing by the gruesome corpses of an unfortunate soldier and an attendant. Apparently, they had been part of a funeral ceremony in which more than 70 participants—musicians, soldiers, and other attendants—had been buried along with their queen so they could serve her in the afterlife. All had been squashed flatter than a Waffle House waffle when the roof of the chamber in which they had perished collapsed.

Eric shook his head at the morbid thought as he approached the solitary case that housed one of the signature items of the museum's collection, the so-called "Ram in the Thicket." Mercifully, no one else was around to admire this incredible object, so Eric ducked behind the case and tried to stay out of sight.

It wasn't long before he felt a slight breeze kiss the back of his neck and heard a soft voice in his ear. "What's the trouble?"

He turned his head and could just barely make out the gossamer outline of Tamanna's head and shoulders. "You're not gonna believe this, but we think Humbaba has gotten loose. Pazuzu thinks he's on the roof. We need to get up there. Can you find a way?"

After a moment's hesitation, she anxiously replied. "Go up the stairs and wait at the top. I'll meet you there."

She rapidly whisked away, and he quickly returned to his uneasy friends. "Okay, Tamanna's on it. Let's get upstairs. She'll meet us there and tell us what to do."

They walked urgently, but not so rapidly as to attract the attention of any other patrons or security guards, of which they had seen exactly none. Stairs to the upper and lower levels flanked the main entrance. Once through the first room of the Middle Eastern galleries they had traversed previously, they turned left and took the first staircase up to a mezzanine, then a single, central staircase that led into Pepper Hall. Eric lingered in the stairwell, out of sight, as he tensely awaited instructions.

Almost ten minutes passed before Tamanna again made her presence felt. "Go down the hall to your left," she murmured. "In nearly the last room, you'll see a glass doorway leading to an outdoor terrace. That's the closest I can get you to the roof. All the other doors are locked, and they can't be opened without a physical key. The glass door on this side of the terrace is locked as well, but the mechanism is operated by a swipe card which I can manipulate so that it opens."

"What about guards? Won't they see us if we try to get out on that terrace?"

"I've taken care of the two museum staff people in that area, one guard, and one young woman operating a booth where you can handle replica items and ask questions. They'll be out for a short while. There are hardly any patrons in the museum, but we'll just have to hope none go by such a remote spot. Hurry and go! I'll be with you."

Eric bounded up the stairs and rendezvoused with the others. "Come on, this way." He led them into the Eastern Mediterranean gallery, then into the room with Roman artifacts, where he saw the now unstaffed table with the replica items.

*I wonder where she stashed the poor woman's body.*

"My brother follows us," Pazuzu gravely announced as they raced into the room dedicated to Etruscan Italy. "He senses me as I sense him."

"Maybe that ain't such a bad thing," Olive suggested. "He may want to be back unified with you as much as you want to be with him."

"Such an outcome would be welcome, but I fear it to be wishful thinking. We may be in grave danger. Make ready. I anticipate the need of your powers in the near future."

On the right wall of the next room, focused on the classical world, a large double glass door stood in an alcove near the elevator. The party came to a halt and peered outside. Other than some metal patio furniture, chairs tucked neatly under the tables, and some trash cans, the terrace seemed empty. The doorway on the opposite side, leading to the museum's library, sat closed and curtained.

Pazuzu didn't hesitate. With both arms he pushed, and the doors flew open, clearly having been unlocked by Tamanna. He boldly strode through, and after a quick squeeze of Siddique's hand, Olive fell in step behind the determined god. Eric stayed with Lotte and Siddique near the doors, holding one open in case in case Olive had to beat a hasty retreat.

Pazuzu reached the center of the terrace, turned, and looked up. For a moment, all was still, but the deity gave an astonished look when a mysterious shape suddenly plunged down and fiercely rammed him to the ground. With lightning quick movements, the two beings tussled, knocking over one of the tables and sending the chairs skittering in different directions.

Olive withdrew and crouched behind some of the other furniture, which provided some modicum of protection from the fray.

With a muscular heave, Pazuzu shed his attacker and tossed him into one of the trellis-topped wooden barriers on the sides of the large patio. The beast skidded to a halt, then stabilized on its hands and knees. Now motionless, Eric took in the wonder of Humbaba, simultaneously repellent and enthralling, with his uniquely terrifying appearance.

The face drew his attention first and foremost, an undulating and pulsing jumble of what could only be described as viscera, the coiled and roiling intestines of some hapless person or animal, exposed by the teeth and claws of a predator in the final frenzied moments before death. Strands of the ropey innards draped from his jowls and across his monstrous neck and shoulders. His black, tear-shaped eyes, void of pupils, looked exactly like the ubiquitous "Grays," pop culture's most recognizable representation of extraterrestrial life. They exuded the ruthless indifference of an insect.

The horns of a bull rose from the pulpy mass of his skull, and his skin bore the scales of a reptile, with thick thorny protrusions on his back. He appeared bipedal, like a man, but the crooked talons of a vulture jutted out on his hands and feet. Perhaps most menacing, Humbaba possessed a long serpentine tail that ended in the head of a strange horned viper, with cruel fangs and dark eyes that matched its master's.

Of all the mystical entities Eric had encountered, Humbaba evoked the greatest dread, a fountainhead of nightmares of the most primeval nature. Even the Afrit and Charun seemed more accessible and comprehensible... more *human*.

*Humbaba the Terrible. The ancients may not have gotten much right about the gods, but they sure nailed this one.*

The revolting entity quickly sprung back into action. Like a leopard, he launched himself at Pazuzu, who had managed to regain his feet. Better prepared for the assault, the god sidestepped his brother's fearsome horns and delivered a stiff kick to the ribs. Humbaba grunted and staggered, but his serpentine tail whipped low and entangled Pazuzu's legs, then the snake's head sunk its fangs into his thigh.

The god winced as he tumbled over and landed full force on his back, but miraculously, he promptly grabbed the slithering ophidian, ripped it free of his leg, and dashed the beast's head on the ground. The pain must have been immense as a bloody chunk of flesh tore away from his quadricep, but the maneuver worked. The snake appeared stunned, and Humbaba's horrendous tail went limp.

Pazuzu quickly swept out with his legs and brought his staggering brother hard to the decked wooden floor of the terrace, then scrambled on top of him. "Huwawa, my brother, cease this purposeless struggle! Why do you attack me? Well do you know that when united, we are mighty, and I sense that you, as I do, struggle to consolidate your powers within an alien body. Give up this senseless battle and rejoin with me. This world has grown only more inhospitable in the centuries that have elapsed since our imprisonment. Together, we may survive, but individually, I fear we both are doomed."

Humbaba's head lolled from side to side, but eventually the monstrous being found his voice. His words gurgled out like mucus from a clogged chest, blurred and mushy, almost indecipherable. "How dare you call me *brother*, betrayer of a thousand promises! My captivity began long before Iblis trapped us!"

"I saved your very existence! Without my intervention, you would have expired among Enlil's precious cedars. Would that have been preferable?"

"No, and countless thanks I gave for your charity, but it came at great cost. I felt enslaved!"

Pazuzu shook his head. "Brother, in all successful relations, one must lead, and one must follow. You have your fortes, physical assets, and preternatural powers that I most assuredly do not possess. Your judgment, however, and your lack of self-restraint, constitute your undoing, in addition to your sometimes feeble reasoning. Why do you think the gods were intent on banishing you in the first place? At the heart of our attempts to edify this aimless and ungovernable species, you remained uncivilized, fit only to live among the beasts! It was fortuitous that Enlil required a guardian for a spot where any mortal who trespassed would forfeit their lives. The task suited you well, but with me, your horizons grew immensely."

Humbaba grotesquely cackled. "Fancy words, fancy words. Always good with speech, you were, and nothing has changed. What 'horizon' grew for me, the privilege of mutely watching you tap my power for the greater glory of *your* name? I could not act. I could not speak. Wonder, it was, that you let me see at all, and, oh... what I saw. Time and again, you let the wicked one go free! Why? You promised me she would meet her end for what she did, but you always let her slip away."

"That is not so! Dimme was wily and cunning, always, it seemed, a step ahead. I could scare her away, but entrapping her remained beyond my capacity, even with your assistance."

"Lies, lies, lies, lies, lies! You became addicted to the image you projected, and to the reverence that came from being the 'protector of pregnant women and mothers.' If only they knew the truth!"

"It *is* the truth! Let me prove it to you. Against all odds, Dimme still survives. I have given my word that I shall hunt her down and bring an end to her."

"Your word is worthless! You promised this to me nearly a thousand years before the fall of Uruk. Why would I believe you now?"

"Because we would have assistance, one who can augment our powers to even greater heights. Additionally, Iblis, Dimme's most potent ally—before he became her ruler—is dead. The path is clear, and when she is gone, we will be among the last remaining gods. Our domain shall be immense!"

"*Your* domain! I will once again be locked away, unable to act, unable to even think thoughts of my own without intrusion! No, *brother*, not again. You lie, but at least one thing you say is true. I am strong, stronger than you. You have never been able to best me in battle, and that is as true today as when we walked separately among the people and deities of Sumer!"

Humbaba viciously swiped across Pazuzu's chest with his vulture's claws, leaving three ragged crimson gashes.

The injured god howled in agony as he savagely clutched his brother by the throat. "Now, child! Lend me your aid as I take by force what is not given willingly!"

Olive scampered out from her woefully insufficient hiding place and stood over the scuffling siblings. As she removed her necklace, Siddique pushed past Eric and, despite his rigid gait, rushed out to join her. Humbaba thrashed and flailed, beating his brother's shoulders and scraping his neck, but Pazuzu desperately held fast. Despite the onslaught, he reached out and took Olive by the hand. Humbaba calmed, his black eyes staring straight up into his brother's resolute gaze.

*This is it!* Eric eagerly thought. *He must be trying to reabsorb his brother now that he's in contact with Olive.*

Pazuzu's endeavor appeared to be working, until Humbaba unexpectedly bucked and again began to claw wildly at his adversary. More troubling still, his scaled tail shakily rose from the ground, and the snake's head delicately probed with its forked tongue.

To Eric's amazement, Siddique dove on the slithering appendage and forced it to the ground between the abominable god's squirming legs.

Olive spared a glance in Siddique's direction, but Pazuzu immediately screamed at her. "Concentrate! The power inside you resists! It covets the strength is has gained and refuses to let it go."

She looked fraught with confusion, clearly unable to determine what to do. She briskly shook her head then closed her eyes, but Humbaba continued to surge with vitality. He kicked at Siddique who still clung to the serpentine tail, and ferociously punched his brother in the cheek. The blow knocked Pazuzu to the ground and severed his tenuous connection with Olive.

"Run!" she screamed, and Siddique pushed the snake away and rolled to relative safety.

With sprightly movements, Humbaba turned from his back to his hands and knees, then vaulted to his feet. His obsidian eyes had just met Olive's, who stood paralyzed in terror, when Pazuzu tried to tackle him from behind. The act clearly saved Olive but failed in its attempt to bring the terrible god to the ground. Instead, the fearsome reptilian tail again found its mark and tore into Pazuzu's side. He bellowed furiously, and for a brief moment, his flesh blurred and flickered, but his power to dematerialize remained beyond his ability to consistently control, and the snake's fangs clung tight.

Humbaba seized his brother's arm, deftly flipped him over his shoulder, and slammed him to the floor. Not satisfied, he mercilessly drove his clawed foot into his stunned opponent's neck, which emitted a distressing *snap*. Humbaba then lifted Pazuzu's body into the air and forcefully threw him like a rag doll at the wooden barrier of the terrace. The brutal impact shattered bones and violently whipped Pazuzu's head, which came to rest in an abnormally horrific position on the ground.

The battle appeared to have ended, and Humbaba the Terrible had seemingly emerged victorious. The repellent being's black eyes bore down onto those who remained on the normally lovely patio, and through the viscus-like tissues of his disfigured face, a ghastly smile slowly blossomed.

# CHAPTER 13

Olive staggered backward to where Siddique crouched near the wall of the terrace, opposite where Pazuzu's ruined body lay. Trembling in panicked fear, she felt the signature tingling, the slight rush of energy from the entity that lurked inside her, but how to harness that power as she had done before completely eluded her. She wrenched her gaze from the terrible god and noticed that Lotte and Eric still stood in the threshold of the glass doors, looks of horror on their faces.

*Maybe we can get away.*

The thought died as she looked down at Siddique, who had expended most of his flagging strength in a valiant attempt to help her. She might stand a chance to reach the door, but he would never make it.

*What good would it do anyway? Dang thing can probably bust through that glass no problem. We are in deep trouble!*

Their predicament became even more apparent when Humbaba began to creep toward them, flexing his hooked claws as the talons on his feet scraped across the wooden decking of the patio. Her shaking increased and her mind spun in fruitless circles, unable to formulate a means of deterring the monstrosity that threatened them.

Siddique suddenly grabbed her arm, shakily pulled himself to his feet, then brazenly stepped in front of her.

She cried out in dismay. "What are you doin'?"

"I'll hold him off as long as I can. You run, save yourself!"

There wasn't time to answer. The beast lunged, and Siddique readied himself in a fighting stance. A millisecond before impact, a blurry shape streaked out of the air and plunged directly into Humbaba's side. The grotesque being tumbled across the floor toward the back of the terrace and overturned another table and chairs before he struck the far doors.

Olive beheld a beautiful woman, completely unclothed, who had appeared as if from nowhere. She whipped her thick, black hair as she turned, a severe look on her face. "Run!"

*This must be Tamanna, the Jinn that saved Eric!*

Olive clutched Siddique's arm, and they hastily tottered toward the exit. Lotte had already gone inside, and Eric held his hand outstretched as his body braced the door open. They'd almost made it when Olive heard a noise and looked over her shoulder.

Tamanna had vanished, and Humbaba had risen and now charged at her across the terrace. His inhuman speed carried him to them in nearly the blink of an eye. Claws outstretched, he leapt into the air, intent on striking them from above.

Panic stricken, Olive forced Siddique to the ground. "Duck!"

The maneuver was pointless as Humbaba had them in his sights, but once again the hazy form of the beautiful Tamanna appeared and stoutly knocked the monster aside. He banged hard into the wall to their right, not far from where Olive and Siddique recently stood. Tamanna rushed forward and leapt into the air, delivering another solid kick to the back of Humbaba's head before disappearing once again.

Olive desperately helped Siddique to stand, but his body hadn't fully healed from his ordeal of the night before. Her friend had just gotten to his knees when Humbaba rallied and again surged to his feet. This time, however, the beast hesitated. He put his thorny back to the wall and darted his gruesome, horned head from side to side as he searched for his unseen assailant.

His hunt unsuccessful, he grimly scowled at Olive. "A pity. I catch a small whiff of what my soon to be deceased brother told me of your power. You'd have made a most interesting meal, or at the very least, I would have ended your ability to hurt me. No matter. That day may yet come, but I have neither the stamina nor the interest in battling your Jinn protector. Unlike the Cedar Forest, this place overflows with humanity. So much energy on which to feed! I am free. I leave you in peace, but rest assured, if we meet again, you will be left in *pieces*."

The terrible god vaulted from the terrace to the museum's roof, and the sound of his talons scuffing across the Roman-inspired tiles receded rapidly into the distance.

For several moments, no one moved, until a great black bird, like a dove bearing an olive branch, landed softly on the trellised wall above Pazuzu's mangled form. Realizing this was probably the raven that Eric and Lotte had also spoken about, Olive helped Siddique to his feet, gently slipped the white medallion back over her head, and then ran to the mortally wounded god.

The others gathered behind her as she knelt and pulled her face close. "Mr. Pazuzu, can you hear me?"

His empty eyes gained a semblance of life as he met her gaze. "I hear, child. I fear my time may be at an end. I overestimated your prowess and underestimated that of my brother."

"How did he get free, and how did he get to be so powerful?"

"I know not, but I believe all too soon a wake of corpses will be discovered in this area. He has fed. Like me, he struggles to absorb and retain energy. Despite his appearance, that is *not* his body. Who it belongs to remains a mystery, even to me."

"What can we do?"

"That is no longer my 'cross to bear,' as the followers of your Nazarene might say. With your energy, I might have had him, but now he is as he claims... free... and there are no gods to check his appetite and oftentimes malicious ways."

Olive felt the sting of shame. "I'm sorry. Really, I am. I *wanted* to help you. I just don't know how."

"Clearly true. I do not blame you. You valiantly faced the challenge, but it was for naught. Now, without me to contain him, Humbaba will inflict suffering upon your kind until he is hunted down and exterminated, or slowly starves. Either way, my part in the saga has come to an end."

"Perhaps not." Tamanna's words surprised everyone. "You're still alive, and you can still exercise your Jinn-like ability to inhabit the body of another."

Unable to move his broken neck, Pazuzu's eyes migrated to her nude form. "My spirit is weak. No one slumbers near enough that I could meld with them. Even if they were, it would be a difficult challenge."

"I disabled a security guard in the next room. He will remain unconscious for some time. We can bring his body out—"

"No!" Lotte interceded. "We're not involving another innocent person in this mess and risk them being killed like poor Harland Cheevers. These are people! They don't deserve a fate like this, and neither do their families and friends who love them—a mysterious and unexplained disappearance, and a horrible death that everyone has to suffer with for the rest of their lives."

Tamanna's eyes narrowed as she appraised her. "All right, Lotte, what do you suggest we do? You've seen what Humbaba is capable of, and if what Pazuzu says is true, many more lives will be lost before we, or someone else, will be able to bring him to bear. We need Pazuzu's help, or this will get far worse before it gets better."

"It has to be one of us," Eric said. "If we don't want to drag anyone else into this, one of us will have to be, like, the *host*... or whatever."

Lotte's eyes widened in horror, but Olive jumped in before she could object. "I'll do it. I've made more promises to more of these dang old ancient gods than I can count. 'Bout time one of 'em takes me up on it. If I had my shit together with this 'power' I've got, we wouldn't even be in this mess."

Pazuzu issued a bloody cough before he spoke. "Your powers are precisely why I cannot merge with you. I would be subsumed, and the entity that lurks inside you would gain even greater leverage toward assuming control. No, it cannot be you. It must be... *him*!" His eyes met Siddique's. "I know his mind from the healing I performed. It would be easiest to merge with him. In fact, he may be the only person with whom I have the energy to successfully complete the transition."

Olive felt her heart skip a beat. "No, you can't take him! I... I can't... I can't lose him... not now... not *right now*."

"There may be no alternative," Tamanna calmly stated, "and I think we have to move quickly."

Olive despairingly looked at her friends. Eric had closed his eyes in obvious misery, while Lotte displayed her usual determined demeanor, tinged with a hint of sadness.

Siddique, however, smiled mildly and stepped forward. "I'll do it. I know it's scary, Olive, but listen to yourself. You were the first one to offer your own life, and had things been a little different, it would be you he took. This isn't the way we thought things would go, but we knew how dangerous all this stuff could be. We got the rewards, all of us: lives that many people would love to have lived, friendships with stronger bonds than any we would have had. All that comes at a price, and now, it's time to pay."

Her mind went blank, the impossibility of the situation exceeding her capacity to comprehend or cope.

Siddique turned to Tamanna. "How do we do this? Don't I have to be asleep?"

She gave a stiff nod. "I can see to that. You won't feel a thing until you wake up, but at that point, it will be Pazuzu's problem, not yours... assuming this works. Just sink to your knees. Lotte, Eric, please catch him as he falls. No need to risk further injury to his body."

With a resigned sigh, Siddique got into position. Lotte and Eric each gently brushed his shoulder as they crouched behind him.

Olive could stand it no longer. "Wait! Listen here, Mr. Pazuzu. If you want my help with your damn brother, then you're gonna have to do something for me! I want him *back*! I want you to promise me that you'll give Siddique back once you've gotten what you want. Find somebody else to take over, somebody wicked, like we do with the Afrit. There seems to be an endless stream of nasty people that come waltzing into our messed-up lives. Take one of them, one that's probably gonna die anyway, and give me Siddique back. I want you to promise that, or else I ain't gonna help you, and if you want to kill me for that, go right ahead! I might as well be dead if this is the way things are gonna be."

Tamanna began to speak but Pazuzu cut her off. "I agree. Without this transition, I shall die, but should I not reunite with Humbaba, that will be my fate regardless. For this, I will still need your help, and perhaps, with time, you can come to master the power within you. This constitutes my sole chance to survive, so I agree to your terms. You have my word."

Olive couldn't believe it. "Really? I mean... umm... I don't know what to say."

"Say nothing, child. Life drains from this mortal body. If we do not act swiftly, all shall be moot."

She turned and fell into Siddique's arms as tears streamed down her cheeks. "If you die, I swear, I'm gonna kill you! I want you *back*, and this time I'm damned well gonna get what I want."

He chuckled. "You look out for me better than I do. I wouldn't ever say something like that to a *god*. You gave me a chance, and I'll do whatever I can to be with you again. Olive, I love—"

"Don't say it! Don't you dare say it until I know that we can live our lives together and I can say it back to you. Save it for later. That's when it's really gonna count." She kissed him deeply, then crawled despondently to Eric's side.

Without a hint of shame at her nudity, Tamanna bent before Siddique and brightly grinned. "For a kindhearted soul, you're tremendously courageous. Can you smile for me?"

Olive could only see the back of Siddique's head, but she pictured his face as she'd seen it so many times, brimming with his good-natured cheer.

With a superhumanly brisk movement, Tamanna forced the heel of her palm directly into Siddique's chin. His head snapped wildly, and he collapsed into Lotte's and Eric's arms, completely unconscious.

"Hurry," Tamanna commanded. "Pull him over so that he touches Pazuzu. That will make the transition easier."

Lotte and Eric quickly complied, but Olive couldn't muster the enthusiasm to move a muscle. It didn't matter. They didn't have far to move him, and everything else relied on Pazuzu. The dying god shut his eyes once Siddique lay beside him, and after a moment, Siddique's body began to buckle and spasm. His breathing became rapid and labored, as if he ran up a steep hill, and his arms and legs flailed outward as if pushing away some unseen tormentor.

*Actually, that's exactly what's happenin'. His body is reacting against a foreign invasion. I went through this when Aicha took me over, except I don't remember it. Just as well. It looks awful. Worst of all, I have to root for Siddique to lose.*

With time, the convulsions lessened, then ceased altogether. Siddique's breathing steadied and his body calmed. Finally, his eyes fluttered, then opened, and he surveyed his surroundings with a disoriented look on his face.

Tamanna squatted beside him. "Great one, can you hear me?"

He blinked several times, then slyly smiled. "I hear. I am with you. The ordeal is over, and I live once more."

Olive shuddered hearing Pazuzu's words from Siddique's lips, void of his signature accent.

"I am weak. I must soon feed, and we must be gone from this place. It will not be long before my brother detects my continued existence. He may decide to return and finish what he started."

Tamanna nodded. "Agreed. Lotte, Eric, help him up and let's get out of here. We're running out of time with the cameras and the unconscious museum employees anyway."

"Where... where am I?" The wheezing voice of Harland Cheevers surprised all of them. "I... I can't move."

In dismay, Olive crawled over to him and took his hand. "Oh, Mr. Cheevers, it's really hard to explain. You're not anywhere near your home, and you're... well... not in very good condition."

"Will I die? I feel like I'm going to die."

Once again, tears welled in her eyes. "I have to be honest with you. I think you're about to die. You didn't do nuthin' to deserve this. You're a good person. All your friends in the Carlos Museum are worried sick over you. They love you, and they were tryin' to help the police find you."

He took that in for a moment, then gave a pained laugh. "It's funny. This isn't how I expected to go out. I always pictured dying peacefully with my favorite music playing beside me."

"What's your favorite song, Harland?"

"Oh, I don't think you'd know it. It's *Awaken*, by a band called Yes."

"I... I'm sorry... I don't know it. *Awaken* is a beautiful title. I'm sure it's a pretty song. Is it by the same band that plays *Owner of a Lonely Heart?*"

He coughed another laugh and blood streamed out of his mouth and down his chin. "Yeah, same band. I don't like that song nearly as much, but I guess it's okay. That was kind of *me*, the owner of a lonely heart. I never found love, except in my music, and the people I met online who liked it too. I met some of them at festivals. That was fun. I guess I didn't have it so bad. Tell the folks at the museum I love them too. I liked being there. All those old things brought me quite... quite a sense... quite a sense of... *peace.*"

Olive wept miserably as Harland Cheevers slipped away. She felt Eric's hands on her shoulders, and she buried her face in his chest, heaving in sorrow. "Why? Why is this happenin'? Why does it have to *be* like this? Why does everything have to be so dang *hard*? Why!"

Her sorrow abruptly morphed to white hot anger. *I'm gonna rip this damn amulet off and I'm gonna tear gawddamned Humbaba apart with my bare fuckin' hands, pardon my fuckin' French! How* dare *he? What makes it so important for* him *to live and Harland Cheevers can't? This is completely ridiculous! This has gotta stop! I'm gonna stop it! Oh, yes... I will.*

"Hey, you okay?"

Eric's words cut through her like an icy sword, dousing the flames of her indignation and bringing her back to the moment. "Umm... yeah, I think so. I just kinda lost it there for a second. I mean, poor Harland.... What a lousy way to die, none of your friends around you, not even knowing where you are. It just—"

"I know, it's awful. We just have to get out of here. Can you stand up and try to get yourself together, at least until we get out of the museum?"

"Yeah, okay. What are we gonna do with his body, though?"

Tamanna cut in. "Leave that to me. I'll take care of Mr. Cheevers and try to clean up a bit. Eric, meet me at the car. The rest of you hurry back to the van and let's get away from here. May Allah protect you from being observed."

Unable to resist, Olive let Eric guide her across the terrace and out the exit. As the door closed, she spared one final glance back at the deformed and lifeless body of Harland Cheevers.

*It almost happened again, that overwhelming feeling when I got really mad. I thought I could do* anything! *Where was all that when Pazuzu needed me? Now, it's too late. Poor Harland is dead, and I've lost the one person who brings any* happiness *into my stupid life. What good is all this so-called* power *if I can't control none of it? Maybe Pazuzu's right and I'll figure it out eventually, but where do I even start, and how? This is hopeless, and if everybody's relying on me to save the day, I have a bad feeling about how all this is gonna end.*

Eric felt a rush of relief when Tamanna's phone finally rang. He swiped and answered. "Hello?"

Lotte's fatigued voice sounded in the speaker. "Eric, we're out of the garage. Pazuzu said his brother headed south, so we're going north to try and get some distance from him and regroup. Is Tamanna back yet?"

"No, I'm still in the garage waiting for her. She should be here soon."

"I hope so. Listen, I'm going to try to find us a place, maybe a house where we can all be together. When you leave, call me and maybe I'll have something. Otherwise, just go north until we can figure out where to meet up."

He agreed and hung up. It had been nearly 40 minutes since he'd gotten back to the car, and he was starting to get antsy. "Where the hell is she?"

"Right the hell here."

Her voice from the back seat nearly sent him through the roof of the Mini. "Shit, you scared me. Sorry, I didn't mean to be a dick, I'm just really nervous. I also feel like crap." He began to face her from where he sat in the passenger's seat, but spying her naked form, he modestly turned away.

"It's all right," she replied as she fumbled to don her clothing in the back of the cramped little car. "I understand. You've been through a lot. I'm amazed you're doing as well as you are."

"Thanks. What took you so long?"

"Well, I had to do something with Mr. Cheevers's body and try to clean up that patio."

"Dare I ask?"

"It isn't pretty. There's a restaurant immediately below the rooftop terrace. I found the back entrance where the dumpsters are located, then I hefted the body down and tossed it into one that seemed fairly full and covered it up. The restaurant was closed, so no one was down there, and fortunately I didn't meet anyone on the stairway or in the hall. The museum is pretty much closed now anyway. I used some cleaning supplies from the kitchen to mop up the blood on the patio."

Eric just shook his head at poor Harland Cheevers's fate.

*Olive is right. This really sucks. Talk about being in the wrong place at the wrong time.*

Tamanna interrupted his gloomy thoughts. "Then I came back here and temporarily disabled the garage's security system. They won't see us leave. Maybe that will help keep us off the suspect list in case the body is found."

"Wow, you've been busy. Harland must have weighed a ton."

"I can be very strong when I expend enough energy. That took a lot out of me, though. I'll need to rest, and I'll need to feed again soon, as will Pazuzu." Now essentially dressed, she opened the door, squeezed out of the back seat, and slipped behind the wheel. "So, where are we off to?"

"Lotte said we need to go north. She's trying to find us a place where we can all be together. I'll call her when we hit the road."

Tamanna navigated the car to the exit, where she rolled down the window and waved her left hand. In short order, the gate opened, and they drove through.

"Wow, that's a handy trick," Eric quipped. "Can we keep you?"

She laughed. "I'm only on loan for now. That machine took only credit cards, and I'd prefer not to enter mine since it's the one I used to rent this car."

They navigated around the garage to 33rd Street headed north, and Eric placed his call to Lotte. "Any luck finding something?"

"Incredibly, yes. I found a perfect place on Airbnb. It's up in Germantown. How coincidental is that? I'm waiting to get confirmation of the booking and instructions for the keys. Just keep driving north, and I'll call you back when I have the address."

He hung up and closed his eyes. His head throbbed, and he felt overwhelmingly tired and shaky.

The phone's ring startled him from sleep, but Tamanna had slipped it out of his hand. He wasn't sure how long he'd been out. She flashed him a sympathetic smile while she quietly spoke with Lotte, then she deftly typed some directions into Google Maps while steering through traffic. Eric realized she had things under control, so he surrendered to the inevitable and fell instantly back to sleep.

Once again, the ring of Tamanna's phone woke him. The little red Mini sat parked halfway on a sidewalk between a large, blueish green apartment building and the back of a row of blocky brick townhomes, each with a single, white garage door blandly encasing the lower level of each unit. The light had faded noticeably, and Eric glanced at the clock on the dashboard.

*Wow, nearly seven o'clock. I've been out for almost two hours.* "Where are we?"

Tamanna shot him a quick glance, brought her finger to her lips, and then silently mouthed *"Nadia,"* before returning to her call. She listened intently for a few moments, then responded. "Are you sure that's a good idea? You've been through a lot, and what magical resources you possessed have been utilized. You can't be of much assistance, and it would only further endanger your life. I don't think —"

Eric could barely make out the voice on the other end of the phone that interrupted her. Nadia sounded pretty insistent, presumably suggesting that she rejoin the party in some capacity.

After a few more faltering attempts to sway her, Tamanna finally seemed to acquiesce. "Okay, okay. You're right. I'm not arguing that. I'm just worried about your safety. This whole situation has become infinitely more complicated than I could have ever anticipated. But you're right, I could use your help if that's what you're willing to do. How soon can you be here?" She paused again. "All right, that's great. I'll text you the address. Are you sure you're up to this? You seem very anxious. Yes... yes... okay, I understand. I appreciate this, really. Like I said, I'll text you the address, and I'll see you Monday night. Goodbye, Nadia, and thank you."

"Looks like she'll be joining us after all," Eric ventured after Tamanna lowered the phone.

She stared out the windshield, a troubled look on her face. "Yes. She thinks she'll be here the day after tomorrow, or possibly Tuesday morning. She's still in the hospital for observation, and the police and the insurance people need to talk with her at some point, so she can't leave and raise any suspicions. She's a brave young woman. I asked too much of her and put her life in grave danger. I almost fainted when you mentioned Ornias at breakfast this morning."

"You know Ornias and Uri?"

"I know *of* Ornias and Uri, but I didn't know they were the Jinn who'd taken up with Aicha Kandicha. If both of them had been at the bridge during the standoff, we wouldn't be having this conversation. They thought they'd tipped the balance with those mercenaries, and they were almost right. It took all the energy Nadia had worked so hard to build up, but she kept you from falling into their hands. Thanks to Siddique — and the Afrit, I suppose — Uri's now out of the picture. That only leaves Ornias, but that's not especially good news. He's a very ancient, very crafty Jinn. You might know of him from the Testament of Solomon."

"Well, Lotte might, but not me. Sorry. I'm not nearly that well-read. I do know that King Solomon was briefly the mortal in charge of the 'Kings of the Jinn.' Utnapishtim told us that, but I know nothing about the Testament of Solomon."

She snorted a little laugh. "It's just as well. The story has so many accretions layered on through centuries, and has been so intermingled with other myths, that it bears little resemblance to reality. At its heart, it's the story of Solomon using his authority to stop the Jinn Ornias from repeatedly and excessively draining the life force out of a young man."

"Why would he do that? It seems like most Jinn are happy to take a little from a variety of people."

"Because some burn more brightly with energy than others. This may have been due to natural variation, or it could have been that this young man had some Jinn heritage mixed with his mortal blood. This is the power that Nadia now offers me. I desperately need to replenish my strength before we face Humbaba again, as does Pazuzu. With her part-Jinn makeup, feeding from Nadia as she sleeps will be infinitely superior to harvesting whatever convenient person I happen upon. She is one in millions, and right now, I need what she has to offer. If I didn't, I wouldn't put her back in this dangerous situation."

"What about Karšift? Could he loan you some energy?"

"Karšift is Jinn, and Jinn don't sleep or close their conscious minds in the way that humans do. Sadly, it's simply impossible. I wouldn't have thought that what Iblis did with Dimme was possible, but divine blood flows in her veins, and he forced her to relinquish her power willingly. Iblis possessed a shrewd but devious mind. It's just as well he no longer haunts our world. Oh, there they are!"

Eric looked where she pointed and saw the familiar white Schneider Industrial Flooring van pull into an alley across the street from where they were parked. The narrow road cut between more rows of squarish, brick town homes.

Tamanna started the car and drove to meet them. By the time they arrived, Lotte had opened the white garage door attached to the first house on the left, essentially identical to those in the row of houses they'd been behind on the other side of the street. Olive had begun to carefully pull the van into the narrow garage space, barely large enough to accommodate their vehicle.

Eric hopped out of the Mini, and he and Lotte embraced by the side of the concrete driveway.

"Sorry things took so long," she said into his shoulder. "I had to wait for the owner to send me the address of the house along with the code to open the lockbox with the keys, so we stopped off at the grocery store to get some supplies. I texted Tamanna the address and told her to meet us here."

"It doesn't matter. I fell asleep. I'm definitely still feeling the effects of getting hit in the head, and then being in a major car accident."

"I know. I think we're all exhausted, but you and Siddique got the worst of it."

"Speaking of, umm... I guess I can't call him 'Siddique' anymore, can I? How is mighty *Pazuzu* doing?"

She rolled her eyes. "Sleeping like a baby, or I suppose *meditating* would be a better description. I have to say, he's the most pathetic excuse for a god I've ever seen. I get that he's been through a lot, but it seems like he's constantly on the edge of completely collapsing. I have no idea how he expects to prevail over his brother. Even with our help, I'm beginning to think this might be hopeless."

"Not hopeless," Tamanna interjected as she joined them, having left the Mini parked in the driveway behind the van, "just difficult. Pazuzu's condition is the result of losing connection with his original, material body. Unlike Jinn, it's not in the nature of the beings of the Abzu and their descendants to transfer their essence into the body of another. In fact, I've never heard of it happening. The energy required just to maintain stasis in this new form must be immense."

Lotte narrowed her eyes. "Seems like that's true of *all* of these supernatural beings, the Jinn included, and it only gets worse when they try something miraculous. They burn through energy faster than I run through my bloody cell phone battery. Not very *godlike*, if you ask me."

Tamanna sharply laughed. "*Godlike*! Remember, Lotte, it's *our* kind who labeled these entities as 'gods.' True, they were only too happy to accept that mantle—and the accompanying adoration—but don't be fooled by their bluster. Powerful as they are, these creatures have limitations, the product of residing in a foreign realm. They're like ants wearing the guise of elephants. They have powers, no doubt of that, but

I don't believe that they've ever fully realized how vast our universe is, or what resources it would truly take for them to rule as gods. Why do you think so many Jinn desire to simply go home? The very act of feeding eventually becomes a tiresome burden, but to cease doing so would mean their end. Even my father, who fully accepted his fate in this world and warmly embraced humankind, felt this way at times. He, like Enki and Enlil, thought a solution could be found, that somehow the promise of those glorious early days could be realized, and he and his ilk could truly live as the gods we made them out be, or at least lead existences of some importance. He was wrong, and his mistakes were costly in the lives of many, mortal and supernatural alike, before he too was killed. This is the danger. It isn't that Humbaba can't be stopped. It's that in ignorance of his own limitations, insignificance, and vulnerability, he'll cause untold damage before he can be brought to heel. It's the price we all pay for the coincidental pairing of our realms, and for being in the wrong place at the wrong moment in the space time continuum."

WILLIAM E. NOLAND

# CHAPTER 14

The house Lotte had found on Airbnb suited their needs perfectly. In addition to the garage, it had three bedrooms, two bathrooms, a living room, and a kitchen, all nicely furnished and clean. The place looked far better on the inside than its generic exterior might lead one to believe.

Olive coaxed the still wary Mutig out of the van while Lotte and Eric grabbed the various backpacks, duffel bags, and groceries. They lugged everything into the kitchen, followed closely by Tamanna, who had roused the recuperating Pazuzu and corralled him upstairs into the house.

The weary god traipsed into the living room and commandeered a love seat near the stairs to the second floor, in which he sat, cross-legged, as he surveyed the room.

Eric found it disturbing to see Siddique's body move in an unfamiliar manner, with unusual and dour expressions that didn't sit well against his friend's normally tranquil demeanor.

It proved too much for Olive. "I need to get out of here," she muttered forlornly. She pulled Mutig's leash out of her backpack, hooked it to the recoiling animal's collar, dragged him reluctantly through the living room, then slunk out the front door with the morose creature in tow.

Lotte rushed out after her, but quickly returned with a discouraged and irritated look. Her dark eyes soon settled on Pazuzu, and she marched to the coffee table and plunked herself down, directly facing him.

Tamanna slipped catlike into a living room chair near the window, while Eric resumed putting away the groceries in the kitchen, not wishing to be too close to the fray, but still in earshot to hear what might happen.

When she spoke, Lotte's words were pointed and direct. "Is what Humbaba said true?"

"My brother said many things," the reclining god mildly replied. "To what do you refer?"

"Oh, please. Spare me! I'm talking about what he said about feeling trapped... enslaved! He said you kept him mute and powerless while you tapped his power. What's worse is that he said you let Dimme go free after you promised to kill her. That's the same promise you made to *us*, among others! Did you lie to your brother, and if so, are you still lying? If you are, then we're walking away from this... all of us!"

"Indeed? You truly think that Olive would abandon me now that I inhabit the body of the man she loves? Go, if you wish. It is her I need, and I have every confidence that she will remain."

Taken somewhat aback, Lotte took a moment, then changed her approach. "All right, look... leaving isn't what any of us are after. Having seen Humbaba, I think we're all in agreement that he poses a threat. We want to stay and help, but you have to be *honest* with us. We have to know the facts so we can act appropriately. We thought your brother would be happy to reunite with you, or at least not be in a position to resist. If we knew he'd gotten loose, or that he believed he needed to battle for his very existence, then we wouldn't have waltzed into that museum the way we did, and we wouldn't be in the mess we're in now. This is why I'm so irritated. If he's wrong about you, maybe we can try to convince him of that, but if he's right, it's an entirely different dynamic. Can you understand that?"

Pazuzu gave a slight bob of his head.

"Okay then, what is it? Is he right about what you did?"

"Right or wrong, he fails to comprehend the larger picture and the motives for my actions. His feebleminded and loutish ways were responsible for his presence as guard of the Cedar Forest in the first place."

"He didn't seem so feebleminded to me on that rooftop terrace at the museum."

"You do not know my brother, or the depravities of which he can be capable."

"How can I? Over the past few days, I've read all the stories that I can get my hands on about Humbaba. They all describe him in different ways, everything from being an intimidating mountain man, to an ogre or giant whose face is covered in the entrails of the foes he slays in battle. I guess that last part is pretty accurate, but it's his... I don't know... his *personality*, for lack of a better term, that I'm more interested in. It seems to vary from the earliest versions of *The Epic of Gilgamesh* to the later ones. Actually, all kinds of details are different. In the most ancient, it's actually Enkidu who slays Humbaba after Gilgamesh had consulted with Enki about how to fool Humbaba into giving up his powers."

Pazuzu let out a sigh Eric could hear from the kitchen. "Lies spread by Dimme to try and preserve Gilgamesh's reputation and to sow the seeds of discord among the gods. I worked for centuries to sway the orators and scribes to tell the tale more accurately, but eradicating false notions among your kind is like chasing a malodorous scent in the breeze. Never will you wrap your fingers around every strand. Some is always bound to still foul the air."

"But you did make progress," Lotte said. "Later versions of the story depict Humbaba with far greater humanity. He even makes a strong case against Enkidu for being cowardly and covetous of Gilgamesh's affection, exactly what you told us when we talked with you in that house in North Carolina."

"Long has it been since I have walked among your kind. I know not how the story of my brother's death has mutated in that time, but what you say aligns with what I heard and saw that day, now so long ago."

"All right, that's helpful. Let's assume that part, at least, is true. If I recall, he also speaks very eloquently about other things in that version. He talks about never knowing his mother or father, and how the mountains reared him before Enlil made him the guardian of his forest. He swears to be Gilgamesh's loyal servant and to build him a palace out of the cedar trees. He comes across as quite sincere."

"He was pleading for his life."

"So, does that mean he was lying?"

Eric stood at the doorway.

Pazuzu closed his eyes and took a deep breath. "My brother was sincere, and it pleases me that the truth of this moment is preserved in your literary heritage. Things are, however, somewhat more complicated. Humbaba never lacked sincerity. He always meant what he said, but like many with only the best of intentions, living up to the standards of one's resolutions can prove challenging. Consider those who aspire to lose weight, or consume less beer or wine, or act with greater kindness. Many can do so, for a time, but often, their nature reasserts itself and they revert to behaviors they swore to have abandoned. So it is with my brother, but his predilection for violence, and his inability to control his voracious appetite, have consequences far beyond those of an overweight, drunken, or callous man. Repeatedly, he killed while feeding. Not one, mind you, but a host of people—entire families, devoured. He was courageous in battle, but even when the day had been won, he reveled in the continued disemboweling of soldiers, friend and foe alike. His bloodlust so consumed him that his visage became permanently imprinted with the shredded entrails of his victims."

Lotte blanched. "Why didn't someone just kill him?"

"Few possessed the power to do so."

"Gilgamesh seemed to have no trouble, although he got help from another god, didn't he? Shamash, right?"

"Possibly. Gilgamesh and Enkidu certainly had divine assistance, but ever did Shamash deny his involvement. Whether this was another of Dimme's lies, or if, in truth, Shamash was in league with her and saw a surreptitious opportunity to diminish Enlil's power as supreme deity by aiding others to kill the guardian of his beloved forest, we may never know."

"Okay, but the fact remains, if enough gods had wanted your brother dead, they could have done it. Why didn't they?"

"Do we kill the lion for preying upon the wildebeest? Of course not. That is its nature, and so it was with Humbaba. Unlike the lion, my brother is a god... precious, rare, powerful, and under the right circumstances, highly useful. Another solution was found, isolating him in a place where only those who transgressed would be slain, and all would have been well had he not crossed paths with Gilgamesh and Enkidu on that fateful day. I saved him, first from death at the hands of the great heroes of your cherished epic, and then from himself. Prior to our uniting, Humbaba and I were minor deities living precarious existences, with intermittent capabilities and little support among either the gods or humankind. Together, we were complete and powerful in ways we were not individually. I cultivated a new guise for us, one that drew upon our now intermingled and enhanced aptitudes, but I could not let my brother express his true nature—could not allow him to slaughter a family of those who had welcomed us into their home! It would have devastated the reputation of my name. I hoped he would have been satisfied knowing that his power stood behind the deity implored upon for protection by pregnant women and mothers."

"Protection from Dimme."

"Precisely. She was already our sworn enemy, and being half-god, half-Jinn, as we were, we knew her ways. We could fend her off and reap the bounty and acclaim of being the 'protectors of vulnerable humans,' among mortals and immortals alike."

"But you didn't *kill* her, and this is exactly what Humbaba is accusing you of. Did she always just 'slip away' as you said, or is your brother right that you fell in love with your role as 'protector of the vulnerable?' This was my question in the first place!"

"And my answer is the same. My brother does not grasp the larger picture, and neither do you. You cannot know the loneliness of entities like us. Being rare, we are precious, but we are also tremendously isolated, and when disputes break out in our peculiar and pugnacious little 'family,' we become increasingly cut off, and exceedingly vulnerable. As something of an outsider, I watched as scores of my brethren were slain, along with countless Jinn, across centuries in a pointless war. The position I held in the mortal pantheon gave me an advantage, and I was loath to give it up. Additionally, in her fiendish way, Dimme is adroit, crafty, and as difficult to slay as any god. Our kind can 'sense' each other across great distances, and because of our shared lineage as children of beings from the Abzu, even when I transmute my form to that of the winds, she can still see me, and I her. Had I planned carefully and struck with overwhelming force, or perhaps enlisted the aid of other superhuman entities, I could have possibly ended her miserable existence, but it would not have been a simple matter, and had I done so, both Humbaba and I would have eventually perished along with all the others, having lost our unique utility. I acted as I thought best, hoping that my gullible and incognizant brother would never realize that I avoided committing myself fully to the task of Dimme's destruction."

Lotte scoffed. "Which is exactly the promise you made to us! So, why should we believe you now, about *anything*?"

The strange god smiled sadly. "Because things have changed. Without the body of my birth, my individual powers are even less imposing than before. I must feed with far greater frequency, and with each meal, I take in less and less energy. I sense Humbaba's lot is the same, or soon will be. He has always been physically, and in some sense, *magically* stronger than I ever was, but he charts an ill-fated course. In stubbornness and lack of foresight, I fear he will die of starvation before he realizes the truth, then all is most assuredly lost. United once more, I believe we will be stable, but the balance between us will not remain as it was. Neither of us would be endemic to the body we inhabit. I would be unable to control him as I once did, though I hope to have the power to intervene before things get too far out of hand. This is something I cannot know with certainty until we have merged, but it remains my only chance, and I intend to try. I told him all of this, but he didn't believe me. So, I pursued the only course remaining. I took action, tried to reassimilate him, and hoped the reality of our changed situation would eventually prove itself to him."

Lotte sat for a moment as she took in the perplexing god's words. "All right, assuming I believe that, what about Dimme? I won't let her live, and no matter what you think about Olive, she's likely to feel the same way. This isn't negotiable with us."

Eric froze, and managed not to react audibly to this. *Shit, Lotte, how many times have I told you that's no way to talk to a god that can rip your head off? But do you listen to me? Noooooo.*

To Eric's surprise, Pazuzu let out a hearty laugh. "You are brave, young one, and you drive a hard bargain. In this case, we already struck the deal in the early hours of this most tiring day. At that time, I gave you my word, and so it will be. Let the situation with my brother not cloud your mind. As I have told you, I will no longer be in control. Humbaba will have his long-awaited vengeance. It will be our task to make sure he succeeds without creating a trail of destruction that will put us all in grave danger. But should you need additional reassurance, I will say this: your kind no longer seek the protection of their children from an ancient god who vanished from your world nearly seven hundred years ago. Preserving Dimme's life confers no benefit to us, and with fortune's aid, her extermination will further increase my brother's trust that we will henceforth be equal. Though Humbaba knew it not, this was the case when we last confronted the malevolent shrew, and last tasted freedom from within my body that we shared. The time for reckoning has been right for centuries, and now shall it be."

Lotte smiled and nodded. "I sense that's the best assurance we'll get, so Eric, you can start to breathe again."

*Right, breathe... no heads being ripped off. Whew!*

She quickly turned her attention back to Pazuzu. "But you have to tell me about this!"

*D'oh!*

"The last time you last faced Dimme, you were trapped by Iblis, right? What happened?"

The tiny hint of mirth that had briefly appeared on the god's visage rapidly disappeared. "As you correctly surmise, it all traces back to Iblis, as so many things do. At the end of the great war, he was quiet for a time, but then covertly restarted his quest to reopen the gate in the Rope of An and Ki that blocked the Jinn from returning home. Fortuitously, all of his attempts met with failure. His first ploy involved the creation of a religion. He was instrumental during the formative years of Zoroastrianism, and helped the Medians overthrow the Assyrian Empire. At the height of his influence, he convinced Nebuchadnezzar the Great to lay siege to Tyre, the seat of power of the Kings of the Jinn, possibly the closest he ever came to accomplishing his goals. After thirteen long years, the great king finally negotiated a favorable settlement, crushing Iblis's plans, and when Cyrus the Great forcibly curtailed the powers of the Zoroastrian Magi in 550 BC, the conniving Jinn was forced underground in Babylon."

Eric grinned. *May the blessings of Zoroaster smile upon you... or not.*

"It was around this time that he began to exploit the abilities of the ashen beast with whom you now associate. Fifty years later, the creature mysteriously wound up in the hands of the Kings of the Jinn."

Lotte nodded. "Yes, we know. Iblis's acolytes betrayed him, at the cost of their own lives. Only a small slice of the Afrit managed to survive, but there are apparently more parts of the beast out there somewhere, trapped inside Iblis's lamp prisons."

"Mmmm. Best they stay where they are. I know firsthand how maddening such an imprisonment can be, and these monsters might prove highly burdensome to control. The treachery you describe set Iblis back terribly. He fled far to the east to avoid the wrath of the Jinn Kings. Some believe he made clandestine forays back into Persia following the chaos of Alexander's conquest, or at points during the rule of the Sassanids. If so, no trace of him was found when Islam swept through those lands in the early seventh century of your common era. They seemed to have great enmity toward the notorious Jinn."

Tamanna's soft voice sounded from where she sat. "That would be my father's doing. As Eric knows, I'm the daughter of Shamhuresh, the Fifth King of the Jinn, who converted to Islam during the time of Muhammed. He wouldn't have tolerated Iblis's presence in Muslim lands."

Lotte seemed amazed, having not known Tamanna's heritage, but Pazuzu merely shrugged. "Nor were the older gods condoned any longer, at least by the common masses. The dangers to our kind increased dramatically as beliefs, and the methods of dealing with the supernatural, became less deferential and more *militant*. As unwelcome in the Christian world as she was under Islam, Dimme fled, as Iblis had, along the Silk Road. I elected not to follow. My brother chafed at the decision, but those in the east did not know my name. I would have been an outcast in unfamiliar territory, unguarded when I fed, isolated and desolate. I eked out an existence in the smallest and most remote settlements in the lands I knew, where the old ways still held. I monitored Dimme from afar, as I do now, but little did I know of her activities, or that, at some point, she became associated with Iblis."

"Right. She told us that he'd accepted her when no others would, showed her the love her family had always withheld. It all turned out to be a lie."

"As it so often is with Iblis. Why they tolerated his continued existence at the end of the war mystifies me. He falsely claimed that he supported the truce and would act to uphold the settlement and end the bloodshed. It seems the more brazen the liar, the more likely they are to be accommodated, even by credulous gods."

Lotte's eyes narrowed. "In the end, though, it all comes back to them—the liars. Dimme turned on Iblis and nearly gave us an opportunity to kill him, and now you'll have to answer to your brother for how you treated him. That's a truth you can't deny any longer. Eventually, it all falls apart."

"Perhaps, perhaps not. True, Iblis is dead, but many such as he are never properly held to task for their falsehoods. Even when they are, they often live long enough to reap the benefits of their mendacity. So it is with Iblis. In the year 1338 of your common era, I sensed Dimme coming ever closer, back to the lands of her origin, and mine. My brother's urgings could no longer be resisted, in large part because I had come to understand that preserving her life no longer proffered any benefit, and that perhaps her head on a platter would gratify the few believers who still remained. Knowing that she prospers in cities, places where population is dense and children, her favored meal, are abundant, I gathered all my strength, then set out to intercept her in a small caravan outpost near Issyk-Kul, a lake in the Heavenly Mountains of Central Asia. I assumed that, as always, she would flee, but I planned to chase her. In such a sparsely populated area, she would have few opportunities to feed, and my persistence would curtail those even further. It would exhaust us both, but eventually she would have to face me, and I felt certain that with the additional strength conferred by my brother's motivation, we could best her."

"But you didn't count on Iblis being there."

"No. How could I have known? I should have suspected something when Dimme uncharacteristically stood her ground in the little settlement, but Humbaba's exuberance overcame me. I sensed we had her and charged in for the kill. She smiled wickedly when I materialized inside the yurt where she awaited me. She was alone, but as I approached, the fire from a small brazier erupted and engulfed me in flame, along with some other, unidentifiable force. Realizing I had been tricked, I attempted to vanish, but the mystifying pressure held me fast. The walls of the yurt were suddenly torn away, and a host of armed men assailed me. Normally, an onslaught such as this would be a minor nuisance, but confined as I was, I truly feared for my life. In anger and frustration, I unleashed a powerful pox upon my attackers, and they fell to the ground, sickened in most horrible ways."

Lotte shuddered. "This is what you did to us in Harland Cheevers's basement in Atlanta. You made us feverish and nauseous."

"It is, for better or worse, the most dependable and fearsome of my own powers. With it, I brought famine to those who defied my will by contaminating their plants or water with disease. Under duress, I can initiate maladies in humans by concentrating infectious elements in the air that your kind cannot see. You were fortunate I was not stronger during our first encounter. You would not have survived. At Lake Issyk-Kul, I quickly identified and distilled the latent capacity of a dangerous pathogen present in the blood of just a few fleas on some nearby rats. It caused the most horrific blackening of my assailant's hands, with great, dark lumps appearing on their faces and necks. They collapsed with weakness and chills, vomiting bile, and I assume later died of their ailments."

"*Alter!* What you're describing is plague... bubonic plague! No one knows exactly where it came from or how it started, but it hit Europe in 1347, and it wiped out nearly half the population. Those men must have been bitten by other fleas and infected more people before they died. The settlement is along the Silk Road, so eventually the disease was bound to travel west. If this the origin of The Black Death, you can't understand the suffering you unleashed."

The terrible god surged forward in his seat. "Speak not to me of suffering! I languished in a prison for nearly seven hundred years, alone with only my thoughts of regret and recrimination! I battled for my existence with the sole means at my disposal, and I lacked the time to give full consideration to the consequences. In retrospect, it came to naught. I dispatched the most immediate threat, but soon, the inexplicable fire singed my flesh, and the mighty force compacted me into an ever-shrinking lump of charred bones and gristle. I lost consciousness, and when I awoke, I had no eyes to see, no ears to hear, no mouth to speak. I could vaguely sense my brother through some tiny and tenuous connection, but only Iblis's voice rang clear in the remnants of our minds. He told us our fate, that we were trapped inside a double-sided amulet that now hung around the neck of one of his slaves."

"Why didn't he just kill you," Lotte asked, having regained her courage after Pazuzu's outburst. "Why lock you away?"

"I asked the same question. For a time, I received no answer, but eventually he revealed what he wanted. He and Dimme had worked together to entrap me. She lent him her power, over which she had limited control, and let him do the job of eliminating her eternal nemesis, which she could never have accomplished alone, but she didn't realize that she, too, had fallen into a trap. Iblis devoured all her energy during the battle, and then ensnared her like he had me."

"Yes, he put an iron collar with gold trim around her neck. The construction was identical to your amulet in the museum in Atlanta. That's how we knew Iblis was involved. The device was horrible. It had spikes that would drive into her flesh when she didn't give him what he wanted."

"Very ingenious. He knew what he needed from her going forward, and that she had to give it to him willingly, even if grudgingly. He never lacked imagination, that one. He tricked Dimme into believing they were allies, and that gave him the opportunity to act on his plan, but he had no such advantage with me or my brother. His only leverage was the promise that if we lent him our strength, he would free us once the gate to his realm had been reopened."

"Did you believe him?"

"Of course not! Neither Humbaba nor I would humble ourselves before Iblis with little to no prospect of ever getting free. For once, my brother and I were united in our intransigence. He packed us away and periodically checked in to see if we had changed our minds. In exasperation and bitterness, he finally severed the connection between the two parts of the amulet, not understanding that the might of his diabolical artifact had been diminished exponentially. Even the thin strands of my brother's thoughts now vanished, but it seems neither of us ever bent to his will. Eventually, Iblis must have lost interest, the experiment with so much promise having never borne fruit. The amulets went their separate ways for reasons unknown, and each wound up as curiosities in your museums. Only his death, or the destruction of whatever item bound the enchantment, freed us, and Dimme alike."

A stony silence overtook the cozy little living room, as if night had suddenly fallen and the entire city had abruptly shut off their TVs, cell phones, and lights, and quietly gone to sleep. Lotte slid from her perch on the coffee table to the nearby couch, and Eric took the opportunity to slip into the room and join her, abandoning the few remaining grocery items that he'd failed to put away. He took her hand, and she gave him a reassuring squeeze, but her eyes remained fixed on the blank screen of the television at the far end of the room.

They sat that way for some time, until Eric started to get bored. He idly picked up the remote from the coffee table, pushed the power button, and scrolled through the guide until he found a college football game that was nearly over. He was about to mute the volume when the picture appeared. The game wasn't being shown. Instead, he saw a breaking news report with the headline, "Chaos Near the Penn Museum." Rather than mute the TV, he raised the volume so they could hear clearly.

"...tracking what seems to be an unrelated event across the street at Franklin Field, home of the Penn Quakers, where two security guards and four grounds maintenance workers were found dead early this evening. No names of the victims have been released and the cause of death is still under investigation, but police are urging the public to avoid the University of Pennsylvania area, and for those in the area already to stay in their homes, and for students to stay in their dormitories. Again, this is a developing situation that comes on the heels of a toddler who went missing in the Penn Museum parking garage earlier in the afternoon."

A distraught woman came on the screen, and bevy of reporters' microphones in her face. "I left Jonah in his stroller while I put his older brother and sister in the car. He was right behind me. I didn't see or hear anyone approach. The garage was almost empty. There were no cars around us. Please, if you know anything about my child's disappearance, I beg you, contact the police. I just want my son back. Please!"

The reporter returned along with a slightly blurry picture of a smiling little boy. "Amber Alerts were activated in the city and across the Delaware Valley, but so far, there have been no reported sightings of little Jonah Davis. If you have any information, or believe you have seen this child, please call—"

Lotte grabbed the remote and hit mute. "You're not going to find Jonah that way. He's been swallowed by an ancient Mesopotamian whale."

Eric was bewildered. "What? You think Humbaba took that kid? Why?"

She sadly shook her head. "Because it's the only logical explanation. That poor woman took her two older children to see the museum and pushed her two-year-old around in a stroller. What do you think the little boy did after he finally stopped fidgeting?"

"Oh, shit."

"Oh, shit is right. He bloody well fell asleep, and he must have been asleep when they went past Humbaba's medallion." She turned to Pazuzu. "Could your brother be in the body of that child? Is this possible?"

"It is," he answered, expressionless. "As I explained, Humbaba's magic is powerful, though sometimes erratic, and I often wonder if his prowess came at the expense of his acumen. He lacks the Jinn-like capability to dematerialize, but he has command over his form in other ways, its size, shape, and other aspects. I harnessed this capability to craft the image of me known best by your kind."

"The ones we saw in the museums," Eric exclaimed, "and the one from *The Exorcist!*"

"I am aware of the movie you reference from the memories of Harland Cheevers. It rivals the falsehoods peddled by Iblis! Do your kind actually believe in such drivel?"

Lotte snorted a little laugh. "See, I told you it was a stupid movie."

Eric squirmed. "It's *not* a stupid movie, but I get your point. It's not meant to be believed. Its purpose is to entertain people by being scary. I can see how you'd be a little miffed about it, though. You're not exactly the 'good guy' in the story."

The god scowled. "I am the very personification of evil, cruelly tormenting a young girl who commits no trespass, save adolescent curiosity. It is an affront to all I ever stood for. Those who depicted me in this way either knew nothing about me, or willfully distorted the truth. Sadly, story or not, this is all the unsophisticated and unquestioning audience of your 'modern' world knows of my once revered name. It is a travesty, worse than the fanciful pretenses in *The Epic of Gilgamesh*."

*So, you didn't like it.*

Eric simply kept his mouth shut until Lotte cut in. "All right, we understand. Can we please get back to Humbaba? Are you actually saying that... *monstrosity*... we saw on the rooftop terrace was the body of a toddler?"

"My brother used the energy of the men he no doubt killed and devoured at the location nearby the museum that was referenced on your wondrous screen. With it, he could assume whatever form he desired. His original appearance was much like mine, that of a human male, but his growth was stunted and dwarflike. He always spent much of his power to increase his height and girth, sometimes appearing gigantic. Over centuries, his barbarity and deviant sensibilities expressed themselves in the various ways you witnessed... snakes, claws, thorny spikes, and, of course, the innards of his victims displayed prominently on his face. This eventually became his most natural form, so it is no surprise that he presented himself that way to me."

"It surprised me," Lotte grumbled. "I also can't believe he'd be so callous as to take the body of a young child. Did he learn nothing from all those years battling Dimme?"

"I tried to tell you the things of which my brother is capable. It is his nature, and this is why he must sometimes be treated harshly. It is my hope that you now understand, and that we act with haste and in partnership to see our bargain through to its conclusion. Mark my words, the killing has just begun, and it will not stop until we bring Humbaba under a modicum of control... or terminate his existence once and for all."

Olive fumbled for her phone that sat on the nightstand by her bed, gave it a tap, and squinted as the screen's icy illumination pierced the darkness.

*Four forty-two a.m. Damn.*

Another sleepless hour had passed since she last checked the time. Despite being dog-tired, she simply couldn't banish the myriad thoughts swirling in her head. She endlessly replayed her failure to supply Pazuzu with the energy he needed to reassimilate his brother, and wondered with dismay how she might be more successful on their next attempt.

*If I can't figure it out, Humbaba might kill Pazuzu again, except this time it'll be Siddique's body that gets broken into smithereens.*

The loss of her friend's support and counsel, not to mention their burgeoning romance, weighed on her chest, making it difficult to breathe and to concentrate. Mutig's continued rejection also rankled. She worried she might have to part with the canine who no longer felt kinship with the abomination into which his once adored mistress had incomprehensibly morphed. The animal remade by Enki had become more than a companion to her. He bolstered her often patchy confidence, and he was intertwined with her aspirations to operate in a world where the ability to defend oneself against physical violence was critical. Without Mutig and Siddique, she once again found herself as she always had been, simply *Olive*, and Olive had never really been good enough.

*This is hopeless!*

"You do not sleep."

The voice shocked her. She shot upright in the bed and her phone skittered to the floor. "What the H-E Double L!"

Siddique's somewhat familiar voice, void of its accent, sounded in the once again darkened room, but his words were guided by Pazuzu. "I did not mean to startle you. I assumed you slept."

She waited a moment for her racing heart to decelerate. "Yeah, can't sleep. Too much on my mind. I'm afraid what happened at the museum might happen again, me not being able to control my powers, and all."

"This concerns me as well. It is why I am here."

"You have an idea?"

She heard the mysterious god walk toward the bed and sit near her on the edge. "Perhaps. I have fed. I am, for now, as strong as I can be, but I need to rest and absorb the energy I have consumed. If I do so in contact with your body, I can simultaneously probe your structure and makeup to gain insight into how I might coax from you what you cannot willingly provide."

"Umm, okay. That don't sound like such a terrible idea. What do you want me to do?"

"Simply lie in place next to me. I must proceed cautiously because of the entity with whom you share a body, but I merely need to observe and study. I will not feed or attempt to assume any sort of control over you... for now. Try to sleep, as it eases the process of exploring your inner architecture."

"I've been tryin' to sleep all night and haven't had much luck yet, but at least this will give me some hope, and maybe calm me down a little. What the heck, let's try it."

"Superb. Remove the medallion from around your neck and we shall begin."

"Woah, hold your horses there, mister. Isn't that kind of dangerous? I wear this stupid thing to keep Aicha from taking control over me... again! What makes you think she won't try something like that while you're sittin' there happily digesting and *probing* me?"

"She lacks the strength," he quickly replied. "If she had the capacity, she would have assumed dominance over your faculties when you removed the necklace on the rooftop terrace. It is still too soon for her, but her path is clear."

"I don't get it."

"Understandable. You are human, and this is beyond the scope of your experience, but consider what you know. A reservoir of mighty energy exists within you, does it not?"

"Yeah, I guess so."

"At times, you have called upon this power to accomplish extraordinary feats, yet at other moments, it evades you. Why do you think this is so?"

"If I knew the answer to that, I'd have probably been able to help you today, or yesterday at this point. Whatever."

"Perhaps, perhaps not, but if you knew, you may have had a *better* chance. Ask yourself, how do you *feel* when the energy flows in your veins?"

"I feel strong, and brave, and focused... like I can do *anything*... and I almost can!"

"And how else do you feel? What do you experience in the moments just before the power surges within you?"

Olive thought back to her encounter with the Jinn-eagle when it attacked Siddique. "I remember feeling all panicky. I didn't know what to do. I had my gun with me, and I thought about shootin' the rotten thing, but that was a dumb idea, 'cause I'd probably just hit Siddique. And then I... I...." Tears welled in her eyes. "I heard my daddy's voice. *Airhead*! That's what he calls me, and he's right—I *am* a dang airhead sometimes, but I hate it when he calls me that, and that I actually call *myself* that sometimes. I *hate* it, and I got so mad. I don't think I've ever been that mad. I almost bit straight through my tongue. Even after that eagle had flown away, I was still so crazy that I almost bashed you—er, Siddique, that is—against the trunk of the tree. I was totally off the wall!"

"And along with your anger came your feelings of might."

"Yeah. That's not the only time, neither. I got mad again, after the fight on the terrace, thinking how unfair everything was for Harland Cheevers, that he had to die, and he didn't do nothin' to deserve it. I wanted to rip this necklace off and make somebody *pay*!"

"Are you beginning to understand?"

"Sort of, I guess. You're saying that when I'm angry, that's when I can get at my powers. I guess that makes sense. I was scared on that rooftop when you called me over, and nervous. I was trying to focus, but I wasn't *angry*. That's why I couldn't help you."

"Correct, and I did not have enough energy or knowledge of your inner fabric to draw out what I needed. The fact remains, Aicha could not take command of you at that moment. Thus, I conclude that she is still too weak to gain ascendency."

"But you think she knows how to do it, right?"

"She offers you her energy when you are angry, or perhaps under the influence of any extreme emotional state in which you abandon your wits. She likely stokes those feelings, and they build into a frenzy, causing you to lose control. You remove the amulet to access her power, but your mind is open and unguarded. Freed from the medallion's paralyzing effects, she extends beyond the space that confines her. If this continues, she will gradually dominate enough of your system that she can reassert supremacy. She baits you with the extraordinary feats you can accomplish, but use them enough, and you will be hers once again."

Olive felt overwhelmed. "So... so what do I do?"

"You must find a way to access Aicha's energy without losing your composure. It will mean exerting dominance over the foreign elements within your system in a methodical, disciplined manner. She will resist, but you must overcome. It will not be easy, perhaps impossible, but it is your only long-term solution, short of turning your back on your capabilities and wearing the medallion for the remainder of your days."

"That's not what I want, but I don't think I can figure this out quickly. Methodical and disciplined ain't exactly my strong points."

"I agree. This is why I propose exploring an alternative method."

"If I'm not wearing the amulet, though, won't she just try to sneak out a little bit while I'm sleeping, or trying to sleep?"

"I will wake you if I detect that, but I surmise that she is still not ready to attempt such a feat. Trust me, I have no desire to see you fall into the clutches of Aicha Kandicha. Without you, all is lost."

With a shrug, Olive lifted the leather strap over her head, placed the white medallion on the bedside table, and lay back down. As always, she perceived a slight tingling, though she still wasn't sure if that was simply her own imagination and excitement running away with her. Pazuzu slipped under the covers beside her, and she felt the warmth of Siddique's body against hers once more.

Suddenly, she froze. "Y'all ain't wearin' any clothes."

"Of course not. I materialized in this room. My garments are elsewhere. I presumed you would not mind sharing a bed with your mate."

"He ain't my *mate*. Well, not exactly. It's kind of messy."

"As are most things with humans. Why you complicate your short lives so is a mystery my kind has never solved. As I sift through the grains of his thoughts, I see that he cares for you, that he wants you, yet he judges himself inferior, and frets that your differences might tear you apart."

"I worry about that too, and not just differences between us, but things that are outside our control, like being judged by your friends and family, or society, or even how stuff that you know in your heart ain't right might still mess with your head without you knowing. There's a whole bunch of things to consider."

"Still, you want him back."

"More than anything. It's like you say about needin' me: I feel like, without him, all is basically lost."

"Perhaps therein lies your answer, and all else is not unlike the stars in the sky—present, and acknowledged to exist, but in great measure, inconsequential."

"Yeah, unless some meteorite whacks into us again like it did when the dinosaurs went extinct. That would be pretty consequential, and so can the ramifications of all those things that bother me and Siddique about our relationship."

"Understood, but even in the infinitely small chance that your world met its end during an unavoidable celestial collision, would you not wish to perish in the arms of the one you love?"

The clarity of Pazuzu's reasoning astonished her. *Could it really be that simple? Is feeling like this how you know you've just gotta let go of all the stuff you can't do nuthin' about and just take a chance?*

Olive closed her eyes, and after a moment, she smiled in the darkness, reveling in the majestic — and utterly insignificant — beauty of the far away stars.

# CHAPTER 15

**Philadelphia, Pennsylvania, Sunday, October 29, 2017**

Eric felt a soft nudge against his shoulder, and a tickle of breath near his ear, as sleep grudgingly gave way to groggy consciousness.

"I have coffee," Lotte whispered as she gently cajoled him from slumber.

It was true. Upon smelling it, he shakily extracted his arm from under the covers and held out his hand.

"There's breakfast downstairs, too," she said, pressing the cup into his palm. "You must be starving. It's nearly noon."

*Holy crap. I've been out for, like, sixteen hours.* The last thing he remembered was stumbling into the bedroom after a quick and much needed shower. Utterly exhausted, he hadn't even bothered with dinner. Now, dim light trickled past the edges of the flimsy, pull-down shade, and he heard the soothing patter of rain against the window.

He took a sip of coffee, and she gently stroked his hair. "How's your head?"

"It still hurts, but I guess it feels better. It's no worse, anyway. What's going on? Where is everybody?"

"Downstairs, mostly. When I got up around nine, I found Tamanna 'meditating' in the living room, trying to assimilate the energy she collected on her little overnight feeding foray. Olive came down about an hour later and told me that Pazuzu had waltzed into her room early this morning wanting to sleep with her."

"Exsqueese me?"

"*Alter!* Not like *that*, silly. He just wanted to be in contact with her, try to get a sense of how much control Aicha has and how they might be able to leverage her magic the next time we meet Humbaba. I'm surprised how calm Olive seems about it. I can hardly bear seeing Siddique controlled this way, let alone having to share a bed with him."

"Seriously. What a mess. Poor Olive. Poor all of us, really. He's our friend too, yours in particular. I hope Pazuzu lives up to his word and lets Siddique go, but I have my doubts."

"I do too, but right now, we don't have much choice but to trust him. In any case, he's still in Olive's room, presumably in the same condition as Tamanna."

"Umm, if all our guardian protectors are basically unconscious, doesn't that make us a little vulnerable?"

"Vulnerable to who? Pazuzu can monitor his brother and will know if he starts coming closer, and the Jinn who hired the mercenaries... what was his name again?"

"Ornias."

"Right, Ornias. He has no idea where we are. Anyway, Karšift is still on the roof. He'll alert Tamanna if he sees anything suspicious. I think we're okay, at least for now. Don't you want some breakfast?"

Lotte's logic and confidence reassured him. Eric stiffly eased out of bed and threw on some clothes, made a quick trip to the bathroom, then stumbled downstairs.

Tamanna sat cross-legged in her familiar chair by the window, wrapped in a thick blanket the Airbnb owners had generously provided.

Olive slouched on the couch, idly watching NFL pregame on the TV. "Y'all finally decided to get up, huh?"

He couldn't resist a slight chuckle. "I had a little help from the coffee fairy. I still feel really weak, but I'm probably just starving. Who's playing?"

"The Eagles play at one o'clock. That'll probably be the game we get here. Falcons play the Jets. I don't really care who your rotten ol' Patriots play."

"Yeah, it doesn't really matter. They'll win anyway."

She clutched her throat and gagged, then stuck out her tongue at him as Lotte handed him a dish of scrambled eggs and heavenly smelling bacon.

"Wow, thanks. This is awesome. Coffee's great too. I should get the shit beat out of me more often."

"I'm sure that can be easily arranged," she replied without a hint of sarcasm. "Sit down. I'll get you more coffee."

He joined Olive on the couch and eagerly started to eat. "Where's Mutig?"

"Got me. Under the kitchen table, maybe, or else upstairs. I don't know what to do anymore. I've tried everything I can to make him like me, but he doesn't want to be near me at all. He acts like I don't *smell* right no more."

"Yeah, that's probably not far off the mark. Lotte told me Pazuzu spent the night with you. She said he was trying to figure out how to access your power more consistently. Any luck?"

"Well, I'm not really sure. He's still sleepin', or doing whatever these crazy things do after they 'eat.' I wasn't about to bug him. We did talk last night, though, and what he told me made sense. Aicha's energy floods into me when I get super angry or emotional. She might even pour gasoline on the fire to make me madder... mad enough to lose my cool and rip off this necklace." She thumped her hand to her chest.

Lotte joined them, sitting on the loveseat Pazuzu had occupied the day before. She passed Eric a fresh cup of coffee and settled back with her tea. "Sorry, I didn't mean to interrupt. Go on."

Olive gave a nonchalant wave. "Once I don't have that thing around my neck no more, all bets are off. I've got power — power to burn — but while I'm using it, Aicha is growing inside of me, gettin' stronger. Pazuzu says that eventually she'll take me over again unless I either never take the medallion off, or somehow learn how to control both the flow of energy and Aicha at the same time."

"It's not unlike my son." Tamanna had opened her deep, brown eyes, but had not otherwise moved a muscle.

Lotte seemed flummoxed. "You have a son?"

"Is it so surprising? I am half-human, and not even Jinn are immune to the passions of the heart. If they were, I wouldn't be here. After nearly eleven hundred years, I finally succumbed to the appeals of one particularly favored lover. Sadly, he didn't have long to enjoy his beloved child. He died while visiting his family near Mount Lebanon... an innocent bystander in the Druze-Christian conflict in the middle of the nineteenth century. Khalil was only seven."

Eric did the math. "That would make him, like, a hundred and fifty years old now."

"One hundred sixty-four, actually. He just had a birthday. His Jinn blood makes him long lived, as does mine, but like Olive, he struggles with what little magic he inherited. Male half-Jinn typically have far less power than the women, and some none at all, which is why I've concentrated my efforts along matrilineal lines."

Olive eagerly cut in. "But you said your son — Khalil — has some powers, and that he has the same problem I do?"

"It's not identical, but similar. Bonafide Jinn assume dominance over their mortal host's neural network, giving them a platform from which to easily express their natural magic. Half-Jinn are different. They inherit power that is alien to their physical bodies, and which they must learn to control. If they possess any magic at all, it usually expresses itself first in an infantile tantrum, where it leaps out, unbidden, to quell the child's fierce desire. They must learn self-discipline to harness their energy on command. This is the training I give to those I accept as students, but many struggle, and some never master the technique. Try as I might, I cannot reach them. It's like teaching someone without lungs how to breathe. I can't understand their experience, so I can't instruct them how to channel their abilities. Khalil had to find his own way. His capabilities are inconsistent, but with time, he has improved. I think his situation and yours are comparable, and that with great effort you might gain access to at least a portion of your powers."

"Do y'all think he could *help* me?"

For several moments, Tamanna closed her eyes in thought. "Khalil has no training as a guide, and since emotional temperaments vary so widely—everything from a slow boil to a volcanic eruption—one half-Jinn's experience may not translate easily to another. With you, there is the added danger of Aicha's threatening presence. Still, it's possible that the things my son has learned could be of benefit to you. You were not born with these gifts, so you lack familiarity with even the most basic and natural aspects of your circumstances. That alone might warrant taking the chance, but I fear that our desperate need for the power you possess makes the decision all too simple. This pains me, because it may put your existence in grave danger if you fail to control Aicha, but if you're brave enough to try, I think it's worth the effort."

Olive didn't hesitate. "I don't know if I'm brave or just stupid, but I know I can't keep on livin' like this. I *have* to try, and I don't have the faintest idea how. If your son is willing to help me, I'm all in."

For Eric, the dreary afternoon passed with blissful and relaxing calm. Tamanna and Olive retreated upstairs to the third bedroom that had surprisingly been left vacant. There, they initiated a marathon Skype session with Khalil. Lotte fetched her laptop, hopped onto the couch beside Eric, and continued to intently review various versions of *The Epic of Gilgamesh*, as well as several interpretative texts that she'd bought online. Eventually, Mutig padded out from under the kitchen table and curled up between them.

Eric felt his tension melt away. *I don't think it gets any better than this. This is what I was born to do – nothing... except scratch this dog's ears and smile occasionally at Lotte.*

To his amazement, she smiled back, a real smile, with teeth and everything. He wondered what he'd done to deserve such favor, or really to deserve having such a vibrant and exciting person in his life at all. Then he ran his hand across the aching lump on the back of his head, and it all became as clear and sharp to him as the gorgeous view out of the giant glass window at 246 Holton Hill Road on a crisp fall day.

*I pay my dues to be here, but this is my life. This is the life I chose, even though I didn't really have much of a choice... not after I met Lotte.*

It dawned on him that at this very moment, he felt more at peace with this "decision that wasn't a decision" than he ever had.

Unsurprisingly, the Eagles crushed the winless 49ers, and much to what he knew would be Olive's dismay, the Patriots dominated the Chargers.

*Her Falcons took care of the Jets, so that'll lessen the sting. I wonder how she's doing up there.*

He didn't dare interrupt for fear of breaking her concentration or intruding into a place or activity where he simply didn't belong. Instead, he settled into the 4:30 Dallas vs. Washington game while Lotte put away her computer and slipped away to the kitchen. Seeing the Redskins take the field brought Blake Harris to his mind. The man would undoubtedly have been watching his favorite team play right now, but for what happened two years ago. Hard as it was, Eric felt a slight pang of sympathy for the desperate and duplicitous man who had threatened him and everyone he loved. Dying in the way he did must have been awful, but it had been necessary to secure their safety, and to placate their infernal ally, the Afrit.

A disturbance on the couch woke Eric from a late afternoon nap. Lotte had returned, displacing Mutig, who hopped to the floor and stared at him expectantly. Eric glanced at the TV. It was halftime, and the Cowboys led 14-13. "I slept through the entire first half."

"You did. You obviously still need rest. I didn't want to bother you."

"Thanks. It looks like Mutig wants to go out. Maybe I'll take him, try to do at least something productive today."

She laughed and gave him a quick kiss, which buoyed his spirits before he trailed out the door with the excited dog into the misty dusk. As they descended the steps, he looked toward the roof of their little Germantown house in search of Karšift, the bright-eyed raven who monitored the area.

*At least, I hope that's what he's doing. I don't see him up there, but he might be trying to stay out of sight. I wonder when he feeds, and what he feeds on? Sleeping pigeons?*

He sauntered down the street, enjoying the cool air and quiet surroundings despite the light rain that intermittently fell, stopping frequently so Mutig could sniff around or pee.

*If he goes number two, I'll have to go back to the house and get a baggie. Should have thought of that.*

Right on cue, Mutig dragged him to a scraggly patch of grass near a driveway and squatted. Eric nervously waited while the poor dog did his business, then tightened the drawstrings on his hoodie against the wind and swiftly steered him across the street. As they hustled back toward their Airbnb, a car appeared in the alley next to the house, its headlights a hazy orb of illumination in the damp air. Painstakingly, it eased into the road, then hung a left in his direction. The vehicle hadn't gone far before the driver clicked on their high beams.

Eric squinted against the onrush of blinding light. "Seriously, dude?" Panic suddenly assailed him.

*If this is trouble, I'm cut off from the house! Even if Karšift sees me, it'll be too late. There won't be anything he can do to stop them from nabbing me... or killing me!*

He frantically tugged at Mutig's leash, trying to get away from the street and into the maze of little yards that ran in front of, and sometimes between, the row houses. The dog seemed to sense his anxiety, and with unnatural apprehension, began to growl and bark at the approaching car. Canine muscles tensed and rippled as he strained at the lead, and it was all Eric could do just to hold on.

The headlights grew steadily closer. The car moved lethargically, far too slow even for this densely populated street in inclement weather. Mutig continued his fearsome display, sometimes choking from the collar around his bulging neck.

Just as the vehicle came within a car's length, it suddenly accelerated. Eric desperately tried to catch a glimpse of the occupants, but the bright headlights obscured his vision, and by the time he could see, the car had whizzed past. "Damn!"

Mutig continued to bark at the fleeing vehicle until a porch light from a nearby house dispelled the misty gloom.

Eric bent and stroked the dog's shoulders. They felt like lumps of granite. "Come on, boy. Let's get out of here. We don't want to cause any trouble."

*Well, any* more *trouble. Those people in the house across the street are gonna find a mess in the morning, but I'm sure as hell not going back to clean that up now!*

They hastened back to the Airbnb, bustled up the steps to the porch, and Eric put the key in the doorknob. Just as he did, he heard the flutter of wings behind him.

He turned and saw that Karšift had landed on the porch railing. "There you are! Did you see what happened?"

The bird cocked its head and flashed him a quizzical look.

"I'm sorry. I must have spaced out, thinking about other things. I didn't mean to go so far. Then a car came around the corner and flashed its bright lights. It seemed like it was looking for something. I don't know, maybe it was nothing, just somebody on the wrong street. I was hoping you might have seen them. You probably don't even understand what I'm saying, do you?"

The inscrutable raven suddenly hopped off the railing and with a quick flutter of his wings sailed across the small porch and onto Eric's shoulder. Afraid to move, he finally turned his head and looked up at the bird who loomed above him.

Their eyes briefly met before Karšift thrust his head into Eric's temple. *'Understand.'*

The creature's thoughts washed across his mind like a gentle breeze that imperceptibly cools the skin on a hot summer's day, not so much words as impressions. "Wow, you can talk, sort of. Who knew?"

*'I came when dog barked. Car already gone. Could have followed, but then cannot watch house. You safe, so came back here.'*

"That's cool. What do you make of what happened?"

The raven's head twitched against Eric's forehead. *'Know not. Many cars come and go in alley. None dangerous, so far. Could be nothing, or maybe noisy dog scared trouble away. Can't say. Maybe don't go so far next time.'*

"Yeah, my bad. Lesson learned. I'm really sorry."

Eric detected feelings akin to amusement in the currents of Karšift's thoughts before the raven launched into the air and disappeared into the murky darkness. He shook his head, opened the door, and slipped inside, Mutig at his heels.

The little house smelled yummy, and he realized Lotte was cooking the German casserole she'd been assembling, with ham and cheese, and just a touch of sauerkraut, which in her hands always seemed to come out better than the restaurant version. He stood for a moment, inhaling the familiar and comforting scents, and tried to decompress.

It wasn't long before she poked her head around the corner. "I heard you come in. Good walk? Are you just going to stand there? Eric, is something wrong?"

His body language having clearly given him away, he slowly unhooked Mutig's leash and took off his jacket. "I'm not certain. We had a run in with a suspicious car. It might have been nothing, but it definitely rattled me... and Mutig. I think he might have actually scared them off, if they were really threatening us at all."

"Who could it have been? It can't possibly be Ornias and the people who attacked us in Middleburg. How could they have found us?"

"You got me. Like I say, it might not have been anything, but something just seemed *off*. One interesting thing did come out of it. I learned that Karšift can talk."

"That doesn't exactly surprise me."

"Why not? How would you know such a thing?"

"Well, it's kind of a coincidence, really. After what happened with Margot, Siddique got really interested in Zoroastrianism and wanted me to explain it to him. Honestly, I don't know that much about it, other than the basics, but I told him I'd do a little research. Imagine my surprise when Karšift's name popped up, described in the ancient texts as a great, black bird — probably a raven. He was apparently some sort of messenger of early Zoroastrianism. Assuming this is the same Karšift, I figured he must be able to communicate at some level."

"Yeah, he can communicate all right. He said we should stick close to the house where he can keep an eye on us."

"Seems like good advice, no matter what really happened with the car. At least you're safe now. Come on, help me make the salad. Olive will be starving when she finally comes down. She's been up there all afternoon."

Eric happily threw himself into the simple and normal task of preparing food. He wondered what it might be like if this were their little house, where they regularly fixed dinner together after their respective days securing flooring contracts or teaching bright-eyed college students the finer points of data-driven archaeological methods. His fantasy of domestic bliss quickly evaporated.

*Nah, it'll never be this simple or quiet with Lotte, not on any regular basis. Even if we ever get all these monsters from another dimension out of our lives, she'll still want more than this. If I wanted this all the time, I should have stayed with Erica, but then I'd have spent every night wondering where Lotte was and what she was doing.*

She gave him a big smile as she passed him an onion to be peeled, and he knew he'd made the right decision.

Salad completed, Eric moseyed back into the living room to check the score just as Olive bustled down the stairs. "How did it go?" he asked his weary looking comrade. "You were up there a long time."

"Tell me about it," she huffed. "I mean, Khalil is nice and all for helping me out, but this was a major crash course! I wanted to stop hours ago, but Tamanna kept pushing me on. She finally let me go because the smell of that food was makin' me hungrier than a tick on a teddy bear!"

Eric laughed. "That'll make Lotte happy. Let's go eat."

"I did learn some things," she continued as they marched into the kitchen. "He gave me words for what I feel when all that energy runs through me, and that helps me separate one sensation from another. He says I'll have to identify and isolate every aspect of what's happenin', and then figure out how to control each detail individually. I think he's crazy. I'll never be able to do that, but I have to admit I learned a whole lot from him and could probably learn a bunch more. I'm just not sure there's gonna be time."

They ate silently, quickly, and gratefully, especially for each other's company in yet another uncanny and perilous situation, though the empty fourth chair at the kitchen table reminded them of Siddique's absence.

Eric finished first. He bussed his plate to the dishwasher, filled Mutig's bowls with food and water, then wandered back into the living room. Dallas had prevailed over Washington 33-19, but something far more urgent quickly caught his attention. "Oh, shit. You both better come see this."

Lotte and Olive darted into the room, and he pointed at the screen. A red banner scrolled across the bottom of the picture. After two passes, they'd all absorbed the message:

ALERT: At least seven people reported missing in the area around Lincoln Financial Field after today's Eagles game. Some eyewitnesses claim to have seen an unidentified animal which may be dangerous. Police ask the public to avoid the South Philadelphia East Area while a search is conducted.

"*Scheiße!* It's just like Pazuzu said. Humbaba isn't going to stop. It's only going to get worse. We need to let the others know what's happening!"

She bounded up the stairs while Eric grabbed the remote and started to flip through the channel guide. He found a local station running an emergency news bulletin that contained interviews with people who had been in the parking lots around the stadium. Some claimed to have seen an unusual creature, slithering deftly between cars, always too fast to be clearly observed. The announcers speculated that the disappearances could be linked to the bodies of the ground crew and security guards found killed, and by more recent reports, horribly mutilated, at Franklin Field yesterday.

"Yeah, bingo," Eric muttered. "This is turning into a bloodbath. At this point, they might call out the Pennsylvania National Guard."

"Exactly," Pazuzu announced as he and Lotte strode into the room. "We must act far more quickly than even I had surmised. Humbaba eats voraciously to maintain his strength, and if it is true that he inhabits the body of a small child who has little knowledge of the world, he has little perspective to understand the dangers of his actions. If your authorities find and kill him with weapons he has yet to fully comprehend, then all is lost. We must strike now, fully prepared, or not."

Tamanna emitted a loud and cynical laugh as she descended the stairs. "Ha! You know we can't best Humbaba in combat. Neither you nor I are at full strength, and I'm not even sure you have the capacity to get there any longer. Even with Olive's help, which is by no means a given, or the energy I could harvest from Nadia when she gets here, it would still be a struggle we'd probably lose. This is suicide."

The agitated god turned to her. "There is another who can help us."

"Ah, yes, the famous Afrit. I have yet to make its acquaintance. There's little question the creature's assistance would be of benefit, assuming we can strike an agreeable compact that doesn't involve your brother's demise."

"Leave that to me," Lotte cut in. "We've bargained ambiguously with the Afrit in the past, and the monster's circumstances and way of operating have changed dramatically over time. I think I can get it to help us, but that's not our biggest problem. Pazuzu, great one, is your brother still in roughly the same vicinity he's been in since the battle at the museum?"

"He has not strayed far from the location in which he finally settled."

"Right, so he *must* be hiding somewhere near the sports stadium. How in the world are we supposed to confront him in an area closed to the public and teeming with police? Also, there are going to be surveillance cameras *everywhere* down there! We can't possibly disable all of them. They'll identify us for sure, and probably link us with the disappearances and deaths. Even if we're somehow able to corral Humbaba, it'll be the end for Eric and me, maybe Olive as well."

All were silent as they pondered Lotte's words.

Tamanna finally spoke. "There may be a way. I have an idea that will take a bit of luck to pull off, but it will give us our best chance. Unfortunately, it all depends on the Afrit. Is the creature still miniscule compared with its normal size and capabilities?"

Lotte shrugged. "We don't know what effect consuming the Jinn-eagle might have had, and there's only one way to find out. I'd been hoping to delay the summoning a bit longer, but it seems our hand is being forced. I guess it's time to find out if our ace in the hole has digested its most recent meal."

Despite the humble surroundings of the narrow garage, the Afrit's portal glistened, just as it had when attached to Lotte's bizarre wardrobe, gone now for so many years. As always, she sat at the apex of the black marble board, chanting under her breath and rhythmically bobbing her head. The candles burned in their bowls, tucked into their slots on the arced stone slab, and near the base of the frame, which had heated and taken on its signature, multicolored glow.

After Tamanna had moved her car, Eric had backed the van out and reversed it into the driveway so they could unload the flight cases that housed the portal and its supporting components. He and Olive now flanked Lotte, while Pazuzu and Tamanna stood in the shadows near the closed door of the garage, curious observers of the ancient ritual to which neither had ever believed they might be privy. All remained silent as the thick and massive pane of glass darkened, and tendrils of billowing ash groped outward toward the flames.

Eric jumped when sparks flew from the black swirls. This had happened before when they first summoned the creature after it had ingested Ninurta, but the display still startled him. At the same time, it also provided some encouragement. It seemed to signal that the Afrit's power and abilities had increased, but along with those enhancements might once again come unpredictable demands.

*I wonder what the damn thing is gonna want now beside its little joy rides into our world. For us to read to it before freakin' bedtime? Actually, that would be kind of cool.*

As the ash coalesced into the monster's head and shoulders, it became clear that this was no longer the imp it had been on their trip south. The molten streaks on its black, pumice-like skin, shone brighter, as did the panoply of blues, oranges, and burning yellows that festooned the beast's wings, and now its eyes as well. When fully formed, the Afrit stood well over six feet tall, not as large as it had once been, but vastly more substantial and intimidating than before.

The creature had always been a frightening presence, but Eric pondered the recent changes in its demeanor, notwithstanding its absorption of Uri's life force. The Afrit had undergone a shattering loss, an experience with which Eric could relate, and in a very real sense was no longer the entity they had come to know. The being had sacrificed a major part of itself to ensure Iblis's end. What portion remained seemed to have regressed back to its transactional ways and self-preserving nature. Amazing as it seemed, he missed the feeling of camaraderie they'd developed with the curmudgeonly brute, and Eric wondered if it would still battle for them with the same zeal it had once exhibited.

Lotte rose and addressed the remarkable wonder before her. "Great one, thank you for answering my call. You look absolutely incredible! Far mightier than before."

The beast gazed downward and flexed its talons, then glanced over its shoulder and beheld the magnificence of its batlike wings.

"We find ourselves once again in need of your assistance. You know of Pazuzu and his quest to reunite with his brother. That didn't exactly go as planned, and now Humbaba is running amok in this city. We need to track him down and subdue him so Pazuzu can bring him under control. Short of that, we need to kill him. Humbaba is extraordinarily powerful. Will you help us?"

Wings and tail quivered as the creature swayed before her. It was impossible to glean any insight into the monster's ruminations from its visage, but it seemed strangely hesitant, wavering even longer than usual.

Lotte flashed Eric a quizzical and nervous look before she turned back to the Afrit. "Of course, you'll probably want to know the bargain. My hope is that we'll be able to bring Pazuzu's brother under control, so our understanding will have to be similar to the deal we made before. I can't offer you a specific victim right now, but we're facing so many dangers, I practically have to start a database to keep up with all of them. Surely, one will present itself soon enough. You can't argue much about how things turned out the last time we made a pact like this. I mean, look at you! I'd hope that you trust me, and like before, if it doesn't work out, I again offer myself as collateral. One way or another, you'll have your spoils."

Eric squirmed with dismay, but the Afrit seemed strangely unmoved. It lifted its horned head to the ratty ceiling of the cramped garage as if it could see the expanse of the heavens beyond. *'Yes, the spoils... always the spoils. It was not until we consumed the energy of beings from realms such as ours that we realized what a quagmire in which we find ourselves ensnared. The power we receive from ingesting those of your kind can make us strong, but it can never match that received from the likes of the malfeasant Ninurta, or now this avian that proved to be much more than a simple eagle. Once again, we are complete – different, yes, but complete, nonetheless. Indeed, this time you lived up to your end of the bargain,* Sadat Alnaar, *but it is unclear whether you can deliver another prize so worthy. If, as is likely, we are diminished by this dangerous otherworldly entity who you ask us to challenge, we see no clear path back to our current state of unity.'*

Eric did a facepalm. *Great. Now Chuckles only wants gods and Jinn for snacks. This is getting to be totally above our pay grade.*

Lotte appeared equally confounded, but it was Tamanna who spoke out. "Just as my father told me. Sometimes he wondered if the Kings of the Jinn had done the right thing, sparing the woeful little creature that turned up at Utnapishtim's door, for whom everything was always 'quid pro quo.' I wonder: who might put me back together if I were broken? Nobody! I'd bear the scars, or I'd die, but I'd do so with the knowledge that I acted in good faith, not for what I might get in return."

The Afrit bristled. *'Who are you to speak in this manner?'*

"My name is Tamanna. I'm the half-Jinn daughter of Shamhuresh, the Fifth King of the Jinn, who protected you from afar centuries ago, though it's doubtful you ever met him. But I'm not talking to you as a Jinn, or a king, or a god. I'm speaking to you as someone who has lived long enough to know when to place your faith in something, and in whom. Your beloved *Sadat Alnaar* has never let you down, and now she even offers her own life as sacrifice to enlist your assistance. What more proof do you need that her heart is sincere?"

*'Never have we questioned her sincerity. We know her heart, perhaps better than any other. Our aim has always been to regain what was once lost and to ensure we are never made vulnerable again. We violated that guiding principle, and it nearly destroyed us. This is simply not our way.'*

"Then change! Creature of fire, the quagmire that ensnares you is one of your own making. Haven't you come to realize that fate delivers unexpected – and often unwelcome – outcomes, causes that bring unforeseen effects? Existence is uncertain, even for powerful beings like you and me. The goal isn't to retreat into some primordial state of perceived 'perfection,' it's to adapt to life as it happens. Yes, much can be lost, but much can be gained as well. It's true that you might be damaged in the battle to come, and that may not be instantly rectified, but you'll earn the gratitude and allegiance of allies who may help you in the future. Dare I say: a measure of friendship."

*'You speak as might a human, which is logical, given your parentage.'*

Tamanna laughed. "And you act like one! I know of your need to visit our world. The Eternal Flame isn't enough for you anymore, is it?

You're as much of a half-breed as I am. What happens to you if we face Humbaba and all meet our end? Who will tend to you then? Think about it, Afrit. What *really* happens if you say no? The changes in you have already occurred. The part of you that acted as it did, sacrificing itself in the Rope of An and Ki, is proof of that. The portion of you that remains simply hasn't acknowledged what that means going forward—or you have, and you don't like what you see."

The Afrit hissed as its wings shot violently outward and the beast's scorpion tail twitched menacingly above its shoulder.

Pazuzu rapidly stepped between them. "Enough of this! Fighting amongst ourselves will solve nothing. Creature of fire, if you demand a god to secure your assistance, I give you one. I have sworn to end Dimme's existence, and I see no more fitting an end than roasting her bones to slake your appetite. It may take time, but if I fail to deliver, you can settle the score with me, since I am responsible for what now needs to be done. Are we agreed?"

The Afrit stood motionless as its anger seemed to morph into puzzlement. *'Has your dark-skinned companion lost his mind? What is he prattling about?'*

Lotte came to the rescue. "Great one, that's Pazuzu, who you met in the house where you later consumed the Jinn-eagle. He's... well... *taken over* Siddique's body. His old one got a little beat up. Well, more than a little. It's a long story. In any case, he hasn't gone crazy, and my desire to see Dimme's end is as important to me as it is to him. But if he doesn't reunify with his brother, that will be a lot harder to accomplish, maybe impossible. He's telling the truth. I know it's a stretch, but it's the best we have to comply with your wishes. What do you say?"

The creature glowered at Siddique, now Pazuzu, and lowered its wings. *'Fate has delivered an unexpected opportunity that sidesteps, for now, the impasse between us. We accept the unconventional bargain with this god, and hope that this engenders amongst you the gratitude of which you speak. Let the rings bind our pact.'*

# CHAPTER 16

Olive clung desperately to her phone as the vista of Philadelphia's lights unfolded beneath her. The Afrit held her close, enfolded in the darkness of its body, from which it had banished all radiant colors.

Still, she shivered. "For a creature supposedly from the 'realm of fire,' you sure aren't very warm! More like gettin' hugged by a dang ol' lump of coal, if you ask me."

The beast made no response.

Lotte had warned her that it would be cold, and they were farther north, as well as later in the season, than when Olive's friend had once similarly flown in the arms of the enigmatic monster. Eric's scruffy but still durable Bruins hoodie helped, but icy late October winds whipped her face and hands, and cut through her cargo pants as though they were made of tissue.

She brought the phone to her lips. "Y'all, I can't take much more of this!"

Lotte was quick to reply. "We know, but we got you as close to Humbaba's location as Pazuzu thought was safe. Just hang on, and he'll give you more specific directions in a minute."

After striking their bargain in the garage, everyone had loaded into the van, save Karšift and the Afrit, who flew in the darkness above. They even brought Mutig along, agreeing that all available firepower needed to be at hand. For fear of alarming Humbaba, who presumably traced his brother's movements, they eschewed the highway and drove slowly and indirectly along smaller streets, toward the patch of land embraced by a bend in the Delaware river where the City of Philadelphia had situated its various sports facilities.

On Pazuzu's instructions, Eric had pulled the van to the side of the road at the intersection of 18th and Wolf Street, where an attractive churchyard cemetery hosted some trees not yet absent their leaves. Olive had disembarked and slipped into the underbrush where she rendezvoused with the Afrit. Together, they sailed into the night sky, and she watched as the van drove off to continue its meandering journey.

Tamanna's plan was simple. The hope was that Humbaba would continue to periodically monitor his brother's whereabouts, or possibly Tamanna, who had revealed her presence to the terrible god during their battle on the museum terrace. As a half-Jinn, the human portions of her composition could be traced, so she remained in the van for now at what Pazuzu deemed a "safe" distance. The rogue god had no knowledge of the Afrit, nor of Karšift, who as a Jinn could not be tracked remotely in any case. Either of these beings could come as close to Humbaba as necessary, but they had no ready way to find him.

This is where Olive came in. Someone had to serve as the relay, relating Pazuzu's directions as he alternated his concentration between the ashen monster and his brother, calculating with ever greater precision Humbaba's exact location. Since Olive needed to be present anyway, it made most sense for her to take the cold and perilous journey.

Tamanna hoped that since Olive posed little direct threat without Pazuzu being present, she would be unlikely to come under direct surveillance. If all went as planned, surprise would be their advantage twice over: once when the Afrit and Karšift, guided by Pazuzu through Olive, located Humbaba and attacked, and again when Pazuzu and Tamanna arrived at the scene, which they could accomplish quickly in their ethereal forms.

Olive shook ever more uncontrollably from the cold. *At least it's a cool view. There's the football stadium. Lots of cop cars are still around there, except....*

"Hey, y'all. It looks like most of the police action has moved away. I see a whole bunch of lights and activity off toward that big bridge to the left, which I guess would be east. Is that where you think Humbaba went?"

"Umm, maybe," Lotte replied. "He's definitely east of you, but it's not clear precisely where just yet. You need to get closer. Can you see the highway between you and the sports stadiums?"

"Yeah."

"Fly over that toward the bridge, and we'll see where Pazuzu wants you to go next."

Olive motioned to the Afrit. "They want us to go that-a-way. Follow the really wide road there, and I'll tell you when to stop."

The creature veered in a southeasterly direction, and soon Interstate 76 roared directly below, still busy with traffic well past midnight. The beast deftly flew just out of sight, but not so high that Olive would lose her precious cell connection.

They passed a wasteland of empty parking lots to their right, and were about to overtake a large casino when Lotte's voice rang in the phone's speaker. "Stop! Pazuzu says he's due south of you right now, about five or six hundred yards away, give or take. He still thinks in cubits, so I'm having to do some quickie conversions. What do you see in that direction?"

Olive rapidly scanned the area. "Well, I can still see the lights of the football stadium and the parking lots around it, but there's a big building in front of them now. I think it's the baseball park. I reckon it's about five hundred yards away. This don't make any sense, though. If Humbaba is over here, why are all the police cars off near the bridge?"

"I have no idea. Maybe he dragged one of his victims off in that direction and the police tracked their cell phone. They may not have any clue where Humbaba has gotten off to, which is probably to our benefit. Get closer to the baseball stadium, and we'll get a more specific location."

Olive directed the Afrit south. The creature clutched her tightly, darted between the casino and another large building, and emerged over another dark and empty parking lot.

"You're very close now," Lotte announced. "Only another two hundred yards or so."

"That's the baseball stadium for sure. You want us to touch down inside? I see some lights on down there. Won't there be security guards, or cameras, and the like?"

"Probably, yes. We'll just have to deal with that later. Is there somewhere you can land that's a bit more out of sight?"

"Yeah, there's a thing that looks like a big shed, and it has a little brick building on top. We'll try that." She pointed out the structure she'd noticed to the Afrit, who circled twice before gliding down and landing gracefully on the asphalt roof.

The creature released its grip, and she scurried to the ledge, where she was quickly joined by the Afrit, and then Karšift, who fluttered to the rooftop gently beside her. Sporadically placed floodlights provided illumination to various parts of the stands and onto the field. To her left, a pedestrian bridge connected the structure they were on with the right field stands. Below, a large courtyard unfolded behind centerfield, surrounded by concession stands, all shuttered.

Again, Lotte's voice sounded, and Olive turned off the phone's speaker for fear of being heard. "Pazuzu says he's nearly due west of you, only about sixty yards away."

The plaza looped around the bullpens that abutted right-center field, almost directly beneath her. Just beyond that, the courtyard widened into an area where a number of picnic tables sat arrayed along the center field wall. "Umm, I don't see him at all."

She heard some back and forth on the phone, then Lotte returned. "Has Karšift joined you? If so, Eric suggests asking him to do a quick fly-by."

"He can understand me?"

"Yes. He can speak as well, as long as he's in contact with you."

She suspiciously eyed the mystifying avian beside her. "Uh, hello Mr. Bird-Jinn-thingy, whatever. Could you please fly around and tell me if you see anything that might lead us to Humbaba?"

The raven's head darted from side to side before he shot into the sky and disappeared. After several tense minutes, Karšift returned, landed on the asphalt, then hopped deftly onto Olive's shoulder.

After pressing his head to her temple, she heard the bird's uncanny thoughts. *'There are parts.'*

"Parts? Parts of *whuut*?"

*'Parts... like yours, but not connected. Legs, arms, body, maybe a head –'*

"Okay, okay, I get it now. Jeez! Where are they?"

*'On big, open field... near wall, in front of trees.'*

"Trees! On a baseball field? That's weird. Are you sure?"

The creature pulled away and darted its head back and forth with agitation.

"All right, all right. Don't go gettin' all upset. I'll take your word for it. Hold on." She put the phone to her ear. "So, we might know where Humbaba is, but I need to get a better look at that center field wall. I hate to say this, but it looks like he's taken some more people, maybe the security guards for the stadium. I sure don't see any signs of life around here at all."

"*Verdammt!*" Lotte muttered. "Keep us posted when you're certain you've found him. We only have one chance at this."

Olive turned to the Afrit, who crouched stonily beside her. "Pick me back up and let's drop real quiet-like onto that bridge, then go into the stands. We can see better from there."

*'As you wish.'*

The ashen beast gently lifted her once more, hopped off the roof, and delicately landed on the footbridge near the entrance to the stands. They shuffled behind the grandstands until she found a staircase a suitable distance away, then descended to the lower level. There, she chose an aisle, and she and her stoic companion crept out into the seating area, all the way to the wall in the middle of right field. She heard the flutter of Karšift's wings as he settled on a seat behind them.

From this vantage, Olive could clearly see that an area of trees, bushes, and a wall of ivy sat just beyond the warning track in dead center field, behind a fence with the "401" distance marker.

"Guess you were right," she whispered over her shoulder at the inscrutable raven, whose eyes sparkled in the light from a floodlamp.

With dismay, she also took in the shapes of various butchered body parts that littered the grass and dirt. Using the calculations she'd made from the bridge, it appeared that Humbaba hid amongst the underbrush in this anomalous little enclave.

She returned to her phone. "Okay, we've got him. What do you want us to do now?"

Lotte relayed the situation to the van's other occupants before responding. "All right, just give us a minute to stop and get ready. On my mark, tell the Afrit and Karšift to attack. All they have to do is keep Humbaba occupied and contained for a few minutes. Pazuzu and Tamanna will be there as fast as they can."

Olive put her hand on the Afrit's shoulder and steered the creature closer to Karšift. "Are you two ready? Humbaba is somewhere behind those bushes and trees, digesting another meal, I guess. Y'all know what to do?"

The Afrit nodded. *'We know. Violence is our vocation, and is the reason your kind has called us forth for millennia. Well do we understand what is expected of us. Only the outcome remains in question.'*

She felt a brief pang of sympathy for the cranky monstrosity. *He is what we've made him, and I'm not sure that's such a good reflection on us. I wish he could see some of the better sides of humanity from time to time, although sometimes I go weeks without seeing much to shout about, so maybe that's easier said than done.*

Lotte interrupted her thoughts. "All right, we're ready. Tell me when Humbaba is engaged, and I'll send the others your way."

"Okay, you mean ol' thing. Go do what you do best and promise to come back to us in one piece."

*'That is impossible. We have not been of* one piece *since time immemorial.'*

She put her hand to her forehead. "That's not what I meant! Oh, never mind. Just go get Humbaba and try not to get too beat up."

The creature launched upward and disappeared into the starless sky, followed promptly by Karšift. For a moment, Olive could see neither of her companions, until the shadowy form of the Afrit crossed the face of a huge, square clock that towered above the concessions plaza. With silent and deadly grace, the beast sailed over the picnic tables, then dove directly down along the ivy-covered wall, into the tangle of bushes and trees at the bottom of the enclave.

Olive had seen cat fights before, and not just the "oh yeah?" stare-down kind, or the brief barrages of batted paws followed by a hasty retreat type. This was like a real knock-down drag-out cat fight, with claws extended, teeth gnashing, fur flying, and a host of snarls, hisses, moans, and other vocalizations that evoked the most depraved and ungodly acts imaginable. The tussle unfolded faster than she could follow as the two screamed over the center field fence and tangled among the dismembered corpses that littered the beautifully manicured grass of the outfield, grasping and ripping at each other's bodies.

It rapidly became clear that the Afrit had injured the gruesome god in its aerial assault, perhaps with its mighty horns. Dark blood oozed from two puncture wounds on Humbaba's side, and he struggled to escape from the onslaught and limp toward the stands to find shelter. His attempts were thwarted by Karšift, who suddenly materialized nearby and fiercely plucked at the demented god's soulless eyes. Humbaba swatted desperately to fend off his avian assailant, and after a brief flurry of wings and claws, the great bird shot upward and out of reach, content to rip away a bloody hunk of viscera from the grotesque mass of Humbaba's face. The god howled in pain before the Afrit rammed him to the ground with a vicious shoulder blow.

Battered and bleeding, Humbaba curled into a tight ball on the grass, crooked talons covering his twisted, wrinkled head as he wailed in misery. "Why do you set upon me so? What quarrel would creatures such as you have with me? I have done nothing to deserve your ire!"

The Afrit planted its cloven hooves firmly in the turf and readied its scorpion's tail. *'You ascribe emotions to us that we do not possess. Like you, we eat to survive in this bleak realm, and you appear to be an especially fulfilling meal. If the paltry resistance you have exhibited represents the extent of your mettle, then our task has proven far easier than anticipated.'*

The prostrate god stiffened. "You surprised me, and you hurt me, but if you believe I'll easily become food for the likes of you, think again!"

Humbaba's scaled skin began to ripple, and the tangle of thorny protrusions on his back undulated as if rocked by an earthquake. Olive watched in terror as the abhorrent being began to rapidly swell and grow. Even the Afrit took a cautious step backward, which proved fortuitous as the suddenly elongated snake that constituted Humbaba's tail lashed out to try and entangle the dark creature. The monster quickly took to the air, but Humbaba unexpectedly vaulted upward and grabbed one of the Afrit's cloven hooves.

The god now stood close to twelve feet tall, and his strength seemed to have increased in proportion to his size. Karšift darted about, trying to find an opening, but Humbaba swung the hapless Afrit in a wide circle, and the bird had to dematerialize to avoid a potentially fatal blow. The rejuvenated god then hurled his captive over his head and plunged the creature headfirst into the ground. Somehow, the Afrit softened the blow with its muscled arms, sharp talons ripping deep divots into the centerfield grass, but the manhandling took its toll. Having been released, the beast again tried to go airborne, but Humbaba reacted too quickly. He brought his taloned foot down on the Afrit's back between its wings, then reached over the struggling creature's shoulders and grabbed its goat-like horns.

The Afrit tried to counter with its barbed tail, driving upward into Humbaba's lower abdomen, but the god's gigantic snake tail swiftly entwined and constricted the dangerous weapon, rendering it useless. With a mighty wrench, Humbaba drove the ashen monster's horns apart until the rightmost appendage snapped and severed near the creature's skull. A trail of dark ash poured from the wound as the Afrit flailed in desperate dismay.

Humbaba hefted the cleaved horn like a great dagger above his shoulder and drove the point downward toward his opponent's exposed back. It had nearly connected when a blur of motion suddenly crashed into the god's arm, drove the weapon from his hand, and caused him to stumble away from his helpless adversary. Olive caught a brief glimpse of Pazuzu's head, arms, and shoulders as he zoomed by and then again vanished into the murky sky.

Before Humbaba could recover, another smack buffeted him from behind, sending him reeling to the ground. This time Tamanna rocketed past, her gossamer form gone faster than Olive could even register her presence. The dazed and dumbstruck deity tried to rise, but a repeated cascade of unpredictable blows rained upon him from his newly arrived and unexpected opponents, until Humbaba lay on his side gasping for breath. Once again, his skin began to pulse and surge, and his size receded from its once gargantuan proportions.

Like a stop motion film, Pazuzu careened unnaturally across the grass in a series of graceless poses as his form incrementally solidified. When he finally skidded to a halt, Siddique's nude body stood majestically just shy of the dirt basepath behind where second base would normally be found when the field was in use.

Olive briefly shut her eyes. *This isn't how I wanted it to be. I can't unsee this. I don't think it'll ever be the same between us again, or maybe there ain't no us no more, anyway. Maybe it just don't matter.* She sadly returned her attention to the conflict, sensing that her role in the proceedings might be imminent.

The Afrit shook its mutilated head and shakily rose to one knee, while Tamanna materialized behind Humbaba, a bit farther out in center field. As usual, she appeared completely unconcerned by her own lack of clothing.

*If there's security cameras filming all of this, they're gettin' a juicy show, that's for sure.*

Pazuzu turned, briefly examined his battered and exhausted brother, then scanned the stands to his right, quickly settling his gaze on Olive's position and extending his arm, palm upward. "Come child, we must act quickly."

She stood and peered over the reinforced chain link fence that ran along the top of the right field wall. The most expedient way onto the field would be to climb over this barrier and then drop down onto the warning track, but it was at least a 15-foot drop. "I'm not sure I can jump that far, and I have no idea where the stairs are to get down to the field. Mr. Afrit, can you please come and get me? Sorry I'm such a wimp."

The ashen beast pulled itself to its feet and launched into the air, but as it did, Humbaba unexpectedly rolled over and grabbed the great horn that had been ripped from the monster's temple. Its glow had returned, ranging from a warm orange at the base to a piercing blue near the tip, and the wobbly god pointed in menacingly at his brother. "I should have known! This dark brute and the bird were only distractions. You were always so clever, weren't you?"

Pazuzu didn't flinch. "Clever enough to have endured longer than many of our kind. It is my hope to be a survivor once again, but I need you for that, brother, just as you need me."

"I need nothing from you! You lie because you covet my power, my strength! Without me, you were nothing, and you will be nothing once again. Leave me be, *brother*. Let us both go our own way. After endless imprisonment, I yearn to be free, most of all... from you!"

Pazuzu dolefully shook his head. "Your freedom will be short-lived. For just one moment, look inward. Reach inside and measure the energy you have consumed, and that which has been expended. You will see the scales are no longer in balance. You cannot even maintain your prodigious size and strength after our assault. You devour an excess to mask the creeping truth, but all too soon, you shall see that I do not lie, and that our only path forward is together. Rejoin with me now, and we shall live in harmony and equality. This I promise you. Forget and forgive the past and let us start anew."

Humbaba staggered to his feet. Behind him, Tamanna crept warily closer, taking a position where she could strike more quickly against their unsteady but still formidable opponent should he attack his brother. The Afrit landed near Olive, and they both awaited the resolution of the tense standoff, while Karšift settled on the railing of the right field wall a few feet from them.

Amazingly, it appeared as if Pazuzu's words had found their mark. With a deep breath, Humbaba's lizard-like skin once again rippled and surged, and the being shrank back to his normal, roughly human-size height.

The words from the mushy mess of his mouth sounded softer, almost wistful. "To start anew. This is what I want as well. So far, I like what I see in this world. Far fewer petty and territorial gods to contend with. For once, we will have the freedom to do as we please. The past holds no charm for me. It is easily forgotten."

Pazuzu smiled and started toward his brother, arms wide.

"But it is not so easily forgiven!" With lightning quickness and utter surprise, Humbaba threw the Afrit's glowing horn. It flew with deadly and pinpoint accuracy, but not at Pazuzu. Instead, the projectile rocketed to the rear, directly into Tamanna's chest where it pierced her heart directly above her left breast.

She grasped at the missile and collapsed to her knees as violent spasms rocked her body, and dark blood surged from her mouth.

Olive watched with petrified shock as Humbaba's lithe, lizard-like body sailed past Tamanna and leapt over the center field fence and back into the trees.

Pazuzu screamed in anger and dismay as his brother shot up the ivy-covered wall and disappeared into the open courtyard. "Follow him! He is weakened. We cannot let him escape now. Come!" In a rapid-fire staccato of motion, he vanished in the direction his brother had fled.

Karšift took to the air but didn't follow Pazuzu. Instead, he sailed out to where Tamanna still twitched on the grass of the outfield.

Olive grabbed the Afrit's pumice-like arm, tears in her eyes. "Take me! Take me to her. Now!"

Together they glided to Tamanna's side, where Karšift sat on her shoulder, forlornly rubbing his crest into her hair. The Jinn's pupils had vanished into her eyelids as she strained from the convulsions. The skin around the wound had turned a sickly gray, and thick blood poured down her chest.

Olive softly touched Tamanna's cheek. "Honey, can you hear me? What can we do? How can I help you?"

The Afrit replied from behind her. *'She cannot speak. Properties in our makeup are noxious to her kind, even with a measure of human blood. Our horn causes the spasms and must be removed for them to cease, though we fear her wounds will prove fatal regardless.'*

"What... what even happened?"

*'It was the being's serpentine tail. With it, he possesses eyes in the back of his head, and even weakened, he enjoys the power of a god. The strike occurred too swiftly, too unpredictably, and with such great prowess as to be unavoidable.'*

"I... I don't think I can do it. Can you... please...."

The beast knelt, put its hand on the embedded horn, and firmly pulled. Karšift instantly hopped onto Olive's shoulder as Tamanna collapsed to the turf, coughing and spitting blood.

Olive delicately rolled the struggling Jinn onto her back, whose eyes fluttered, then partially opened before she took some gurgling breaths and tried to speak. Olive had to put her ear to Tamanna's mouth to hear the faint whispers of her words.

"I'm here... for now. I... I should have seen that coming. Too close. I just got too close."

"It's all right, don't worry about that. Is there anything we can do?"

"I... I rather think not. Pazuzu might have helped me, but he's gone. Even paralyzed, I could still hear. He's right. You need to follow Humbaba... may be... our only chance."

"We can't just leave you here sufferin' like this!"

"Suffering is... nearly over. Tell Karšift to... disable the security cameras. No need for subtlety, just destroy everything. And the creature of fire... tell it... tell it to come back for me when the task is done. Whatever remains of me, I give... as spoils... with my allegiance... my gratitude... and my friendship... one half-breed to another. Tell it... tell it... tell...."

Olive wept softly as the wisp of Tamanna's final words caressed her ear. She felt a surge of sadness from Karšift before he launched from her shoulder and took to the air, seemingly aware of the final undertaking his longtime companion wished him to complete.

After a few moments, the Afrit gently brushed her arm. *'Has she expired?'*

She wiped her eyes and nose on the sleeve of Eric's Bruins hoodie. "Yeah, expired. She's most definitely *expired*. She wanted us to go help Pazuzu track down his stupid brother. Karšift is gonna disable all the security shit so our faces aren't plastered all over *Good Morning America* tomorrow—especially yours, which will convince half the damn population that Satan walks among us! Anyway, we've gotta go, but we can't leave Tamanna just settin' out here. Take her to the roof where we first landed. They won't notice her so easily up there. We'll come back for her body later, and if we get killed, it's not our damn problem no more!"

The Afrit slowly rose, took Tamanna's lifeless body in its arms, and flew toward the upper deck of the stadium past right center field. Olive sat morosely on the beautiful grass until she heard Lotte's barely audible voice.

She reluctantly pulled the phone out of her pocket and brought it to her ear. "Hello. I'm here."

"*Alter!* Olive! What in the world is going on? We were afraid you'd been killed!"

"I'd be so lucky."

"What?"

"Oh, I'm just kidding. I'm fine, obviously. It's just that... well... umm... Humbaba got away. Yeah, he's back on the loose. Pazuzu is following him, and me and Chuckles are about to take off after him too. I'll let you know which direction we go when we're in the air."

"All right, we'll follow along if it doesn't take us too close to the police. What about Tamanna and Karšift, where are—"

"Oops, here comes the Afrit. Gotta go. I'll update you when I can. Bye!" She slipped the phone back into her pocket. She just couldn't face a big explanation right now; it was simply too much to process. There would be time for that later.

*Unless we really do get killed.*

Disturbingly, she wasn't completely certain whether such a fate might actually be preferable to the avalanche of harsh realities that swiftly and unexpectedly seemed to have subsumed her old life forever.

# WILLIAM E. NOLAND

# CHAPTER 17

Olive and the Afrit again went airborne. They lurched upward, over the trees in the center field enclave, and then past the big, square clock that overlooked the courtyard. The incredible vista of downtown Philadelphia briefly flashed by, until the Afrit swerved sharply left, over more sprawling parking lots and what appeared to be the Philadelphia Eagles practice facility, before reaching an area of swanky townhomes. There, they veered left yet again, over a large, forested park.

'There,' the Afrit blandly reported. 'Either Pazuzu caught up with his brother, or the wretch chose to make his stand. Either way, they appear to be locked in battle in a cluster of trees. What do you wish us to do?'

"Hold on," Olive replied. She carefully fished her phone out of her pocket and put it back on speaker. "Lotte, it's me. We found 'em! They're in some big park. I think it's west of the baseball stadium. The Afrit says they're fightin'!"

After a pause, Lotte responded. "Okay, we know where you're going. That's FDR Park. The problem is, it's *huge*. Pazuzu obviously needs help, so you'll have to go down there, but try to tell us where you land. If there are no police in the area, we'll come and help, assuming we can find you."

"Roger that!" She clutched the phone to her chest and looked over her shoulder at the Afrit. "They want us to—"

'We heard. Prepare for our descent.'

"Wait! Not just yet. There's somethin' I gotta tell you in case... well... if I don't make it out of this."

The creature stilled the beat of its wings and glided in a gentle circle above the darkness of the park.

"It's about Tamanna. She told me she wanted you to come back for her body."

'This was understood. Leaving her body there raises suspicions among your authorities, not to mention our severed horn, which we must also retrieve.'

"Yeah, but it's not just that. She wanted you to... like... *take* her—as spoils, assuming there's anything left to take. Maybe she thinks some of

- 229 -

her Jinn energy will still be in her body for a while. I don't know. That's just what she told me to tell you. Also, she said she was giving this to you with her allegiance, and gratitude, and friendship... as one half-breed to another."

The ashen beast continued to silently sail in the crisp breeze.

"I remember what she said to you, back at the house. She sounded mad, but I don't' think she hated you. I think she was trying to tell you somethin'. My momma would talk to me that way sometimes. She called it 'tough love.' I called it *an ass whoopin'*, even though she hardly never spanked me. She just wanted things to be better for me, and I think that's what Tamanna wanted for you. Problem is, the only person that can really make things any better is yourself, so you have to live with gettin' criticized all the time, then figure out who really has something to say, and who's just being mean. It ain't easy. Anway, that's what I had to tell you. Sorry if I got off track. We can go now."

Like a roller coaster, the monster instantly dropped at breakneck speed. Olive felt her heart in her throat and instinctively shut her eyes in terror, but then remembered she had to see where they were going. The wind lashed her face and tears streamed from her eyes as she frantically looked around. The last thing she saw before they touched down — with astonishing finesse — was a long strip of brick office buildings off to her right.

The Afrit let her go, and Olive quickly scampered behind a bush while the creature rushed into the darkness of the trees. After catching her breath, she again took her phone off speaker and put it to her ear. "We're on the ground. It all happened so fast that I'm not exactly sure where we are, but there's a big row of brick buildings off to my right, near a road that loops around the park. I can still see the tops of them over the trees, maybe... I don't know... about two hundred and fifty yards away, something like that. Good news is, I didn't see any police cars around here, at least none with their lights on."

"All right," Lotte replied. "I think we've got you. We'll get as close as we can and come join you, if possible. If the battle is still going on, Mutig might be of some use."

The riotous cracking of branches and the rustling of leaves abruptly broke the quiet of the park.

"Oh, it's still goin' on, okay. Holy damn!"

Near the tree line into which the Afrit had disappeared, a whirlwind of motion now emerged. Illumination from the tall buildings nearby, along with ambient light from the city itself, helped Olive make out several forms locked in combat. It took her a moment, but she was finally able to discern Humbaba's shape, once again towering over his assailants, though not as colossal as before.

Seeming to remember the gigantic god's capabilities, and perhaps taking a page from Karšift's book of tactics, the Afrit deftly fluttered out of reach, periodically swooping down and striking with his barbed tail at Humbaba's grotesque head before darting to safety. Pazuzu struck by materializing briefly for a flurry of body blows, before falteringly vanishing once more. The combat was clearly taxing his already erratic powers.

*He's using a lot of energy on this, and it don't seem to be doing much good, although it looks like Humbaba ain't as strong no more neither. If Tamanna was here, we might actually have him, but right now, it just looks like a stalemate, and it may be just be a question of whose battery runs out first.*

Eric gunned the van as they raced westward on Oregon Avenue.

"Slow down," Lotte cried. "We don't want to be stopped by the police."

He dialed it back slightly, but still chafed with urgency. "You said left on 20th, right?"

"No, left. You had it right the first time, unless... oh, forget it. Left is correct. Here it comes."

Amazingly, the light was green, and at this time of night, no traffic snarled the roadway. He banked onto 20th Street, sped under the mass of I-76, and then bore right onto Penrose Avenue.

Lotte consulted her phone. "Perfect! In a few blocks, we'll reach Pattison. Take a quick left there, and then we'll get onto Gateway Drive."

"Then what, turn right onto Portal Avenue?"

"Very funny. It's pretty coincidental, though, isn't it? Anyway, just follow Gateway, and that will take us straight to the buildings Olive saw."

At an intersection near a 24-hour Sunoco station, he navigated left, followed Pattison for about a block, then squeaked onto tiny Gateway Drive past a sign advertising "The Enclaves and Gateway Towers." The road took them around the park on their left, as Olive had described. They rounded a large bend and passed a little cement fountain on an island that divided another intersection to the right.

Eric slammed on the brakes. "What the fuck?"

A small gatehouse blocked the road to the buildings ahead.

"*Scheiße!* That wasn't on the map! Umm... just go right and hop over the curb near that fountain. It's not that high. We'll have to go back the way we came and try to find somewhere to park."

He crossed the island as she suggested, but instantly had another idea. The road onto which they emerged was divided like a highway, with a thin strip of grass separating the stretches that ran in opposite directions. As there was no fence, he carefully steered the van across this patch, then turned left toward a graffiti strewn bridge.

He parked amongst a line of idle cars, trucks, and utility vehicles near a cluster of scraggly roadside trees. "How's this?"

"It'll have to do. Grab Mutig and let's go!"

The dog seemed eager to be free of the van as Eric fetched him and rolled the side door shut. They scurried across the two roads, still essentially void of traffic, passed the cement fountain again, and ran to the embankment that separated Gateway Drive from the park. Here they encountered a roughly six-foot chain-link fence.

Mutig began to whine and tightly pulled at the leash in Eric's hand. "He can sense them out there. Let's get him over the fence, then we'll figure out how to get in. I think I can pick him up." He unwrapped the lead from his wrist and began to hand it to Lotte, but Mutig tore away, ran back near the cement fountain, then rocketed back toward the fence. Just shy of the embankment, the dog leapt and easily cleared the top of the barrier. Without hesitation, he streaked off into the darkness.

"Whew!" Lotte whistled. "That's one way to do it. Come on, put your fingers together and give me a boost up. "

"What about me?"

"You're tall and strong enough to pull yourself over."

"No reverse psychology this time?"

She smiled. "You need motivation? I'll tell you what, you get yourself over that fence, or I'll never make coffee for you again."

"*Touché.* Just wait for me once you're over there."

It happened in the blink of one of Humbaba's frightful eyes.

After a seemingly endless barrage of feints and parries, the Afrit accomplished what the tenacious, but not nearly as combat proficient, Karšift had failed to achieve. Olive watched in wonder as the creature's barbed tail sliced across one of the wicked god's menacing black pupils, which popped like a water-filled balloon and discharged a gush of ichorous bile. The dreadful being screamed and stumbled backward, feebly clutching at his writhing face.

Sensing his brother's weakness, Pazuzu stutteringly rematerialized and tried a new strategy. He grabbed Humbaba's serpentine tail as it gnashed at the Afrit, trying to keep the beast at bay. Caught off guard, the snake couldn't resist. Pazuzu wrapped it around its master's legs, gave a mighty tug, and Humbaba fell like one of the towering cedars of Enlil's once great forest.

Neither of the two allied entities hesitated. Each descended on the fallen deity, delivering the most merciless of beatings. Humbaba clawed at the ground, trying to pull away from the fusillade, but his own tail still entangled him, and one clawed hand still pressed at his sagging eyelid. His position hopeless, he soon ceased his resistance, and lay bleeding and moaning amongst the fallen leaves.

The Afrit straddled Humbaba's legs and stamped down a mighty hoof right behind the viper's head, securing it to the ground. Pazuzu sat on his brother's chest, grabbed his wrists, and forced his arms to the ground.

The pummeled god gave little resistance.

"Now you are mine," Pazuzu announced, no sign of joy in his voice. "Shall you come to me willingly, or must I force upon you what is best for us both?"

Humbaba's words were more garbled than ever, but he needed only one to communicate his message. "Never... never...."

"Very well." He raised his head slightly. "Come, child, I sense you nearby. I have need of your energy. Quickly. Now!"

Olive gulped. She felt the same as she had on the terrace at the museum, frightened, nervous, and completely clueless as to how to summon her power. Tamanna's son, Khalil, had spoken to her of energy nodes, positive and negative flow vectors, and isolating and controlling synaptic junctions. She barely understood the terms, let alone how to put them into practice. Equally alarming, she felt no strong emotion, and she sensed that trying to summon one artificially, like a high school actor feigning tears, would be a worthless sham.

She reluctantly rose from her hiding spot and trudged out to meet her fate.

Once she stood by him, Pazuzu secured one of Humbaba's arms with his knee and took her hand. "Concentrate, child. Everything is at our fingertips, but it is all up to you."

*Great... just what I* didn't *need to hear right now.*

She grudgingly slipped the leather strap of the milky white amulet over her neck and deposited it into the pocket of the hoodie. The familiar tingling immediately started, and she wracked her brain trying to think of something that might make her angry, or sad, or *something*. She thought of Tamanna's wrenching final words and gesture, but she'd already shed her tears over the Jinn's sad fate, and they had never been especially close companions to begin with. Likewise, her burning and longstanding anger at her father seemed to have vented itself in the trees above her mother's house when she rescued Siddique. To her amazement, however, she did make out the tenuous pull of Pazuzu's power within her.

*Looks like he might have figured something out last night, other than how to really creep me out!*

The tingling sensation increased as she felt a rush of energy surge through her body, though it seemed unfocused, and she couldn't tell how much actually aided her mighty associate in his precarious struggle.

Humbaba began to twist and tremble as Pazuzu set about wrenching the life force from his brother's body. The cost of the wounded god's resistance was clearly apparent as his scaly flesh began to ripple and his proportions once again diminished.

"More," Pazuzu bellowed. "I need more! Do not hold back from me what you promised!"

"I didn't promise nothin'!" Olive retorted. "I told you I'd do the dang best I could, and that's what I'm doin'. I ain't holdin' back nothing! I can't just be super angry, or super sad, or whatever, at the drop of a hat. It don't work that way!"

"I care not how it 'works,' merely that it does. Perhaps your feelings might be different if you knew that should you fail me, you'll never see your *precious* Siddique again."

Olive's blood ran cold. For the briefest of moments, she pondered what exactly the needful god had meant. Was he saying that if he failed to reunite with Humbaba and died, Siddique would die with him, or had he implied that he would actively kill her friend in retribution for her nonperformance? In the end, it didn't matter. For her, it was the way he said "precious" that really tweaked her. In a flash of anger uncharacteristic for Olive, but all too symptomatic of Aicha's unwelcome infestation, she began to pull her hand away, but as she did so, she gave Pazuzu a small dose of the power he so craved.

Where he must have expected the warmth of a smooth and steady flow, she felt her energy rip into him like an icy dagger, tearing into his body with a devastating jolt. He screamed, yanked his hand from hers, and tottered from his perch atop his brother.

With what strength he still possessed, Humbaba instantly lunged into action. He shoved the still shuddering Pazuzu aside, then roughly threw his legs strongly apart, mercilessly ripping his serpentine tail to pieces, but freeing himself from being entwined. The surprised Afrit briefly lost its balance, and Humbaba deftly flipped onto his belly, then propelled himself upward with his mighty arms, as if performing a superhuman push up. The cluster of cruel spikes on his back smashed into his ashen opponent, and the creature madly flailed its wings to try and break free.

Before the Afrit could pry itself loose, Humbaba drove backward and mashed the creature into a tree trunk. The dark brute howled in fury, but quickly countered with its barbed tail, slashing across the back of Humbaba's leg. Blood gushed from the wound as the god shrieked in agony, and he rapidly twisted his back free and tumbled to the ground. The Afrit wobbled unsteadily as loosened ash poured from the myriad puncture wounds on its abdomen.

Pazuzu had regained a modicum of composure and began to painstakingly pull himself toward his brother. Humbaba tried to rise and flee, but his injured leg gave way, the deep gash having almost severed the limb entirely. He desperately craned his neck, trying to pinpoint some means of escape with his one remaining eye, and Olive's heart sank when the anguished god's singular gaze settled on her.

*Uh, oh....*

Before she could react, Humbaba launched himself in her direction with his good leg, aided by his powerful arms. She had no idea if he would kill her and try to ingest her energy, or take her prisoner, but either way, she knew she was in deep trouble. She found herself paralyzed by fear, surely a dire emotional state, but not one that allowed ready access to her reservoir of power.

With a little hop, Humbaba the Terrible's wide arms engulfed her, and his clawed hands tore at her back. The stench of death enveloped her as the great jowls of slimy viscera crushed against her face. She felt her feet leave the earth as he whipped her like an empty sheet blowing in the wind, and gasped for breath as his mighty grasp forced the air from her lungs.

She nearly passed out before the mighty pressure ceased and she unexpectedly felt herself plunge to the ground. Stars spun in her eyes as she gulped in oxygen. As her vision gradually returned, she became aware of a ferocious tussle just to her right. Shaking her head and sparing a quick look, she saw that Humbaba grappled in the grass and leaves with some creature that had locked its jaws near the deity's gruesome neck.

*Mutig!*

The dog snarled and gnashed as blood spouted from his foe's throat. Humbaba raked against the canine's sides with his claws, but Mutig held firm. The wretched god's skin bubbled and seethed, and once again, Humbaba began to shrink before Olive's eyes.

*Mutig's got him! He'd draining out the last of Humbaba's reserves!*

Just when victory appeared to be literally in her savior's clutches, the dog reared up, yelped in obvious pain, and let go his death-grip. To Olive's horror, the slithering tail of the snake had plunged its fangs into the canine's side.

*Oh, crap! He shrunk down to regrow his freakin' tail!*

The serpent wasn't as large as it had once been, but its bite proved severe enough to command Mutig's attention. With a blistering movement, the viper drew back and struck again, this time in the meaty lower thigh of the dog's hind leg. Mutig yowled in distress and tried to catch the malicious appendage in his jaws, but his movements had become clumsy and uncoordinated.

*He's been poisoned! I hope not enough to kill him!*

Humbaba fiercely hooked his claws around the animal's neck and began to savagely twist.

The effect was instantaneous. A blinding and all-encompassing anger obliterated all but one thought from Olive's mind. "Let go of my gawd damned *dog!*"

She set upon the threatening deity with murderous abandon, slamming her fists into the squirming gristle of his face and trying to sink her nails into his one remaining eye. Humbaba reacted by whipping Mutig's limp body into her shoulder. She pitched to one side but broke her fall with an outstretched arm.

The injured dog fell to the ground beside her. For a split second, their eyes met. The woozy canine held her gaze for the first time since she'd returned from her fateful trip to Massachusetts, but Olive couldn't enjoy the moment. She was still far too furious, and she knew that Humbaba's venomous tail was now free to strike at her. She quickly pivoted, interposing herself between Humbaba and Muitg, and sought the deadly viper before it could attack.

To her surprise, the menacing tail was nowhere to be seen, but Humbaba ferociously seized her arm and pulled her face toward his. "*There you are! This* is the power my brother sees in you, and now it's *mine!*"

With horror, Olive realized her terrible mistake. In her frenzied state, her mind lay open, just as it would have for Pazuzu had she been overpowered by emotion, allowing him access to her energy. She tried to clamp down on the rage that impelled her, but it wasn't so easy, likely due to Aichia's machinations. Before she knew it, Humbaba voracious craving had infiltrated the meagre defenses of her mind. Like parched earth in a rainstorm, he began to soak in the torrent of her power.

In panic, she did the only thing left to her. She drove her hand into the pocket of her hoodie and clutched the milky white medallion. Instantly, the flow of energy ceased, and the chaotic abomination of Humbaba's twisted thoughts jettisoned from her mind. The abrupt suspension of her connection with the ravenous god hit her like a sledgehammer. With the last of her fading consciousness, she felt herself collapse face first into the carpet of crisp, fallen leaves, hand still pressed tightly against the precious amulet.

Eric stumbled behind Lotte as she raced through the park. Though he kept it to himself, she had slightly overestimated the current state of his physical prowess. Still weakened and woozy from the blow he'd received from Rashid on the bridge, among other injuries, he'd narrowly scaled the chain link fence, and the jolt upon landing had done him no favors.

*Running is the last thing I need right now. I'm not even sure what good we'll be when we get there. I mean, it's not like we're gonna square off against Humbaba... at least I hope we don't!*

They only had a vague sense of where the combatants were, assuming they hadn't moved. Olive had told them the long row of buildings was to her right when she and the Afrit had landed, and they'd scaled the fence just to the north of those. Once clear of the trees, they dashed through an open meadow until the expanse of high-rise structures loomed beside them, then cut left.

Zigzagging to avoid a copse of trees, they chanced upon a worn trail that took them due east between a series of thickets. When they emerged on the other side, Eric heard noises. Lotte had clearly heard them as well, as she veered off to in the direction of the sounds, following the path at first, but then once again cutting across country. They sailed over another, wider dirt track, then ran a bit farther, before Eric felt Lotte grab his hand and pull him behind the ancient stump of a tree.

Whatever was happening, it was just another twenty or thirty feet away. Eric listened as he heaved for breath. The familiar swish of the Afrit's batlike wings sounded above him, and periodic snarls came from the ground just beyond their tenuous hiding place. He also heard Siddique's unaccented voice, meaning Pazuzu was still in charge.

"Brother, give up the struggle. Your energy is as depleted as mine. You are injured and cannot walk, and you lack the capacity to overcome such a serious wound. The dark beast that flies above you will slay you with certainty if you do not surrender. Do you truly hate me so? Without me, you would not be here now. You would have died in the Cedar Forst at the hands of Gilgamesh and Enkidu. Please, listen to me, before it's too late."

Humbaba grotesquely cackled, "Fancy words, fancy words. Always the same for poor Humbaba — abandoned, banished, shunned, and then imprisoned. No, *brother*, not again. I have another idea. You were surely right about one thing. This girl at my feet shelters surprising power. For the briefest instant, I felt it surge in my veins. When she wakes up, I'll have it all, or I'll tear her apart! And if either you, or your foul new ally, comes near me, I'll do the same. Then you'll be as good as dead, won't you? Without her, you have no chance of taking me back by force."

"I fear that won't be possible in any case. Her command over the energy she possesses is too erratic, too subject to passions she cannot control. You will discover this yourself when she awakes, then you will kill her, and then nothing will stand between you and the creature of fire. You and I will both meet our end here in this place if you do not come back to me willingly. It's down to that."

Humbaba emitted a sadistic hiss.

Lotte shot Eric a look of distress, then peered over the top of the stump. She briefly surveyed the situation as Eric creakily rose to join her, but before he'd gotten into position, she'd risen and had begun to slip around their meagre barrier.

He grabbed her wrist. "What the hell are you doing?"

"This has gone far enough. I won't let Humbaba take Olive for nothing like this."

"So, what do you plan to do about it? Even the freaking Afrit can't attack him, or he'll kill her."

"I have another idea. It's a long shot, but it's the best I've got. Trust me."

She pulled away, and Eric's head reeled from the unfathomable fact that the love of his life was walking head on toward a desperate and dangerous entity. Had he possessed the strength and quickness, he'd have stopped her, but by the time he realized what had happened, she was gone, and all he could do was cling to the top of the timeworn stump and fretfully watch. In the dim light, he could see Humbaba's shape kneeling over Olive's limp form. Pazuzu crouched a short distance away, clearly exhausted from the pursuit and ensuing battle with his brother, while the Afrit still flitted above with agitation.

*Funny, I don't see either Tamanna or Karšift, but they might be flying around invisibly. Wish I could do that.*

He was more concerned about Mutig, who he also couldn't locate.

"Humbaba," Lotte announced, as she rapidly closed the distance between them. "Listen to me. I have no weapons, and no ability to harm you. I just want to talk. Actually, I'd like to ask you a question, if you'd do me the honor of answering."

The injured god looked at her with a mixture of loathing and bewilderment. "Who are you? Where did you come from?"

"It's a long story, but I'll make it short. My name is Lotte. I'm a friend of Olive's, the person who's unconscious at your feet. She told me where she was, and I followed her here. I don't want her to die. I don't want you or Pazuzu to die either. This whole situation is really quite insane. I'm hoping we can talk. I'd like to understand more about you... about how you *feel*."

The gruesome entity once more emitted his phlegmy chortle. "How I *feel*? What can this possibly mean, and how can knowing this bring resolution to our deadlock?"

She shook her head. "I'm not sure, but I've read nearly everything about you that our mythological and historical documents have preserved. With so many different versions and various interpretations, it's hard to tell fact from fiction, which makes it really difficult to comprehend the truth. Please, if you would, tell me if these are your words: 'I have never known a mother, no, nor a father who reared me. I was born of the mountain. He reared me, and Enlil made me the keeper of this forest.' Did you say that to Gilgamesh as you begged for your life?"

Humbaba's icy, one-eyed stare became distant. "Yes. I told him I would be his servant, and that I would build him a palace from the trees of the forest. Enlil would have looked away at the loss of a few of his precious cedars to see peace restored. Gilgamesh was ready to accept my offer, but conniving and envious Enkidu lied and told him fate would not be kind to him if he spared my life. In the end, reports of my death in part led to Enkidu's well-deserved demise, but by then, it was too late for me. Of what consequence is any of this?"

To Eric's horror, Lotte strode right up to the menacing brute and gently touched his shoulder. The fearsome snake tail slithered over her hand, but she didn't flinch. "None of what happened with Gilgamesh is of any consequence just now. It's what you *said* that struck me, something that was obviously very important to you, very important *about* you, that you'd bring it up at such a delicate moment. From the mists of ancient history, your words resonated with me as if I'd spoken them myself. I also lost my mother. Unlike you, I knew her, and I loved her more than I can say, but I heard you talking just now about feeling abandoned, the first of several injustices you told your brother that you've suffered. I suspect it's the most fundamental as well, and I know how horrible it feels, because I felt it too, and I reacted exactly as I think you did. I retreated inward and shunned contact with others, fearing they too would all abandon me in the end."

"A reasonable assumption, no?"

"To an extent, I suppose, but that kind of isolation only takes you so far. You may have felt relatively safe on your own in the Cedar Forest, just as I did when I pushed people away. That has its limits, though. I reached mine when I met the creature flying above our heads right now. That beast almost killed me, and I needed help to figure out how to stop that from happening. As luck would have it, the whole experience wound up being my path back to myself, back to being able to trust again."

"Lucky you," he sneered with disdain. "If this is your attempt to make me trust my brother, you have failed!"

The snake tail deftly wrapped around her wrist and slinked up her arm, but she seemed not to notice, or care. "No, that's not my point. I'm talking about abandonment. I'm talking about how that *feels*, and the extremes that pain can drive you to just to be rid of those feelings. But it never really goes away, does it? You always feel it in the pit of your stomach, an emptiness that can't be filled. Before you take my worthless life, just be honest with me, like I think you were honest with Gilgamesh. The agony of never knowing your mother, of feeling abandoned by her, has driven a lot of what you became, hasn't it?"

The Afrit delicately landed near Pazuzu, seeming as eager to observe what happened next as everyone else. All became very still.

Eric tried to calculate how quickly he could intercede to try and save Lotte, but almost instantly deduced that it was hopeless. He steeled himself for what was to come.

To his relief, Humbaba spoke with strikingly measured words. "What sense is there in denying the obvious? Of course, anger has ever driven me, and the bloodlust dulls the desolation, for a time. Eventually, I became unfit for 'civilization,' and an inconvenience to the gods whose power over humans depended on their newly imposed 'order.' I embraced my role as protector of Enlil's domain. Enough fools tested his power that I remained sufficiently entertained."

"But that sense of abandonment still ate at you, didn't it? It never went away, and it's absolutely awful, isn't it?"

"Yes. Awful. Poor Humbaba. I have never known a mother nor a father who reared me."

"That's terrible, really. I truly understand, and I feel for you. You're not a monster. You coped as best you could, but let me ask you: does the pain you experience justify inflicting that on others?"

Humbaba tensed and the coiled viper jerked Lotte closer. "What are you implying?"

"I'm asking you a simple question. Is all the death that you've dealt to alleviate your misery justified? Can you understand that the people you kill have spouses, families, and children who all experience the full gamut of suffering that you have when their loved ones are torn from their lives? Think about the mother of the toddler whose body you now inhabit. How do you think she feels?"

"This is not my concern! I am a god! I can do as I please."

"Does this really *please* you? Humbaba, are you actually happy, or have you simply found a way to self-medicate with violence? You know as well as I do that none of this is necessary. You're part Jinn. You don't have to kill to feed, but you do. That's what hurt people do... they *hurt* people! I know. I did it myself, and it doesn't make me proud, but it does help me understand. I know how easy it is to fall into the trap of pushing everyone away and indulging the worst side of yourself because there's so much pain inside. The problem is: no one can go it alone, even you. You'd have died in the Cedar Forest had it not been for your brother, and whether you believe him or not, he's telling you the truth about the dangers you're facing now."

"Back to this, are we?"

"Yes, we're back to this. You've convinced me that deep down, you're not a monster, but you continue to act like one! Think about it. What would have happened if Gilgamesh had taken you up on his offer? As his servant, do you think he'd have been any more tolerant of your rampant killing sprees than the gods had been? You'd have had to learn discipline—which seems to be out of the question--or he'd have been rid of you, and it's unlikely that your brother would have been hiding in the trees to save you. Now you're faced with the same problem. You have no idea what humanity has become since being entrapped by Iblis. We wield forces you can't possibly comprehend, and if you keep slaughtering people like this, they *will* track you down. To survive, you have to change your behavior, and you and I both know that you can't do that alone. You need help, and your brother remains your best chance, as you are for him. He's fading away. He can't live indefinitely inside an alien body without your support, any more than you can survive in the body of the little boy you stole."

Humbaba pushed her away in disgust and she tumbled to the ground.

"Like it or not, that's the truth! Dimme, your sworn enemy, takes children from their mothers that way. I know. She took mine, and I want her dead for it! Think of all the suffering she's caused to you and countless others. Do you still want to see her pay for what she did? If so, your best bet is lying at your feet unconscious at this very moment. Olive may not be able to control her powers right now, but given time, I think she can learn to give both you and Pazuzu the energy to destroy Dimme. But she can't help you if she's dead, and she won't help a god of *carnage*, and neither will I. Is that how you want your name remembered? Is that who you are?"

Eric shook his head in disbelief. *The hell with archaeology. Lotte should have been a freakin' lawyer!*

Pazuzu unsteadily rose and walked to his brother, arms wide in supplication. "The girl has recounted with great eloquence all that can be said. I have no fight left in me. The choice is yours. I will no longer stand in your way. If you think you can avoid the dark being that lurks behind me, take your chance. Win or lose, you will not last long. Like me, you will soon expire. Believe that or not, as you will, but know this: I failed you. I overlooked what this sharp-minded mortal discerned from your immemorial words, and the bleak truth of the sentiment behind them. It is a mistake I regret, and given the chance, one I shall not repeat. This city we are in has a special meaning in the ancient tongue of the plucky Hellenes. *Fila Delfia*, the City of Brotherly Love. It is a fitting place for us to reunite, or to say our final and fond goodbyes."

He lowered his head, exhausted, and seemingly defeated.

Humbaba shakily stood on his good leg and surveyed those assembled around him, then shambled to his brother and pressed his face close. They stared at each other for a long moment before the terrible snake tail unexpectedly struck out with lightning quickness and clamped onto Pazuzu's abdomen, while Humbaba's talons grasped his shoulders. Pazuzu briefly winced, but then steadied and threw his hands onto his brother's chest. Both mighty entities began to shudder and convulse, and then Humbaba's gnarled and misshapen form began to shrink. Pazuzu gingerly followed him to the ground, never losing contact, and finally kneeling when his brother was no larger than....

"A toddler!" Lotte sounded almost in tears as the form of a very young boy emerged from the undulating remnants of Humbaba's terrible incarnation. Pazuzu briefly cradled the unconscious youngster in his arms before placing him gently amongst the leaves next to Olive.

WILLIAM E. NOLAND

# CHAPTER 18

Eric ran as fast as he could to join Lotte, then helped her pick herself up. "What the hell just happened?"

"It is done," Pazuzu mildly replied "Humbaba rests inside me now. I can already feel his energy stabilizing and enhancing my ability to control this body."

"The body you promised to give back," Lotte said stiffly.

The god got to his feet, clearly more vigorous than before. "I intend to keep that promise, but doing so now is out of the question. It will take time to fully reassimilate our patterns and ingest enough energy to undertake another transfer."

He closed his eyes, and his body became tense. Then, his skin began to ripple as Humbaba's had. Siddique's nude form began to lose focus, replaced by features vastly more fearsome and inhuman. Great claws emerged in place of hands, horns emerged on his head while his eyes bulged, and his mouth elongated into a snarling canine snout. The picture was complete when great wings unfurled on the unnerving entity's back, and the tail of a scorpion flicked dangerously over his shoulder.

*Wow*, The Exorcist *actually got him almost perfectly. Ha! Stupid movie, my butt!*

Arms wide, Pazuzu exuberantly raised his glimmering eyes to the sky. "Ah, much better! Now, I can fly again, a far less taxing means of travel. You have certainly delivered impressively upon your promises to me. I thank you, all of you. I will find you when I have recovered enough strength to complete the remainder of our bargain. Until then, I bid you farewell."

"Wait," Lotte sputtered. "Are you insane? You can't fly around like *that*! People will see you and think you're a demon, which actually may not be far from the truth."

"No one shall lay eyes upon me," he chuckled. "As you see, my skin is obsidian like that of your beloved Afrit. I can fly at night undetected. By day, I shall hide and rest, or assume the shape of your human companion and walk amongst mortals. There is much to learn about this curious new world."

"But... but... where will you go, and how long do you expect to be gone?"

"Like your unconscious friend, you ask many questions simultaneously. It matters not where I go. Upon deeming myself fit to resettle in another body, I can easily find you from anywhere. When, exactly, that may be, I cannot say, but by your measures of time, it could be months, perhaps years."

Eric felt like he'd been punched.

*Years! Olive might as well never wake up, because she's just gonna die when she hears this.*

Lotte seemed equally distraught. "This is *terrible*! I'm sorry, this just isn't what I expected — any of us, really. I accept some of the blame. We should have been clearer on this point, though I'm not really sure what choice we had. It's just that our friend, Siddique... it's... it's not so simple. What about *his* life? He can't just disappear without any explanation for who knows how long. People will think he's dead, and they'll be asking us what happened. This is a disaster."

"The misunderstanding is regrettable, but never did I lie, and at this stage, no alternative exists. A successful transfer is not assured even under the most favorable conditions. I have been lucky twice. I will not attempt it again until I have greater confidence in success."

Lotte turned to Eric, a look of desperation on her face. "What do we do?"

"You're asking me? I don't know. Maybe we could ask him if he'd at least come back home with us. He could take Siddique's form and help us tie up some loose ends, let people see he's not dead before he goes wherever it is he wants to go."

Her eyes went wide. "Eric, that's brilliant!"

*Really? I thought it was kind of lame, but it was the best I could come up with on short notice.*

She shot her attention back to Pazuzu. "Listen. You say you can assume Siddique's shape whenever you like. What if you come with us and take his place? This world is wonderful, but it's also dangerous, and very different from the one you're used to. We can help you understand it, learn how to live in it on a daily basis, and if more trouble comes our way, you'll be close by to help us as well. By night, you'll be free to fly and feed — or do whatever it is you do — but at other times, taking on Siddique's persona will help you, and help him once you give him back control over his body. I know he doesn't have the most exciting life, but his existence is low profile, exactly what you need while you recover. What do you say? I beg you, please think it over."

The majestic god was silent for a time. More than once, he turned his piercing gaze to the Afrit, who stood, sparkling and statue-like, in the spot where it had landed. Finally, Pazuzu returned his attention to Lotte. "Time has wrought many changes, and the world I knew is long gone. My existence here will henceforth be of a different nature, and I can think of no superior alternative that would ensure my safety during this delicate time of acclimation. You have served me well, and your counsel may yet be of benefit. I shall try. That is the best I can offer. For now, let me fly free, and soon I will meet you back at the house we shared."

Lotte sighed with deep relief. "Agreed. Thank you! You can't imagine how grateful we are for your indulgence. Be cautious. You know enough of the dangers our world presents. I'd hate to see all our work come to nothing."

Pazuzu gave a slight nod, then eagerly rocketed into the sky and disappeared above the treetops into the night sky.

Lotte rushed to little Jonah while Eric made a beeline for Olive. As he knelt beside her, he saw Mutig pressed underneath her. The dog lifted its head and emitted a little whimper.

"Holy crap. Hold on, boy. Let me just get her off of you." Eric tenderly shifted Olive's body and rolled her onto her back.

The movement seemed to rouse her, and she coughed and then opened her eyes. "What happened? I feel like a car ran me over. Shit! Where is it?"

"Where's what?"

"Oh, nothing. I thought I'd lost the stupid amulet, but it's right here." She extracted her hand from the pocket of Eric's hoodie, exposing the white medallion, and he helped her quickly slip it back over her neck. "It's startin' to come back to me. If I hadn't had this thing, Humbaba would have drained me dry, and I'm not sure the Afrit or Pazuzu would have been able to stand up to him."

"Well, that was lucky. When we got here, you were already unconscious and we had no idea why, or what was going on. I still have no clue where Tamanna and Karšift are."

She gave him a sorrowful look as Mutig dragged sluggishly to her side and began to lick her cheek.

Eric noticed bloody puncture wounds on the dog's hindquarters. "Oh, shit! Mutig is bleeding. We have to get him back to the van, see how bad this is. He may need to—"

Olive touched her finger to Eric's lips. "That blood's nothin'. Mutig got bit by Humbaba's tail, except the snake was really small cause he was runnin' out of power. It was the poison that stopped him, but if he ain't dead yet, I don't think this will kill him. It just needs to wear off. But... but... *she's* dead."

"Who's dead?"

"Oh, God. Tamanna, sweetie. I'm so sorry. I know you kinda liked her and all, but she's gone. Humbaba got her."

At this, Lotte turned and scooted over to them, Jonas in her arms. The child appeared to be in deep sleep, chest rising and falling in relaxed and steady intervals. "What are you saying? How could he kill a Jinn? Why couldn't she vanish and get away?"

"It just kinda *happened*," Olive muttered. "Basically, he threw a broken off piece of the Afrit's horn at her so fast, she didn't see it coming, and the magnetism in the ash infected her body. Plus, he pretty much pierced her heart."

Eric's mind went numb. *She saved my life... everybody's lives. She gave her life for us, almost fifteen hundred years of existence so that we could live. Was it worth it?*

The Afrit's voice penetrated his haze of misery. *'Her body must be retrieved from the building where she perished. She gave instructions that we are to take her... as spoils. Should any energy remain inside her, she wished it to be ours.'*

"It's true," Olive affirmed. "Those were her last words."

For once, even Lotte seemed speechless. They all sat in stunned and remorseful silence until the Afrit spoke again. *'We will take our leave. Dawn approaches, and with it, a greater threat of discovery. Like the ragged god, we shall return to the abode where you summoned us, and take what has been offered.'*

"Hold on," Lotte cried. "You have to do something else as well."

The Afrit gazed stonily down at her.

"You have to take *him*." She ratcheted to her feet and held out sleeping Jonah. "If we're somehow seen dropping off this child, it's all over for us. You seem to have a way of avoiding unwanted attention. We need you to drop this boy in a safe spot where he'll be found by the police. They're everywhere to the east of here, toward the rising sun, near the great bridge. Please, do this for us."

The ashen monster looked indifferently at the child Lotte presented, then wrapped its talons around the boy's neck and abdomen and drew him close.

"Shouldn't we cover him up somehow?" Olive urgently asked. "The poor kid's totally naked, and it's cold as all get-up out there. He'll freeze. Here, I'll give him my hoodie."

Lotte emphatically stopped her. "No! That sweatshirt has Eric's and your DNA all over it, probably mine as well. Plus, it's covered in blood, probably Mutig's from when you were lying on him."

Eric inspected closely and saw that it was true. *Damn. I've had that thing a long time, but that may be the end of it.*

Lotte turned back to the Afrit. "Just fly close to the ground where it's a bit warmer and keep him close to your body."

Olive gave a little snort of disdain. "Fat lot of good that'll do. That nasty ol' thing is cold enough to freeze the balls off a pool table."

Lotte just shook her head. "There's nothing for it. The Afrit doesn't have far to go, and the child is totally passed out from exhaustion, which is definitely for the best. I hope he never has any memories of what happened. In any case, thank you, great one. This will make things far simpler."

Like Pazuzu, the Afrit took to the air and quickly vanished from sight.

Eric got up and put his hand on Lotte's shoulder. "That was quick thinking about Jonah. We'd have had a hard time dropping him off somewhere without our van being filmed by multiple cameras. They'd have tracked us down for sure. Actually, what you did with Humbaba might be the fanciest persuading I've ever heard you conjure up. What the hell made you think that would work?"

She scrunched her lips. "Think? That's giving me a lot more credit than I deserve. I was in a panic, and I knew something had to be done. It was getting pretty clear that Pazuzu's logic wasn't working. It seemed like a more 'emotional' approach might be in order. Of all the things I've been reading up on lately, Humbaba's lines about his mother in *The Epic of Gilgamesh* stuck with me the most, like a little window into his soul that I could easily relate to."

A look of distant sadness crossed her face, and Eric took her in his arms.

"It wasn't just that, though," she said into his shoulder. "It was also what Pazuzu said yesterday about Humbaba never lacking sincerity, or not trying to change his ways, but rather having difficulty maintaining his resolve once he'd made a decision. I thought that, just maybe, if I could get him to feel a bit of empathy, make him understand that the people he hurts, or their loved ones, suffer as immensely as he does, that he might make a sincere but spontaneous choice. It wouldn't matter if he changed his mind later. By then, he'd be with Pazuzu, and we'd have done what we set out to do. I had no idea it would actually work. Honestly, I was sort of stalling for time, hoping Tamanna might come to the rescue. I have no idea what I'd have done had I known.... So awful."

Eric bit back tears. "Yeah, awful. Listen, if we don't want to end up in jail, we probably need to get out of here."

"We do, but I think we're going to have a hard time scaling that fence, and I don't think Mutig is in any condition to be jumping it again. There has to be another way out of here."

"Let me check Google Maps and see what looks like the quickest exit." He got out his phone and called up FDR Park while Lotte hauled Olive reluctantly to her feet. "Okay, I think the best way is to go north, toward Pattison. Looks like there's a main entryway there. We can follow the trails we found. They'll take us right to it."

Lotte and Eric supported a feeble Olive as the three friends trudged through the darkened park, Mutig limping closely at their heels.

What should have taken ten minutes took more than double that, and by the time they shambled onto a paved road that led to the exit, Olive was near exhaustion.

She collapsed onto the curb, and Mutig instantly curled up at her feet. "Y'all, I'm sorry. Can we just rest for a while."

"I'm not sure that's a good idea," Lotte replied, nervously looking around. "This part of the park seems more developed and might have cameras, or even security guards. I think it's best we get out of here as quickly as possible."

Olive's head slumped in dismay, and Eric cut in. "Why don't you two just hide out of sight behind a tree for a few minutes. I'll go get the van and park on Pattison. The street seems dead this time of night, and I'll watch out for police cars. I'll come get you, and that will give Olive time to rest, and cut off another half-hour walk."

"I'll go with you," Lotte offered.

"I think it's better if you stay here. If there are guards, and they find Olive, you and your silver tongue might be able to talk our way out of trouble. Besides, what could happen to me? All the monsters have been accounted for at this point, and if I get robbed, it's better you're not around anyway."

She shrugged. "All right. For once in your life, you actually make sense. Just be careful."

He smiled and gave her a quick kiss, then set out for the main road.

Pattison was a major six lane thoroughfare, and a smattering of cars still sped past in both directions. He exited the park across from South 20th Street and, despite there being no sidewalk on the south side of the street, he hung a quick left and hugged the fence near the trees, which shrouded him in relative darkness. It was only a couple of blocks before he reached the familiar turnoff to Gateway Drive, which he followed back to the intersection with the cement fountain.

He breathed a sigh of relief when he saw the van sitting parked where he'd left it by the side of the road, blending in amongst the various inactive construction vehicles near the ratty old bridge. He jogged across the street, quickly unlocked the door, hopped in, and started the engine.

Intending to once again go straight across the narrow, grassy median, he'd just begun to pull out into the street when a car's headlights suddenly appeared from behind one of the utility trucks, blazing on high beams. The vehicle careened past the van, nearly colliding with the front bumper, then squealed to a halt, blocking him in.

"Shit! Is this the police?"

He suddenly felt a strong, bare arm wrap around his neck. "Follow that car. Flash your lights to acknowledge that you'll comply. Do it now, or I'll snap your neck."

The man's voice had an accent of indeterminate origin, vaguely Middle Eastern, but the lilt of his words reminded Eric of how Aicha Kandicha had spoken. There was no uncertainty in his meaning or of his sincerity. The man's arm steadily tightened, forcing Eric to make a choice while he still had the capacity to do so.

*This is probably Ornias. He wants what he's wanted all along, to get one of us for questioning – torture, really, but whatever. If he gets what he wants from me, maybe he'll leave Lotte and Olive alone, especially once he learns the truth that the stupid scroll and key are long gone, and that the Rope of An and Ki won't be sending him home anytime soon. If I die now, that chance is wasted.*

He pulled twice at his blinker to flash his bright lights, and he felt the death grip around his neck loosen slightly. He took his foot off the brake and followed the car before him as it steered into the road. They'd barely cleared the bridge when the vehicle veered right onto South 26th Street and began to speed up.

"Where are we going?"

The man didn't answer.

To the left, a sprawling, dirty, industrial zone unfolded, seemingly larger than FDR Park. The right side of the road was lined with thick trees, and an occasional building interrupting the dense greenery. Eric slammed his foot on the brake, surprised that the car in front of him had stopped abruptly. It backed up slightly and then signaled for a right turn. There wasn't a true road here, just a dirt track through the trees. The vehicle inched forward, then pulled to the side and glided to a halt, sheltered amongst the underbrush.

Eric compliantly parked behind.

"Shut off the engine," the man commanded.

Eric did so, wondering if he should try to make a break for it, then try to get lost in the industrial area across the street. *Probably a bad idea. I think I'm just gonna have to take whatever this asshole has to dish out.* "Okay, what now?"

"Get out of the seat and come back here... slowly. I don't want to kill you, but I will if I must."

Eric didn't doubt it. He unbuckled his seat belt and sidled into the back. The man quickly pushed him to the floor and kept a stiff arm on his shoulder. Even in dim light, Eric could see he was totally nude.

*Yep, Ornias for sure. He clearly snuck into the van in his immaterial form. How the hell did he find us?*

The lithe, bald man sat with his back against side of the van. He didn't move a muscle, save his head, which craned from one side to the other, scanning the front of the vehicle, then back through the largely empty cargo space.

Outside, Eric heard the car's door open and close. After some stuttering footsteps, a loud knock rang out on the van's side door, followed by a brusque query. The words were not in English, but the voice was unmistakably Rachid's.

"Open it," Ornias directed, "and don't do anything foolish."

Eric slid the door open with resignation and beheld Rashid, rifle at the ready, thermal imaging goggles positioned under his helmet. The man spared him a quick glance and seemed to frown slightly before he hopped into the cargo space and rapidly pulled the door shut.

Ornias eagerly asked him some questions, again in a language Eric couldn't understand, and Rashid responded in kind, seeming to indicate the negative by shaking his head.

A few more words passed between them, then Ornias turned his attention to Eric. "Very well, then. We seem as safe as possible for now, but time is short. Shall we proceed?"

"Look, I know you're gonna get what you want out of me. I won't last fifteen seconds under torture. I'll answer your damn questions truthfully, I promise. Just tell me what you want to know!"

"It's too late for that, and in any case, we lack sufficient time. There's no telling when another one of your unanticipated protectors might appear from nowhere. I'm simply going to have to take what I want."

Rashid cautiously cut in. "Ornias, is that truly necessary? This one has been—"

"Silence! Do your job and keep watch for those who made a mockery of you and your 'top-notch team' back at that bridge."

"The female Jinn wasn't supposed to be there. You were tricked, and we paid the price."

"True, but all the more reason not to dally any longer with these insignificant interferers. I'll get what I want, and we can be done with them. This ridiculous game ends now!"

Eric began to tremble. "What does that mean? I guess it means you'll kill me, right?"

"There are fates far worse than death, my friend. If it is any consolation, I will swear upon the name of any god you like that I will not take your life. Better?"

He gulped and didn't really feel much better.

"Sadly, I cannot promise that my method will be without pain, or without *other* consequences. But here we are, and if you are ready... here we go."

Put simply, Eric wasn't ready, but he could never have been prepared for what Ornias had in mind, so it didn't really matter.

After an indeterminate period of complete incoherence, he oddly found himself conscious of the fact that he was now *unconscious*. He guessed that he'd been knocked out. Ornias must have hit him, like Tamanna had hit Siddique on the rooftop patio. It all happened so fast, he couldn't remember, and he wasn't sure why he remained aware, like the experience of a lucid dream. All he knew was that he could feel the presence of another being, someone inside his mind, sifting through memories as if they were inspecting the drawers of his dresser. He tried to see, tried to experience what this intruder was after, but he couldn't "move," for lack of a better word.

Suddenly, he had the sensation of falling, of spinning downward, ever downward, faster and faster. He anticipated an impact at some point and knew it would be painful. He was quickly proven correct. He made contact with *something*, or something made contact with him. It wasn't solid. Rather, it was more like a barrier of sorts, like passing from one zone into another, and in this new place, the feeling of plunging was replaced by an incomprehensible agony.

He could feel the intruder intently watching as the very strands of his mind were ripped open, cruelly exposed for anyone to see. For the one who observed — Ornias, presumably — all was as clear as the words on a page, divided neatly into chapters, and carefully indexed by various topics from the most mundane to the exceptionally important, easily referenced and located in the text of his life.

Eric knew he could stop it, knew he could close things back up and keep the secrets of his mind to himself, but somehow, he had been fiendishly sequestered in one section of his memories, one subject that while intermittent over the course of his life, overrode all others with its magnitude and immediacy. He found himself immersed in the topic of *pain*.

It wasn't simply physical pain, though that was surely present. Memories he didn't even know he still possessed rushed by, like the severing of his umbilical cord and the cold of the world assailing him after the warmth of his mother's womb. Skinned knees, stubbed toes, paper cuts, hammers to the thumb, that stupid leap in third grade off the swing set at its highest point onto the asphalt below, play fights with schoolmates that went a bit too far and left mottled bruises that lingered agonizingly for days, along with a host of other petty but painful experiences, washed over him—not one at a time, but all at once, every instance happening simultaneously.

To this was added the more severe injuries, those dealt by baseballs on rocky infields, a couple of bad falls from bicycles, strained muscles in the gym, and, of course, wounds he'd endured from battles with enemies both mortal and immortal in the pursuit of keeping the dangerous artifacts out of nefarious hands. The Afrit's claws in his thigh, the table across his back, his manhandling by Charun, and even worse, Ninurta. He felt the concussion from the kamikaze explosion of the stalwart Afrit in the Rope of An and Ki, and more recently the wound to his head from Rashid's baton. All pummeled him nonstop, ripping at his very sanity, but that wasn't even close to being the worst of it.

The physical agony paled in comparison to the emotional. Every embarrassing moment, every slight that separated him from his peers, every instance where he didn't measure up, from baseball, to geometry, to German, to the complex and seemingly incomprehensible social interactions of school, now replayed in fast forward and endless repeat before his eyes, pinned wide open like Malcolm McDowell's in *A Clockwork Orange*. Unremittingly, he relived the bitter humiliation of his first semester in college, and guilt beset him as the terrible choice he'd made that ended his grandmother's life, as well as taking the life of the man in the house above the Majlis Al Jinn, persistently scrolled past.

*Why did I hit him so hard? Couldn't I have just knocked him out?*

He'd entirely blotted out the fact that he'd never even come close to having a girlfriend before meeting Lotte, having been too shy, too insecure, and ultimately, in his mind, too undesirable. Now those feelings flooded back to him, as did the epiphany of his infinite inadequacy once he'd inadvertently entered her celestial orbit. The gutting he'd endured when they broke up again tore into his soul. He found himself permanently locked in his little red Mazda 3 on Holton Hill Road after he'd dropped her off for the final time before they both went off to college. The vehicle still retained its glorious new car smell, but that scent was stained with his tears, knowing that the girl who had actually made his pathetic life worth living would soon be on a plane to England, and almost surely, the rest of her life without him.

Then, as if nothing joyful or uplifting had happened since he and Lotte reunited, the anguish of losing their child presented the *pièce de résistance* in this banquet of torment. He watched mutely as blood again blossomed in the beautiful, clear waters of the Abzu, and as Lotte savagely wailed and shrieked until she was hoarse, into the waves of the uncaring sea.

This presented the ultimate torture. He couldn't bear it. The loss overwhelmed him, made him wish he, too, were dead, that he had never been born, never existed at all, and that his memory could just be wiped away forever, so he wouldn't have to remember such utter and complete despair. He realized that, in a sense, this was exactly what was happening. Imprisoned in misery, no other thoughts or actions were possible. The totality of these horrible sensations would sweep him away, hopefully sooner than later.

*Or what if they don't stop? What if I'm trapped like this forever? This is hell. I'm in hell... the real hell... probably inflicted by Jinn on clueless people for millennia. I guess I better get used to it. They say it's endless and that there's no escape.*

Without warning, the unbearable thrashing ceased.

The deluge of images slowly faded, though the ache from the battering cascaded through his body and rang in his ears, like the noise after a loud concert. For a while, this constituted the extent of what he could see, hear, and feel, but after an indeterminate time, the sound of deep, ragged breaths caught his attention, along with the voice of a person, chanting slowly and soothingly. This he recognized as Rashid, speaking in his native tongue.

Eric tried to get up, but found he couldn't move his limbs, couldn't even feel them. He attempted to speak, but the words caught in his throat, causing him to choke.

"Ah, you're alive." His enemy's words were strangely warm. "Go slowly. The ordeal you experienced surely taxed you to the limit. You're safe now, at least for the moment."

With his limbs immobilized, Eric endeavored simply to open his eyes. The task proved difficult, but eventually the familiar surroundings of the van's cargo space came into focus. The dome light had been turned on, providing illumination to see, but it took him a moment to digest what was happening.

Ornias's bald head hovered over Eric's right shoulder. Eyeless sockets gaped at him as the man twitched and shook. The flesh on his cheeks had blackened and begun to flake off, as had most of his shoulders. Rashid crouched firmly behind the suffering Jinn with one arm wrapped around his torso, keeping the twitching body from collapsing onto Eric where he lay on the floor.

"Wh... wha... what? What... happ.... What happened?"

"I killed him," Rashid mildly replied, "or I'm in the process of doing so."

"Wh... why?"

"Why? Because I can no longer be party to this insanity. Had I known it would end this way, I'd have never gotten involved, but it wasn't always like this, and the money... the money was impossible to pass up."

"How... how did you... find us?"

He sadly lowered his head and his thermal imaging goggles pointed to the floor. "The woman whose car fooled Ornias. I believe her name was Nadia. After your Jinn friends attacked us near the bridge in North Carolina, a police car arrived. I was injured, but not dead, and I was still heavily armed. They had no chance, never even saw me. I took their vehicle, which turned out to be the key. Through the police radio, I was able to track Nadia's appearance at a nearby police station, and to which hospital they took her. When the police were finished with her and she was discharged the next day, we followed her. She took a taxi to a rental car shop and got on the highway headed north. We captured her when she eventually stopped at a rest area, and forced her to find out where you had gone."

Eric sputtered in disbelief. "I... I'd have never gone along with that. I wouldn't betray my wife and friends like that. No way! I'd rather die."

"Brave words, but you heard Ornias. There are worse fates than death. I imagine you experienced some of that after he knocked you unconscious."

Eric tightly shut his eyes, shuddering at the memory of his recent ordeal.

"I see you did. I'm sorry, but this was the only way."

"Wha... what do you mean?"

"Nadia was defiant, like you. She also said she'd die before being disloyal to her mentor, but Ornias promised her something far worse, and unlike you, she knew what that meant, and that he had the capacity to deliver. Rather than kill her, he threatened to leave her alive, but trapped in a coma, untreatable by human medicine. She'd live out her days alone—conscious, but locked away, unable to move or communicate. It would be an endless torture of tedium, day after day the same, or perhaps made more abominable by some additional machination concocted by Ornias. Seeing what you've now seen, what would you have done?"

*I have to admit, experiencing agony like that for years on end truly would have been a fate worse than death. That may be what he had in mind for me, once he'd gotten what he wanted.*

"I... I don't know."

"Mmmm, not so confident now, are we? I can hardly blame you. I'm not certain I could have faced such a brutal sentence. Nadia made the right choice and cooperated, preferring dishonor, and then death, to the horror Ornias proposed. I thought all would be well after she made the call and we located your whereabouts, but then... everything changed. Ornias struck her unconscious as he did to you. At first, I thought her dead, but I was wrong. Instead, he penetrated her unprotected mind and left her in exactly the state he'd sworn to refrain from inflicting. I couldn't believe it. Why? Death, I can understand. She posed a threat if we left her alive, but what purpose could this possibly serve? I realized then and there that I'd given my allegiance to the wrong master, one who could inflict such cruelty to satisfy a petty grudge."

"Why didn't you kill him then, or just leave and never come back?"

"I could probably have slipped away later, but Ornias knows far more about my life than I do about his. My family and friends would have been in grave danger. A quick phone call to the endless supply of guns for hire in Morocco, and that would have been that. As for killing him, in that moment, I was completely unprepared. It wasn't until he'd committed the act, and I saw the rising and falling of Nadia's chest with breath, that I realized what had happened. By then, Ornias had regained consciousness and would have easily been able to resist any assault I could have mounted. I had to wait, bide my time, and hope for another opportunity when he was feeding, or again penetrating the mind of another victim. Jinn are vulnerable during such periods, which is why they employ mercenaries such as me to watch over them, just as I was doing this very night."

"So, I was bait. It's not actually the first time I've been bait. I didn't think bait had such a decent life expectancy."

Rashid smiled. "I tried to get him to question you, then let you go. Unlike Nadia, you couldn't hurt us any longer, once Ornias had gotten what he wanted. Presented with the opportunity, however, I didn't hesitate. I killed Nadia when he made me drop her body near a dumpster behind a restaurant, partly praying that he wouldn't see me do it, and partly praying that he would and bring an end to my worthless life. It's certainly no less than I deserve."

He thrust his right shoulder and Ornias jerked and spasmed before letting out one final, desperate howl from his desiccated mouth. The cry ceased when his head ripped free of his neck and shoulders and tumbled to the floor of the van. Rashid's fist punched through the dusty debris that rained from the mortal wound, clutching Naomi's brass knuckles with the fearsome iron barb. She'd crafted this item to be a Jinn killer, and it had worked with extraordinary efficiency. Black tendrils already snaked their way down the Jinn's chest, recalling Aicha Kandicha's condition when Eric had inadvertently killed her, and her poor host, with a rusty rail spike.

Rashid released Ornias's now lifeless torso, then drove his weapon into the Jinn's kidney and twisted savagely. Once satisfied, he released his grip on the blood-stained brass knuckles and dusted himself off. "That will do it. I'm glad I had the foresight to take that weapon from Naomi's corpse as I was searching the SUV for useful items before I fled. Here's another thing I picked up along the way, something you might like back."

He reached to his belt, unholstered a pistol, and casually tossed it to the floor of the van. "Your little Glock 19. I thought about keeping it as a memento, but being shot isn't exactly among my fondest memories. Perhaps it will give you greater pleasure."

"It's not really mine. The owner will be super relieved the police didn't find it. She gave it to me to use if I got desperate. Despite what you might think of me, I didn't take any *pleasure* in shooting you."

He smiled. "I know. I hoped you'd be happy to remember that I didn't die. In any case, I find it time to make haste once again. I haven't seen them, but I suspect your Jinn friends will be close on your trail, and this time, I don't think I'll be as lucky to escape with my life. You'll be paralyzed for some time—as are all who the Jinn touch in this way—but that will wear off... fairly quickly, I think, as you're already able to speak. I hope the memory of whatever distress Ornias brought to you soon fades as well. I struck as quickly as I thought safe. You surprised me, all of you. If you truly have the favor of ancient gods, as I've been led to believe, they chose their associates wisely. Good luck to you, Eric. You don't mind if I call you Eric, do you?"

# CHAPTER 19

**Atlanta, Georgia, Saturday, November 11, 2017**

Olive washed down the last of her Varsity chili dog with a swig of Coke, then reached for a french fry and held it out for Mutig. The dog quickly vacuumed the morsel out of her hand and devoured it before resuming his expectant vigil in the passenger seat beside her.

"Nun-uh. That's all for now. I don't want you gettin' sick on the plane, though I doubt you'll even notice... unless we crash. Enki sure did make you tough!"

He cocked his head, and she scratched under his chin.

She felt wonderful being back in Mutig's good graces, though she realized he'd never truly abandoned her. He'd been there for her when the chips were down, launching into combat with Humbaba to try and save her life. What the magically endowed animal had clearly questioned was whether she would be there for *him*—she who had become tainted by the mysterious scent of another.

*It's okay, boy. I'm still me... basically.* She didn't bother voicing the thought. *I guess I proved myself by saving him. Yeah, like all it took was for me to risk my own life. Whatever. All's well that ends in a well, so they say, sort of. I gotta say, though, if this is ending well....*

Just as Eric had once warned her, Olive had an entirely different perspective on life compared to just two years ago. She'd witnessed nearly incomprehensible, sometimes shattering events, including being party to the killing of others. Moreover, her very existence on Earth had been forever altered.

*Mutig wasn't wrong not to trust me. I don't completely trust myself no more. Pazuzu asked me not only who I was, but what I was. I'm honestly not sure. What have I become?*

She had no answer but held out hope that the journey upon which she was about to embark might be a step in the right direction, in spite of the dark specter of death that hung over the undertaking like a foreboding storm cloud.

Her phone chimed, and she opened it and glanced at the text. It was from Claudia:

*Leaving now. Meet you at airport ~30 mins?*

She glanced at the clock and ran a quick calculation before she thumbed out her reply:

*Better make it 45. See you then.*

She had another chore to complete before driving her Jetta one final time to its new owner. Claudia seemed nice, an education student at Georgia State University who had responded to the Craigslist advertisement, and she was overwhelmed when Olive had offered to pass the already inexpensively priced car to her for free.

*Honestly, it ain't such a great car no more, but I guess it's got a few miles left in it. I certainly won't be needin' it where I'm going.*

Olive eyed the peach pie that sat in its paper wrapper on the tray that clung to her open window.

*The time has come.*

Loss and grieving had been Olive's constant companions since the fateful night in Philadelphia. This would be the final act that, at least for a time, would bring this process to a close, though it would still take time to fully banish from her mind the sad litany of events that had brought her to this moment.

After what seemed like an eternity waiting behind a tree in FDR park with Lotte and the wondrously durable Mutig, whose wooziness was rapidly abating, Eric had finally called them and relayed what had happened. Nearly another hour passed before he regained enough control over his faculties to drive back to them, at which point Olive grudgingly took the wheel and cautiously steered back to the house.

When they arrived, Karšift and the Afrit awaited them, hiding out of view behind some trash barrels. The creature had retrieved its broken horn, and of greater import, Tamanna's body. Eric completely lost his composure when he saw the gaping and desiccated wound on her exquisitely beautiful chest. Olive spent the remainder of the night consoling him, leaving Lotte to cope with the fire portal, and the beast who wished to return to its realm bearing the spoils of its labors.

The next day, Olive felt it her duty to contact Khalil about his mother's death. His shock and sadness pierced her heart. He mourned not only the passing of his sole remaining parent, but of an entity that had impacted events with a subtle and efficacious hand for centuries. She was, he said, irreplaceable, and the world would miss her, whether it knew that or not.

A burgeoning anger at the god who had sent his mother on her fateful mission forced him to abruptly end their call. Without saying it outright, Olive strongly sensed that Khalil also blamed her, along with Lotte and Eric, for what had happened. She could understand his resentment.

*Was my life really worth saving? Plus, Tamanna would still be alive if I'd been able to help Pazuzu. So much for gettin' Khalil's help with gettin' control over my stupid* powers *now. Man, it can't get any more rotten than this!*

She was proven woefully wrong when, later in the day, Lotte broke the unexpected and unwelcome news that Siddique's return to consciousness after becoming a vessel for Pazuzu, and now Humbaba as well, would not be forthcoming. Moreover, it seemed the rejuvenated god would be assuming Siddique's persona and life, and that the timeframe of this arrangement appeared uncertain and seemingly interminable.

This was the final indignation. She packed up her few things, grabbed Mutig, and left the little house in Germantown, barely saying goodbye to her friends.

*Friends. Are they really my friends, or are we just stuck together in this endless cycle of* suck? *How can I even see them if Pazuzu is gonna be around, rubbin' my face in what* might have *been? Maybe I'm better off without any of them, or really anything at all in this putrid excuse for a life!*

With Mutig in tow, the bus wasn't an option, so she grabbed an Uber to the airport and rented a car. Frustration and discouragement plagued her on the road back to Atlanta.

*My job sucks, my living situation sucks — I mean, sorry, Mom, but really, I want be out on my own — the most promising relationship I've ever had has been messed up by a two stupid Mesopotamian gods that can't get their shit together, and my friends think it's fine if he... they... whatever... just live my potential boyfriend's life for the next who-the-hell-knows how long. Seriously, am I being punished for my sins, or something?*

Once home, she didn't even bother to return to work at the station, sensing she'd exhausted what little latitude for which she might once have qualified.

*So much for a career in law enforcement. McDonalds, here I come!*

Her phone rang and beeped regularly over the next week or so, mostly calls and texts from Lotte and Eric. She ignored them, just as she fended off her mother's increasingly anxious concern by hiding in her room. She needed time to sort things out, but in truth, there was nothing to sort out. No answer to her dilemma lurked in "introspection," or a career change into a wasteful and depressing dead end.

At one time, she might have agreed with Siddique's assessment that their unusual little group of friends had lived enviable lives. At this point, all that seemed ill-considered and naïve.

*Or maybe he was right, and all that stuff does come with a price.*

"Boy, I'm payin' now, that's for sure!"

Mutig stirred where he lay beside her on the bed in her room, shades drawn to keep out the remorseless reminders of life that accompanied the daylight.

"You paid too, didn't you? You're sort of like me, all bent into something you were never supposed to be. One thing's for sure: there's no goin' back, for either of us."

The dog morosely laid back down as the sound of her phone indicated a text message. Against her better judgment, she gave it a casual glance. To her infinite surprise, it came from Khalil. His message was simple and direct:

*What are you going to do?*

She had no idea, and in the absence of other promising options, plus an irrepressible curiosity, she returned his message.

The plan he offered made sense, even if it meant making herself utterly dependent on the person who harbored anger about her association with his mother's death. It also meant giving up just about every aspect of her current life, but as she'd come to realize, there wasn't much to salvage — perhaps nothing at all.

Olive snatched the peach pie off the tray, slid a portion gently out of the paper wrapper, and took a bite. She then opened the Youtube app on her phone and typed in the song she needed.

Her eyes went wide when she saw the picture on the video, presumably the cover of the record it was from. "That dude is buck naked! What kind of stuff is this, anyway? I mean, nice lookin' butt and all, but if this is some kind of wacky porno music, I'm not going through with this!"

She was about to push play when she was again taken aback. "Fifteen-and-a-half minutes! What the.... Who do they think they are, Beethoven?

And who the H-E Double L has time to listen to a fifteen-minute-long song? Somebody with nothing better to do with their lives, *that's* who! If I'd known this, I might not have done it. I sure hope the Car Hop doesn't come back to get the tray and sees 'naked butt boy' on my screen. That would be too embarrassing! It's for Harland, though, so here goes."

She started the video of Yes's *Awaken*. The music began with what sounded like classical piano that morphed into a gentle melody before a soft and ethereal soundscape unfolded.

The vocals, when they came in, jolted her slightly. "Gawd, he really does sound like an elf on helium! I wonder if he's the naked guy on the cover. I guess I could get used to his weirdo voice if I got to see a nice-lookin' *derrière* all day." She gave Mutig a little wink.

The piece struck her as somewhat abstract, especially the lyrics, which sounded like a hippie Book of Revelation, but when the tempo picked up and it started to rock a little, she began to settle in.

This was the best she could do. She'd barely known Harland Cheevers, really hadn't known him at all, but now she thought about him. He'd once seemed so frightening, but he turned out to be so nice, so considerate and tenderhearted. It's clear that life hadn't always gone his way, but he'd been there for his parents as they aged, and he seemed to have never done any harm. His last thoughts were of his friends at the museum and the people he'd known at his music festivals. Those things brought him joy, as did being amongst the ancient artifacts that surrounded him most days.

Olive could relate to that. Old things brought her a sense of comfort as well, but the past would have to wait while she immersed herself in an unfamiliar and potentially dangerous future. She needed to learn how to control forces that might kill her, or potentially even worse, unleash a malignant entity back into the world.

Despite his displeasure with her, Khalil had proposed that he aid her in gaining command of the powers within her, just as he would help her navigate the perils of modern Tyre. He'd already orchestrated the myriad delicacies of her presence in Lebanon, as if by magic.

None of these changes would be easy on her, but the decision to leave had come as a relief. It would separate her from a life that had, in many senses, gone off the rails. There was nothing to reclaim from the wreckage, not now, at least. Some distant tomorrow might hold different opportunities, but she couldn't sit at her mother's house in Marietta, working a crappy job and waiting indefinitely for Siddique to return.

*I'd go crazy. I have to do somethin'!*

A feeling of unease came over her.

*We always feel like we gotta do something, don't we, but who knows if what we decide to do makes things any better? It's like what Lotte was sayin' back in the Carlos Museum: cause and effect. We do what we think is right, but who knows if it really is.*

Olive had always tried to do what was "right," but forces seemingly beyond her ability to control, both internal and external, had interceded with distressing frequency and impact.

*Maybe that's just the way it is. Things sure didn't work out so well for poor Harland, and that started long before a dumb ol' god basically stole his life! Still, though, he tried to make the best of it. He went to work, he did social media, he had his music – such as it is – and he went to all those concerts. He didn't just sit around doing nothin'. He had his friends, and they missed him and were worried about him.*

The song on her phone reached a dramatic crescendo before returning to the ethereal lightness of the earlier, opening section. Olive choked back tears and repeatedly stroked Mutig, who had curled up beside her.

*Huh, friends. In the end, that's all he really had. Go easy, Harland. You were a good person who deserved better, and I'll never forget you, or this long-ass song you made me play. Actually, it wasn't nearly as bad as I thought it would be.*

The music ended with a gentle bluesy lick. She wiped her eyes and glanced at the time. She needed to get to the airport to meet Claudia, but she took a moment to pull up her text conversation with Eric and type a message:

*Who do your sucky Patriots play tomorrow?*

He and Lotte knew she was leaving tonight, and where she was going, but they had few other details. She placed what remained of the peach pie on the tray, along with a ten-dollar bill, and hailed the Varsity Car Hop.

Her phone pinged with Eric's reply:

*Broncos, in Denver. Falcons play the Cowboys.*

She smiled.

*I'll miss it... traveling. Update you when I'm in Rome on layover. Send me the final score.*

The Car Hop cheerfully hustled to her window. "Y'all done?"

"Yep, I'm done. Thanks. It was real good. I'll be back some day... I hope."

"I hope so too. Thank you very much! Y'all have a fantastic night!"

She rolled up the window and glanced at her phone as she started the engine. Eric had answered her request:

*Will do.*

## South Boston, Massachusetts, Saturday, November 11, 2017

Eric sat behind the wheel of his Mazda, not so patiently waiting for Lotte to return. Things were getting somewhat easier, but being alone was still hardest. No distraction, it seemed, from sports blab on the radio to mindless Youtube clips, could keep his thoughts from going... *there*, exactly where he didn't want to go, but where his mind invariably drifted, unbidden and undesired.

The wavering of the flashlight on Lotte's phone caught his attention as she emerged from the scraggly underbrush near the train tracks and rounded the corner of the building. Once more, an impish Afrit, not much larger than a pigeon, flew in Boston's night sky.

Upon returning from Philadelphia, Lotte and Eric had deposited Pazuzu, freshly reunited with Humbaba, into Siddique's apartment. Unwilling to leave their menagerie of irreplaceable artifacts in the charge of the unpredictable god, they'd had little option but to return the items to their former hiding place in South Boston. Aside from them, no one who had seen the space they'd rented in the repurposed warehouse could still be counted among the living—technically—so they felt relatively safe. They had to trust that Olive would keep Aicha contained, but with few other immediate options, there wasn't much of a debate.

Eric watched as Lotte skipped up the steps to the loading dock and disappeared inside to lock up. He was about to start the car when his phone pinged. To his amazement, Olive had texted him.

*Wow, wasn't expecting that. I wonder what she wants. I hope it's not trouble.* He laughed when he saw her message. *Sucky Patriots, huh?*

Despite the prattle on the radio, he had no idea who his team was playing tomorrow. He'd checked out of sports—along with just about everything else—since his experience with Ornias. He put on a brave face for work because he had to, especially if he wanted to keep tabs on Schneider Industrial Flooring's newest employee: Pazuzu, King of Demons, Bringer of Famine, Layer of Base Coat for Subflooring.

*Actually, he's having Humbaba do most of the work. He says it's a good way to give him a sense of control and to prove that things are different now. Pretty clever. I sure as hell hope it works.*

He knew Olive could look up the game easily, but he was overjoyed having finally heard from her, so he played along and checked tomorrow's games on ESPN.

He'd just finished typing his reply when Lotte hopped in the car. "Texting with somebody?"

"Yeah, Olive."

"Really?"

"Yup. I'm as surprised as you are."

"What does she want?"

"Nothing much. She asked me a dumb question. I think she just wants us to know that she doesn't hate us... anymore."

"That would be awfully nice. I really feel terrible, it's just... what else were we supposed to do? If everything gets sorted out eventually, this will have been for the best."

"Yeah, I know, and she does too. It just stinks in the meantime. I still can't even believe any of this is actually happening." His phone dinged again, and he glanced at Olive's reply.

"What does the say?" Lotte asked.

"She's gonna text us when she's in Rome on layover."

"Well, that's a good sign. Maybe we'll get a little more information. I know it's hard, but I hope she keeps the channel open. We need to know what's going on."

He nodded vaguely as he typed a quick response. *Yeah*, you *need to know*. At the moment, Olive's troubles were as far from his mind as football. He decided to change the subject. "So, how'd it go?"

"How did what go?"

"How'd it go with Chuckles? Was he happy you were willing to stamp his passport again so he can joyride on planet Earth?"

She scoffed. "Oh, right. Honestly, you got me. Things have been quiet since we got back... too quiet. I thought it was best to at least check in. I got a response pretty quickly, but the bloody little thing flew off and barely said a word to me. Funny, I've been getting that treatment a lot lately."

"Huh?"

"Exactly. 'Huh' has pretty much been your response to everything for the past two weeks. I know you had a terrible experience, but you're not the stupid Afrit! You actually *know* you have feelings, and that you have someone you can talk with about them. It would be nice if you took advantage."

He shivered and started the car to get the heater going, even though he knew that wasn't the genuine source of this particular chill. "I know.

It's just... hard. I don't really want to think about it, but I do anyway. I can't help it. It just takes over, and suddenly, I'm back... *there*. I don't want to be *there* ever again, and talking about it is like reliving it. Plus... I don't know... I just don't think you'd be particularly happy with some of the things I've been thinking. I know I'm not."

She put her hand on his thigh. "Try me. I know this is difficult, but I think this is eating you alive. We're in this together. You've been there for me countless times, and it's cost you. I want to be there for you, and I'm afraid of what might happen if you can't get your head around this. You hear me?"

He heard her. He knew she was right, and it wasn't just because she was *always* right. A door in his mind had been opened to a room that, for most people, remained forever locked. In it, all the things that ever hurt you lurked and brooded, whether you were aware of them or not. Just knowing such a place existed, irrespective of the exact contents, was enough to make Eric's skin crawl.

He'd seen Hell, not the imaginary Hell used by ignorant phonies to coerce you into *their* concept of "good" behavior, but the real Hell, where all the hurt you'd experienced clung to the hull of your life like infinite layers of barnacles. With time, despite your best efforts to stay on track, the ship no longer steers true, and eventually, enough detritus might accrue that you actually get dragged into the depths. This he now knew, because it had been revealed to him, and in some perverse way, certain things started to make sense.

He turned up the car's heater and took Lotte's hand in his. "Okay, but you're not gonna like what I tell you."

"I'll like it even less if you *don't* tell me."

"Yeah, that's probably true. All right. I don't know how to put it nicely, so I'll just say it: Dimme was right." He felt her pull back—try to extract her hand from his—but he held firm.

"Dimme was right about what!" she finally snapped.

"We taste better when we're young, before all the shit builds up and freakin' *poisons* us. You can't believe it. I didn't... not until I saw it myself. It's all there, Lotte. Everything. Every ache and pain, every broken heart, every mistake you ever made, every regret you ever had. It's all inside you, and it has power. It influences what you do, whether you know it or not."

She took a deep breath, and he felt her inch a bit closer. "You might be right, but we're not supposed to see all that, experience all that, least of all having it come at you in the same instant. Under normal circumstances, our bodies and minds are built to handle these things. Not to contradict your esteemed Doctor Freud, but the evidence suggests that this is *exactly* what dreams are for. They're a safety valve that helps you process the stress, and pain, and grief, and who knows what else, in a healthy way so you can live your life. What Ornias did to you is beyond what any human should have to endure."

"Hmmm, dreams. I hardly ever remember mine, except the ones that everyone gets where you haven't been to class all year and you find out today is the day of the final exam — geometry, probably — and you have no idea where the classroom even *is*, and you're completely naked, and your mother is there, trying to — "

"Wait a minute! You're completely naked and your *mother* is there?"

"Yeah, isn't that what normally happens in dreams like this?"

"Umm, I don't think so. Not that I've heard of, anyway. That's pretty weird, and definitely TMI!"

"Sorry. I probably need counseling, or maybe we should skip that and just go straight to the electroshock therapy."

She snorted a little laugh. "Don't be so hard on yourself. I have freaky dreams too, especially over the last couple of weeks. You think your mother being there is bad, try having *Afrits* pop up all the time. Well, that's not really what it's like, except when the damn thing wants something. It's more like I just feel this 'presence,' like the monster is watching me, there in the background, but just out of sight. I'm sure it's just stress, but it's very odd."

"It's very *creepy*. I can try and make an appointment for you at the electroshock clinic. Maybe they do two-for-one deals."

She giggled and put her arms around him. "There you are. I knew you were in there somewhere. I'm sorry this happened to you. I really am. I don't know what to say to make you feel any better. I'm not even sure if words would do the trick, but I'll say this: Ornias gave you the very worst of what's inside you, but that's not all there is. There's good stuff, too — lots of it — and if you got a steady dose of that instead of all the nasty bits, you'd probably feel like you'd achieved nirvana. Neither side tells the whole story. It all seems lopsided right now, but if there are forces inside of us that unconsciously influence what we do, you can't overlook the good ones. They count too, despite what fucking *Dimme* might say, and you have to find that perspective. If you have trouble doing that, just look at me. Not to brag, but I think I've been a pretty good thing in your life. Well, mostly, anyway. We don't have to talk about anything at all. There's lots of fun things we can do without speaking."

She held him tighter, and despite the cavalcade of horror and torment that unremittingly pressed against his consciousness, he remembered for the first time in two weeks that there was, perhaps, a semblance of good in the world. "Fun things, huh? What exactly did you have in mind?"

"Well, it's not too late to go for ice cream."

"It's freaking thirty-five degrees. Aren't you cold?"

"Nope. Anyway, this is now part of your program. You'll increase your happiness by making me happy. Isn't that a great solution?"

He couldn't really argue. Much as he might actually believe that he could benefit from counseling, he knew that Lotte was the only person he could seriously talk with about what had happened. She was his lifeline, and he needed to lean on her until he could regain his balance. He threw the car into reverse and began to consider what flavor ice cream he might like.

*Vanilla,* he finally decided. *Vanilla would be nice. I just need to get back to vanilla.*

<hr />

## Dorchester, Massachusetts, Saturday, November 11, 2017

We sit atop a mammoth structure made of steel, a great container that stores energy with which the humans in this region heat their homes or cook their food. It is painted with swashes of color that evoke the image of a rainbow. A millennium or more has passed since we glimpsed a real one. Back then, we could not differentiate colors, nor appreciate the simple wonder of sunlight refracted in droplets of water, the opposing forces of fire and water, briefly married with remarkable effect in the sky of this so often gloomy world.

The massive expanse of water that leads back to the lands we once knew laps at the nearby shore and disappears into the darkness of night, but it is to the perpetually crowded roadway that our eyes are drawn. Cars weave and stagger by like supplicants on a nighttime pilgrimage, expectantly marching with blazing lanterns toward their moment of veneration, seemingly unaware that another throng intently proceeds in the opposite direction. As with the rainbow, this panoply of headlamps also constitutes a marvel, one of human manufacture, not unlike the gleaming city toward which the vehicles on the road travel, or from whence they emerge.

The opulence of this metropolis obscures the drab routine of the lives of its occupants. People sweat and toil amongst what their ancestors would consider miraculous, but they hardly ever notice. Perhaps our age, and the scope of what we have seen — and will yet see — gives us greater perspective, though it may be that we are simply attracted to such bedazzling displays because of their similarity to the Eternal Flame. Either way, the strange charms present here stir complex and compelling urges within us, and we continue to find ourselves needful of this "material" plane.

The realization brings us little delight. We bear the stamp of all that fortune has dealt us. The powers of gods and Jinn course through our molten fabric. They grant us unparallelled resilience and might, but this energy possesses its own proclivities, the aspirations of earthly beings amplified by the potency of near immortals.

Now, what little remained of the daughter of Shamhuresh imbues us with her intoxicating essence. We find the sharp-tongued Jinn's gesture unexpected and puzzling, particularly given the testiness of our lone interaction. Yet ever did she find at least one commonality between us.

*Half-breed.*

Much as it pains us, there is truth in her words. That once "greater" portion of ourselves that blew itself apart in the Rope of An and Ki knew that the time was past when we could lock ourselves away in the plane of fire. Our existence would have been an endless and lonely misery of longing, with madness a near certainty. We are, it appears, doomed to straddle two realms forevermore.

*Better, perhaps, to put an end to things?*

For all the travails we have endured, never have we given as much credence to such a thought as now. Still... here we are, gazing at the beauty of a traffic jam. We cling to our existence, just as do the pathetic souls who plead and haggle as we transport them to our altar as spoils. Logic dictates that we are not yet ready for an ending of such *permanence*, but if this is accurate, what distresses us so?

We grow weary of our perch and take flight, high into the air, above the great gas tank, and the massive ocean, and the shimmering roadway, and the pulsating city. She knows it not, but we follow her — our *Sadat Alnaar* — she and her dull but stalwart mate. From afar, we watch as they revel in their wearisome routines, oblivious like all the others of the wonders around them, and how precocious little time they have to enjoy them.

When she sleeps, we touch her dreams. Lightly... ever so lightly. Just enough to breathe in, if only for a moment, the heaving needs, and yearnings, and pains, and passions that unconsciously roil within her psyche, and the inner lives of all her kind. This is part of what we need from this Middle Realm. Being awash periodically in these mortal drives keeps us sane and helps stave off the unruliest of our impulses.

*Yet, it is more than that.*

Once, we could leave everything behind, taking only that which we needed to survive. This is no longer the case. We know now what it means to be *destroyed*, the experience of loss nearly beyond comprehension. Someday, all too soon, the spark of life will inevitably abandon our *Sadat Alnaar*, and our memories of her will need to sustain us, if they can.

*How utterly human.*

We see with crystal clarity how much for us has changed. Our dependencies here will be ceaseless, and our course is charted into near eternity.

*We know the future, Tamanna Ibnat Shamhuresh, daughter of the Fifth King of the Jinn. We know, and we acknowledge what that means for us going forward, and we confess to you, in the darkness of this lofty place, and with the assurance of confidentiality which only* death *can bring, that we do* not *like what we see. We do not like it one bit, yet no alternative presents itself to us... for now....*

*For now....*

# THE END

(...although Eric's and Lotte's adventures will continue. To help ensure that happens, please consider leaving a review on whichever site you typically purchase books online. Your support is critical to the success of independent publishers like Evolved Publishing, and independent authors like William E. Noland. Reviews send a strong signal to potential readers and encourage online booksellers to promote the titles. If you'd like to see more books like this one, leaving an honest, heartfelt review is one of the best, and most sincerely appreciated, forms of support that any loyal reader can offer. Thank you so much.)

# ACKNOWLEDGEMENTS

I'm surprised to be reflecting on the release of my fifth book. When I started writing, barely four years ago, I couldn't have imagined all of this was inside me, waiting to get out. Perhaps the most gratifying thing about this experience is how I feel I have improved as a writer, and I have one person to thank for that, my editor, and in a sense, my coach in the art of writing, Dave Lane (AKA Lane Diamond).

Dave has been a more than patient teacher to a student that doesn't always get it on the first try (or the fifth) and doesn't always pay attention to smaller details. Over time, however, his suggestions and encouragement have opened my eyes to ways of expressing ideas with far greater effectiveness and engagement. The results are clearly evident to me in these pages, and I hope to you, the reader, as well.

Thank you, Dave. I'm not a graduate of Dave Lane University yet, but I'm happily making progress.

I also can't say enough thanks to Kris Norris for rendering the covers to all my books. This most recent was probably the hardest, but it also may be my favorite, and it would never have happened without her knowledge, expertise, and inspiration.

I learned long ago through music that no one can do it alone, and I'm glad I have such excellent support in my writing endeavors.

# ABOUT THE AUTHOR

William Noland combines a lifelong love of speculative fiction with a passion for history, sociology, and psychology. Engaging and entertaining, Noland's stories carry his hallmark of strong character development that weaves through every book in this page-turner series. In addition to writing, William plays in multiple rock bands and loves international travel and reading. He lives in Massachusetts with his wife and two cats.

**For more, please visit William E. Noland online at:**
**Website:** www.WENoland.com
**Goodreads:** William E. Noland
**Facebook:** @WENoland.Author
**LinkedIn:** www.linkedin.com/in/william-noland-103804140/

# WHAT'S NEXT?

William and his team at Evolved Publishing are fast at work on Book 6 of the "Uncommon Bonds" series. Stay tuned to the web page referenced below to keep up to date.

# www.EvolvedPub.com/UB

# MORE FROM WILLIAM E. NOLAND

### PLAYING WITH FIRE
### Uncommon Bonds - 1

*An ancient entity, trapped and suffering; a girl who inexplicably hears cries of anguish in her dreams.... What's their connection?*

### HAMMER TO FALL
### Uncommon Bonds - 2

*A grainy photograph and a cry for help begin a new descent into terror for long-separated friends Lotte Schwarz and Eric Schneider.*

### FROM THE BEGINNING
### Uncommon Bonds - 3

*A devastating flood and a chance encounter trigger a rapid-fire series of events that again pit Lotte Schwarz and Eric Schneider against challenges both mortal and supernatural.*

### DAY OF JUDGMENT
### Uncommon Bonds - 4

*Be careful what you wish for, as notorious success may lead to unintended scrutiny and even more otherworldly dangers.*

# MORE FROM EVOLVED PUBLISHING

We offer great books across multiple genres, featuring high-quality editing (which we believe is second-to-none) and fantastic covers.

As a hybrid small press, your support as loyal readers is so important to us, and we have strived, with tireless dedication and sheer determination, to deliver on the promise of our motto:
## QUALITY IS PRIORITY #1!

Please check out all of our great books,
which you can find at this link:
## www.EvolvedPub.com/Catalog/

Thank you!

www.ingramcontent.com/pod-product-compliance
Lightning Source LLC
Chambersburg PA
CBHW022207030726
47494CB00021B/1938